Heroines Behind the Lines

CIVIL WAR
BOOK 3

YANKEE *in* ATLANTA

JOCELYN GREEN

MOODY PUBLISHERS
CHICAGO

Published in association with the literary agency of Credo Communications, LLC,
Grand Rapids, Michigan, www.credocommunications.net.

This is a work of fiction. Names, characters, places, and incidents either are the prod-
uct of the author's imagination or are used fictitiously, and any resemblance to actual persons, living or dead, businesses, companies, events, or locales is entirely coincidental.

Edited by Pam Pugh
Interior Design: Ragont Design
Cover Design: Left Coast Design
Cover photo of girl's hair and face copyright © StockLite/Shutterstock;
         of girl's cloak and blouse © 2012 Klubovy/iStock. All rights reserved.
Author Photo: Paul Kestel of Catchlight Imaging
Maps of The Atlanta Campaign and the City of Atlanta: Rob Green Design

LLibrary of Congress Cataloging-in-Publication Data

Green, Jocelyn.
  Yankee in Atlanta / Jocelyn Green.
    pages cm. -- (Heroines behind the lines, Civil War ; Book 3)
  Summary: "When Union soldier Caitlin McKae wakes up in Atlanta wounded in
battle, the Georgian doctor believes her only secret is that she had been fighting for
the Confederacy disguised as a man. In order to avoid arrest or worse, Caitlin hides
her true identity and makes a new life for herself in Atlanta. Trained as a teacher, she
accepts a job as a governess for the daughter of Noah Becker, a German immigrant
lawyer who enlists with the Rebel army to defend his homeland against Sherman's
army. This story is about two families torn apart by war, two hearts divided by love
and honor. In a land shattered by strife and suffering, a Union veteran and a Rebel
soldier test the limits of loyalty and discover the courage to survive."-- Provided by
publisher.
  ISBN 978-0-8024-0578-4 (pbk.)
1. United States--History--Civil War, 1861-1865--Fiction. 2. United States--
History--Civil War, 1861-1865--Women--Fiction. I. Title.
  PS3607.R4329255Y36 2014
  813'.6--dc23
                          2013047170

We hope you enjoy this book from River North Fiction by Moody Publishers. Our goal
is to provide high-quality, thought-provoking books and products that connect truth to
your real needs and challenges. For more information on other books and products
written and produced from a biblical perspective, go to www.moodypublishers.com
or write to:

River North Fiction
Imprint of Moody Publishers
820 N. LaSalle Boulevard
Chicago, IL 60610

1 3 5 7 9 10 8 6 4 2

Printed in the United States of America

To Jason and Audrey
It is only distance that separates us.
And to divided families everywhere.
May your hearts be joined even if your hands cannot be.

God sets the lonely in families.
Psalm 68:6

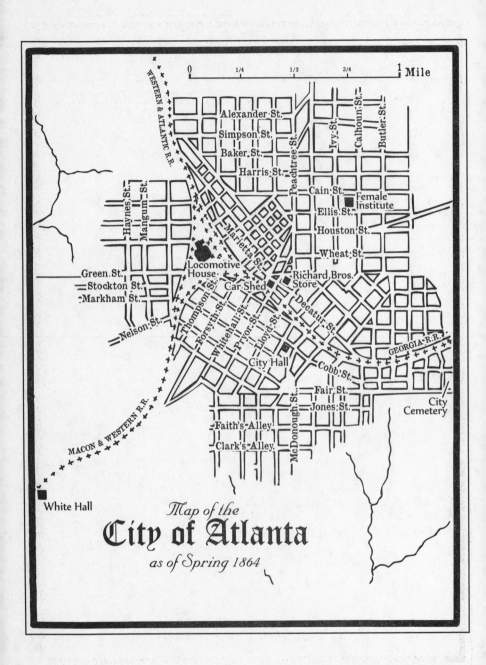

0   1/4   1/2   3/4   1 Mile

WESTERN & ATLANTIC R.R.

Alexander St.
Simpson St.
Baker St.
Harris St.

Peachtree St.

Ivy St.
Calhoun St.
Butler St.

Cain St.
Female Institute
Ellis St.
Houston St.
Wheat St.

Haynes St.
Mangum St.

Marietta St.

Locomotive House

Green St.
Stockton St.
Markham St.

Car Shed

Richard Bros. Store

Thompson St.
Forsyth St.
Whitehall St.
Pryor St.
Lloyd St.

Decatur St.

Nelson St.

City Hall

Cobb St.

GEORGIA R.R.

McDonough St.

Fair St.
Jones St.

City Cemetery

Faith's Alley
Clark's Alley

MACON & WESTERN R.R.

White Hall

Map of the

City of Atlanta

as of Spring 1864

Map of the
Atlanta Campaign
Tennessee / Northern Georgia
and Environs, 1864

Contents

A Note on the City of Atlanta

S o far as civil war is concerned, we have no fears of that in Atlanta." So proclaimed the *Atlanta Daily Intelligencer* shortly after a Georgia convention voted to secede by a margin of only 2 percent. The day after the vote, the earth literally cracked, rattling Atlanta but causing no damage. "May not its coming and passing away so easily," wrote the paper's editor, "with the clear and bright sky, be symbolical of the present political convulsion in the country, which in the South will pass away so easily, leaving the spotless sky behind."

He could not have been more wrong. Founded in 1836 as a dusty frontier town at the end of the railroad tracks, Atlanta soared to significance during the Civil War—or War Between the States—becoming the second most important city in the Confederacy, after Richmond. As it rose in prominence as a manufacturing, transportation, medical, and government center, the population surged from 11,000 people before the war, to 20,000 by 1863. The booming city was home to both the upright and the unsavory, to staunch Rebels and secret Unionists. As war encroached upon the city, every able-bodied man was pressed into service.

A small portion of Atlanta enjoyed extravagant wealth. Most were middle-class families, many driven to poverty and homelessness by the end of the war. But before Sherman's army ever set foot in Georgia, and regardless of their loyalties, the women on the home front were squeezed by the blockade, hunted by hunger, plagued by uncertainty, and still played hostess to refugees and convalescents. Though their strength is often passed over in the tale of Sherman's fire, they were heroines behind the lines.

As Atlanta rose on the tide of war, so it would be crushed by it. *Yankee in Atlanta* is a story of conflicting loyalties, divided families, and hearts refined by fire.

Prologue

The Virginia Peninsula
Saturday, May 31, 1862

Not now. Please, not now. Rebel bullets ripped through the sulfurous fog hovering above Caitlin McKae's head. Her middle cramping violently, she prayed her anguished bowels would not betray her. *Not now.*

"Don't let them take my leg, please! I'd rather die on the field!"

"We're getting you out of here, Marty!" Caitlin fairly shouted as she and the other three stretcher bearers carried the wounded soldier a quarter mile to the rear. Sweat poured from beneath her kepi and inched across her tightly bound torso. River water from the rain-swollen Chickahominy soaked through her brogans, and she faltered more than once in the red clay quagmire.

Head pounding like a fusillade, Caitlin slogged back through the mud to pluck more wounded comrades from the spongy earth, wondering how long this desperate battle for Richmond had lasted so far. Had an hour passed? Two hours? Three? Suddenly spent, Caitlin doubled over, gripping her knees. Her stomach heaved, though it had no contents to vacate.

But her body wasn't through. Her insides churning, Caitlin was left with no choice but to break away to the furthest pine tree she could make it to and find relief in relative privacy behind its trunk.

Before she could reach it, a lead ball tore through her arm. The twisting pain in her middle paled as fire blazed through her right bicep. The bullet had ripped completely through.

Caitlin's thundering pulse dimmed the sounds of battle as she dropped to her knees. With fumbling fingers, she unbuttoned her jacket with her left hand, wriggled free of it, and wrapped it around her bloody shirtsleeve. *I could go back. I can still hold the stretcher with my left hand.* But she couldn't. Strength sapped from her body, her limbs felt as though they'd been filled with lead.

Flat on her back now, Caitlin tried to steady her breathing. *The sky is still blue,* she told herself. *Somewhere, far above me, where bullets cannot reach and cries cannot be heard, the sky is still blue.* The haze of gun smoke thinned, and she caught a glimpse of Professor Lowe's balloon *Intrepid* hovering in the sky, with Lowe inside, reporting Confederate troop movements to General McClellan. Her eyelids drifted closed and she imagined herself there. *But if I were, I would cut the lines tethering it to the ground and sail away, far away from war and disease and death. If only it weren't for Jack.* Her thoughts trailed into a blank expanse as welcoming as the sky.

Mud splattered her face as another bullet pierced the ground next to her. Suddenly, her ears tuned to the musket fire still rattling in the air. Rolling over, Caitlin dragged herself into the pine trees, leaned against a trunk, and felt the earth shudder with the booming of artillery.

"God, when will it end?" she groaned through gritted teeth.

"Soon."

Caitlin turned toward the gravelly voice and found a bearded Rebel soldier. Mosquitoes hummed near his bleeding stomach. He would die within hours, even if he were in a hospital. "You're bleeding, too." He nodded to her crimson-soaked arm. Her jacket-turned-tourniquet must have fallen off when she'd crawled here for shelter. "Take mine. I'll not be needing it now."

"Thank you," she breathed, and let him help her tie his jacket to her arm. Gooseflesh raised on her skin as the sweat filming her body turned cold.

"Can you read?" He handed her a small New Testament with Psalms and Proverbs. "Do you know the one about the valley of the shadow of death? I reckon that ought to do." His face was so pale. Surely he was in that valley now.

Though her mind began to cloud, with her left hand, Caitlin opened the cover and saw it had been inscribed with the soldier's name and regiment, the Eighteenth. She flipped to Psalm 23, and forced her voice through chattering teeth. "Yea, though I walk through the valley of the shadow of death, I will fear no evil: for thou art with me; thy rod and thy staff they comfort me. Thou preparest a table before me in the presence of mine enemies . . ."

Caitlin's eyelids refused to stay open. She was sinking, deeper, as though the Virginia swamp was swallowing her whole. Her grip loosened on the Bible in her hand, and her consciousness slipped fully beyond her grasp.

———

Atlanta, Georgia
Thursday, June 19, 1862

Lips cinched, Caitlin McKae fought the instinct to reach toward the smoldering pain in her arm—the pain that had dragged her back to consciousness and told her she had survived.

Where am I? She shook her head, hoping to clear the fog. Flies droned lazily about the room. Muffled voices swam toward her from the hallway while the air sat thick and heavy on her skin. Beyond the shuttered window, locomotives bellowed and chugged.

Where is Jack? "Please," she prayed through cracked lips. "Keep him safe . . ."

"Well looky here." The door creaked, and a wedge of light broadened on the floor, framing a stocky silhouette. The odor of corn liquor seeped from his grey uniform as he stepped to her bedside, peering past his mustache at her. "Look who's finally awake. I got a whole heap a questions for you, girly-girl."

Oh no. Her hand flew to her heart, felt it hammering against her palm with only one threadbare sheet between. The binding around her chest was gone.

"That's a fact." He chuckled. "Your secret is out now, so you might as well fess up directly." One hand flexed around a club while the other rested on a revolver in its holster. His lips curled into a grin.

The alarm clanging in Caitlin's mind rivaled the screeching steel of a steam engine grinding to a halt outside.

"Ain't you got something to say for yourself? For starters, how could such a pretty girl such as yourself come to this? Leastwise, maybe you was pretty once." He reached for her, wearing the same possessive expression she had seen too often before.

"Don't touch me," she whispered, trying in vain to knock his hand away. When he laughed and called her "playful," she spit in his face, dormant anger and fear combusting in her veins.

Cursing, the officer ground his club into her bandaged arm. A gasp escaped her as searing pain ushered her back to the moment the bullet first tore through her flesh.

"George Washington Lee, you get out of here this instant!" The club fell away, and Caitlin, nearly breathless, blinked up at the blessed interruption—a silver-haired woman, blue eyes blazing, cheeks flushed. "How dare you treat her this way?"

"And just who is she, Miss Periwinkle?" Coughing racked Lee's body until he dabbed his mouth with a handkerchief. "She reeks of espionage."

Caitlin sat up, pulling the sheet up over her chest, and swallowed the moan bubbling up from the pain.

"Of course not." The woman jabbed her finger toward the man, as she stood with one fist propped on her ample hips. "She has more patriotism in the tip of her freckled nose than a regiment of conscripts. Why else would she fight for the cause?"

"I am not a spy," Caitlin broke in.

Lee's eyes brightened. "You see! You heard it for yourself, she is a Northerner!"

"She's Irish, and you know as well as I do that we have plenty of immigrants in these parts, and them as loyal to the cause as you are." Her tone was thick with disdain.

"I would beg you to remember that as the provost marshal of this fine city, it is my oath-bound duty to ferret out deserters, spies, foreigners, Northern sympathizers, and any other such like as would be harmful to the good of our country."

"Humph!" Miss Periwinkle snapped opened the wooden shutters and light flooded the small space. "You'll not bully me or anyone in this establishment or you may find the good doctor not nearly so inclined to oblige that nasty cough of yours. Now good day to you."

"Do be advised, Miss McKae." Colonel Lee leaned against the doorway again. "We do not abide spies in our midst."

"I told you, I am not a spy."

"Funny. That's what all seven of those Yankee devils said, all the way to the gallows. The Andrews raiders said they were Union soldiers, but they were dressed as civilians when they tried stealing our train. As I said, we do not abide spies. No matter what they're wearing." His eyes seemed to bore through hers.

Though she did not blink, Caitlin hugged the sheet to her chest as she watched him leave.

Miss Periwinkle bustled back to Caitlin's side. "I'm so sorry about that, dear. Rude introductions, indeed."

Blood still rushing in her ears, Caitlin wore a tight mask of counterfeit composure as Miss Periwinkle prattled on. "I'm Prudence. Now drink this tea of dandelion root for the pain in your shoulder. I do wish we had some opium for you, but Lil Bit says our tea will do nicely."

"I do wish you'd stop calling me that around the patients, Prudence."

A white-haired gentleman stepped to Caitlin's bedside, one hand cradling a pipe and the other resting on the stethoscope about his neck. "Older by fourteen months, and my sister still won't let me forget it." The doctor placed the stethoscope on Caitlin's chest, listening. "You gave us quite a scare, my dear."

"What happened?" Her voice creaked. She struggled to sweep the remaining cobwebs from her mind.

"Quite simply, the Richmond hospitals ran out of room after the Battle of Seven Pines, so they shuttled all who could safely be moved down to us. You've had a hard go of it, my girl. Your wound was only part of your trouble. By the time you arrived here, you were in the throes of typho-malarial fever, and unconscious. I imagine you had been for days. Do you remember any of this?"

Caitlin pressed her fingers to her aching forehead while snatches of memory flickered over her. The wrenching abdominal pain, headache, nausea, fever, and chills. The bullet that tore through her arm, and the Rebel who gave her his jacket as a tourniquet. "I remember some," she whispered, mind still reeling. Slowly the pieces fit together.

She'd been reading the Rebel's Bible, marked with his Georgia regiment, when she passed out. Slowly, the pieces fit together. It must have been in her hand when Confederate medical officers found her with her wound wrapped in butternut grey, an apparent Southern casualty. To Jack and the rest of her own regiment, she was now missing in action.

Dr. Periwinkle unwound a bandage on her upper arm. "It's a miracle the ball passed through you without shattering the bone," he murmured while inspecting the entry and exit wounds. "There is still risk of infection and secondary hemorrhage." He paused, stroked his handlebar mustache downward. "But you'll be fine. You remind me so of my own daughter, when she was about your age, Miss McKae."

The words pricked Caitlin's ears. "How do you know my name?"

Prudence raised her eyebrows. "You told us yourself, dear. But you

16

were in the fever's grip and I reckon you've forgotten the worst of it."

Her heart plunged. "Where am I?"

"Periwinkle Place boarding house. Since war came, we care for convalescents here, too. Wounded Rebels come in from all over to us, on account of our railroads. Lil Bit brought you to me directly so you may recover with privacy, now that you won't be soldiering anymore."

"The South has sent its sons to war—including mine—but we need not send our daughters." The twinkle returned to the doctor's eyes. "Your patriotism does you credit, child, but it's time you just get well and stop pretending to be someone you're not. No more soldiering, all right? You're safe now, in Atlanta."

Atlanta. The Gate City to the South.

Caitlin's spirit flagged, but her face betrayed nothing. She may be able to get well here, but to stop pretending and reveal her true identity would never do.

Then again, this would be the last place anyone would look for Caitlin McKae.

Including Jack. The void he left in her heart ached already. And yet, the price she had paid to be with him had exacted a toll only another veteran could understand. Closing her eyes, she allowed herself to imagine a life without marching, drilling, fighting, suffering. A life so far from her past she could stop looking over her shoulder for it.

She would start over again in Atlanta and make this place her home, at least until she had the means to leave. She had reinvented herself before. She could do it again. She would have to.

This is not the end, she told herself. *It is only a new beginning.*

17

"ATLANTA HAS BEEN since the commencement of the revolution—a point of rendezvous of traitors, Swindlers, extortionist, and Counterfeiters. The population as a predominant element is a mixture of Jews, New England Yankees, and refugees shirking military duties."

—COL. GEORGE WASHINGTON LEE, Provost Marshal of Atlanta

"WE HAVE LEARNED our lessons well—can cry when we would laugh—and laugh when we would cry ... The face must keep its color—white or red—though the heart stops beating or flames up in scorching pain."

—CYRENA STONE, Unionist Atlanta resident

Act One

LOYALTIES IN THE BALANCE

Chapter One

Atlanta, Georgia
Sunday, July 5, 1863

raitor.

A rifle butt slammed between Caitlin's shoulder blades, pitching her forward on the narrow plank. Stumbling, she righted herself again, wrists bound behind her. A dangling rope brushed her face.

How could you?

She squinted up at the voice, edged with hatred yet still familiar. *Jack?* Blood streamed from his chest.

His hazel eyes blazed. *You did this to me.*

No!

If you do not stand with me, you stand against me.

The noose was around her neck now, burning like live coals. *It is only distance that separates us!*

He shook his head, his hair curling over one eye. *It is everything that separates us. The chasm can never be crossed.*

Caitlin looked past Jack to the shallow grave behind him. The seven bodies of the Andrews raiders lay decomposing into one brittle mass. But there was room for one more. Terror pulsed in her ears.

I had no choice!

You made your choice. To be one of them.

I am one of you!

You are neither.

A single kick to the scaffold beneath her feet, and—

"Jack!" With a scream in her throat and fists clenching her collar, Caitlin burst from her nightmare into the hot breath of Atlanta. *Surviving in enemy country is not a betrayal!* She railed against her recurring dream. *I am not a turncoat!*

A knock on the door. "Caitlin? It's me, Minnie." She knocked again. "I haven't got my key." Caitlin sat up and rolled her neck. The residual fear of her nightmare dissolved under her roommate's muffled drawl. "You didn't fall asleep on your books again, did you, honey?"

At nineteen years of age, Minerva Taylor was four years younger than Caitlin, and she called everyone honey, whether she was truly fond of them or not. As the Atlanta Female Institute's music teacher whose pupils ranged from the talented to the uncooperative, it was a capacity that proved to be as diplomatic as it was habitual.

Caitlin tripped on a dog-eared book as she went to open her door. "What else is a Sunday afternoon for if not reading and napping?"

Minnie shook her head of perfectly coifed sunshine-blonde hair, her face radiant in spite of the pockmark scarring. Parasol in hand, she stepped into the room and shut the door behind her, muting the rowdy conversations of the other boarders at Periwinkle Place. "Reading for pleasure I could understand. But something tells me you're preparing for your classes. On a Sunday!" She plucked the worn volume from the floor. "Why, we're almost out for the summer! You're such a bluestocking!"

Caitlin's grin faltered. Her classes were the best thing about Atlanta. When they ended for summer break, she would sincerely miss teaching.

Perhaps the Southern sun had addled her brain for her to not hate living here the way she once did. Atlanta had given Caitlin what New York City could not. A way to survive without marrying. Or soldiering.

She pasted a smile back into place. "And who's to say I don't find pleasure in *Paradise Lost*?"

"You would." Minnie laughed, her grey eyes dancing. "But tell the truth. It's in your curriculum too, isn't it?"

"What kind of a literature instructor would I be if it weren't?" The fact that Caitlin was a literature instructor at all was no small miracle. But the Atlanta Female Institute was only three years old and, with the war calling the men away, in dire need of teachers. Caitlin had been offered the position vacated by an enlisting soldier as a personal favor from the principal to Dr. Periwinkle. That they believed her to be a Confederate veteran had worked to her benefit, as well.

"What about you?" Caitlin asked, twisting her shoulder-length, cinnamon-colored hair back into place beneath her pins. "Don't you play the piano and sing when you're not in class?"

"Of course I do. But this?" She read the text with a hint of vibrato: " 'Live while ye may, Yet happy pair; enjoy till I return, Short pleasures; for long woes are to succeed . . . ' That's just morbid, honey!"

"What's morbid is how you completely murdered the iambic pentameter!"

Minnie shrugged. "I've got to let you be better than me in *something*. Aside from shooting a gun, that is." Her dimples deepened in rosy cheeks, as they always did when she teased.

"Let's leave the past where it lies. I've certainly won few friends with mine."

"I know you don't like to talk about your soldiering in the army, but the truth is, I only wish I were as brave as you so I could lick some Yankees myself!"

But Caitlin had not felt brave in battle. Not with lead tearing toward her and cannons shaking the earth beneath her. Not with men unraveling around her like rag dolls in the mouth of an unseen beast. Not with her lifeblood seeping out of her. She'd been terrified then, and the recollections jangled her still. "Never wish for a fight, Minnie. It is a horrid thing."

"But for a just and righteous cause such as ours—"

"For any cause."

Minnie laid a hand on her arm. "I've upset you. I'm sorry, honey." Her gaze traveled to the white line on Caitlin's jaw, likely assuming it was a mark from the war, and Caitlin did not correct her. "Come, let's go for a stroll."

By the time they stepped out onto Alabama Street, Caitlin's heart rate had almost returned to its normal pace. Apple peels and peanut shells crunched beneath every step along the busy dirt road where soldiers swarmed between local residents and travelers.

When two Rebels half-bowed in their direction, Minnie trilled the chorus of the ever-popular Bonnie Blue Flag. "Hurrah! Hurrah! For Southern rights, hurrah! Hurrah for the Bonnie Blue Flag that bears a single star."

Caitlin smiled at her friend's beautiful soprano voice, but could not stop the Battle Cry of Freedom from running through her own mind at the same time.

The Union forever! Hurrah, boys, hurrah!
Down with the traitors, up with the stars;
While we rally round the flag, boys, rally once again,
Shouting the battle cry of freedom!

"That one's looking at you," Minnie whispered.

Caitlin kept her gaze straight ahead. "Not likely. Or necessary."

"Don't you want to find a beau?"

"No."

"Why ever not? With your education, you could secure quite a husband."

"With my education, I don't need a husband." She arched an eyebrow. "I can make my own way."

Minnie's jaw dropped. "You don't mean you'd rather have 'single blessedness' instead."

"I most certainly do."

Their conversation stalled at the corner of Whitehall Street and the railroad tracks. Knots of women and old men huddled in silent groups outside Wittgenstein's saloon.

"What is it?" Minnie asked a woman nearby.

"There is news." She nodded to the second floor of the building, the *Atlanta Daily Intelligencer* office. "If we can but survive the waiting for it."

Minnie blanched and gripped Caitlin's hand. "Father." *Jack.* "Pray, stay with me until we hear."

Hours passed, and the sun glared haughtily down upon them, baking all those who waited, exposed, below it. Sweat pricked Caitlin's scalp beneath her palmetto hat and bloomed beneath her arms.

Prudence Periwinkle stood on the fringe of one cluster, clutching a bottle of smelling salts the way young mothers press babies to their chests. Horses swished their tails and pawed at the red dirt road, and the people choked on dust and suspense and fear.

No one spoke.

All eyes were on the arched door leading up to the *Atlanta Daily Intelligencer* office, waiting. News from the West reported that Vicksburg had surrendered. The Confederacy lay cut in two. But every breath still hinged on the news that would come from a little town in the North called Gettysburg.

Minnie's whispered prayers were for her father, while Caitlin's only thought was of Jack.

"There it is!" someone cried.

In the shadow of the door's alcove, someone reached out and fed a ream of papers to hungry hands. Finally, the casualty list had arrived.

The sheets of names passed through the crowd, sending up wails and moans from nearly all who touched them. When it was Minnie's turn to read them, her hands shook so fiercely she thrust the pages into Caitlin's hand.

"Please," she whispered, eyes squeezed shut. "Thomas Taylor. Quickly, quickly, I can't bear another moment."

Caitlin scanned the tiny columns of names, the fresh ink now blurred and smudged. Hastily, she skipped to the *T*s.

And found the name.

"He is . . ."

Minnie's eyes popped open, and Caitlin labored to force out the words. "He was . . ." She shook her head. "He is at peace."

For a moment, Minnie sat in silence, as if frozen by the incomprehensible news. Then her face crumbled, yet she did not make a sound. Caitlin wrapped her arms around Minnie, and the grief of a father's daughter bled out onto her shoulder. Caitlin's face was wet with empathy.

Around them, sorrow thickened in the air, souring every breath. Caitlin tasted no victory in their despair.

In the edge of her vision, she saw a woman drop to her knees in the dusty road. Heart hammering on her ribs, Caitlin looked once more at the casualty list, slowing when she found the *P*s.

Pelton, Pemberly, Pendleton, Periwinkle . . . Blood rushed in Caitlin's ears. *Periwinkle, Stuart.* Dr. Periwinkle's son. Prudence's precious nephew, the one she helped raise and love as a mother would have done. Gone. Prudence bowed down on the street, clawing fistfuls of dirt and letting them crumble over her silver hair.

The war would not come to Atlanta, they said. But from the fields of Pennsylvania, its long fingers wrapped around its throat with an iron grip. The sons of the city had been slain. They had even been defeated.

The fissures in the House of Dixie were running deeper, yawning wider. How long would it be before it came crashing down, as the crack in Edgar Allen Poe's "House of Usher" had sent it rushing into the sea?

And if I am here when the Confederacy collapses, will I be saved by the North? Or will I go down with the South?

Words from her nightmare reverberated in her spirit. *You are neither.*

Caught between two nations desperately at war, Caitlin McKae was on her own.

———

New York City
Sunday, July 5, 1863

"Jesus loves me—this I know, For the Bible tells me so." Ruby O'Flannery rocked her one-year-old son and relished his warm weight on her lap. "Little ones to Him belong—They are weak, but He is strong." She hummed the refrain and mused what a difference the truth of the song had made in her life, and in his. Before he was born, she had not wanted him, for reasons too painful to dwell upon. Now however, she could not imagine life without him. He had brought joy back into her life and laughter to her lips.

Aiden's eyes drifted closed, and his dimpled hands loosened their grip on the zebras from his wooden Noah's Ark set. Pressing a kiss to his pillowy cheek, Ruby laid him in his crib and gently brushed copper curls off his forehead.

"Sleep well, darlin'" she whispered.

Ruby tiptoed out of the room and descended the wide walnut staircase of the Waverly brownstone just as a knock sounded on the front door. Caroline Waverly, her employer, was reading in the rear parlor, but no matter. This caller was for Ruby—the only caller she ever had.

She opened the door, a smile already on her lips, to see Edward Goodrich still in his Sunday best. He was not devilishly handsome—she wouldn't trust him if he was, given her previous experience with that sort. But he was genuine. Kind. His coffee-colored eyes were deep and warm, not mischievous—and certainly not lustful, thank heaven.

"Is he down?" Edward looked past her to the stairway.

"You just missed him. You know, sometimes I wonder if you come here for our Bible studies or to play with my wee babe." Tilting her head in mock disapproval, her smile didn't fade. "Come in, come in."

Edward hung his hat on the hall stand, swiped a hand over his caramel-colored hair, and followed Ruby. She stopped in the kitchen to pour two glasses of lemonade before they went to the garden for their Sunday discussion. Ever since she had come to work for Caroline last year as the maid, she could not get enough of this beautiful space. Growing up as the daughter of a potato farmer in Ireland and as an immigrant living in New York City tenements for years, nature's beauty simply had not been part of her life, until now.

Shaded by a maple leaf canopy, Ruby and Edward sat at a wrought iron table flanked by hydrangea bushes drooping with white blooms. The rest of the garden was splattered with vibrant hues: yellow primroses, pink and red roses, and, hugging the tree trunks, green-and-white-leafed hostas.

"Thank goodness for the shade," Edward said as he shrugged his shoulders out of his tan broadcloth suit jacket and tugged at the cravat at his throat. Not a single breeze stirred the air. "Still, it beats the heat of Washington, doesn't it?"

"Aye." She sipped her lemonade, the glass already sweating in her hand. Ruby had first met Edward in Washington City the first year of the war. He was a hospital chaplain there, and she was there to be close to her husband in the Sixty-Ninth New York regiment. She had lodged with Sanitary Commission nurse Charlotte Waverly, her employer's daughter, and Charlotte's sister Alice. Now Charlotte was co-director of a Rhode Island military hospital, and Edward . . . Ruby sighed as she looked at his lean, care-worn face. Edward's plans had been altered by news of his father's accident at the shipyard. He had stepped into a coil of rope, which tangled around his legs when the pulley yanked up. Not only did his legs break with the force, but when his body hit the block at the top, his arms, which had been raised to cover his head, broke too. Edward requested a transfer to New York so he could care for him at his home only a few blocks from the Waverly residence. Lucky for Ruby, he also helped her understand the Bible during Aiden's Sunday afternoon naps. Ruby's faith was about as old as her toddling son, and though eager, it was not always sure-footed. She was grateful for Edward's guidance.

Edward laid his black leather Bible on the table and leaned back, stretching his long arms behind his head. "So, Ruby. What shall we talk about today?" She had insisted long ago that he dispense with calling her Mrs. O'Flannery. After all, she was just an Irish immigrant, a servant. His family employed people like her.

"I read about a Samaritan in the gospel of Luke chapter twenty-one."

"Ah. One of my favorite parables." He leaned forward on his elbows. "What do you think it means?"

"Well, the lesson seems to be that we should help people in need. But I stumble over the 'thees' and 'thous.'" She'd been working on matching her Irish tongue more to American-English speech patterns like Mrs. Waverly's, but the poetic language of King James sometimes stumped her.

"It takes some getting used to. You've gleaned the main point, but let's dig a little deeper. The first two men who found a man stripped, robbed, and beaten on the road were Jewish religious men. They knew the right thing to do, but they didn't do it, because it wasn't convenient. The third man was a Samaritan. Do you know what that means?"

Ruby shook her head.

"Samaritans were despised by the Jews. But it was the Samaritan who loved his neighbor when the religious leaders chose not to. That should alarm us. See, we can be full of Bible knowledge, but if we don't love our neighbor, we still aren't pleasing Jesus."

"Who is our neighbor?"

Edward's smile broadened, and faint lines framed his eyes. "Anyone who God has brought into your life. Friends, family, Mrs. Waverly, but even those you meet at the market, or perhaps people you knew before you came to work here. Many times it isn't convenient to love your neighbor, but that doesn't mean we shouldn't."

Inwardly, Ruby shuddered. *I've spent this year trying to forget my past entirely. Am I really to go back and care for those in the tenements now?*

The French doors opened and Caroline rustled out into the garden with Dickens, Charlotte's cat, beside her. "I do apologize for interrupting." She sat on a stone bench opposite Ruby and Edward, her olive-colored day dress billowing from her waist. "But I've made up my mind. I'm going."

Ruby's eyes widened. "To Gettysburg?"

Edward's eyebrows arched. "What's this?"

"The fighting at Gettysburg. If the papers can be believed, it was by far the worst battle of the war to date." Dickens jumped into her lap. "The need is desperate and the resources few. Charlotte asked me to join her; she says I can be of use just by stirring a cauldron of stew. For once, I said yes." She paused, stroking Dickens's marmalade fur.

Aiden's fussing floated out the open second-story window now, and Edward gathered the empty glasses from the table. "I'll get him, if it's all right with you."

It was. Edward's limp was barely perceptible as he ducked into the house.

Ruby turned back to Caroline. "What about her hospital in Rhode Island?"

"Olmsted insists he must have her field hospital experience on hand." Frederick Olmsted was the executive secretary of the Sanitary Commission. "Her co-director can manage without her for a time."

And I'll thank God I can stay right here. Where there was bloodshed, Charlotte was keen to go. But Ruby had seen enough of battlefields and army hospitals to suit her. She'd never forget the sea of wounded at White House Landing, Virginia, where she watched her own husband die right before her eyes just hours before Aiden was born.

Edward returned to the garden, carrying Aiden like a sack of flour and blowing kisses on his round belly. The baby giggled and squealed, squirming until his little feet stood on the soft grass. Stooping, Edward let Aiden grasp his fingers while he practiced walking.

30

"She'll be in New York tomorrow, and from there we'll travel on together and stay as long as they need us. Olmsted is already there by now. So is Dr. Lansing."

Ruby nodded. At least Charlotte would catch a glimpse of her fiancé, then.

Edward sighed. "Where there are men—especially wounded men—there should be chaplains."

"I'm sure there are, dear. And the Christian Commission has sent delegates, too." Caroline patted his shoulder. "The spiritual welfare of the entire Army of the Potomac is not up to you. The patients in New York's hospitals are lucky to have you here, and so is your father. And so are we." She glanced at Ruby, then back at him. "Edward, will you look in on Ruby and the baby while we're gone? Between Sundays, too? I'm letting the cook have some time off so she can visit her family. I'd feel so much better leaving if I knew I could count on you."

"Of course you can." Aiden sat on his foot as Edward straightened and grinned at Ruby. "That's what neighbors are for."

"Aye." Ruby nodded and chuckled. "Whether it's convenient or not."

Chapter Two

Atlanta, Georgia
Monday, July 11, 1863

I'm sorry. If there was any other way . . ." The principal trailed off, mopped his brow with a kerchief.

"You're closing the school?" Caitlin gripped the wooden bench that supported her. Sunlight bathed the Atlanta Female Institute's chapel, and in the silence suspended between the principal and his six staff, Caitlin heard echoes of the 140 girls who had begun and ended every day by singing here.

"They need the building for a hospital."

Caitlin caught Minnie's narrowed gaze, unspoken questions passing between them.

"And soon. The news from Gettysburg . . ." He shook his head before pinching the bridge of his nose. "And Vicksburg . . . as the hospital center of the South, we must prepare. They are taking our school. As I said, if there was anything I could do . . . but there isn't."

Caitlin clasped Minnie's hand and whispered, "What will you do?"

"What else can I do? I'm going home. Grandfather will be all alone now, and I'm sure he'll be grateful for the company." Minnie tucked her fingers in the pleats of her unevenly dyed black dress.

Caitlin's heart sank. "Home" for Minnie was a plantation in Tennessee, near Chattanooga. She would lose her job and her friend all at once.

"I'll see you back at Periwinkles," Minnie said. "I need to determine arrangements for the students I'd planned to teach over the summer break."

Nodding, Caitlin rose and exited the chapel's double doors.

"Miss McKae."

The deep voice, like the distant gallop of cavalry, could only belong to Noah Becker, the German immigrant lawyer who taught modern languages part-time. She need not slow her gait for him to reach her in three long strides.

"Yes?" Impatience edged her voice.

"Where can you be off to in such a hurry?" Sunlight shone on his tobacco-brown hair as he looked down at her, his hat in his hand.

"Nowhere."

"I'm headed that way, too. Share my carriage and you'll get there even faster." A grin softened the features of his angular face and teased a grudging smile from her lips. With a slight nod, she fixed her straw bonnet onto her hair, and he placed his hat back on his head. Together, they left the institute and found his tethered team.

"It is hard news." Mr. Becker said as he assisted her into the carriage. "Do you grieve for a loved one at Gettysburg or Vicksburg?"

Was it a test? "I grieve for all of them, of course." Silently, she breathed a prayer for Jack.

"Of course." Red dust lifted off the road as hoofbeats plodded down Ellis Street. The closer they drew to downtown, the more Caitlin's nose pinched. Ever since the casualties from Gettysburg had twitched across the telegraph wires, the air had soured as women dipped their dresses in pots of pungent black dye.

Mr. Becker sighed. "I don't know how to say this delicately."

"Speak your mind."

"Without an income, you will soon run out of money for boarding." Caitlin groped for a reason to contradict him. She found none.

He continued. "I have a large house."

"How nice for you." Heat scorched her face as the wicked words slid out. She had not intended to be so discourteous.

Mr. Becker chuckled. "Come now, lass, hear me out."

She laughed at the slight German accent layered on the Irish word and bade him continue.

"You are not from here," he began, and her heart lurched. "Neither am I. I've lived here for years, but though I have adopted Georgia as my homeland, some days I'm not altogether certain *it* has adopted *me*. I don't blend in—never could speak like them."

"Nor can I."

"So I noticed." He laughed again. "Your Irish accent sharpens when you're agitated. Otherwise, you just sound like a Northerner."

The honeysuckle cloying in the air suddenly lost its charm. "Say your piece, Mr. Becker."

He cleared his throat and turned the corner onto Peachtree Street. "I understand what it's like to be more of an outsider than an insider. To be on your own when most people have families—large ones—for built-in support."

"Are we going somewhere with this or is it more like our carriage ride?"

His steel-blue eyes grew serious. "You need a place to live. And, as I said, I just so happen to have a house."

"I don't need your help, Mr. Becker."

"You miss the point entirely. I need you. I'm going to enlist. Live in my house while I'm gone." No flame of eagerness flared in Noah's countenance, no prediction of speedy victory passed his lips. A lump shifted in his throat. "Can you think of any reason why you should not? When

34

the war is over, the school will certainly reopen and you'll have your position back. But in the meantime . . ."

"It wouldn't be proper, I'm sure."

"Nonsense. You wouldn't be alone. Bess does the cooking and cleaning, and her husband, Saul, cares for the property and horses."

"Your slaves?" The words bolted from her before she could rein them in. Of course they were his slaves. She hazarded a glance at his countenance, wondering if her obvious feelings on the matter had condemned her already.

Mr. Becker shifted the reins in his hands. "I hire them from their master in Decatur, about eight miles from here. They sleep in their own quarters above the kitchen and carriage house, and I pay them honest wages for their work. The percentage they pay back to their master is not up to me. As far as I'm concerned, they are merely servants . . ."

But not free. This time she bridled her tongue.

"Does that make me Simon Legree?"

Caitlin turned away from him at his reference to *Uncle Tom's Cabin.* She'd be lying if she said the novel did not color her perspective.

Shoulders sagging, Noah dropped his voice to a whisper. "I operate under the law, even if I don't agree with it." Faint lines fanned from his eyes, and Caitlin wondered just exactly what his opinion was. But, "The 'peculiar institution' is not the debate I intended to have right now. Please." His tone tugged at Caitlin. "Will you come?"

Make your own way. Depend on no man. Her mother's voice rattled in her spirit. "I thank you for your offer, Mr. Becker. But I will find a way to weather this storm without relying on your charity."

He nodded, jaw set. "Shall we simply enjoy the fresh air and continue the ride then?"

Caitlin agreed, and settled back into the seat, swatting a trio of flies away from her face.

The clanging rhythm of wartime factories signaled their approach to the clogged center of town. The carriage lurched haltingly along the road, navigating between cabs, wagons, omnibuses, and the steaming calling cards horse-drawn conveyances inevitably dropped behind. Four railroad lines converged in Atlanta, and the citizens never forgot it. Day and night, iron horses belched and screeched. Every departure carried away railroad supplies, saddles, shoes, percussion caps, rifles, ammunition, swords, and more. Every arrival brought more wounded and refugees. The city nearly choked on the business of war.

Caitlin did not care for downtown Atlanta. The inherent odors of a population outgrowing its sanitation sysem were not new to her. What New York didn't have, however, was Confederate soldiers stationed along the dusty streets, doffing their caps to her as she rode by. Had her regiment battled with their brothers? Would those Rebels raise their guns against her if they knew? She dropped her gaze to her calico-covered lap.

"Here we are." Mr. Becker drew rein and the carriage stopped.

Caitlin looked around, confusion grooving her brow. "But why?" They were near the railroad tracks, surrounded by boxcars. Grimy children played in the dirt and women hollered at them from the shadows. Some of the refugees had brought pets or pianofortes with them. Most had trunks and cookware. All of them looked hungry.

"Welcome home." He was not smiling. "Without a residence, this will be your only realistic option."

No. "I'm staying at Miss Periwinkle's boardinghouse—"

"How long can you stay without an income? She might let you stay for free because she's so fond of you, but you'd be taking money from her by taking the place of a paying customer. Would you do that to her after she already looked after you all last summer during your convalescence?"

Caitlin's throat went dry. Without Prudy and Dr. Periwinkle, she would have withered away long ago, in spirit as well as body. Taking money from Prudence was no way to return the favor. And if Periwinkle Place was not an option, neither was the Trout House, Atlanta Hotel, or any of the other lodgings that curried no affection toward Caitlin.

"Take a good look, Miss McKae. Do you want to join them in the boxcars? You'd have to share the space with four other families, but at least you'd have a roof over your head. They say you get used to the smell."

She glared at him. Everything in her being revolted at this place. The filth of living without proper water closets, the deafening shriek of the never-ending trains, the aimless purgatorylike existence. How quickly the tide of her life could turn on her!

Mr. Becker grasped her trembling hands in his. "Come away with me, Miss McKae. This is no place for you."

Maybe it was, though. After all she had done, maybe this was exactly the place for the likes of her.

A train wailed and the earth rumbled with rolling freight as Mr. Becker's large hands tightened over hers. *Why would God put a lifeline in my hands if He did not intend for me to use it?* He had shown her the way out before. Perhaps He was doing so again. But to be indebted to a man grated on her no end.

"It is not charity." Mr. Becker said, as though he could read her mind. "It is business."

———

Noah's palms grew damp on the leather reins as they rode past city hall and turned right on McDonough Street. Oak trees dappled the road with shadow while pink-and-red blossoms sizzled across crape myrtle branches. Soon they would be home. The thought of having a woman in his house again should not set his nerves on edge this way. This was nothing like the last time, so many years ago. Entirely different circumstances.

Entirely different women. He slid a glance toward Miss McKae, but saw only the tip of her nose poking out from the bonnet that shielded her. Not that he needed to see her face to remember her molasses eyes, the faint spray of freckles—and the thin scar lining her jaw on the left side. The little spitfire had a story to tell, that much was certain. Whether he would ever hear it, however, remained to be seen.

37

"I would ask something of you while you're here. I would ask you to teach a little girl. Just one child, seven years of age."

Caitlin blinked. "Only one pupil? Is that all?"

His full lips flattened for a moment. "Not quite all. I would ask that you care for her as your personal charge."

Caitlin tilted her head, squinting at him, and he feared she would say no. His heart dipped. No other woman would be right for the job. Her students not only loved her, they learned from her. What's more, she made them *want* to learn. And yet she did not coddle them like their mammies had. She taught personal responsibility as well as any subject in the curriculum. It was what set her apart.

As they drew near to his home, she finally spoke. "Who is she?"

"Papa!" The door on his white, black-shuttered plantation plain home slammed shut behind Analiese. She flew out onto the columned porch, braids streaming out behind her. Rascal, his coonhound, loped in her wake, his tail wagging his rear end. "You're home!"

Noah slowed the carriage to a halt in the boxwood-lined drive, and when Ana came close enough, he swung her up onto his lap before reaching down to scratch Rascal behind the ears. Ana's forget-me-not-blue eyes sparkled as she wiggled down between him and Caitlin on the bench.

"Yes, Dear Heart, and I've brought a friend. Analiese, this is Miss Caitlin McKae. Miss McKae, this is Analiese. My daughter."

Caitlin's gaze flashed over his bare ring finger, but mercifully, she did not ask for an explanation.

"Pleased to meet you. I am seven years old and I am missing two things. Can you guess what they are?" Ana grinned broadly.

"Let me see now." Caitlin tapped her finger to her chin.

"I'll give you a hint. It rhymes with 'beeth'!"

"Oh!" Caitlin threw her hands in the air. "Then it *must* be . . . a wreath!"

"No . . ." Ana shook her head.

"No? How about a sheath?"

Ana giggled.

"Not a sheath, then. Hmmm. What else rhymes with beeth . . . Meeth? Seeth? Leeth? Why, do you know, Analiese, that I am missing all of those things myself? I have no idea what they even are!"

Laughter bubbled out of Ana as she rocked back against Noah. "Teeth! Teeth! See?"

Caitlin's eyes widened as she studied the gap-toothed smile. "I do see! One smile minus two teeth. Now if only you were missing an eye as well, you could wear a patch and look just like a pirate."

Ana squeezed one eye shut and grimaced. "Like the pirates in *Robinson Crusoe*? Like this?"

Caitlin's eyebrows lifted. She raised her eyes to meet Noah's gaze and said: "Yes." Her smile hitched in his throat. She had given him her answer.

He planted a kiss on Ana's pecan-colored hair and without turning to face him, she patted his knee while chattering on to Caitlin. She smelled of sunshine and magnolia petals and innocence. She was the best part of his life.

And he was leaving her.

Chapter Three

New York City
Monday, July 13, 1863

*T*he city seemed far away as Aiden pointed happily at the
fluffy sheep grazing in Central Park. Ruby smiled and let him stumble
ahead of her. Green grass was far more merciful to a wee lad's knees than
were the cobblestones and sidewalks in their own neighborhood. *And
not a lamppost in sight.* For if there were, Aiden would certainly careen
right into it.

She watched him for a signal that he had run off enough energy to
justify going home. The sun had licked the dew from the ground already, and Aiden's curls were beginning to cling to the nape of his neck.

Her mind wandered to the work awaiting her at the brownstone.
She needed to iron the apple-green promenade gown she'd just finished
sewing for Mrs. Kurtz before she arrived later today to pick it up. *And
with four flounces on the skirt, it will take some doing.* Ruby had to make

sure the gown was absolutely perfect. Mrs. Kurtz had four daughters, all of whom appreciated well-made clothing. If she could please Mrs. Kurtz, more business was sure to follow.

Before becoming a domestic, Ruby had been a needlewoman who sewed shirtsleeves for Davis & Company. Since working for Caroline Waverly, however, she had tried her hand at sewing complete custom gowns when her domestic duties were complete. Her first gown, created for Caroline, had been a remarkable imitation of a fashion plate in *Godey's Lady's Book*, which quickly generated orders from several of Caroline's friends. This week, with her employer gone to Gettysburg, perhaps Ruby could finish at least two of them. The more she could store up for Aiden's education, the better. He would be the first in her family to have any, cost her what it may. She was no stranger to sacrifice.

"Almost time to go, Aiden. Can you say goodbye to the sheep? What does a sheep say?"

"Moo!"

"Close."

Ruby turned her head toward the voice and smiled to see Edward driving his horse and buggy toward them, his hair at odds with the breeze that riffled through it.

"I didn't expect to see you here!" Ruby bent to hold Aiden's hand as Edward climbed down from the buggy. And she certainly never expected to see him in public without his hat. "Is something the matter?"

He shielded his eyes from the sun with his hand and scanned the park. "Not that I can see."

Ruby's lips quirked up. "Tell that to your neck." Dark pink blotches had bloomed on his fair skin.

Edward's hand flew to his throat for a moment, then dropped in apparent resignation. "It is not my most fetching characteristic, granted." He shook his head. "How much better would it be if, occasionally, I grew large biceps instead of large splotches the very color of peonies?" Edward curled a fist over his shoulder and frowned.

Ruby hid her laughter behind her hand, but the gleam in his eyes told her it was exactly the response he wanted. Though he was a learned man, and far above her social class, he always set her at ease.

"Up, up!" Aiden pulled on her skirts.

Edward knelt down beside him, plucked a white-blossomed wild-flower from the grass, and placed it in the boy's chubby hand. "Now, give that to your mother," he whispered, and scooped Aiden up, propping him on his hip. Aiden held out the tiny flower, and Ruby took it.

"Thank you." Ruby smiled, knowing full well the poor thing would be wilted beyond redemption by the time they arrived home.

"His idea. Headed home?"

"Aye."

"Good. Keep the omnibus fare, I'll take you myself."

"But you just arrived! Didn't you?"

"I've seen enough. Come, there is room on the bench for all of us. But I'll need this one to help me drive." Edward bounced Aiden on his hip and the baby gurgled with delight.

Once seated on the plush leather bench with Aiden settled on Edward's lap, Ruby drank in the scent of freshly mown grass. Birdsong flitted through the air as the buggy wound its way through the Green and the Playground, around the Pond and along the wooded Promontory until exiting through the southeast Scholar's Gate. It was not a leisurely pace.

"Thank you, Aiden. Now, back to your mama." Ruby guided Aiden's chubby legs over to her own lap and noticed Edward's smile was tight. He drove Justus a little faster than usual, and his gaze constantly roved the periphery.

"Are you worried about your father being home alone?" she tried.

"Hm? Oh. No, Schaefer is capable." Ah yes. Ruby had forgotten Edward shared the nursing duties with his father's manservant.

Suddenly, his jaw set as he stared straight ahead. Then she heard it, too.

"Fighting? On Fifth Avenue?" Ruby looked around, bewildered. She'd grown used to these scenes along the Bowery and in Five Points. But in midtown Manhattan? She clutched Aiden closer. "What's happening?"

"I was afraid of this. Hang on." He snapped the reins above Justus, and the buggy lurched over a broken cobblestone. "I think it's coming from a few blocks east of here, at the provost marshal's office. Just need to get past it and get you home."

"What? Please tell me, what's going on?"

Edward flattened his lips. "Lincoln's draft. They've drawn names, you see, to force men to refill the Union's dwindling ranks. They were in the papers over the weekend. Many of those selected come from working-class families. Many of them are Irish. They can't afford to pay the three hundred dollars it would take to buy their way out."

"Oh no."

Edward nodded. "That's what they thought. But that's not the end of it." He sighed. "Black men are exempt." He glanced at her. "They can volunteer in colored regiments, but they won't be drafted."

Dread knotted in Ruby's chest. The tensions between her people and the free blacks had been simmering for years. Free blacks complained that Irish immigrants were replacing them in the service trades—domestic servants, dock and railroad laborers, and more. The Irish felt themselves to be considered lower in the social strata than former slaves and clamored to climb over them. If blacks were exempt from the military draft and Irishmen were sent away, the jobs would go to the black community.

"They will want blood for this." Aiden squirmed in her lap but she held him firm. Pushing down the rising swell of fear, however, proved to be far more difficult.

"I pray not. But I fear it's likely."

Edward strained to see what was happening up ahead. *Lord, help us. Protect them. Show me the way.* Wasn't that always his recurring prayer? War had taught him that God didn't always show him the way *around* trials. Sometimes, He showed him the way *through* them.

43

Justus whinnied and twitched his mane as the phaeton approached a crowded intersection. *Too crowded.* "All right, boy, let's find another way." But just as Edward began to wheel the buggy around, a tide of men came rushing up from the cross street behind them. They were the men who kept the city going. Brawny men, corded with muscles and streaked with grime. They had poured their sweat into the railroads, machine shops, shipyards, and iron foundries. Their women had come with them, tattered and taut with tension, with crowbars and glass bottles for hands. The Black Joke Fire Engine Company No. 33 was here too, in full regalia, blistering, no doubt, that their traditional exemption had been revoked, as well.

Years of anger and frustration that had been banked up against the privileged class now blazed forth. A sooty-faced man broke a cobblestone from the road and hurled it over Edward's carriage and into a blurry group of policeman. Justus skittered sideways. Another cobblestone sailed overhead, and another, each one drawing shouts and screams from both sides.

Without a sound, Ruby shoved Aiden to the floor between her feet and trapped him beneath her knees. Lunging forward and clutching the dash rail with a knuckle-white grip, she covered her son's body with her own.

"Steady," Edward said. But the horse was not steady. He was young. *And frightened out of his wits.* Backward, forward, sideways Justus stepped. Rioters and police seethed and clashed. Crowbars, clubs, fence posts, paving stones all sought their prey with primal rage. *God! All is madness! This is not a battlefield, it is Fifth Avenue, New York City!* Justus reared and the carriage teetered on its left wheels before staggering back into place.

"Whoa, Justus!" Edward pulled hard on the reins, but Justus was beyond calming. Eyes wild, he reared again and pawed at the air, twisted frantically in his harness.

"Jump, Ruby!" She straightened, and Edward snatched Aiden from the floorboard. He grabbed Ruby's elbow and jerked her to her feet.

"Now!" With Aiden digging his fingers into Edward's throat, Edward boosted her out of the phaeton and leapt to the ground after her, right as Justus came crashing down to the pavement on his side.

Aiden's cheeks were wet on Edward's neck. "Get back! Steer clear of the horse!" He handed the baby to Ruby, and in the next instant, Edward was on the ground, unhitching the buggy's harness from the stunned horse. If Justus rioted like the rabid crowd around him, the phaeton would be a dangerous weapon, capable of injuring both Justus and anyone in his path.

"Steady, boy, steady." Edward stroked the horse's neck and grabbed the reins below his bridle.

"There's a three-hundred-dollar man!" The voice sounded far away, until a strap of leather tore across his flesh. "Down with rich men! Can't buy yer way out o' this!"

Stunned, Edward stumbled before whirling around to face his attacker. *A soft answer turneth away wrath.* "Friend, you have reason to be upset, yet I have no quarrel with you. I would never buy a substitute, I serve myself as—"

"How does it feel to be beaten down, laddie?" The belt sliced through the air again and raked through his side, stealing the air from his lungs as fire spiked through his core. "Never mind, don't tell me. I already know."

Justus jerked the reins out of Edward's hands and bolted.

Another man sneered, a club clenched in his fist. All around them, people were shouting, screaming, kicking, pulling, shoving, punching. The jagged edge of a broken cobblestone came down on the back of Edward's head. He dropped to his knees, waited for the world to stop spinning and for his breakfast to settle back down in his stomach.

"Edward!" Ruby screamed from the edge of his vision. He pushed himself back up and turned to her. Strands of red hair whipped about her flashing green eyes. Her dress was striped with axle grease.

"Got yerself a little wench, too, I see. Only she looks a mite better fed than mine, that's what."

Ruby flinched as the slur landed upon her like a handful of dung. But it put steel in Edward's spine. He thrust himself between her and Aiden and the angry men.

"Leave them alone now, gentlemen." Surprising, how steady one's voice could be when one was in such pain.

They howled with whiskey-scented laughter. "'Gentlemen!' How do ye like that? Well, *kind sir,* I'll tell ye what. It makes no difference to me who's under my belt so long as I get a sound thrashing in. Ye'll take her share, then, will ye?"

"Gladly." If the Shepherd King David could slay lions and bears for the sake of his sheep, surely Edward Goodrich should be able to stand a leather belt for two in his keeping. After all, it was only last September he'd taken a bullet meant for his friend Dr. Caleb Lansing, his lingering limp a daily reminder. It seemed he had quite a knack for getting in the way.

"Edward!" Ruby shouted again and stepped closer, holding Aiden tight. "Patrick, Seamus, Kevin!" Edward feared she had gone mad. "Aye, I know you lads, and more's the pity! Shame on you! You are threatening an innocent man, a chaplain with the army! He has served his time and still serves the wounded right here in New York's hospitals!" Her voice strengthened with every syllable, and her Irish accent sharpened, puncturing through the din of men grumbling into their beards. "I'm one of you, I am, we come from the same land! And I have scratched out a living with my belly clawing for food, same as anyone here, that's what. I'm sorry about the draft, lads, really I am, but if you beat this man for the wrongs of another, then—then God have mercy on your souls, for the law won't, that's what!"

A crowbar clattered to the ground, and Ruby turned to face a bright-cheeked woman in a threadbare purple gown, holding her hands out to Ruby, palms up, as though begging for alms.

"Ruby?"

Ruby squinted toward the voice.

"Bedad! It's Ruby Shannon O'Flannery!" Black hair falling into her eyes, she turned to the men. "Get out of here, you're fightin' your own, you are! It's Ruby, don't you remember? Shoo!" The woman swung her broken bottle in a wide arc around her. "Her Matthew fought with Sean and the lads in the 69th straight off! Died in Virginia, he did! You'll do as she says! Ruby, darlin', you're home at last! I thought I'd never see you again, that's what. Look at you now! My, how time has been kind to you." Tears glazed wobbly paths down her cheeks and gathered beneath her trembling chin.

Ruby gasped, and Edward strained his ears to hear her whisper, "Emma!" She shifted Aiden's weight to her other hip and patted his back as his little shoulders heaved with sobs.

"Oh!" Emma clapped her hands over her heart. "Such a bonnie wee lad, Ruby!"

Emma reached for Ruby, and with but a moment's hesitation, she took Emma's grimy hand. The women embraced, Aiden sandwiched between them, until at length, Ruby pulled back.

Edward cleared his throat. "And to whom do I owe my surprising rescue?" The ache in his back and ribs intensified as the crowd ebbed away, and he struggled to keep it from showing in his face.

Emma snorted. "Go on, now. 'Twas Ruby making the lads think twice with her own speech first."

"Well. I am Edward Goodrich." He reached out and shook her hand, noting with some alarm that her nails were painted even brighter than her face.

"This is Emma Connors," Ruby offered. "My neighbor."

———

New York City
Wednesday, July 15, 1863

"How bad is it?" Ruby swung wide the door and let Edward push through it, his shoulders sagging with the knowledge of good and evil.

"Apocalyptic." Shadows clung beneath his red-rimmed eyes. "Very, very bad."

"Come sit down. Eat."

Edward followed her into the dining room and eased himself into a chair. Ruby tossed a colander to Aiden, who happily practiced sitting in it and getting out again while she scurried into the kitchen to scoop biscuits and stew into a bowl for her chaplain friend.

"Eat first, then tell me." She set the steaming dish in front of him, fully aware they were steaming just fine without it. All windows and doors had been locked shut ever since Monday.

He bowed his head in silence, then began his dinner. When he closed his eyes and sighed with the first forkful of roast beef, she realized he probably had not eaten a decent meal since their harrowing escape on Monday morning. A policeman had caught Justus by the reins before he had left the block, and once the crowds had dispersed, they were able to take him and the carriage home after all. Emma begged to see Ruby again, and Ruby had agreed. *Later*, they had agreed, as Emma picked up her crowbar.

Mrs. Kurtz had not come on Monday for her gown, nor did she come yesterday or today. The rioters had broadened their targets to include not just policemen and draft officers, but Republicans, the wealthy, and blacks. People had died. Perhaps they were dying still.

Ruby sat quietly as Edward ate. His eyelids drooping, he sipped his black coffee before leaning on his elbows and looking her square in the eyes. Ruby detected no warmth in them now, only the darkness he had seen here, in their own city. "I don't know where to begin."

"With your father." Ruby squeezed her hands together in her lap. "How is he?"

"Fine, thank you." He paused, spinning the saltshaker around on the table. "Some mansions on Fifth Avenue have been looted and burned, and some homes just a few blocks from here were destroyed, too. They cut the telegraph lines. Sacked Brooks Brothers for its profiteering with uniforms made from shoddy. Thousands of rioters broke into the armory, took carbines—rifles—and then burned the building down even though ten rioters were still inside."

"Did they escape?"

"No." Folding his hands in his lap, Edward pressed his lips together for a long moment before continuing. "They have made barricades in the streets. I believe they are truly at war. With New York. Including its children." He shook his head. "They burned down the Colored Orphans Asylum, Ruby." His voice wavered.

Nausea rolled Ruby's stomach as she cast a blurry glance at Aiden. Were her countrymen really so vile? "What happened?" she whispered.

"Thank God they all escaped alive and by the guidance of an Irishman, word has it. Paddy McCafferty? Do you know him?"

Ruby shook her head, although she wished she knew this heroic Paddy rather than the rioters she had called by name on Monday.

"Well, the boys and girls are safe, but they'll need a different home. Actually, I fear most of the city's black residents will be looking for another home if they aren't safe in the arms of Jesus by now."

Ruby sucked in a breath. "What?"

"Have you not read the newspaper?"

"Only the headlines. I'd rather hear it from you." She pinned him with her gaze and watched the struggle behind his eyes. Was she selfish for asking him to repeat what he had seen?

"Whatever violence you can imagine an Irishman doing to a freeman, it has been done."

She blinked. "I can imagine quite a lot." *Destroying their property. Beating them. Mutilating them. Drowning them. Shooting. Lynching.*

"It has been done." He spun the saltshaker still, with trembling hand. "Many times over."

The words cost him, she could tell. Edward fell into silence then, and Ruby did not pull him out. She only sat at his elbow, watching Aiden roll around on the rug, his bottom wedged in the colander, and wondered how long her son would believe the world was a beautiful place that existed to make him happy. She wondered what he would do when he discovered it did not. Would he reach for the bottle? Or a gun? Or a noose? Did his Irish blood condemn him to a life of violence? *No, please, God.* She would raise him different than that. Besides, he was only half-Irish. At least, as far as she knew.

Edward leaned back in his chair and winced, snapping Ruby from her reverie.

"Has anyone treated your wounds yet?"

He grimaced as he leaned away from the rungs of the chair. "You mean there is something that can help these stripes feel better?"

"Aye," she said. "Comfrey leaves boiled into a tea should help." She had used them countless times to soothe Aiden's cuts and scratches. "You just soak linen strips or towels in the tea and place them on the wounds."

"Can you help me?"

Her heart skipped a beat. What had she done? She couldn't help him, she couldn't touch a man, not even this man, not *any* man, not after—her eyes squeezed shut against the sneering face that surged before her. She could almost smell his pomade and whiskey. Ruby shook her head, trying to loosen memory's tentacles from her spirit.

"It's just that—I don't have any comfy tea. Can you make it for me?"

"Comfrey."

"Comfrey sounds comfy to me." The corner of his mouth tipped up.

"All right. I'll go make it. It will take a few minutes."

By the time Ruby returned carrying a tray of tea-soaked linens, Edward had fallen asleep lying on his stomach on the rug in the rear parlor, Dickens curled next to him. Kneeling down beside him, she could not bring herself to rouse him from his slumber. It was what he needed most of all.

She looked at the towels, already cooling. They really should be applied when quite warm to do the most good. *Come now lassie, you can do better than this. It is only Edward. You are a widow, not a maiden.*

Gingerly, Ruby tugged up his shirttail to expose the tracks the belt had left on his back. The damage may not have been so great save for the brass buckle digging its tooth into his skin before tearing through it. She cringed at the sight. No, she was not cut out to be a nurse like Charlotte, or to visit the wounded in hospitals nearly every day like Edward did. But God help her, she should be able to lay comfrey-soaked strips on top of these scabbed-over gulleys through his flesh. Really, she didn't even have to touch him.

Ruby spread the cloths over the inflamed stripes and sat back on her heels. It was a victory, and she thanked God for it.

Aiden toddled over, tin colander in his chubby hand, and Ruby scooped him up before he could climb on Edward or pull the cat's tail. "Come, darlin'." She kissed Aiden's temple as she peeled his little fingers off the handle. "It's time we get you to bed."

Ka-boom! Ka-boom! Ka-boom!

Edward jerked awake and stumbled to his feet, wet towels peeling from his back as he did so. His heart hammered against his ribs as comprehension knifed through his drowsiness. New York's troops had come back from Gettysburg.

Ka-boom!

And were firing cannons at the rioters.

Quickly, he swiped up the towels that had fallen to the carpet and dropped them on the tray at his feet, then rushed to the bottom of the stairway.

"Ruby!" he called up. "I've got to go now. Lock the door behind me!"

Edward slammed the door shut after himself and bounded down the steps. The twilight sky was stained a dirty orange, and thick with the smell of turpentine, a choking reminder of the buildings the rioters had torched. The black community downtown had fared the worst, by far, as had the restaurants, saloons, and brothels that had served them. Sidewalk bonfires consumed furniture in these neighborhoods, and kept the skies glowing even after the sun had set. The waterfront had all but emptied of dark-skinned New Yorkers.

But it was the cannons that concerned Edward now. They seemed close, only blocks away. He jogged on Sixteenth Street east toward the sound, through Union Square Park, past Lexington Avenue, and Third Avenue—and stopped.

Bronze, short-barreled howitzer cannons gleamed as they spewed grapeshot into the barricades erected at First Avenue. Clouds of gun smoke belched from their mouths, and the taste of saltpeter bit on Edward's tongue. The earth shuddered, reverberating in his chest.

The rioters engaged desperately. When a chink was punched through the barricade, bricks came hurling out of the open windows of the tenement behind it. Then came the sniper fire. Soldiers who had survived the battle of Gettysburg and then a hard march back up north were being felled by their own neighbors.

"Fix bayonets!" The order jolted through Edward like lightning. *Bayonets?* "Charge!"

"No wait!" But Edward's voice was lost in the cacophony of the charge. Did they understand that the building surely held more than just the snipers and stone throwers? That women and children could be huddled in the corners? Visions of the Irishwomen he'd seen on the streets since Monday flitted through his mind then. Women, in fact, had been the ones who crowbarred up the tracks of the Fourth Avenue commuter rail line above Forty-Second Street. They had beaten policemen until they were unrecognizable.

But of course, those women did not represent the whole. There had to be more like Ruby O'Flannery among the Irishwomen. They just weren't the type to be seen. They were the type to hide and pray for it all to pass on by.

"Wait!" Edward cried out again, and pushed through the gap in the barricade and into the bowels of the tenement building. He ran into room after room, calling, listening, looking. Until finally, he heard it.

"I mean you no harm!" It was not an Irish accent. Perhaps the reason she had been spared the soldiers' steel blade.

"I am coming, just a moment!"

Edward found her then, exactly as he had imagined her. Small, unthreatening, yet threatened. "Can you walk?" Edward helped her to her feet.

"I believe I twisted my ankle."

"Here, let me help you." He wrapped his arm around her waist and ushered her outside. She was so very thin, her weight was nothing for him to support. She was draped in rags, but her hair was pulled neatly into a bun.

"Are you hurt elsewhere? Other than your ankle?" He eased her down onto a barrel while the firefight continued inside the building.

She stared at his face, eyes growing wide. Her bony hand fluttered to her heart. "George?" she whispered. "It's me, Vivian! You have found me!"

"No, I'm sorry, dear woman, you must be mistaken. My name is—"

"Of course, of course! It has been so long you see, and you look so much like your father. You are Edward." Tears glossed her eyes. "My, how you've grown!"

Edward cocked his head and studied her.

"Edward Goodrich. My nephew." She clasped his hand in both of hers. "I never thought I'd see you again. You look just like your father did at your age. Oh! I can scarcely believe he sent you for me, after all this time!"

But Edward had not seen this woman, ever. His father was an only child, like Edward. At least, that's what he'd always said.

A few more soldiers jogged up to the tenement, one of them shouting above the rest. As they drew closer, the shouting became louder, more frantic.

"That's my building! That's my home! Hey! My mother's in there!"

Vivian whipped her head toward the shouting, eyes blazing. She stood on her good foot.

"Jack?"

The soldier froze.

Vivian shouted again, waving her arms. "Jack! Jack! Over here!"

Edward stepped back and Jack ran to her, engulfing her thin frame in his arms, and she wept onto his dusty blue frock coat. "I can't believe you're here! My son, my son, oh thank You, God, my son is home!"

She pulled back and removed his kepi, brushed his saddle-brown hair to the side. "It's you," she whispered. "Look at you. Nineteen years old now, and taller, too."

"And Caitlin? Is she here?" Jack looked over his mother's head, scanning the faces around them.

Her smile wilting, two lines appeared between her eyes as she shook her head. "She'd been sending me money for months—never put a note with it, and never a return address, but I recognize her handwriting on the envelope. It's just the sort of thing she would do, too. Then all of a sudden, the money stopped coming. That was more than a year ago."

Jack dropped his chin to his chest and scuffed the dirt with his brogans. "I thought she'd made it home before me."

"From where?" The words leapt from Vivian's throat as her bony fingers clutched his biceps. "Jack, do you know where your sister has been?"

"She was with me." The boy's voice quivered. "But I—I lost her. She's missing in action." He winced at his mother's strangled gasp. "But she might be all right. If Caitlin is alive somewhere—anywhere at all—she will survive."

Eyes squeezed shut for a moment, Vivian's lips trembled even as she nodded. Whatever she whispered in her son's ear as she embraced him once more, Edward could not hear.

"Come," Edward said as soon as Vivian released Jack's neck. "You need food and rest." Clearly, she needed more than that. But at least, it was a start.

Chapter Four

Atlanta, Georgia
Thursday, July 16, 1863

"Many years ago there was an emperor who was so excessively fond of new clothes that he spent all his money on them.'"

The low rumble of Noah Becker's voice drew Caitlin in from the porch and to the doorway between the main hall and the parlor. Slowly, she sipped her cup of raspberry tea and drank in the scene. The room was dressed for summer, with reed mats on the pine floor, and bleached linen slipcovers protecting the sofa and upholstered chairs from the dirt and dust that clung to summer's breeze. Ruffle-edged white sheers sashayed in front of open floor-to-ceiling windows. A gilt-framed mirror hung on picture molding over the fireplace between gold leaf candle stands with crystal accents. In the middle of the room, flanked by two slipcovered chairs, a tea table proudly displayed a decorative oil lamp.

But the real centerpiece of the room, Caitlin thought, was Ana nestled in her papa's lap on the sofa, her head resting on his shoulder, her gaze fixed on the pages from which he read. Evening's rosy glow filled the room as pink champagne would fill a goblet, but the warmth radiated from father and daughter, alone.

"Life was very gay in the great town where he lived; hosts of strangers came to visit it every day, and among them one day, two swindlers." The rich, melodic timbre of Noah's voice proved that reading to Ana was not a chore, but a cherished ritual, much like teatime had been with Caitlin's mother.

Unobserved, she knelt on the reed mat for the rest of the story, and her eyelids slid closed. Her own father held her tenderly on his lap and read to her, once upon a time, as well. Of course, Da's accent was Irish, and Noah's was German—but the two men held two important things in common. They had chosen to leave the lands of their births to adopt America as their home, and they loved their daughters.

Yes, Caitlin had been known once, and treasured. Tears pricked her eyes. For more than two years now, she had sheathed her true identity. She was beginning to forget what it felt like to be loved for who she really was. Unbidden, her mother's face now surged before her. *Poor Mama.* She, too, had been truly loved once, and maybe that was the curse of it. Da had loved Mama with every thread of his being, and though she gave up her privileged standing to be with him, she thrived as his wife. They had been so happy together in Seneca Village—Da, Mama, Caitlin, and her brother, Jack, four years her junior. Life overflowed with simple pleasures.

When Da died, he took the light of day right with him. At the ages of seventeen and thirteen, Caitlin and Jack were stunned by grief. But Mama had been crippled by it. If Da could see what became of her then . . .

Caitlin opened her eyes again to wiggle free of memory's grasp, and focused on the fairy tale instead.

"'But he has nothing on!' at last cried all the people. The Emperor writhed, for he knew it was true but he thought 'the procession must go on now,' so he held himself stiffer than ever, and the chamberlains held up the invisible train."

Ana sucked in a breath before releasing it in a belly laugh.

"Ja, der Kaiser ist sehr absurd, nicht wahr? All right, to bed with you."

Noah stood and reached his open hands back behind his shoulders. Ana clasped them and scrambled onto his back. With her legs squeezed around his waist, she wrapped her arms around his neck and kissed his cheek.

"How many more sleeps until you go, Papa?"

Caitlin's heart seized in the silence that followed, and she retreated to the porch to respect the privacy their moment required.

"Take your cup, Miss Caitlin?" Bess smoothed her yellow kerchief over her hair before offering calloused hands.

"Oh, I can take it to the kitchen myself, thank you." Caitlin would never feel comfortable accepting slave labor.

A smile brightened Bess's shining brown face, and faint wrinkles fanned from her eyes. "No need for that, now. Mr. Becker pays me to clean. And I'm headed to my quarters for the night, which just so happens to be above the kitchen. Land sakes, you're holding on to that dish tighter than a noon squint!" Her rich voice bubbled with laughter. "Come on, now."

Reluctantly, Caitlin relinquished her teacup and watched Bess shake her head all the way to the kitchen, muttering something about "that strange white lady" as she went.

A sigh escaped Caitlin as she eased into a rocking chair and gently swayed to her own lazy rhythm. Soon, the muffled voices of Bess and Saul talking in their quarters floated to her on the breeze, punctuated by a rare burst of masculine laughter echoing in the house behind her. Somehow, it only made Caitlin's heart heavier for Noah and Ana. With their hearts knit so tightly together, the unraveling from each other would prove that much more painful when the time came for him to leave. It would be easier, far easier, if Noah and Ana didn't get along so well.

Get out! I don't want to see you here again! You've done enough! The last words her mother had spoken to her slammed against her memory, bruising her just as much as they had the fateful night they had been hurled. Rippling bitterness gave way to a wave of regret for what had happened next.

"Do you mind if I join you?" Noah stood over her, framed by a sky flaming with broad strokes of marigold and magenta.

Liberated from her grim recollections, she smiled into Noah's red-rimmed eyes. "Please do."

He dropped into his rocker as if his energy had gone to bed without him, and stared out over the gardens. A chorus of tree frogs and crickets mingled with the creaking of their wooden rockers.

"You are the center of her world, aren't you?"

"She is the center of mine." He kneaded the back of his neck. "It is almost frightening. Can you understand?"

"Love is risky." She paused. "You have something to lose."

He nodded, slowly. "I also have something to fight for. Die for, if necessary."

"Mr. Becker—" She sought his eyes. "You have someone to live for. You are no use to her in the grave, you know."

Shadows sagged on his face. She should tread lightly. And yet— "What would she do if something happened to you? Where is the girl's mother?"

Noah leaned forward, elbows on his knees, and stared at the white-washed floorboards between his feet. "She is—gone." His voice was rough.

Caitlin scolded herself for bringing it up. "I'm sorry. Has it been long?"

"Ana never knew her mother. We do not speak of her," Noah added, his tone leaving no room for debate.

"As you say." She paused, gauging his mood before forging ahead. "But have you no other family to care for Ana?"

"I hired you to care for Ana." He leaned back again in his rocking chair, breathing deeply as pine-scented wind swept through the porch.

"Have you forgotten so quickly how you came into your good fortune?"

He smiled, but Caitlin did not return it. "That is not what I meant. In the event—"

"I know what you meant!" His voice was restrained, but only as a bridle keeps a stallion in check. He pushed himself out of his chair and began pacing the length of the porch. "I know what you meant," he said again, quieter this time. "Do you suppose I have not considered all the possible outcomes of my decision? Do you think I have not imagined my precious child as an orphan forced upon the charity of those who would see her as a mere duty?" His footsteps fell heavier upon the floorboards, thudding like a distant drum. Caitlin's chair stilled as his agony drilled into her with every word, every step.

"Then . . . must you go?"

He gripped the back of his rocking chair with both hands and expelled a sigh. "How many men do you see in this city?" He shook his head. "Let me rephrase that. How many men between the ages of eighteen and forty-five do you see here, other than the five hundred soldiers stationed in Atlanta?"

It wasn't many. Not since last fall, when the Confederacy had broadened the age range of those eligible for the draft in the second Conscription Act. Some men were exempt. Physicians with more than five years of experience, for example. Railroad and foundry workers, salt laborers who produced twenty bushels of salt per day, telegraph operators. City government officials and ministers. Professors and teachers with more than twenty pupils—*Oh*.

"You're eligible for conscription now that the institute closed, aren't you?"

"I'll be hanged first rather than be forced into it. If I'm going to fight, I'll go of my own accord, with my honor intact."

Caitlin turned her gaze heavenward. A deep blue curtain had lowered in the sky, banking the blazing sunset. If only its beauty could also extinguish the dismay now kindling within her. Enlistment would separate Noah and Ana for three years, or until the end of the war. Unless of course, he did not survive. Caitlin's heart buckled at the thought of Ana losing her adoring father, as Caitlin had lost hers. *Mourning clothes fade. Grief doesn't.* The sharp edges might dull with time, but the ache never disappeared. There had to be another way for them. It could cost up to two thousand dollars, likely a few years' wages. But if he had the means, he could legally be exempted from service to a dying cause.

She rose from her rocking chair and edged closer to Noah. "Have you considered a substi—"

"No, no, I would never pay another man to take my place." His eyes glinted like steel in the twilight. "My conscience would not permit it. If he were killed, or if his family suffered in his absence . . ."

His unyielding eyes were the flint to Caitlin's fear for this tiny family, sparking a burning anger in her gut. She was angry that she, a Union veteran, had taken pity on this Rebel recruit. She was angry that her pity had compelled her to suggest a route that was less than honorable, even in her own estimation. And she was angry that even though honor cost him everything, he was willing to pay the price. *And for what?*

"*Your* family will suffer in your absence, Noah Becker, you stubborn mule of a man!" Her words flew roughshod ahead of her. "As a matter of fact, I tend to hate draft dodgers, deserters, and anyone else who would shirk their duty because it does not suit them to be inconvenienced. But in your case, I'd think you might feel some duty to your own daughter, considering you're the only kin she has in this world." She had plowed ahead too far. She knew it.

Noah walked away from her, then circled back. "My duty to Ana includes being the kind of man a father should be. A man who chooses to sacrifice, a man who gives himself to the greater good."

"What greater good? The Confederacy is crum—" She caught herself, looked around, cut her voice low. "It's crumbling, Mr. Becker. I know it isn't popular to say it, but surely you know, surely everyone knows it, the way everyone knew the emperor in your story was walking around naked but refused to speak the truth. With the defeats in Vicksburg and Gettysburg, we are as exposed as that arrogant emperor.

Yet no one speaks the truth. The House of Dixie is falling."

Breath pulsing against her corset, she awaited his rebuttal. Then she remembered she could be arrested for the speech she had just made. Nausea wormed through her middle. Noah knew the law. Would he prosecute? *Surely he cannot support all the South stands for, not if he "operated under the law" without agreeing with it.*

Moments moved like molasses. But he did not deny her treasonous words. Instead, "I'd rather die for something I believe in, than live as a coward for the rest of my life."

"And just what is it you believe in, that is worth the cost of your life?"

"My family, Miss McKae. My home." A wry smile bent his lips. "This is why I need to fight, and now, more than ever. You're right. Most of Tennessee has been lost to Rosecrans, and if General Bragg cannot hold Chattanooga, the bluecoats will pour into Georgia." He slacked a hip against a column and looked out into the darkness. "I must help defend our state from the ravages of war. Our city. And yes, our home. When I fight, it will not be for the sake of slavery. It will be to protect all I hold dear." He turned and faced her then, though night masked his expression. "*That* is my duty to Analiese." His voice cracked on his daughter's name.

Caitlin's throat ached as she wiped the tears from her face. "I will do my utmost for her in your absence."

"I am indebted."

"You will come home."

His silence lashed her heart.

———

Noah's head throbbed. Lately, he felt so much older than his thirty-one years, especially in the oppressive solitude of night. It was here, caught between sunset and the coming dawn, that he found himself tangled in the web of his own convictions.

Caitlin had retired to her bedroom upstairs hours ago, and here he

61

sat at his desk in the office, bathed in the eerie halo of a "Confederate" candle. At least this particular version didn't require the use of any precious matches. Sweet gum globes Saul had gathered from the woods, floating in a shallow bowl of melted lard, glowed when saturated, without being lit. The candles that gave off brighter light—twisted rags soaked in beeswax and twined around a bottle—Noah reserved for winter's shorter days.

Not that I will be here. He leaned down and stroked Rascal's fading red coat, the old dog's snoring barely penetrating Noah's thoughts. His reasons for enlisting were sound. The timing was right. Everything he had said to Caitlin was true.

At least in some interpretation. *When I fight, it will not be for the sake of slavery,* he had said. *It will be to protect all I hold dear.* Noah dropped his hands to the armrests. No, he was not fighting for the sake of slavery. But he was fighting with and for the Confederacy. It was only natural. This was his country now. The land for which he had left his family and the Rhineland.

"No, not this," he muttered to himself.

He did not immigrate to a confederation, but to the United States of America, the best example of democracy in the world. The Germany in which he had grown up was a conglomeration of large and small principalities, many of them ruled by absolute sovereigns. The land seethed with territorial rivalries. There was an aristocracy, and there were masses of downtrodden peasants. At sixteen years of age, Noah and his older brother, Wilhelm, dropped their university textbooks and took up the tricolor flag—black, red, and gold—that had been so long prohibited. They proudly became revolutionaries in 1848, for the unification of Germany into one nation-state, and equal rights for all citizens before the law.

And now, a mere fifteen years later, Noah would volunteer to fight for the right of the United States to disunite. Perhaps he had already aligned himself with slavery by prospering in a state that prospered by slave labor, and in a city that did not trust its colored people. The few free blacks in the city had a nine o'clock curfew. They were not allowed to carry canes or pipes. There was even a law against vagrancy, loosely defined as wandering or strolling about or leading an idle or immoral life. The first offense resulted in two years of slavery. The second offense: permanent reenslavement.

If Wilhelm could see him now . . . During the Revolution, they and the other revolutionaries had been so zealous for equal rights, they did not even want to use formal titles, like "Professor" or "Doctor." Instead, they would simply call each other "Citizen," an attempt to break down a class system that divided them so sharply.

Ridiculous idea. But the principle of equal rights for all people was not. It was fundamental.

According to the Confederacy's vice president, Georgia native Alexander Stephens, however, it was slavery that was fundamental. Stephens had said so right here in Atlanta on March 21, 1861. Several thousand people heard him outside the Atlanta Hotel, and two weeks later he gave the same speech—his "Cornerstone Speech"—in Savannah. The transcript had been printed and reprinted in newspapers across the South.

Eyebrows knitting together, Noah rifled through some papers until he found the edition of the *Southern Confederacy* he was looking for. The print was difficult to read by the glow of sweet gum globes, but his memory aided him well. Speaking of the Confederacy's new government, Stephens had said:

. . . its foundations are laid, its corner-stone rests, upon the great truth that the negro is not equal to the white man; that slavery subordination to the superior race is his natural and normal condition. This, our new government, is the first, in the history of the world, based upon this great physical, philosophical, and moral truth . . .

Those at the North . . . assume that the negro is equal, and hence conclude that he is entitled to equal privileges and rights with the white man. If their premises were correct, their conclusions would be logical and just—but their premise being wrong, their whole argument fails. . . . They were attempting to make things equal which the Creator had made unequal.

Noah slammed the paper down and pinched the bridge of his nose. His lawyer-trained mind could argue both sides of the debate between states' rights and federal power. He also disdained Lincoln's political angle in exempting four border states and parts of Louisiana and Virginia from the Emancipation Proclamation—not that the rest of the South paid any credence to what was considered a toothless document of a "foreign government," anyway. But he could not stomach that the Confederate White House had proclaimed slavery as its cornerstone.

His bitter abhorrence for it was flavored with hypocrisy. Before he rented his own slaves for his own household, before he had been a revolutionary and an academic, he had known what it meant to work another man's land and give him half the proceeds. He had been born into a family of tenant-farmers, working on an estate in a castle, not as slaves, but like serfs.

It was why he and Wilhelm and thousands of others rose up against the class system.

And now here he was, participating in it all over again. Only this time, he was in the master class. Did reaching the upper echelon of society squelch the fire behind his former principles?

I did not come here to become rich, he reminded himself. *I came here for asylum!* If he had wanted wealth, he would have planted cotton and tobacco. If he wanted status, he would have purchased slaves, dozens of them, rather than just renting two.

Hypocrite. Pain twinging behind his eyes, Noah tucked the *Southern Confederacy* on a shelf behind a volume of Christopher Marlowe. *Now, Faustus, must thou needs be damned? And canst thou not be saved?* The haunting lines hissed in his soul. Noah Becker loved law and order. But this time, whether he followed his fledgling government's laws or not, he felt doomed.

His spirit dimmed like the spiky sweet gum balls barely gleaming in the bowl. Soon their light would be out completely.

Rising, he took up the crude candle and used it as a guiding light as he padded upstairs, Rascal following behind him. Quietly, he nudged open the door to Ana's room and peeked in. *Just as I thought.* She had wrapped herself in her sheet like a cocoon. With one hand, he loosened it. Her cheek was damp with perspiration, but he kissed it anyway before stepping out of the room.

The weight of his love for her crushed all doubt that there could be any other choice but to fight for her protection.

Forgive me, Brother.

Heavily, Noah entered his own chamber across the hall. He'd be exhausted in the morning, again. And yet, it could not come soon enough.

Chapter Five

New York City
Friday, July 17, 1863

*E*yebrows plunged downward, Edward Goodrich fastened the last of his uniform's brass buttons into place. He was running ten minutes behind in getting to work and more than a couple of decades behind in meeting the rest of his family. If, he reminded himself, the woman he met and brought home with him two nights ago could be trusted.

He had peppered the woman, Vivian, with questions. She'd known almost everything about his father, George, right down to his bulldog frown and knuckle-cracking habit. She had known that Edward had grown up without a mother, but with a succession of nannies. She knew that Edward's grandparents had been killed together in a carriage accident near their home in Buffalo, New York, and that George had sold everything and moved to New York City at the age of twenty. She claimed she had come with him. In any case, Vivian knew as much about George as Edward did.

"No. More," Edward growled as he brushed the lint off his jacket. Now Vivian was staying in a bedroom on the second floor while her son, Jack, remained with his regiment somewhere in New York City.

Six thousand troops now filled the ravaged metropolis. Third Avenue was lined with Seventh Regiment pickets. The Eighth Regiment Artillery Troop had their mountain howitzers trained on the streets around Gramercy Park. The 152nd New York Volunteers bivouacked in Stuyvesant Square.

Edward should be relieved he and Ruby and Aiden had survived the draft riots—"the largest single incident of civil disorder in the history of the United States," the paper had said. Death toll estimates varied wildly, from less than four hundred up to one thousand.

The staggering loss was not all that churned his belly. *How could George keep family a secret? Why would he let his sister live in need?* Edward had taken George off his laudanum so he could emerge back into coherency. All day yesterday he had been confined to his chamber as the effects of the drug wore off. If he didn't feel inclined to come out today, Edward would personally escort him. He needed some answers. Now.

Edward's lips pressed together as he left his dressing room and headed downstairs. *Lord, help me not judge him yet. Please bring him back so he can explain himself.*

The clinking of silverware on china trickled down the hall. Edward cleared his throat before stepping into the dining room. Sunlight bounced off the crystal chandelier and danced between the candlesticks on the rosewood table.

"Good morning." He smiled at the brittle-looking woman in front of him. Judging by the nearly empty Wedgewood plate in front of her, Cook's eggs and toast had been to her liking.

"Oh my!" Vivian drew her hand to her mouth for a moment, her chocolate-colored eyes round. "Don't you look grand! Oh! You must forgive me, Edward. It's just that you look so much the way I remember George the last time I saw him. Of course, he didn't see me. It was at the harbor, and he was in his uniform, shipping out for the Mexican

War. The uniform is different of course, but other than that . . ." She trailed off. "It's just so good to see you again."

"Vivian?"

Edward swiveled. His father was in his wheelchair in the doorway, with a wide-eyed Mr. Schaefer right behind him.

Recognition flickered over George's face. "Is it really you?" His voice was gruff.

Tears glazed Vivian's sunken cheeks. She stood. "It's me, George. Your sister is here."

"How?" George finally said, and the confirmation lit a fire under Edward's collar.

"It was Edward."

"Edward!" George snarled. "What have you done, boy?"

"What have I done? Aside from coming home to care for you, you mean? Aside from watching out for our neighbors during the worst mob uprising in our history?"

"You know exactly what I mean. Now *out* with it."

"I heard cannons firing on civilians Wednesday night and went out to see what I could do about it."

"You always did think of yourself as such a hero. Did you fire a weapon while you were there?"

"Of course not."

George laughed darkly. "Whoever heard of a hero who wouldn't stand up and fight like a man?"

"George!" Vivian gasped.

"Milksop."

Edward grit his teeth and prayed for composure. "The troops were shooting into the building. They charged with bayonets, with the aim to root out all the insurrectionists."

George grunted. "Rightfully so. Hope they dispatched them to Lucifer, too."

"Your sister was in the building, in mortal danger. I brought her out. She said I resemble you."

"In appearance only. This boy is so unlike me, sometimes I wonder if he is my son at all."

"George, George!" Vivian twisted her hands together. "What has happened, brother, for you to speak so unkindly?"

George glared at her then, his silence charged. "You shouldn't have to ask."

Vivian circled the table and took Edward's hand. "You shouldn't have to find out this way."

"He wasn't supposed to find out at all! There was no reason to! You chose your path, woman, and it led you away from me when you married that dirt-poor common Irish bloke. I told you what would happen! Now get out!"

"She stays." Edward's voice was edged with steel. "Unless of course, she can't stand sharing a roof with you. We have room. She is family."

George shook his head. "Not any—"

"She is family," he said again, louder. "She stays. Now if you'll excuse me, I'm late for work."

"See if some of the courage of those wounded soldiers can rub off on you today!" George's voice chased after Edward as he slammed the door behind him. If only it were as easy to shut out the bitterness taking root in his heart.

"Get me out of here," George muttered to his manservant. "I'll breakfast in my chamber."

"Very good, sir."

Vivian watched helplessly as her brother, once so tall and strong as an ox, was wheeled away.

She was alone. Again.

Vivian McKae had dreamed of seeing her big brother again. But in her dreams, he had wanted to see her, too. Why had she not imagined it would turn out this way? Why had she not guessed that his home would be a cave, and that he would be a shell of a man himself? It was not his physical injuries that concerned her, but the damage that had clearly been done to his soul.

Still standing, she propped her fists on her slender hips. She had work to do.

Mr. Schaefer passed by in the hall, on his way, she presumed, to the kitchen. By the time he reappeared with a tray of food, she intercepted him.

"I'll take that to him, thank you."

He frowned. "Thank you, but I should do it myself. I'll need to feed him, too, you understand."

"I can do that, too. We're family." She took the tray from the servant before another protest could form on his lips, and favored her sore ankle all the way down the hall to George's room.

She tapped on the door before pushing it open. His wheelchair was pushed up to a small round table in front of the dormant marble fireplace. His face was drawn, his charcoal hair, peppered with grey, slightly askew. George's spirit seemed as lifeless as his limbs. But somewhere in there was the brother she had once known.

"Let's try this again, shall we?" she said as she sat the tray on the table and removed the cover. She pulled a needlepoint chair close to him. "Good morning, George, it's so good to see you again. How long has it been? Twenty-three years? Twenty-four?"

"Not long enough." He glared at her, his grey eyes cold and drooping as much as his mustache. "Where's Schaefer?"

"I told him I could take care of you. Just as you took care of me."

"Now listen, I told you—"

"Oh hush. I'm not being sarcastic. There was a time when you did care for me, and very faithfully I might add. I would have been lost without you right after Mother and Father died. But you brought me to New York City with you and provided for me out of your own salary. Do you remember that?" Vivian had been fourteen years old at the time, and George twenty. He had managed the sale of their father's entire estate and the relocation from Buffalo to New York City.

71

She smiled at the memory, and he frowned in equal proportion. "I adored you, George. Do you hear me? It's what little sisters do. You were the sun and the moon to me before I married James."

He grunted and looked away.

Her gaze landed on heavy velvet drapes still encasing the windows. "Let's let some sunshine in, shall we?" She crossed the room and shoved the curtains apart. Light spilled onto the floor.

"This room will bake like an oven later with the sun coming in like that."

"Then I'll draw the curtains later. Hungry?" She returned to her seat and picked up a piece of toast smothered in raspberry jam.

"I seem to have lost my appetite."

"Are you certain?"

"Terribly."

"Then do you mind? Thank you." She took a bite of his toast and relished the jam on her tongue, raspberry seeds and all.

"Congratulations, Vivian. Just look at what's become of you."

She swallowed. Tucked a strand of black hair back into its bun. Yes, she was thin. And dressed in a threadbare, patched calico dress. But she was clean since availing herself of George's water closet.

"You look like dung."

Vivian dabbed a linen napkin to her lips, hiding the tremble of her chin. "Sticks and stones."

"No. Truly. You are the very embodiment of the slums. Starving. Sallow. And I dare say you look older than me though I know you are only forty-three."

Dishes clattered as she slammed her napkin on the table. "I asked you for help!"

"I *did* help you."

"Only when it suited."

"And you didn't suit yourself?"

Vivian sighed, placed her hands in her lap, and squeezed fistfuls of her thin skirt. "It broke my heart that your Sarah died when Edward was only one. No one could have guessed that she would have contracted yellow fever on her trip to New Orleans with you. I was happy to help raise him. I loved him, I loved you. I still do."

"The devil you did. You left us."

"Not for three years."

"You left us!" he shouted, eyes blazing, jowls quivering. "You left me. After Mother and Father died, after Sarah died, you left me."

"I was nineteen!"

"I was your brother! I was your family!"

"You still are."

He shook his head. "No. No. You chose poverty over provision, an immigrant laborer over me and Edward. I'll never understand you."

"I chose love, George. Surely you can understand that." *And heaven help me, I choose to love you again, too.*

"Love. What do you have to show for it?"

"Enough happy memories to live on for the rest of my life. A son and a daughter." She would not let her mind wander past James's death.

"Yes? And what has become of the children of a poor immigrant who feeds his family love instead of food?"

"Jack is a soldier. Like you were, George. He is brave and courageous, and has served his country honorably."

An eyebrow jutted into his forehead. He sniffed. "And the girl?"

"Caitlin—" she broke off. Her mind whirred with possibilities until she clamped down on them. "She is strong and smart." Her throat closed around unshed tears.

"And?"

"And she will be fine." *Please God . . .* "Are you sure you don't want any toast? Eggs?"

"I told you no. You might as well eat it yourself; you look as if you hadn't eaten since before the war started."

She shook her head. Suddenly, she wasn't hungry either.

———

Outside Atlanta, Georgia
Saturday, July 18, 1863

Out here, away from a city swollen with war and throbbing with nationalism, away from rutted roads that pulsed with people, away from fevered factories and screaming trains, Noah Becker could remember what he had loved most about America.

Closing his eyes, he inhaled the pine scent carried by wind that hushed through the trees like a mother to her child. Sugar Creek gurgled and glittered in the sun, hugging banks unsullied by man's progress. The clink of his horse's bridle, the drone of cicadas, the drilling of a pecker-wood from some unseen branch—it all harmonized in one resounding theme: possibility.

"It's beautiful here." Caitlin's soft voice drew him from his reverie, but did not jar him. She seemed to belong here as much as the dogwood and viburnum did.

"Yes, it is." He indulged in her velvety brown eyes. The breeze tugged a strand of cinnamon hair from beneath her straw hat, and he fought the urge to brush it from her cheek. She hooked it behind her ear and popped a freshly picked blueberry in her mouth. Her gaze drifted toward Ana and Saul, who stooped to help the girl find sweet gum globes despite his arthritic joints.

"I'm afraid we didn't come here just to gather." He pulled his der-ringer pistol from one pocket, along with a lacquered wooden box. "You need to learn to be the predator or else I fear you may be easy prey. While I'm gone." He added the last phrase more as a reminder to him-self than to clarify what he meant. *I'm leaving,* he often found himself muttering. *I'm leaving.* In truth, he may never come back.

All the more reason to equip Caitlin for her task.

"The lawyer is telling me to shoot someone?"

Noah smiled at the irony. And at the freckles dusting her nose. They made her look so innocent, he almost felt guilty placing a gun in her hand. Unfortunately, it was for the best. George Washington Lee's gang of ruffians patrolled the street with roving eyes and twitching clubs, hunting for anyone without a pass, and anyone who could be considered disloyal to the Confederacy.

"Just showing that you're armed can dissuade most to leave you alone. I hope you never have to use it." Noah turned the walnut-handled pistol over in his hand, his thumb grazing the intricate pattern in the metal. Sunlight sparked in Caitlin's eyes as she watched.

"Now," Noah continued. "If you do need to pull the trigger in self-defense, calculate your timing carefully. The derringer is for close-up shooting so I'm afraid you will have to let the threat get close before you shoot."

"How close?"

"Between three and twelve feet." He nearly cringed even as he said it. If a perpetrator was that close, he could reach her in a fraction of a second. "It fires just once and takes two minutes to reload. So make your shot count." Noah caught her gaze in his. "If anyone threatens your safety, or Ana's, you defend yourself. I don't care what color the uniform. I don't care if he's wearing a gunnysack. You stay in control of the situation with a steady hand. Understand?"

She nodded.

"Don't invite trouble. Don't go out after dark, don't go anywhere near the Athenaeum Theater, or the Car Shed. If you catch the scent of whiskey, you turn tail and go the other direction . . ." He took a breath. "Just use common sense. Stay safe. I'm counting on you."

"I understand."

I hope you do . . . Noah did not tell her about the spike in criminal activity he and the mayor had discussed. The court docket more than doubled in the last year with disorderly conduct, illegal liquor sales, prostitution, larceny, and food theft, even out of the commissary. Attempted murders doubled this year, arson tripled. Fornication, bigamy, and adultery cases were all on the rise. Atlanta was slipping back into its frontier ways of unpunished crime and vigilante justice.

"Now to load the pistol. It will be better if you do it yourself. I'll walk you through it."

Caitlin took the derringer from him, hefted the weight of it in her small palm.

"Make sure the hammer is in the down position, resting on the nipple." He pointed to each part of the gun as he named it. "Next, the gunpowder. That goes in the barrel first, about a teaspoon." He took a metal flask of powder from the lacquered box and handed it to her.

Caitlin measured out the gunpowder and carefully poured it down the barrel, threads from her frayed sleeves fluttering against her slender wrists. "Like that?" She handed the flask back to Noah, and he replaced the lid and set it back in the box.

"Good." Reaching back into the box, he retrieved a tiny cloth patch and a round lead ball. "Keep the pistol pointed in a safe direction. Now put the patch over the muzzle of the barrel and then seat the ball over it."

She did so.

Then, before he could do it himself, Caitlin plucked a small ramrod from the box. He arched his eyebrows.

"Isn't that next?"

"Indeed. We use the ramrod to tamp down the patch and ball so it sits on top of the powder at the base of the barrel."

Caitlin had finished that task by the time he finished his explanation. She placed the ramrod back in the box, then half-cocked the hammer. Noah sat back and watched as she reached back in the box for a percussion cap and fit it on the nipple.

"Have you done this before?"

Color leeched from her complexion. "This is the first time I've seen a derringer."

She certainly seemed to be catching on quickly. "Fine. Why don't you practice firing it?"

Caitlin screwed her mouth to one side, but nodded.

Noah climbed out of the buggy, then helped Caitlin down. With the horse tied to a young hickory tree, Noah and Caitlin swished through bluestem and switchgrass until they were a safe distance away.

"What's my target?" she asked.

"That dead tree over there." He pointed in the opposite direction of his horse and buggy. "Do you see the knot on its trunk? See if you can hit that." It wasn't far—maybe ten feet away, at the most.

He stood beside her, breathing in the faint, sweet scent of chinaberry soap. Strands of her shoulder-length hair tugged free from their pins and reveled in the wind, curling around the scar on her jawline. The thin white ribbon troubled him. She already knew what it was to be in danger. She had escaped it—at least once—but barely. What would happen if Caitlin met a threat again?

With a deep breath, she raised her arm, aimed, and fully cocked the hammer. She squeezed the trigger and the pistol bucked in her hand as a loud *crack* announced her mark.

Noah stared through the vanishing smoke at the tree for a moment before striding over to inspect her work. His fingers raked the shaggy bark until one of them sunk into her bullet hole. *Bull's-eye.* "How did you do that?"

Caitlin dropped the pistol into her pocket. "You are a capital instructor." Plucking her hat off her head, she twisted her rebellious locks back up beneath their pins, and smashed the hat back down on them.

Suspicion jarred Noah. She taught literature. She should have been far more tentative with a weapon. "Is there anything else you'd like to tell me?"

He had not intended to growl, but her darkening eyes showed him that he had. Her eyebrows plunged downward.

"No." She spun away from him and stalked off.

Just as Susan had, every time they had an argument. *Or a secret.* It drove Noah mad then, and it drove him mad now. A nest of hornets swarmed his belly.

"Where are you going?" he bellowed. "The buggy is *that* way. Unless you'd rather walk the two miles home."

She froze, lifted her face to the sun and shook her head. When she turned back around to face him, the anger in her eyes seemed to match his own.

"Leave the barking to Rascal, would you please?" She strode past him.

"What did you do, where did you live, before moving to Atlanta?" He bridged the distance between them, the tall grass tugging at his trousers. A fight he could handle. An utter withdrawal, he could not abide. "I would beg you not to walk away from me when we're having a conversation."

"We aren't."

Fire smoldered in his veins. He wanted to grab her hands, forcing her to stand still and talk this out like a grown-up. "You have secrets," he said, at length. "Too many secrets. You are a suspicious character in Atlanta, and you had best be more careful!"

"Are you still vexed that I forgot my pass on Monday?" She crossed her arms. "That was an honest mistake, and it ended just fine."

"Because I was there. Don't you realize what I'm saying? I'm not going to be here anymore to watch out for you! You with your Northern accent, and your short hair—"

Caitlin let it whip defiantly about her face, the pins guiltless of doing their job. "I don't have slaves to spend hours pinning up my long hair."

"And your obvious hatred of slavery in a state that relies upon it, and your unladylike marksmanship . . . you will land yourself in prison, and for Ana's sake, I simply must beg you to watch yourself."

She looked again toward Ana, whose falsetto giggles mingled with Saul's baritone chuckle over some secret joke thay shared. "I would never do anything to put her in harm's way. I promise you that."

"Just—please. Learn to be a little more responsible."

Her features turned to stone. The light in her eyes snuffed out. "I freely admit I could use lessons in many things, Mr. Becker. Responsibility is not one of them."

Noah sighed. It was not how he had wanted their outing to end. When he offered his hand to help her over the wheel and into her seat, she turned away from him.

Just as Susan had.

Chapter Six

New York City
Sunday, July 19, 1863

*W*ith the scent of lemon oil still lingering in the parlor, Ruby glanced at the clock and swiped a white-gloved finger over the mantel, checking one last time for dust. *Six o'clock.* The guests should be arriving soon.

Caroline had arrived home on Friday, all but overflowing with stories from her time nursing with Charlotte and the Sanitary Commission at Gettysburg. Ruby, in turn, had shared tales of their living through the draft riots. When she mentioned that Edward had discovered a long-lost aunt, Caroline had insisted on them both coming for dinner. Edward's father declined to join them.

Ruby's heart thudded against her corset as she checked her appearance in the hall mirror. Why should she be so agitated? *'Tis only Edward,* she told herself. *And his aunt.* She straightened her maid's cap over her dark red hair before smoothing her apron over her skirt. This would be the first time in weeks Edward would see her as a maid. A reminder to both of them that they were not equals, as perhaps she had pretended while Caroline was away. When he came to dine, she would eat in the kitchen with the cook.

For shame. She scolded her reflection, green eyes snapping. The arrangement had never bothered her before. Had she grown ungrateful for the bounty of Caroline's generosity? May it never be.

Knock knock knock.

Ruby drew a deep breath, then opened the door. A smile bloomed on her face as she noticed Edward's aunt wore the dress Ruby had made and sent over for her, free of charge, as soon as she heard she was in need of clothing. Her gaze scanned from the hem up, satisfied that the sage-green belted poplin dinner dress fit her frame so well.

And then she gasped.

"Vivian? Vivian McKae?"

Vivian covered her mouth with her hand.

"'Tis me, Ruby!"

"Is it really you?"

"Aye! But what—you canna be—" Ruby frowned, looking from Vivian's face to Edward's, and could not decide which of them looked more surprised.

"Well!" Edward removed his hat. "I was about to say, Ruby, this is my aunt, Vivian McKae. But it seems you need no introduction!"

With no thought for propriety, Ruby threw her arms around the older woman's neck, laughing in disbelief.

At length, Edward cleared his throat, his coffee eyes sparkling. "May we come in?"

"Oh! Forgive me! The McKaes were our neighbors when we lived in Seneca Village, you see! Before they evicted us and used the land for Central Park. I used to tend to her children!" Ruby stepped aside and ushered them through the door.

"Welcome, welcome!" Caroline swept into the entryway. Aiden stumbled along behind her, sending Dickens scurrying for safety.

"Good evening, Mrs. Waverly!" Edward bowed. "I have the pleasure of introducing to you my aunt, Vivian McKae."

"How do you do, Mrs. McKae?"

"Charmed, I'm sure. But please do call me Vivian."

"And you must call me Caroline. This is Ruby O'Flannery, and behind me we have her son, Aiden."

"Oh! He is just precious, Ruby!"

Edward caught Caroline's gaze. "You're not going to believe this, but Ruby and my aunt were neighbors years ago."

Vivian bent down and reached her hand out to Aiden, who promptly grabbed her finger. "Such a beautiful son; you and Matthew must be so proud!"

Ruby's heart dropped into her stomach. "Matthew has passed on." *And if he had not, he would certainly not be proud of Aiden. Or of me.* "The war."

"Oh, God rest his soul. I'm so very sorry, dear. Jack is fighting, too."

"Is he? He always had so much spirit. And Caitlin? How is your bonnie lass?"

A shadow passed over Vivian's face, and she shook her head. "I have not heard from her in quite some time."

"She is teaching out West then? I remember she had her eye on that."

"That isn't—that isn't likely."

A chill passed over Ruby. *Does Vivian not know where her daughter is?* It didn't make sense. *That lass was the one holding the family together after James died. What in heaven's name had happened?*

"Wherever she is, we shall all pray God keep your daughter safe, Vivian. Now. Shall we move to the dining room?"

Ruby scooped up Aiden. "I'll let Cook know you are ready to be served. Enjoy your meal." She bobbed in a curtsy.

"Thank you." Caroline nodded. "Unless—" She looked between Ruby and Vivian. "I know this is rather unusual, but considering you two have a bit of catching up to do . . . Ruby, do join us at table this evening, won't you?"

Ruby's heart grew wings and fluttered heavenward. "Aye—I mean yes, I'd like that very much."

"Aiden, too." Caroline leaned in close. "Why don't you tell Cook not to plate the dinners tonight, just set the covered platters on the table and we'll serve ourselves so you're not going in and out between courses. Then go change, dear. I'm sure you'd feel more comfortable if you weren't in your maid's uniform."

"Yes, mum."

"We'll wait for you." Edward held out his hands to Aiden, and the boy lunged to him.

When Ruby returned to the dining room in her lace-trimmed lavender poplin gown, Edward seated her between Aiden's highchair and Vivian at the large walnut table. As he sat across from her, candle-light gleamed in his deep brown eyes. His smile warmed her more than usual. *Vivian McKae is Edward's aunt!* She could not believe it.

As soon as Edward finished blessing the food, the dinner party began eating their salads. Ruby cut her tomatoes and cucumbers into tiny pieces and set them on Aiden's wooden tray. She watched out of the corner of her eye as juice and seeds squished between his fingers. *As long as it doesn't land in his hair . . .*

"It's so lovely to meet Edward's family," Caroline was saying. "He's been such a joy to have around these last several weeks."

Vivian beamed at her nephew. "I always knew he'd grow into a fine young man."

Ruby watched Edward's face. He smiled, but she could not quite read what was behind it. He had told her some of the story, how he'd found her, and how his father had wanted to cut her out of their lives. How very odd the whole thing was.

Aiden banged on his tray for more food, and Ruby cracked open a hard roll, allowing the steam to escape in wispy curls before pinching hunks of the soft white bread for her son.

Conversation ebbed and flowed around Ruby as she did her best to keep Aiden happy, or at least quiet, between her own bites of stewed mutton chops and mashed potatoes. But by the time Ruby passed out the lemon cheesecakes that had been waiting on the sideboard, not one of them had mentioned the draft riots, though the troops patrolling the city now exceeded ten thousand.

"I did receive some news yesterday." Caroline dabbed her napkin to her mouth and smoothed it back onto her lap. "It's my daughter Alice." She flicked a gaze to Edward and Vivian. "I hope you'll forgive me for speaking so candidly, having just met you, Vivian. But as a mother yourself, I'm sure you understand. Alice is with child."

"That's wonderful!" Vivian clasped her hands.

Caroline put up her hand then, and Ruby's heart skittered. "It goes hard with her. Jacob asks me to come to them at Fishkill."

Oh no. "You will go soon?"

Caroline nodded. "As soon as arrangements may be made. I'll take Dickens with me, of course. Jacob says you and Aiden may join me."

Ruby locked eyes with Edward until he looked down. His fork broke off a piece of his dessert and pushed it around his plate.

"If you come, you will come as guests," Caroline continued. "The Carlisle estate has servants aplenty already, and need no other help."

Suddenly, the lemon cheesecake was too tart for Ruby's taste. She sipped her goblet of water slowly, as her mind raced. The fresh air and countryside would be so good for Aiden, Ruby was certain. But to leave now would be to forfeit all the clients she had built up during the last eighteen months. Surely they would find another seamstress to sew for them in her absence, and who was to say whether they would bring their business back to her when she returned?

She turned and looked at her son. What was best for him?

The question scraped at her. Surely he would find it best to run and play on the wide, smooth lawns of the Carlisle estate, to have a mother who had time and energy to play with him, rather than endlessly diverting his attention with a toy so she could steal a few moments to stitch a hem.

She sighed. *But my stitches are turning straw into gold for his education.* A mother who plays with her toddler all day long is all very well and good until it is time for him to enter school and she has not the money to pay for it. She must think of the long-term investment rather than the short-term indulgence.

"Ruby?" Caroline's voice was gentle. "You have a choice, you know. You are not required to come. Just realize that if you stay, I'll not be here to help with Aiden. Keeping your clients well-supplied with the latest fashions will be much more of a challenge."

Her heart sank. Caroline was right. And what was the use of staying here if she had not the time to—

"Clients?" Vivian's eyes flashed.

"I've been sewing dresses, saving money for the lad's future."

"What a grand idea! You are so wise to do so. If it's someone to watch your son you need, look no further. You watched Jack and Caitlin for me many a time. Now it's my turn to return the favor."

"And I'll be glad to help whenever I can. If you choose to stay, that is." Edward arched his eyebrows.

"Well, my dear boy, if she stays, you'll be back on duty to check on her as you did while I was in Gettysburg," Caroline said. "Can you manage that?"

"I am at your service." Lines crinkled around his eyes. "And hers."

As he held her in his gaze, something rippled through Ruby. Just as quickly, she dismissed it. Edward was a good man. And someday, he would make some woman—*a woman far better than myself*—a very good husband. In the meantime, they could at least be neighbors.

"In that case . . ." Ruby's face warmed as three pairs of eyes fixed their attention on her. "Give my best to Alice. I rather think we'll stay."

—•—

Atlanta, Georgia
Monday, July 20, 1863

"King, this is the only time I'm going to say this. I really wanted to be your friend. But you've enslaved your people."

Caitlin watched from across the chess board as Analiese pointed her bishop at Caitlin's king. To Ana, chess was not just a game. It was theater.

"I'm trapped! I'm trapped!" Ana pinched a pawn by its head and shook it, sending up a fake wail to match the drama of the moment.

"Now you're captured!" Caitlin swooped in with her knight and plucked Ana's pawn from the board. The girl howled in mock despair.

"Miss McKae? A word, please."

She looked up, and flinched at the sight of him. He stood tall, his eyes darkened to gunmetal grey the same shade as his flannel shirt. A cartridge box sat on his waistbelt, his Spiller and Burr .36 caliber revolver in his holster. He'd get something resembling a uniform when he mustered in at camp, along with a haversack and canteen, Caitlin knew. But at this point, if a Rebel soldier didn't bring his own weapon, he'd have to wait to pick one off a Union body at the next battle.

"Papa?"

"Just a moment, Dear Heart. I'll come in and talk to you."

Caitlin's hand was on her heart as they stepped into the hallway. "Now?"

He nodded, and her nose pinched as she cast a glance over her shoulder at Ana, still prattling away with the chess pieces. She turned back to Noah and waited for him to speak.

He cleared his throat. "While I'm gone, I expect more refugees will be passing through Atlanta. With Rosecrans at Tullahoma and Bragg at Chattanooga, there will inevitably be a battle, sending thousands more refugees this way."

"I expect so."

"You are to let them in."

She blinked. "For a week? A month?"

Noah kneaded the back of his neck. "As long as they need shelter. And food. You are to feed them as well as you can. If a stranger comes to this house in need, you are to let her in, as I have taken you in. As I was taken in myself."

Caitlin paused. "Excuse me?"

"I know what it is to be a refugee. After the revolution—" He waved his hand as if to reach across the ocean, to his former life. "In Switzerland, France, England. For two years. Were it not for the kindness of others, I would never have survived at all, let alone come to America. Let it never be said that the house of Noah Becker turned away a refugee. Please."

"You were a refugee," she repeated, and a new perspective layered itself upon what she thought she knew of this man.

Noah smiled ruefully. "Yes, an outcast. At least, that's how it felt for a very long time. Of course, since I will not be here, I would only approve of your taking in women and children."

"*Only* women and children?" Somehow, they laughed at this. Virtually all refugees were women and children, with nearly every man in the army.

"Do I have your word? You will do your best? I realize I am asking much of you. I need you to be hospitable on my behalf."

Caitlin pursed her lips, but nodded.

"Papa? Do you want to play with me?" Ana slipped her small hand into his, and tugged him into the room.

Noah's heart skipped a beat, and his stomach rolled. He could not put off this goodbye any longer. When Noah pulled his daughter onto his lap and kissed her cheek, Caitlin shut the double doors to the room.

"When will you be back?" Ana tucked her head under his chin, her silky hair soft against his throat. She picked at his buttons.

"It will be a long time, I'm afraid." He kissed her hair and marveled that she still had dimples for knuckles at the age of seven.

"How long?"

Noah sighed. The truth was so hard to bear, even for him. "Three years, or until the war is over."

"Oh my! I think that must be about one hundred days!" Her two missing front teeth gently lisped over the words.

"Ach. *Ist das wirklich wahr?* Three hundred sixty-five days in one year, so three years is . . ."

"More than one hundred." Her hand dropped into her lap.

"It is more than one thousand."

"Oh! I think we will never reach the end of that!" Ana's voice wobbled. "Who will tuck me in at night? Who will be my Papa while you're gone?"

The question sliced through Noah's heart, and tears bled from his eyes. *Lord, how will I ever get through this?* "I will *always* be your Papa." He forced the words around the lump lodged in his throat. "No matter what. And you will always be my daughter."

Her bright blue eyes shone with tears. "I will miss you too much, Papa!"

"I'll miss you too, more than you know."

"Wait." Ana climbed off his lap and scurried to one of the chairs.

When she returned to Noah, she held out a little doll, made of a handkerchief draped over a cotton ball and tied with string around the neck. She had drawn eyes, a smile, and hair on the head. "This is for you. I made it myself."

"Ah! Why not keep it so you can play with her?"

"No, Papa. She is for you. So you can remember me. She can keep you company when you get lonely, too." Ana pressed the doll into his hand, and closed his fingers over it.

"Thank you." His throat closed around his voice. "I love you, Dear Heart." He wrapped his arms around her. "Be good for Miss McKae. Do what she says. Your heavenly Father is watching over you."

Suddenly, her little face knotted, and she fled the room, each footstep on the stairs stomping on Noah's heart. His empty arms and lap felt cavernous, cold. Would he ever see Ana again?

He could not dwell on such a question, not now. He waited at the bottom of the stairs, listening, to see if she would come out again and call his name. She didn't.

It was time.

Out on the porch, he found Caitlin sitting on the front steps, her patched-over plaid dress fanned out around her. Rascal leaned into her, and she scratched behind his ears while his wagging tail whapped the floor. The door clicked closed behind Noah, and she rose to meet him with red-rimmed eyes.

"Ana's run to her room." His voice was thick.

"She will come back. And so will you."

"She gave me this." He opened his palm to reveal the doll. "To keep me company when I get lonely for her."

Caitlin laid a hand on his arm. "I'm sure you'll miss her, but I will write you the little things she says—when she plays chess, when she says her prayers at night."

"You must tell me when her new teeth come in. And how she progresses in her studies."

"Of course."

"Promise." Noah placed his hand over hers. "You will tell me what I'm missing. And you must tell her how much I love her even when I cannot."

"Yes, yes, I will. And I'll take care of her as if she were my own."

He nodded. "I trust you." What choice did he have? "I trust you. I'm giving you my Heart, you know."

Her brown eyes swam in unshed tears. "I know," she whispered.

"Thank you." Noah dipped his head to touch the top of hers. "The Lord bless thee, and keep thee: The Lord make His face shine upon thee, and be gracious unto thee: The Lord lift up His countenance upon thee, and give thee peace."

He stepped back and smiled at her, a lump bobbing in his throat.

Without thinking, he hooked a strand of her hair behind her ear, then cupped the side of her face in his hand, her scar barely grazing his palm. "Take care of yourself," he breathed.

Then, as if the floor beneath his feet was suddenly ablaze, he whispered, "Goodbye, Miss McKae," and left.

"IF THE WAR CONTINUES four years longer, it seems to me those who escape death from bullets or pestilence must die of excitement, for there you see nothing but war. You eat war; you hear war; you talk nothing but war; and when you retire to your bed you dream of war. You wake tired of war but the despot has you by the throat, with a thousand bayonets bristling round you, and you must fight or do worse."

—SALLIE CONLEY CLAYTON, Atlanta resident

Act Two

EATING WAR

Chapter Seven

Atlanta, Georgia
Saturday, September 26, 1863

Eleven dollars a month.

That was what Caitlin had to work with from Noah's new salary as a private in the Confederate army. He had left her with some savings, but at the rate of inflation, they would burn through that in short order.

Caitlin's lips cinched as she studied last month's grocery receipt at Noah's secretary in the office.

1 lb. black pepper . . . $10
1 lb. coffee . . . $10
1 ham . . . $54
5 lbs. flour . . . $50
2 lbs. butter . . . $20

And she had eleven dollars a month. Out of this money, she had to pay Saul and Bess their wages, plus her own? What would be left? Even if she could spend the entire sum on food, how much would that get?

Winter was coming. They would need fuel for the fireplaces. A dress without holes in it would be nice, too, for both her and Ana. But purchasing one was absolutely out of the question, with the simplest merino gown costing no less than four hundred dollars.

Pulse trotting, the print in front of her swam in her vision. Raggedy clothing she could handle. Starvation she could not. She had known hunger before, and had sworn she would never taste its bile again. Yet here it was, stalking her, chasing her, its rotten breath hot on her skin.

Caitlin raised her eyes and looked out the back window toward the detached kitchen. What she saw, however, was already behind her.

If only she could leave it there.

Hunger felt every bit the same here in Atlanta as it had in New York City. If she closed her eyes and listened to the traffic nearby on McDonough and Fair Streets, she could imagine herself as part of the crowd, next to her father again in a hackney, on their way to another prayer meeting at Burton's Theater on Manhattan's Chambers Street. Three thousand people gathered daily to pray and hear Henry Ward Beecher speak there, while thousands of others sought heaven's gates all over the city. Most of them were desperate. All of them were hungry.

Like a contagion, the Panic of 1857 had spread throughout the city, the country, and even into Europe. When the New York stock market crashed, its victims fell by the thousands, until, by the end of October, one hundred thousand people were out of work. The McKaes' neighbors in Seneca Village—railroad workers, merchants, foundry mechanics, garment workers, coopers—were hard hit. When maritime construction and the shipbuilding industry collapsed, nearly three-quarters of the city's shipbuilders were laid off. Including James McKae.

Mama added water to the milk to make it last longer. She filled everyone's plates but her own. Only when Caitlin said she wasn't hungry did Vivian allow herself to eat. It was all Da could do to keep thirteen-year-old Jack from joining his friends and stealing bread.

"Therefore take no thought, saying, What shall we eat? or, What shall we drink? or, Wherewithal shall we be clothed? Your heavenly

Father knoweth that ye have need of all these things," Da had said to his family, quoting from the gospel of Matthew.

She tried to match her faith to her father's. When he went to prayer meetings, she went with him. Where he saw a revival, however, she saw a sea of gaunt faces gathered to plead for work. For bread. For life itself.

One day, when Da asked her if she'd like to go to the prayer meeting with him again, she said no. She should be scrounging the city for work, any work. Her neighbor, Mrs. O'Flannery, sewed for a living. Maybe there was still some needlework to be had. "Going to meeting won't feed our family," she had told her father, feeling so wise for her seventeen years.

"Darlin,'" he said, his calloused hand on her cheek. "Prayer may not always change our circumstances. But it always changes us." He smiled. "That is why I go. My faith is not a talisman. 'Tis the anchor in the storm."

They were the last words he ever said to her. He had intervened in a street fight after prayer meeting, and a blow to his head stained the cobblestones crimson with his departing life.

Vivian all but disintegrated with grief, and Jack grew more violent and unpredictable than ever. It was up to Caitlin to hold her crumbling family together. While Vivian rocked from sunup to sundown in the corner, Caitlin cleaned, laundered, and cooked what little there was to be eaten. She hounded Jack until he found honest work, though the wage was criminally low. Together, somehow, they survived.

And then they learned their neighborhood was to be razed to the ground. The city leaders would build a Central Park, and give the work to thirty-six hundred of the city's down-and-out. They would build it on land that included Seneca Village.

There was no other place to go but to the tenements, where hunger clawed at their vitals. Life was reduced to the search for food. It was barely living at all.

"Miss McKae?"

Caitlin opened her eyes to see Ana standing beside her. "Yes?"

94

"Didn't you hear me?"

"No, darlin', I'm sorry. What did you say?"

"I said I'm hungry. Can't I have something to eat?"

New York City
Monday, September 28, 1863

"You're sure you don't mind coming?"

"I already told you, I insist upon it." Edward Goodrich helped Ruby up into the Concord buggy before turning back to the Waverly parlor window and waving at Vivian and Aiden. "My aunt has been itching to watch Aiden, anyway."

"Well, in *that* case." Ruby laughed, relieved. "'Tis so kind of both of you to help."

"It's her pleasure, I'm sure. And mine."

The buggy rocked into motion. The cool wind washed over Ruby, ruffling her hair in her snood. Maple leaves the color of fire scraped and swirled along the cobblestones to music all their own.

She glanced at Edward. "Most people still don't want to set foot anywhere near the Irish tenements, you know."

"But you do."

Ruby cast her gaze on gracefully arched branches dripping with autumn splendor the way some women dripped with jewels. "To be honest, I never wanted to go back there again after I left. But then I saw Emma."

"Ah yes. The unlikely heroine of the mob."

Ruby covered a giggle with her hand. "Very unlikely. We used to be friends, she and I. At one point, she was better off than I was—at least in terms of being able to pay the rent. She tried to help me."

"How did she do that?"

Ruby took a deep breath. "How does a woman in poverty try to help herself? There are only a few roads to take."

"Sewing?"

Ruby laughed through her nose. "Emma found a quicker way to make the money she needed." She hoped that in the silence that followed, Edward could guess at her insinuation. The mere fact that she would not name it should say a great deal. Prostitution was not considered suitable conversation for a chaplain. *But then, perhaps it should be.*

Edward frowned. "But—you said she tried to help you?"

Ruby rolled her lips between her teeth for a moment before responding. "Recruit me. I should have said, she tried to recruit me."

The telltale pink blotches began creeping up from under Edward's blue wool collar. "I see."

Her stomach burned as they bumped along over the cobblestones. She hadn't meant to upset him. "I said no, Edward." What would he do if he knew the rest of Ruby's tale? She shuddered.

His sigh was audible. She bristled.

"Please don't judge her too harshly. She was hungry. In truth, starving. She felt she had no other option. She didn't know she could pray to a God who would show her a different way. Her compass was not her conscience, but her stomach. Sometimes you can't hear anything else over its growl."

She slanted a glance at him. He nodded, but kept his eyes straight ahead as they passed hackneys, carriages, and cabs. "Jesus had compassion on the sinful woman who He urged to 'go and sin no more.' How can I judge Emma, if she wants to turn from her ways?"

"That's what we're going to find out, I hope. Whether she wants to turn from her ways. She was my neighbor once. I could be a neighbor to her still. Right?"

Edward smiled at her, his brown eyes warm. "Exactly. I'm proud of you, Ruby." She returned his smile and quickly turned away as tears pricked her eyes. She'd never heard those words before.

Once they arrived at the brick tenement building, Ruby suggested Edward wait with the horse and buggy. *They have a way of wandering off in this section of town.*

96

In a whisper of grey muslin, Ruby entered the building as Matthew O'Flannery's widow, and felt herself swept back in time to the days when she, too, was hunted by hunger. Her eyes strained to see in the darkness, and she could almost feel her posture hunching forward once again, as had often happened as she bent over her sewing by candlelight for eighteen hours a day. Ruby squared her shoulders, as she knocked on Emma's door.

It clicked open. "Well, hello, darlin'." Emma's brother Sean leaned against the doorframe, a half-empty bottle dangling from his hand. His shirtsleeves were rolled up, tight against biceps made thick with manual labor.

"Hello, Sean. Glad to see you're back safe from the war."

"Aye, I am, at that. You're looking well. Pity Matthew isn't here to see you. Lucky for me, I've got me own eyes."

And they are full of mischief, that's what. Heat singed her cheeks. "Is Emma in, please?"

"Sleeping off last night's work. But don't go—"

"Get out of the way, you big lout! Let her in!" Hair combs swinging in loose curls by her face, Emma swatted her brother before tightening the belt on her robe. "Why, Ruby Shannon! You came!"

With a grunt, he stepped aside, and Ruby stepped back in time as she entered the room. The women sat on wooden chairs in the front room while Sean went to the back room.

"I thought you'd never come, darlin'." Emma beamed, and Ruby felt like crying. Her friend had aged beyond the two years that had come between them. Her watery blue eyes were bloodshot, her skin sallow. Yet a purple satin hoop skirt gown hung on a peg in the corner, and pots of rouge lay scattered on the table, signs she still plied her old trade.

"Such a bonnie lass, you are! What have you done to save yourself from the likes of me?" Emma laughed, and Ruby forced a smile.

"I found a good job as a domestic."

"Oh! Well, no house would take me now, that's sure!" She cackled again, and Ruby could not contradict her.

"But that's not what happened first, Emma. First, I found grace."

Emma squinted at Ruby. "Bedad! You mean you found religion? How could you, after what you've done?"

"No. Grace. It's different . . ."

Emma shook her head. "There is not enough grace for me, darlin', and that's sure."

Ruby's own words came back to her then, words she had spoken in bitterness when Charlotte Waverly had tried to tell her about God's amazing grace for her. *The Lord wants nothing to do with me,* she had snapped. *There is no "Amazing Grace" in my life. I am still lost, and will never be found. I am still blind, and will never see.*

Emma pinched a pleat of Ruby's ribbon-trimmed grey dress. "Other than the color, which is ghastly if you don't mind my saying so, this is a lovely gown. Does it come in green silk? Red satin?"

A smile quirked Ruby's lips. "I made it myself, lass. I still sew, I don't just quit with the sleeves now. I even have a small business running where I make gowns for other ladies in Manhattan."

Emma's jaw dropped open. "Go on with you, now! They pay you well, do they?"

"Aye, they pay for the materials plus labor, and they're not stingy like Davis & Company or Brooks Brothers. I almost have more work than I can manage."

"Do you now? But you don't look nearly so hunched over and stooped as when you only made sleeves. How can you be doing this?"

"I'm not working in the dark anymore, that's what. And I only take in the work I want, and set my own deadlines."

Emma whistled. "If that don't beat all. Say, could you help me hem up my working dress? It's gotten a mite raggedy as of late."

"Don't tell me you can't hem your own dress."

She shrugged. "To tell you the truth, I never saw much reason for it. 'Twasn't hurting business any. Just thought I might feel a little better without my tail dragging in the dirt, you know?"

Suddenly, the germ of an idea sprouted in Ruby's mind. Why hadn't she thought of it before? The House of Industry taught women in poverty how to sew for this very reason. Of course, they wouldn't accept anyone but the "worthy poor," so Emma would not be admitted. But Ruby could teach her.

"How would you like to learn how to make your own dress? A sensible, attractive visiting dress or at-home gown. You choose the pattern from *Godey's Lady's Book* or *Harper's Weekly*, then we shop for fabric and get to it."

Emma slanted her eyes. "I'm no hand at sewing. I'm no hand at anything."

"You could be if you tried. We could do it together. And then, you'd have a trade. Another door open to you."

With a wave of her hand, Emma seemed to dismiss her. "All doors have shut to me, save one. And you know 'tis the one what pays the best, it is."

"You can make your living without selling your soul."

"Who says I've got any soul left at all?" Her eyes were as hollow as her cheeks.

Ruby grasped Emma's hands. "You don't fool me, Emma Connors. I've known you for years, I have. This—" She gestured toward the purple gown drooping in the corner. "This is not who you really are, deep down."

Emma bit her bottom lip. "What if it is? Oh, I admit, I used to hate it. But I've grown used to it, I have. Got no complaints, mostly." Her gaze dropped, and Ruby's followed it until landing on yellow-grey blooms on Emma's wrists.

"Saints alive, it doesn't have to be this way!"

A slow smile curled Emma's lips, her vapid eyes mirrored what Ruby had once felt herself. *I deserve nothing more than this.* Ruby hugged her then, and Emma's cheap perfume tasted stale in her mouth. *Lord,* she prayed, *help me show her what grace looks like. Help me love her like You do.*

"Please," Ruby whispered. "Just tell me you'll come make a new dress for yourself with me. We'll chat about old times, you and me. 'Tis all I ask."

At length, Emma nodded. "All right, Ruby darlin'. Now off with you. I've got an appointment to get ready for."

Ruby's stomach roiled, but she let it go. Showing God's grace to Emma would be a journey, and she would take it one step at time.

———

Uh-oh. This isn't good. Ruby's puckered expression told Edward that the fellow walking her out of the tenement was not a welcome escort. The man easily kept pace with her hurried footsteps, speaking in low tones quite close to her face.

Edward hopped down from the buggy, ready to intervene, but Ruby held up her hand, palm out, to stop him. Her green eyes flashed. *Why would she tell me to stay if this bloke is bothering her?*

When the man grabbed a handful of her skirt and jerked her into his arms, Edward shot toward them, bracing himself for a pounding. The man was taller and more muscular than he by far.

"Kindly let the lady go, sir."

"Edward, you don't have to do this." But of course he did. Didn't she know that by now?

"What business do you have with ol' Ruby here? Paying customer, are ye? I'll get in line if I have to."

"No, Sean, stop it! I told you I don't do that!"

"Emma says you did. Tsk tsk. What would Matthew say?"

Tears clung to Ruby's eyelashes as she pivoted between Sean and Edward. Comprehension grooved Edward's brow. *Was this Sean actually accusing Ruby O'Flannery of being a woman of the night?* The idea was ludicrous! He offered his arm to her. "Let's go."

Her hand trembled on his arm, and Edward covered it with his hand.

"He's drunk, he is," she whispered.

"Hoo-wee! The view is even better from behind! Whatever you've been doing to fill out those curves, Rubes, you just keep on doing it! I never did like a skinny wench!"

Ice-cold anger clamped over Edward's chest. He turned around, though Ruby pleaded with him not to. "I would beg you to keep a civil tongue in your head, sir. Do you not realize you speak to a widow and mother?"

"Oh yeah?" Sean's eyes popped open wide. "When the cat's away, the mice do play!"

Vaguely, Edward registered a pull on his arm. But he would not be moved. He would not turn the other cheek this time, though he wore red crosses on his uniform collar even now. "Just what are you insinuating?"

Sean laughed. "Ain't insinuating nothin', Chappy. I'll say it outright. That lady on your arm there? She may look healthier than most, but don't be fooled. She's a whore. And that's a fa—"

Nearly blind with fury, hands that had never sought violence curled into rock-hard fists. A blow to Sean's face split his lip like ripe fruit. Sean staggered, then plowed into Edward's nose with a crack. Ruby screamed. Blood trickled down, and Edward licked it off his lips, the metallic taste detonating years of pent-up frustration he had never allowed himself to vent. For the first time in his life, Edward Goodrich stood up to a bully.

At least, until the bully knocked him out.

Chapter Eight

New York City
Sunday, October 4, 1863

*E*dward Goodrich felt as foul as the weather rattling his second-story sitting-room window.

Glowering, he eased himself back into the rosewood armchair, squinted at steel-grey clouds slung low over Manhattan. Thunder rolled like a drum inside his chest while rain sprayed the house like shrapnel. He brought his fingertips to the ache in his nose, and winced. But it wasn't just the throbbing reminder of his fistfight that bothered him. No, it was something much deeper than a mere shiner and a broken nose.

Hypocrite.

How could he tell his flock to love their neighbor when he had instigated a fistfight? Edward had always turned the other cheek before. But when Sean had implied the very worst about Ruby, he lost his self-control.

"No, I didn't," he corrected himself, leaning forward with his elbows on his knees. He had *wanted* to hurt Sean, and badly. The venom in his own spirit startled Edward. Was he really so vicious? Did he have more in common with his father than he realized?

A soft knock at the door, then Aunt Vivian rustled through it. She was again wearing the dress Ruby had made for her without realizing she was sewing for a former neighbor. He curved his lips into a deliberate smile.

"Not convincing." Vivian laughed quietly. "May I join you?"

"By all means." Edward stood until his aunt had seated herself in the armchair opposite the tea table.

Vivian flinched at the sight of Edward's pulpy black eye. "How does it feel?"

"Not as bad as it looks." Edward sighed. "I'm usually not a fighter, Aunt Vivian."

"I know that."

"I don't believe violence is the way to solve things." He drummed his fingertips on the armrest. "I do have a knack for getting in the way of trouble."

"For the ones you love."

Edward looked up, then, into Vivian's rich brown eyes. "What did you say?"

"Love makes you do things you might never do otherwise. It makes you sacrifice, or fight, or chase, or even push away." A faraway look shadowed Vivian's face for a moment.

Edward cleared his throat. "I care for Ruby like a shepherd cares for his sheep. Shepherds fight bears and lions to protect their lambs."

"True."

"Or like a sister."

"I see."

"I told Caroline Waverly I'd look out for her. I'm just keeping my word."

Vivian arched her eyebrows. "The young man 'doth protest too much, methinks.'" Her voice was soft as silk, but the quote from *Hamlet* stung. *The question is, does it sting because it's true? Am I making excuses for how I feel toward Ruby?*

"It's all right to care more for her than you would for the average sheep in your care, you know. Ruby is a fine woman. I've known her since she first came to this country at the age of nineteen. She is responsible, industrious, she loves the Lord, and she happens to have a son who seems to adore you."

Beautiful. Edward checked the word before it escaped his lips. *You forgot to say she's beautiful.* Her heart and spirit were even more becoming than her appearance, although that was lovely to behold, as well. Her face surged before him now, emerald eyes sparkling, russet hair shimmering in coils heaped on top of her head, swept away from the collar of her grey dress. "She is in mourning."

"The second stage of mourning. And she'll be done with that soon enough."

He shook his head. "We are very different, she and I."

"In what way?"

Edward stood and paced the room. He could scarcely believe they were having this conversation. "I can't explain it."

"You communicate abstract truths for a living." Vivian's tone bordered on impatience. "Do try."

He rubbed the back of his neck and grimaced. Truth be told, he had barely bothered to imagine himself with any woman at all. But when he had, he had conjured up a woman from a good family, with a long-standing membership in a church, with refined tastes, yet compassionate to the plight of those less fortunate than herself. *Someone, in fact, more like Charlotte Waverly.* He cringed as the thought raised its head. He had ceased thinking of her in that way long ago.

"We have very different backgrounds, for one thing—"

Vivian stiffened, sat up a little straighter in her chair. "You mean she is Irish. An immigrant."

The look in her eyes chilled his warming face. He had insulted his aunt and Ruby both.

She rose, lifted her chin. "I see. You are more like your father than I realized." It was the worst epithet she could have given him. And he deserved it. "When I met James, he was working on one of the ships in your father's shipyard. I didn't go looking for love, but when I found it, I had the good sense to hold on tight. Yes, he was Irish and the Goodriches are English. Yes, he made his living by the sweat of his brow rather than by business acumen and sound investments. But he was a good man and did right by me right up until he died." She swallowed hard. "We were happy together. When he smiled at me I felt God's love shine down on us, as well. And by looking at Ruby, I have a feeling she feels the same way about you."

Alarm clanged in his mind. Had he led her to believe he felt something he did not? "Are you quite cert—"

She raised her hand to cut him off. "I can read a woman better than you can, so there's no use arguing. Now, I'm not telling you to run off with her willy-nilly. But if your heart is opening to Ruby, don't let your prejudice against the Irish slam it shut."

Prejudice? The word stabbed. Hadn't he been the one to reach out to Ruby with the Bible studies? Hadn't he gone to the tenements and helped Vivian herself out of harm's way? *Prejudice!* The label snagged and itched. Surely it did not belong on him.

But Vivian was not done. "She may indeed have a hard past, one you cannot relate to. But are we not all equal in God's eyes? Or will you preach love for your neighbor on Sundays but wallow in law and judgment every other day of your life?" Vivian's breath heaved by the end of her speech, and Edward stepped back from the force of it. *Wallow in judgment? I never!*

Crossing the room to meet him, she took his hands. "If I've put too fine a point on it, it's only because I love you, Edward. I just want God's best for you." She wrapped her arm around his waist. "If you are truly not interested in Ruby as anything more than a neighbor, that's fine. Just don't mislead her."

Edward told himself to nod. "I understand." But inside, he still smarted.

By the time the rain let up and he prepared for his Sunday afternoon Bible study with Ruby, however, the sting had faded. After all, it was not romance he had in mind with Ruby, but ministry.

Truly.

Later that night, with her belly full of steak, green beans, and melt-in-your-mouth rolls, Vivian McKae kissed her brother and nephew good night, and quietly stole up the stairs to turn in early. She had trudged too far down memory's path today. Exhaustion thudded at the base of her skull.

Or was that her conscience knocking?

A sigh brushed Vivian's lips as she unpinned her hair and changed into her flannel nightdress. How she had loved James!

All the more piercing your betrayal.

Vivian covered her ears, but in vain. This voice, the one whose forked tongue slithered deep into her spirit, was the demon she went to bed with every night. Instead of James's strong arms reaching for her in the night, pulling her close to the muscular curves of his chest, the cold scales of this invisible beast writhed around her spirit, strangling her.

"My heart had already died within me, I did not give him that. That belonged to James alone."

Yet you gave him your body to bruise, beat, and bed.

"In the confines of marriage, yes. I had to. I had to. We were evicted, we were starving, Jack would have turned to vice, Caitlin would have given up her future for the pursuit of bread. I needed a husband!"

You broke James's heart.

"If he was watching from heaven, he would have understood. I did it for our family. I did it to survive."

By the skin of your teeth. And that a miracle in itself.

Vivian rose from her chair, and knelt before the window. She saw only her own reflection. She had aged since marrying James, and even more since she had buried him. But her eyes were the same as they were every night when she waited for Bernard to come home in a drunken rage. She had let him beat her until he was spent so no harm would come to Jack and Caitlin. Always, always, she was careful not to cry out for fear of waking them.

It was for Caitlin that she was most concerned. She was eighteen and beautiful when Vivian had agreed to marry Bernard. It had only taken a few weeks to discover her second husband's character, and that was black as soot. If given an opportunity to be alone with Caitlin, Vivian had no doubt he would have his way with her, especially if he was drunk.

Jack quit school to work at age fourteen, but Vivian insisted Caitlin keep on with her dreams of becoming a teacher. *Depend on no man,* she had told her, over and over. *Make your own way in the world.*

When Caitlin saw a magazine article about a new program that trained young women to teach in the West, and then paid to send them there, she and Vivian both seized upon the opportunity. Caitlin attended the tuition-free six-week training at the Hartford Female Seminary in Connecticut, then came home to await her assignment.

That was when they heard the news that shattered Caitlin's hope. The National Board of Popular Education ended its program to send teachers west. She was trained, but had no place to teach. New York City was already saturated with teachers and those who were begging to teach. So Caitlin stayed and tended Vivian's wounds instead. *I fell down the stairs,* Vivian lied. *I burned myself on the stove.* No one mentioned James again. It was as if that happy life they had once known had never been at all.

A year passed, and Caitlin was still stuck in the tenements, still tending her weak and battered mother. Then another year passed. And another. Until finally, Vivian had scraped all her strength together and yelled at her own daughter to get out and find a life for herself. The stunned look on Caitlin's face haunted Vivian still.

Vivian touched the glass pane with her fingertips. *God protect her, wherever she is. Bring her home safe. Please.*

Weariness tugged her toward the canopied bed. Vivian gathered up the pillows, and stacked them neatly on the plush carpet. After she finished in the water closet next to her bed chamber, she brought a clean towel with her, rolled it up tightly, and placed it beneath her neck as she snuggled down between the lilac-scented sheets.

She had good reason not to sleep over a pillow. *Not since*—but she would not think of that now.

Chapter Nine

Atlanta, Georgia
Monday, October 19, 1863

Caitlin tucked her feet beneath Rascal's warm body, the rag rug that had formerly been under the workroom's table now in a tangle of sewn-together strips on the table in front of her. Twisting them tightly, she dipped them into a bowl of liquid beeswax, rosin, and turpentine. The days were only getting shorter, and there were no candles to be had unless one made them at home.

Ana sat across from Caitlin at the work table, elbows resting on the *First Reader for Southern Schools* open in front of her. When the wax had cooled enough, Caitlin carefully pressed the warm waxed strips around a glass bottle, from the base to the neck.

"Why don't you read aloud, Ana."

The girl sat up a little straighter. "All right. Lesson Twenty-nine. 'The man's arm has been cut off. It was shot by a gun. Oh! What a sad thing war is!'"

"That's enough." Ragged crimson memories from the Battles of First Bull Run and Seven Pines exploded in Caitlin's mind. Horrific scenes that had been engraved on the parchment of her soul. Certainly it wasn't good for Ana to dwell on such things with her own father in the army. "Let's read something else for your lesson. Do you know where *Robinson Crusoe* is?"

"Papa's office, I'm sure." Her bright blue eyes sparkled.

"You may fetch it. We are sure to find ample supply of spelling words in the text."

Ana's chair scraped the floor as she stood. "Hoora—"

"Shhhhh." Caitlin's hand stilled on the wax until it burned her fingertips. "Do you hear that?"

Rascal pushed himself up, nails clicking on the bare wood floor, nose in the air.

The hoofbeats grew louder.

Caitlin and Ana hastened out of the workroom, down the main hall and out the front door in time to see a pair of Rebel soldiers galloping down their lane toward them. As they drew rein in front of the porch, Caitlin clutched the railing, knees weak. What could they be doing here, unless it was to bring news? *They would not bring glad tidings.* She cupped Ana's shoulders in her hands.

"Did Papa get shot?"

Caitlin closed her eyes, bracing herself. Her grip on Ana tightened.

"I don't rightly know," said one of the soldiers. "But if he's in the Army of Tennessee he more'n likely ain't got any shoes."

Caitlin blinked. "Shoes?"

"Yes ma'am. Our boys in grey have been marchin' barefoot. Bragg sent us here on the express purpose of finding shoes to bring back to camp around Chattanooga."

"Is that all?" Caitlin nearly dropped into the rocking chair in relief. "You may find shoes in Atlanta, but they are as much as five hundred dollars a pair now!"

The man smiled. "Not for us. What the army needs, we're taking.

It's for the good of the Confederacy. I have orders to search your house for any shoes not already on feet." He pushed past her and into the house while his companion waited outside with the horses. She could hear Rascal barking but knew he'd never bite.

When the soldier returned, he held Noah's Sunday shoes over his head triumphantly. "Thank you kindly, ma'am. Much obliged." He tossed them in a haversack. "Now for the horses."

"What?" Caitlin's palms prickled with sweat. How would they get out of town to gather firewood, berries, plants?

"Army needs them. We'll pay you in Confederate bonds, re-deemable after the victorious conclusion of the war."

Caitlin chased after the soldiers into the carriage house where Saul was currying Noah's matched pair. His hand dropped as soon as he saw the uniforms.

"See here, boy. Get those horses ready to ride."

Boy? Saul was a grandfather by now, not that he'd ever seen his children's children, Bess had told Caitlin. She held her breath as he stood erect, eyes sparking. "They ain't mine to give. They Mr. Becker's." He turned and fed one of the horses an apple from his hand.

"Don't waste our time." One of the soldiers brandished his pistol at Saul, yanking a scream from Ana's throat.

"Do as he says," whispered Caitlin, thinking only of Saul's safety. He obeyed her, but with the fire of Mount Vesuvius in his eyes. She felt sick.

"Here." The second soldier thrust a note into Caitlin's hand. It was a promise for a quarter of what the horses were worth, redeemable after the Confederacy won the war.

The horses now bridled and saddled, the soldier took the reins for both in one hand, then led them out of the carriage house. Handing the reins to his mounted companion, he climbed back into his own saddle. "Your country thanks you. And sleep easy, ma'am. For we will be victorious in the end."

They rode off then, leaving Saul alone in the carriage house and

Caitlin and Ana coughing on clouds of dust raised by horses they would never see again.

"It's all right, Miss McKae." Ana slipped her hand into Caitlin's. "If Papa and his friends need the horses, they should have them."

Caitlin nodded mutely and shuffled with Ana back into the house, her loyalties at war within her.

From the table in the main hall, she picked up yesterday's *Intelligencer* and looked for clues as to the true condition of the Southern armies.

> *Never has the South shown so much her ability to maintain her independence than the present time . . . While our cause is brightening in its aspect, that of our enemy is becoming daily more desperate.*

The editor's optimism did not resonate with Caitlin. Apparently, it did not resonate with the North, either. For there, in the same issue of the *Atlanta Daily Intelligencer*, was reprinted an article from the *New York Herald*.

> *Atlanta is the last link which binds together the southwestern and northeastern sections of the rebel Confederacy. Break it and those sections fall asunder.*

Caitlin's pulse trotted. If the Union army came to Atlanta, they would crush it, or die trying. She had run to war, and run from war. Now, it was running after her.

That night, in her dreams, she saw both Jack and Noah, lying in the blood-soaked mud. Ana was there, too, reciting lesson twenty-nine from the *First Southern Reader* over their torn bodies of abbreviated lives. "The man's arm has been cut off. It was shot by a gun. Oh! What a sad thing war is!"

Caitlin awoke to the sound of her own scream.

New York City
Monday, October 24, 1863

A gentle rain tapped on the windows, and Ruby O'Flannery hoped it was a portent of the cleansing work that may someday happen in Emma's heart. The women sat at the table now, their heads bent over Emma's new dress in the making. The fire crackled in the friendly kitchen hearth, scenting the air with woodsmoke. As they traced the pattern on olive-green merino wool, Ruby silently thanked God that Caroline had granted permission to use the Waverly brownstone for this purpose. If she never saw the tenements—or Sean Connors—again, she would count herself blessed indeed.

"I'll feel like a different person in this gown, I will!" Emma grinned.

"Aye, that you will. You might even *be* a new person in it." Ruby winked at her friend. "How we dress ourselves matters, you know. 'Tis a signal not just to others, but to ourselves, about who we are. When my dress is dirty and full of holes, I feel poor and desperate, so I act poor and desperate. When my clothes are neat and tidy, I feel clean and decent, I do." She did not need to point out what Emma's garish low-cut silk gowns said about her.

Emma snapped her head up. "Bedad! When we call a woman 'loose' or 'upright'—that's talking about the corset being loose or tight, ain't it?"

Ruby nodded. "The way you look sends a message. What kind of message do you think *this* dress will send?"

A sly smile spread on Emma's face. "Not my usual, that's sure."

"Aye. You're right about that, darlin'." Ruby laughed.

She enjoyed being with Emma when they were sewing together. But she missed her friend Edward. He still came to check on her, but always brought Vivian with him. Maybe he was just quieter when Vivian and Ruby were chatting. Or maybe he had cooled toward her for a different

113

reason. *A good name is rather to be chosen than great riches.* Had Sean's words tarnished her name irreparably in Edward's mind?

Emma chattered on, and Ruby nodded absently as a cold thought penetrated her mind. Ruby was no more than a project to Edward. Just like Emma was a project for Ruby.

A knock at the front door, and Emma jolted. "Is it three o'clock already? I told Sean to pick me up if it was still raining. That'll be him now, it will."

Swallowing her distaste for Emma's brother, Ruby led the way to the door. "Same time next week? See you then."

"That you will." Emma kissed her on the cheek. "Many thanks, lassie."

Ruby pressed a hand to her fluttering stomach, then opened the door. "Afternoon, Sean."

"Fine day for a promenade in the park, eh, Ruby?" With a scab still crusting his lower lip—compliments of Edward's fist—his smile did not stretch far as Emma ducked under his umbrella. "How's your friend? The chaplain?" But he did not look at her. His gaze went over her head, roving hungrily from left to right.

"Goodbye, then." Ruby closed the door and locked it before leaning against it with her back. Their footsteps faded quickly, and she peeked into the parlor at the mantel clock. If she hurried, she could clean up in the kitchen before Aiden awoke from his nap.

A clap of thunder rattled the windows, and Ruby froze, waiting for her baby's cry. It didn't come. *Thank goodness.* Aiden was cutting a tooth, and it had been keeping him up at night lately, which also made the days far less pleasant. Soaking a washcloth in cold water for him to chew on helped some, but it was not enough. Both baby and mama were exhausted.

Dreaming of her own bedtime already, Ruby returned to the kitchen and folded the wool they'd been cutting today. No sooner had she stacked the pieces than another knock sounded on the door. *Strange.* When Ruby stepped into the hall, a loud banging behind her catapulted her heart into double time. She spun around to face the French doors leading to the garden. There, dripping wet, was Sean.

"What do you want?" She shouted through the glass.

"Emma forgot her gloves." He shrugged. "Can you let me in, please? If you hadn't noticed, it's a wee bit humid out here."

"Where's Emma then?"

"Running late as usual. I sent her back with the umbrella. Told her I'd fetch her bloomin' gloves and catch up to her." Lightning split the sky behind him. "Come on, Ruby, don't make me wait. If I catch pneumonia out here, it'll be on your head." His attempt at a smile screwed into a grimace instead. Sean would break the glass just to have his own way if he was in a black temper. Scowling, Ruby let him in and pointed to a patch of floor just inside the door. "Wait here while I go look for them."

"As you wish!" He tipped his hat to her, sending a stream of rainwater splashing onto the rug.

Rolling her eyes, Ruby ducked back into the kitchen and lifted every fold of fabric until she found Emma's gloves under the bolt. "Here you go, I found—"

He wasn't where she had left him.

Her heart hammered against its cage. "Sean?" She walked down the hall, looking in the dining room, the library, the rear parlor, until she found him in the front parlor. Hands folded behind his back, he gazed up at an English landscape oil painting hanging above the sofa. He half-turned, and caught Ruby's gaze in the mirror above the marble fireplace.

"You sure are livin' like a queen in her castle."

Ruby's mouth went dry. She shook her head. "No, you're mistaken. I am the lowly Irish maid. The queen is just not here."

His eyes flashed, and she bit her tongue for its thoughtless remark. "That's what Emma says. It's quite a set-up." He swiveled slowly around, as if calculating the worth of every item.

Ruby's skin crawled. "Here are Emma's gloves. Now go."

"'Tis raining harder. Surely you wouldn't turn me out just yet."

She grabbed an umbrella from the hall stand and thrust it at him, wishing it was fitted with bayonet. "Take it. Emma can return it to me next week. She'll be wondering where you got to."

Sean stepped toward her and grabbed the end of the umbrella. "I don't take orders from anyone. Not from skinny-necked lieutenants. Not from my sister. Not from you."

Ruby flinched.

"Sure is a lovely place. And you're a lovely woman." His gaze raked her body, igniting fire in her veins. "And here we are all alone."

"I told you, I'm not that kind of girl anymore."

"Old habits are hard to break. At least, I hope they are, in your case." He stepped closer, until he was near enough that she smelled whiskey on his breath, saw whiskers bristling from his jaw. In his eyes she saw every man who had ever violated her. Stolen her soul, piece by piece.

It would not happen again. *Old things are passed away; behold, all things are become new.* "I am a new person now. And I'll not be havin' any of your vile talk. There's the door, now go."

"How about a tip first?"

"For what?"

"For not ravaging you right here on the floor, for starters. On account of I'm such a gentleman, I am."

"You'll not have a dime."

"I'm not talking about a dime. I'm talking about something a little more valuable that the missus would never miss."

"Help you steal from Mrs. Waverly?" Ruby was incredulous. "I'd never!"

Aiden cried out, and Ruby's heart nearly stopped beating.

The devil's grin slithered across Sean's face. "Aye, the little bastard! I almost forgot you had him. Let's see the wee babe. Though I doubt I'll see any likeness of Matthew in him." He shoved Ruby into the corner of the doorframe, and pain sliced the length of her back. He was on the staircase in a few long strides.

"Don't you touch him!" Ruby screamed and clambered up the stairs after him, clawing at his ankles. He turned, gripped her wrists and twisted, until her hands went numb and released their catch. Then his muddy boot slammed squarely into her chest and sent her crashing against the walnut banister and down the stairs.

The room swayed. She struggled like a capsized ship in high seas to right herself. Her hand pressed against the pounding in her head and came away wet with blood. Her back cried out in pain.

But it was nothing to the cry of her son, growing louder now, more frantic. When her vision focused, the rest of the room fell away. Fear released itself in a hot trickle down her leg.

Sean suspended Aiden over the second floor railing by his feet, with nothing but air between the baby's head and the main hall floor below. "What's he worth to you?" Sean shouted over Aiden's screaming.

"Everything!" She was sobbing now, pushing herself up to her feet, stumbling with her arms outstretched to the place where Aiden might drop.

"Then let's have it."

"Put him down!"

Sean let go of one foot, and the baby swung like a pendulum, choking on tears and mucus.

Ruby's anguished scream echoed in the hall. "He is innocent!"

"But you aren't. Or else he wouldn't even be here." He laughed. "Promise me."

"P-Promise you what?"

"Everything."

"Carry him down the stairs to me safely and I promise you, I promise you, what I have is yours. So help me if you harm a hair on his body, I will kill you myself."

"I doubt that." But he heaved Aiden up over the railing and carried him under one arm down the stairs. "You can have no idea how fun it is to watch you squirm."

Ruby staggered toward him and snatched Aiden out of the madman's arms. "Shhh, shhhhh, you're all right now, Mama's here, it's all right." His tiny shoulders hiccupped with sobs that mimicked her own, and his face was red and swollen. Ruby's heart shattered as she squeezed his sweaty little body against her aching chest. If she had lost him . . .

"We can all be bought, Ruby. You're no different. Now, if you please. You did promise." He fingered the top button of her collar.

She jerked back. "*I* am not for sale."

"Then what exactly did you promise me?"

When Sean finally disappeared back into the rain, it was with everything Ruby had earned and saved for Aiden's future.

She was cast down, but not destroyed. Ruby's price had already been paid—but not by Sean. *For ye are bought with a price: therefore glorify God in your body, and in your spirit, which are God's.*

Sean did not own her, and neither did her past. God did.

Ruby O'Flannery would never give up her body to another man again.

———

Atlanta, Georgia
Thursday, October 29, 1863

Damp morning air seeped through Caitlin's tattered dress even as pine branches crackled in the kitchen fireplace. "I can do this," she told herself, frail wisps of woodsmoke curling into the air around her.

Two refugees—a pretty, yet spoiled young woman a few years older than Caitlin, and a kind, warm lady about Caitlin's mother's age—had come knocking on the door in the last week, and Caitlin had welcomed them in, though it meant two more mouths to feed. Soon after they arrived, she had had no choice but to let Bess and Saul go. There were no more horses for Saul to care for, and barely any food to cook. If Caitlin could do the work herself, that would be only four bellies to fill instead of six.

I can do this.

The first want of the day was always coffee, and as they had none left, a substitute would have to suffice. It seemed as though every issue of the newspaper brought with it a new recipe:

Rye, boiled, dried, and ground like coffee.

Irish potatoes peeled and sliced very thin, roasted and ground.

Sweet potatoes cut into chunks and dried in the sun, and ground.

Dandelion roots, washed, diced, and roasted until dry and dark brown, ground.

Ripe acorns, washed, parched until they open, roasted with bacon fat. Okra seeds.

Corn.

Shelled peanuts, toasted or roasted until almost black, ground into powder.

Peanuts Caitlin had, as did most Atlanta housekeepers. Scooping a few handfuls onto the table, Caitlin sat on the stool and pressed the flat blade of a knife on the shells to crack them open.

When enough peanuts had been shelled, Caitlin placed a tray of them to roast on the grate over the fire and stood back. Her gaze skittered around the kitchen, making a mental note of their supplies. It did not take long, thanks to the thieves who had helped themselves to her supplies last night before Rascal's toothless barking had scared them away. Besides peanuts, there was corn and cornmeal. Potatoes. Some rice. A little dried meat, not much. Some sorghum. Just three eggs left from the last time the yeoman farmers passed by. Caitlin had no idea if they'd ever be back. The poor white folks who lived outside of town used to roll through here regularly, selling corn, sorghum, and eggs out of their buckboard wagons. But ever since the Confederate government imposed a tax-in-kind on yeoman farmers and plantations alike, forcing them to hand over a portion of all they grew, the farmers had kept out of sight for the most part.

No matter. She would make do. Heaven knew she had done it before.

Let's see, three eggs, four people. She could use one to make cornbread, and boil the remaining two, dividing them lengthwise to make sure each person received an equal portion. A grim smile curled her lips. It sounded like one of the story problems from Mr. Johnson's *An Ele-*

mentary Arithmetic. *If one Confederate soldier can whip 7 Yankees, how many soldiers can whip 49 Yankees?*

A Confederate soldier captured 8 Yankees each day for 9 successive days; how many did he capture in all?

If a merchant sells salt to a soldier's wife at $50 per bag when the going rate is $90 per bag, how much money would the merchant lose selling four bags to soldiers' wives?

If two boiled eggs must feed three women and one child, what fraction should each person eat?

"Half an egg each." It was not so unusual anymore. Jefferson Davis was quoted in the papers as saying that he could see no reason for not eating rats, for he thought they would be as good as squirrels. The idea made her ill as she hung a pot of water over the fire.

Outside, Rascal barked. When he grew more frantic, the back door of the house slammed, followed by footsteps running toward the kitchen.

"Miss McKae! There's someone else at the door!"

No eggs in the cornbread then. Three boiled eggs divided by five. That would be . . . three-fifths each. Oh how she could use a real cup of coffee.

"Come, come!" Ana tugged on her skirt, and Caitlin followed her around the house to meet the new refugee on the porch.

As they rounded the corner, she wiped her hands on her apron and tucked her hair behind her ear. Pebbles punched through her thin soles as she walked. "May I help—"

The woman turned. "Hello, honey."

"You!" Caitlin ran to embrace her. "Minnie Taylor, am I ever glad to see you! What brings you back to Atlanta?"

"The Western & Atlantic." She smirked, her dimples popping into place. " 'Live while ye may, Yet happy pair; enjoy till I return, Short pleasures; for long woes are to succeed.' "

Caitlin shuddered as Minnie quoted *Paradise Lost.*

"Turns out Milton was right, honey. He just didn't know he was talking about the Confederacy." Her grey eyes drooped to the bundle at her feet. "I don't suppose you'd have any room for a refugee like me?"

"Of course we do." Caitlin squeezed Minnie's shoulders. "But what about your home? Didn't you have a plantation?"

"Appropriated for some federal officers during the siege of Chattanooga. All the slaves freed. Grandfather's gone, too. Enlisted in the army to take my dead daddy's place. There's nothing for me there anymore. I couldn't think of anyplace else to go."

"I'll take care of you now, Minnie."

"No, honey. We'll take care of each other, with God's help."

Caitlin nodded, though God had not bothered Himself much about her family before. The two women circled back around to the kitchen, Ana at their heels until she spotted a rabbit in the brush and decided to stalk that instead.

"Oh!" said Caitlin when she saw the peanuts nearly blackened over the fire. With a rag, she snatched the tray off the fire and set it on the table.

"Heaven help us, what are you fixin' to feed us today?"

"Only the finest peanut coffee in the South." Caitlin winked at Minnie as she scooped the charred peanuts into a wooden mortar and ground them with the pestle. She then poured the grounds into the percolator coffeepot and ladled hot water in over it. "We'll let it brew while the eggs boil, then we'll go in and you can meet the others."

"The others?"

"Two more houseguests here, indefinitely, from the Chattanooga area as well. One is named Naomi Ford, and the other—"

"The other" burst into the kitchen then, smelling of rose hair oil and reeking of indignation. Her nearly white-blonde hair was arranged in three rolls of varied sizes over the top of her head, on each side of the part.

"Why, I'm simply ravenous! Where are your Negroes? If I were you I'd whip them up one side and down the other for making us wait for breakfast!"

Caitlin grit her teeth before responding. "I told you, I've let them go."

"You what? You can't free your slaves, it's against the law!"

"They were never mine to begin with. We rented their time and service from their owner in Decatur. I've simply stopped employing them so I have more money for food."

"They weren't even your own slaves?" She threw up her hands, then laughed, shaking her head. "What kind of a home is this?"

"The kind that takes in a stranger without a Confederate shinplaster to her name." Caitlin's tone was sweet as sorghum. "Now. Your breakfast will be ready shortly. I'll pour you a cup of coffee now, since you're here, and then we can eat in the dining room soon."

She sniffed. "Fine. What are we having?"

Caitlin glanced at Minnie and stifled a laugh. "For you? Three-fifths of a boiled egg, peanut coffee, and cornmeal crackers if I can just get around to making them." She should not be so amused at the look of horror on the woman's face.

"Why, I never! Do you know that where I come from, breakfast is no less than six courses? Melon, fried perch, chicken in cream gravy, poached eggs on toast, porterhouse steak with tomatoes and mayonnaise, oatmeal, corn muffins, sugared peaches! Tea, coffee, and chocolate!" She groaned, eyes closed, with a hand on her tightly laced corset.

"It's a wonder you ever left such a place." Caitlin poured coffee into a tin cup and handed it to her, an impish grin on her face.

"Well I wouldn't expect the same fare here of course, not in these times, but I do declare I was hoping for a little more substance than this!"

"You're getting three-fifths of a boiled egg, peanut coffee, and crackers. Enjoy."

Minnie stepped forward, laughter in her grey eyes. "By the way, I'm Minerva Taylor. It's a pleasure to meet you. I'll be staying here for a while, too."

Caitlin and Minnie watched as Susan sampled the peanut coffee—and spit it out onto the floor, by way of Caitlin's skirt.

"I'm Susan." Eyebrows drawn together, she pressed the back of her hand to her pert little mouth until she recovered. "Susan Kent. Charmed, I'm sure."

New York City
Monday, November 2, 1863

"Shhh, shhhh, Aiden, shhhhh." Ruby swayed with her baby on her hip, but of course it did nothing to soothe his swollen gums. "I'm sorry, Emma, he's cutting a tooth. Our sewing lesson may be over for today." She smiled apologetically. "I'll be right back."

"Poor little lad. Don't be sorry; he can't help it a wee bit, now can he?" Emma's voice floated down the hall as Ruby headed to the kitchen, where a washcloth was steeping in cold orange tea—a suggestion from Vivian. She wrung out the cloth and handed it to Aiden to chew on.

He calmed, and Ruby breathed a sigh of relief. "Does that feel good, darlin'?" He nuzzled his head under her chin as she carried him back to meet Emma.

"You're such a good mama, Ruby. I could never do it."

"Yes, you could. God gives strength and grace for what you need, when you need it."

"Aye, for you he does."

"Not just for me. You—" She stopped cold. Was she hearing things? "Emma, is Sean coming for you again today?"

"No, lass. He's comin' for you."

"What?" Ruby gasped. "I—I told him not to come back again." She had done far more than that. She'd gone to the police station and asked them to patrol the brownstone periodically, in anticipation of Sean trying to break in. But the answer, thanks to her Irish accent, had been no. *Your people curried no favor with us by beating uniformed officers to a pulp last summer.*

"Sean told me you had an argument, he did. I'm sorry for it. But he wanted to apologize."

Ruby's pulse galloped. "No, no, I won't be alone with him again.

123

I'll not have him in this house!"

Emma's brow wrinkled. "'Twas that bad, was it? Well then never mind. I'll stay with you. Just step outside on the steps, in full view of the street traffic, in broad daylight. He won't rest until he's said his piece, and you might as well hear him now with me than later when he's been sloshing in his drink again."

Ruby's eyes narrowed with doubt.

"Trust me, he'll come back again later without me if you don't hear him now."

Ruby shifted a glance toward the door. "Do you think he's sober?"

Emma nodded.

"Fine. We'll settle accounts and put an end to it then." Ruby laid her hand protectively on Aiden's head as Emma opened the door. November wind scraped their faces as they stepped outside.

"Make it fast, Sean, it's cold out here." Ruby leveled a glare at him.

Freshly shaven, and smelling of musk, he removed his hat and spun it by the brim in his hands. "I'm sorry for last week, Ruby. Truly. 'Twas the devil drink, it was."

"Pay me back by never coming here again."

"Don't ask that of me, Ruby, please. I know it may not seem like it, but I'm keen on your company. What I mean to say—"

Aiden fussed, and Ruby cooed to him.

"I want to court you, Ruby."

She jerked her head up. "Go on, now." Even Emma's eyes were wide.

"If I do it right and proper, there ain't nothin' wrong about it. 'Tisn't like you're married, which is more than you could say for yourself—"

"Sean Connors!" Emma jabbed him in the ribs. "That's no way to sweet talk a lady!"

"Do you have to be here?" Sean snarled.

"That she does," Ruby said.

He sighed. "Truth is, Rubes, I've had my eye on you ever since you and Emma were first friends. I wanted you then, but I'd not cross Matthew. He's not here now. I am."

124

Ruby's ears tingled. "I don't believe what I'm hearing," she muttered into Aiden's coppery hair, chafing his arms to keep him warm.

"Did you want to be unmarried for the rest of your life? Or did you have another fellow in mind?"

I would rather be alone than with you. She knew better than to say it.

When Aiden fussed again, Emma took him from Ruby's arms and tickled his nose with the fringe of her shawl.

"I need to get a blanket for him," Ruby said. She slipped inside and grabbed a shawl for herself off the hall rack, plus the blanket on the parlor rug, before returning to the front stoop. "Get away from my son." Her tone smoldered with warning.

Sean stepped back from Aiden, hands up in mock surrender. "I wouldn't hurt a fly." He smiled. "He needs a father to show him how to be a man, that's what."

Ruby scowled as she draped Aiden's blanket over his back. "You're not the one for the job."

"Don't tell me you've set your cap for the chaplain! Such a namby-pamby, that one!"

Edward wasn't brawny, true enough. But, "He's a gentleman."

"Aye, too gentle for the likes of you. If you hadn't noticed, I don't believe preachers are in the habit of marrying prostitutes!"

"And I am not in the habit of being courted by a man who treats women so shamefully! Get out."

Emma handed Aiden back to Ruby, and whispered, "I'm sorry, lass. He's a hard case, he is."

Sean slapped his sister, hard. "Shut your trap."

Ruby recoiled, pressed Aiden tighter to her.

And then she smelled it. She leaned closer to Aiden's mouth.

"Whiskey?" Her voice cracked with disbelief. "Did you give my son whiskey?"

Sean shrugged, eyes glinting. "Just gave him a little nip on his rag for him to suck on, that's all. Cures whatever ails a man. See how quiet he is now! I do believe he fancies it."

Trembling with rage, Ruby no longer needed her shawl to keep warm. "Leave us now or you can go to the deuce!"

His muscled arm shot up, his fingers dug into her throat right in front of Aiden's eyes. "That's no way to talk to a man."

Ruby struggled for breath, even as she noticed Aiden watching Sean's every move.

"Mama?" He dropped his rag and patted his dimpled hand on her cheek. His breath smelled not of milk, or crackers, but of the demon alcohol.

Carriage wheels clattered along Sixteenth Street just yards from where they stood. Finally, Sean released her and stepped back. "See? It's like I said. Someone needs to show the lad what it takes to be a man."

Sobs choked her when Sean's hand did not, and she slumped to the cold stone, clutching Aiden. Hatred and fear twisted together, lassoed her heart and plunged it to the depths of her spirit. The fury in its place startled her.

"Mrs. O'Flannery?" All three heads turned toward the speaker, a brougham driver who drew rein in front of the Waverly residence. "What's going on here?"

Sean placed his hat back on his head. "See you around, Ruby. You too, laddie." He winked at Aiden, and Ruby's toes curled. She could not even bring herself to look at Emma as they left.

"Ruby?" Vivian McKae climbed down out of the brougham and swept up the steps. She knelt in front of Ruby before turning back to the coachman. "Mr. Biggs, I do believe I'll stay a while. I'm sure you can use the carriage house and come warm yourself inside."

Ruby nodded, then allowed Vivian to help her to her feet. With the older woman's arm wrapped around Ruby's shoulders, they went back inside the house and made it to the rear parlor before Ruby crumbled onto the sofa.

"I'll put on the kettle." Vivian bustled out and returned again in moments. "Edward said you called off your Bible study with him yesterday, so I came to see how you are. But I can see plain as day what the answer is."

Vivian's lips flattened as she looked at Ruby's throat, still radiating with pain. She pushed a strand of hair from Ruby's forehead, her fingertip snagging on the scab on her temple.

Tears misting her eyes, Ruby grasped Vivian's hand, while her other arm still circled Aiden. "Vivian, so help me, if he touches my son again, I just might kill him or die trying." Her words shocked her. How would they sound to Vivian McKae, whose marriage to James was the happiest one Ruby had ever witnessed? "I need help."

"You need to leave."

Chapter Ten

Outside Chattanooga, Tennessee
Tuesday, November 3, 1863

*D*rumming rain soaked through Noah Becker's shell jacket, plastering his shirt to shivering skin as he stood picket duty along the swollen Chattanooga Creek. The last time he'd served as sentinel, he was a boy of seventeen years, atop a castle besieged by the Prussian army, from which he could see the Black Forest, the mountains in which Baden-Baden was nestled, and the Rhine valley with its rich fields and vineyards.

Once again the revolutionary, Noah mused, but stopped short of further comparisons. Ankle-deep in standing water here in the valley between Tennessee's Lookout Mountain and Missionary Ridge, all he could think of was drying out. That, and his growling stomach.

Though the Union army was under siege in Chattanooga, it was the Rebels who suffered most, with little shelter and less food. In fact, Noah's Sixty-Sixth Georgia regiment was the newest here, and the only one with the luxury of tents. The men Noah passed who had been here longer looked sick, hollow-eyed, and heartbroken. They lived on the parched corn that had been picked out of the feet of officers' horses.

Rain streaming from the brim of his felt hat, Noah squinted across the creek at the boys in blue. Some had oilcloths or India rubber blankets draped over the heads, some only their forage caps between them and the rain. The orders, on both sides, were not to fire unless fired upon, or unless one of them tried to cross. They were close enough to have conversations, which often led to friendly exchanges via private truce. Southern tobacco for Northern coffee, and both armies thrilled with the swap.

Sloshing footsteps tramped toward the sentinels, and Noah's chest expanded. Relief had arrived.

Back in his tent, Noah peeled off his Sibley jacket and shirt and rubbed his skin down with the corner of his blanket.

"Howdy-doo and gootin tag, Herr Becker." Ross, a long-bearded private from north Georgia, had taken a shine to Noah, and delighted in twisting English and German speech together. He was a yeoman farmer before enlisting as a hired substitute. "Ask me why I might be your *bester* friend right about now."

Noah eyed him wryly before pulling a dry shirt over his head and slicking his hair off his forehead. "All right. Why?"

Ross pulled out an envelope. "Say biddie!"

Noah's heart leapt to his throat. "*Bitte.*"

Ross handed it over. "Do I hear a donkey?"

A chuckle escaped Noah as he shook his head. "*Danke. Vielen dank.*"

Ross beamed. "You're so biddie."

"*Bitte sehr,*" Noah corrected him, then retreated to his bedroll with the envelope fairly burning in his hands.

After pulling off his saturated brogans and socks, he tore into the envelope. He had only to read the first line before he realized he had been holding his breath for this moment for weeks.

Dear Mr. Becker, We keep well, and pray for your safe return every night.

He scanned the text hungrily at first, then went back and savored every word, a range of emotions flaring within his spirit as he did so. Longing to tuck his daughter into bed again himself, resignation over the loss of his horses, concern for Bess and Saul. Noah was gratified that Caitlin had accepted three refugees from the Chattanooga area into his home so far, and so pleased that one of them was Minerva Taylor. Though his interactions with Miss Taylor had been limited at the Atlanta Female Institute, he had always thought her a cheerful spirit, and no doubt Caitlin had need of the companionship.

At the bottom of the page, Caitlin mentioned that the price of stamps was regrettably high. He knew what she meant. Frequent correspondence should not be expected.

And now, Caitlin wrote, *I have a young lady here who wishes to speak with you.*

Noah flipped the page and Ana's childish scrawl immediately blurred in his vision. She had drawn a small but familiar and comforting picture for him. Ana holding Noah's hand, standing in front of their house. An oval-shaped Rascal was in the picture, too. Noah blinked the moisture from his eyes and read on.

Miss McKae says I'm doing very well in my lessons. Would you like to see what I can do? I will do my next lesson for you here. This is from Mrs. Moore's Dixie Speller:

> *This sad war is a bad thing.*
> *My pa-pa went, and died in the army.*

Noah's brow furrowed. This was Ana's spelling lesson? Chills rippled over him.

> *My big brother went too and got shot. A bomb shell took off his head.*

> *My aunt had three sons, and all have died in the army. Now she and the girls have to work for bread.*

I will work for my ma and my sisters.

I hope we will have peace by the time I am old enough to go to war.

If I were a man, and had to make laws, I would not have any war, if I could help it.

If little boys fight old folks whip them for it; but when men fight, they say "how brave!"

I would not run away like some do . . . I would sooner die at my post than desert.

If pa-pa had run away, and been shot for it, how sad I must have felt all my life!

Well Papa, how do you like my spelling? My hand is tired and I am out of room but I love you so so so so very very much. I love you to the stars and back. Love, Ana

P. S. I like having the new ladies stay with us very much. Except maybe for Miss Kent. She snaps at Miss McKae and looks at me funny sometimes.

Noah squinted at the words. Miss Kent? *No, no.* It could be a mistake. Ana could have misspelled the name. He studied the words again. Even if the name was Kent, there was no reason to believe it was Susan Kent—let alone the same Susan Kent he had married eight years ago. No reason to believe Ana's mother had returned for her, with him not there to stop it.

I would not run away like some do . . . I would sooner die at my post than desert.

Chapter Eleven

New York City
Wednesday, November 4, 1863

Guilt sitting like a stone in his stomach, Edward rapped his knuckles on the door to the second-story sitting room. "Ruby?"

Vivian had informed George he'd have two more houseguests, and then Edward and Biggs had moved Ruby's things over, including Aiden's crib and Ruby's rocking chair, so they could stay in George's master bedroom. The attached water closet gave her privacy, and being on the second floor instead of the third allowed her to hear when Aiden would awaken from his naps. Besides, George would not need his old bedroom until his legs had fully healed, and by that time, Caroline would likely be home anyway, so Ruby could move back in with her.

Edward wanted her to feel comfortable here. Safe. It was why he moved his own bedroom to the third floor, so Ruby, Aiden, and Vivian could have the second floor to themselves at night. And he knew better than to barge in on Ruby without knocking, even during the day. Sean had barged in on her enough already. *More than enough.*

"May I come in?"

"Aye," came her answer, and Aiden's babbling followed.

Heart thudding, he sat down on the sofa with Ruby, with Aiden stacking blocks on the Persian rug at their feet. A fire crackled in the marble fireplace, casting a bronze glow on Ruby's hair.

"I need to apolo—" His words fell away when his gaze dropped upon the yellow-edged purple marks on her neck. A lump drove sharply into his throat. "I'm so sorry," he whispered.

Her green eyes glimmered. "'Twasn't you that did it."

"But I said I'd check in on you, make sure you were safe." He could barely squeeze the words out around his dismay. "I hate that this happened to you."

"'Tisn't your fault. You can't be with us all the time. But God can." She smiled, and his jaw slacked.

"You don't blame Him for what happened to you?"

She shook her head. "'Twas He who brought us to a safe place. He brought us back to you."

Warmth spread through his chest as he looked at her. She was battered, but not broken. Perplexed, but not in despair. *Beautiful.*

Ruby's face hardened as she watched Aiden play with his blocks. "He almost killed my son's body. Then he tried to get his soul." She shuddered.

"What do you mean?" The hair on his neck rustled.

"Monday on the front steps. When I went in to fetch a blanket and shawl, Sean doused the washcloth I'd given Aiden to chew on with whiskey from his flask. My wee babe! Tasting whiskey! If the child develops a taste for alcohol I don't know what I'll do."

Edward stared at Aiden's cherub face and shook his head, blood boiling in his veins. Alcohol was the cause of so many men's demise. To introduce it to a baby was just pure evil.

"That's not all." Ruby rolled her lips between her teeth, and her nose pinked. Her chest heaved with breath before she could speak.

"Sean hit Emma in front of him. He choked me as I held the baby, and Aiden watched. He said he was showing him what it meant to be a man." Tears spilled down her cheeks now. "I've lost all my money for the lad's education. What if I can't protect Aiden from the influences of the street, and he grows to be just like Sean, or even like Matthew, who lashed out when he was drunk? Drinking liquor and hitting women, as if that's just what men do. If I tell Aiden that's not what it means to be a man, who will he believe? His mother? Or grown men?" She covered her face with her hands while Aiden remained busy building squat wooden towers, ignorant of the struggle clearly rending his mother's heart.

And Edward's. He reeled at the mention of Matthew. *Her own husband struck her?* Even if it was rare, the idea made him sick. The thought of Aiden becoming hardened and given to vice shook Edward—he could not imagine the pain Ruby felt. This wasn't just about one man, or one attack. It was about a legacy that needed to be broken.

"I will help you show him," he offered. "Respectable men do not go to the bottle for solace, but the Lord. True men don't hurt women. They protect them, cherish them, extol them. Proverbs says a virtuous woman is worth far more than rubies. Real men understand the treasure with which they are blessed." Tenderly, he laid a hand on her shoulder, his thumb lightly grazing the bruise on her soft neck. For a moment, his words netted in his chest as he drank in the trust and hope he read in her glossy eyes. "Aiden will never see me hurt you, Ruby. He will see me treat you the way you deserve to be treated."

Ruby was a treasure indeed.

Atlanta, Georgia
Thursday, November 12, 1863

Weak light blinked fitfully onto the pages of a Sir Walter Scott Waverley novel, from which Caitlin read aloud to the parlor full of women.

It had quickly become their evening routine to read to one another, passing the long winter nights by escaping to another world. At least, those who could hear the words over their growling stomachs. Ana sat opposite the tea table from Caitlin, diligently pulling the candle's twisted-rag wick away from the bottle as it burned down.

> *He found Miss Bradwardine presiding over the tea and coffee, the table loaded with warm bread, both of flour, oatmeal, and barley meal, in the shape of loaves, cakes, biscuits, and other varieties, together with eggs, reindeer ham, mutton and beef ditto, smoked salmon, marmalade, and all the other delicacies which induced even Johnson himself to extol the luxury of a Scotch breakfast above that of all other countries. A mess of oatmeal porridge, flanked by a silver jug, which held an equal mixture of cream and butter-milk, was placed for the Baron's share of this repast . . .*

"Oh, stop, honey, can you please? Or skip that part and move on to something else?"

Caitlin looked up toward Minnie's voice.

"My belly's crying out in envy is all." She laughed feebly.

"Sorry, Minnie." Caitlin's own mouth had started watering at the first mention of coffee and warm bread. But since she could almost taste the fictional menu, too, she hadn't minded. "Would you like to take over? Or Naomi? Susan? It's time I get Analiese to bed anyway."

Caitlin stood, and Ana reluctantly did the same. "Is your room all picked up?"

"It's as picked up as I want it to be." Ana ground her toe into the thick carpet.

Caitlin suppressed an exasperated sigh. "That's not what I asked. Is it picked up the way it is *supposed* to be?"

"No. Miss Kent says I shouldn't have to do that."

"What?" Caitlin's skin tingled. "Susan, is that true?"

Susan rose, but in the shadows Caitlin could not read her face. "Yes, it is. I never picked up as a child. That's what your slaves are for."

Caitlin bristled. "You'll forgive me for saying so, but one of the main reasons Mr. Becker hired me as Ana's governess was that I believe in taking responsibility for ourselves. Each of us should clean up our own mess." It was a lesson Susan would do well to learn herself.

"I disagree." Susan's voice was cold, hard. "I will say it again. That's what we have slaves for. That is, that's what I had slaves for. Obviously you can't afford to keep them here."

"And I wouldn't even if I could. But we are skirting the matter now. I am Ana's governess. You will please refrain from undermining my authority." She turned to the girl. "Please go pick up the rest of your things. I'll be up in a moment to see that it's been done before tucking you in for the night."

"Annie, don't do it." Susan's voice rang out, but Ana's footsteps faded up the stairs nonetheless. Fire kindling in her bones, Caitlin stalked over to Susan, who couldn't even remember Ana's name right. "What in heaven's name do you think you're doing?"

"You speak of undermining your authority. I say you are undermining our Southern way of life. I don't know who you are or where you come from, but it's plain as day you're not from Dixie."

"Susan!" Minnie gasped. "Being a Southern woman is not about being pampered and petted, and consumed with our own selfish vanity while waiting on others to pander to us."

"Oh! How convenient for a woman without a single suitor to say! Little wonder, though, with those pockmarks all over your face." Susan's words leeched into the air like poison.

Caitlin's jaw dropped. But Minnie held her own.

"Your own tongue betrays you, Susan. A true Southern woman demonstrates ladylike behavior: cheerfulness, a gentle nature, and service to others as a source of happiness and satisfaction for oneself. You possess none of these qualities. If you had any true breeding at all, you would show—or at least have the good sense to feign—traits of the true woman."

"You will cease speaking to me in that way."

"I will not. Clearly you need an education. Amiability, piety, a desire to please others. Cleanliness, neatness, patience, industry, kindness, modesty, politeness, respect for elders, obedience. These are the characteristics we should be cultivating in Ana, not laziness and self-importance. Above all, ladies are not to become vexed, let alone show it."

"I don't have to listen to this." Susan seethed. "Just who do you think you are?"

"Minerva Taylor is an instructor at the Atlanta Female Institute, my friend, and a guest in this home." Caitlin held her voice steady. "As are you, may I remind you."

"Oh no. I'm much more than that, make no mistake."

"Really? And just who might that be?" Naomi pushed herself up from the sofa and crossed her arms, the maturity of her forty-some years evident in her matriarchal gaze.

An unearthly glow lit Susan's bright blue eyes. Eyes, Caitlin realized, that were the very color of forget-me-nots. The resemblance to Ana's was truly remarkable.

No. The impossible idea sliced through her. *She is gone,* Noah had said. Susan could not be—

"Annie's mother." Susan lifted her chin. "I'd say that gives me a sight more authority around here than you have, wouldn't you?"

Caitlin's heart plunged as her throat grew tight. "I don't understand."

"How simple can you be? We're divorced. He left me. Took the child and left me."

Divorced! What kind of a man takes a woman's baby from her? Caitlin wondered. *But what kind of a woman returns to find her long-lost daughter and does not scoop her up into her arms at once?*

"How can we be sure you're her mother?" Naomi asked evenly.

"Her birth date is January 14, 1856. I'll never forget it because I thought she would be the death of me on her way out. The doctor had to break her right collarbone to get her out, and I suspect there is a bump where the bone healed."

Caitlin's heart skipped a beat. Ana had grown so thin lately, Caitlin had, indeed, noticed a curious bump just where Susan had said it was. *Could she have made up the story to match?* Impossible. Susan was never with Ana when she bathed or changed clothes.

"Mama?"

All heads turned toward the voice that crept from the doorway. Ana had not obeyed and gone to bed after all. She had heard every word.

"You're my mama?" she asked again, her fingers pinching the bump in her collarbone.

Silence pulsed in the shadows. Caitlin held her breath.

Finally, Susan spoke, as though exasperated. "Well? Aren't you going to put the child to bed?"

Atlanta, Georgia
Friday, November 13, 1863

"Do you think I should sleep in Mama's room with her instead?"

Caitlin tugged Ana's nightgown down over her head and looked into the girl's questioning eyes. "Did she ask you to?"

"No . . ." Her eyes rolled sideways. "But maybe—maybe she just forgot! I know! Why don't I just go ask her? She's in the parlor; I can be fast as a flash."

Reluctantly, Caitlin nodded, and Ana rushed out of Noah's room, where she and Caitlin had been sleeping ever since Minnie came to join them. Surely he wouldn't want a total stranger sleeping in his own room, Caitlin had reasoned. It must be better that Caitlin and Ana sleep here while Naomi, Minnie, and Susan took the other three rooms.

Moments later, footsteps whispered in the hall until Ana came back and wrapped her arms around Caitlin. "She's a light sleeper. I don't want to wake her up."

Caitlin clenched her teeth before her true opinion of Susan Kent could escape. "That's very considerate of you. And you know your Papa would be happy to know you are keeping his bed warm. I am always glad that you keep me company, too. What would I do if I had a bad dream and you were not here?"

Ana smiled. "Grown-ups don't get scared. That's silly."

"Certainly we do! So I will have to thank Miss Kent for being a light sleeper. That way I can keep you with me."

Sighing, Ana pulled away and unplaited her hair. "Do you think my mother loves me?"

The question pierced. A child should never have to ask such a thing! Worse still, was the suspicion needling Caitlin's heart. "I think she doesn't know you very well yet. I think she is far from home and perhaps Miss Kent is scared too."

Ana frowned. "Scared of what?" Her eyes popped wide, and her horsehair brush stilled on her hair. "Scared that I might not like her? Or that I'm angry she waited so long to find me? Scared that Papa might not come home?"

The humble fire behind Caitlin hissed and crackled. She was grateful shadows veiled her face. "I don't know her very well either."

"I'll be as kind as I can be to her in the morning. Do you think she'd like me to draw a picture for her?"

"I should think she would love that."

"Then I will draw one for her and one for Papa. Can you send it to him tomorrow?"

Caitlin assured her that she would, then pulled back the counterpane as Ana scrambled beneath it. Together, they prayed for Noah, the refugees under their roof, and for peace. "Please God," Ana added. "Help me be very very good so Mama will learn to love me."

Tears pooled in Caitlin's eyes as she kissed Ana goodnight. Instead of joining the others in the parlor now, she decided to turn in early herself. Suddenly, the fatigue she'd been fighting all day won out.

Once she was settled in bed herself, questions hammered inside her mind. What had happened between Noah and Susan? Had Susan always been so disagreeable? If so, why had Noah married her at all? He had seemed so honorable, so committed to his family. Then why would he have abandoned Susan and taken her infant daughter with him?

Every question seemed to dredge up another one, like fishing line snagging only the flotsam and jetsam of a wreckage. Real answers only drifted further away. Tomorrow, she would write Noah and ask him for the truth.

Gently, she turned onto her side and stared blankly at the orange glow spilling from the fireplace. She should not be surprised that Ana was desperate for her mother. Caitlin often wished she could have her own mother back, as well. But she was gone. Just like Da. Just like Jack. Noah may never come back, and now little Ana would turn from her if only Susan would open her arms to her.

Caitlin begged sleep to cover her, but it proved to be as thin as her worn-out dress. It was certainly not enough to mask what she did not want to see.

Herself at twenty-one, peeling potatoes with her mother in their kitchen. Her hair in a braid reaching her waist. Completely oblivious to how the course of the night would change the course of her life forever.

"Maybe it was meant to be that the board is no longer sending teachers out West," Caitlin said. "Otherwise who would take care of you and Jack? Surely not Bernard." As a police officer, her stepfather often worked late, and sometimes didn't come home at all. When he returned smelling like cheap violet water, Caitlin seriously doubted the nature of the business that detained him.

"Jack enlisted today," Vivian said, and Caitlin nearly dropped her peeler.

"He what?"

"He's seventeen years old. No longer a boy." But her voice faltered against the backdrop of New York's Seventh regiment marching off to war this very moment.

"Of course he's a boy! Seventeen years old, that's—that's not old enough to fight in a war! How could you let him do such a thing?"

"I could not stop him if I wanted to." Vivian's sigh seemed weighted with resignation. "In truth, perhaps he is better off in the army than he would be here in the city."

But since when had the army been a positive influence on an impressionable young man whose father had left his life at the age of thirteen? What would become of Jack? She gripped the edge of the counter. Her mind reeled as a band struck up a rousing march outside.

"It's time to move on from this place, for you too, dear. You must stop thinking about me, and go live your own life. You mustn't let me hold you back. I'm fine." But Vivian wasn't fine. It seemed whenever Caitlin was not present, she had an accident of some kind. Burned her wrist on the skillet. Tripped and banged her head onto the table. A book toppled out of the bookcase and hit her. Was her mother's clumsiness just another sign of residual grief, as Caitlin's insomnia had been?

Then Bernard came home with bloodshot eyes and a leer for Caitlin that had made her skin crawl. Vivian stepped in front of her. "Home so soon?"

"Yeah." He scratched his stubbled jaw and tossed his hat on the coat tree. "And I'll take some of that grub if you haven't burned it to tarnation yet."

He stumbled closer and grabbed Caitlin's braid before she could back away.

"Let her alone." Vivian's voice was low. She turned to Caitlin. "Get out. Now."

"Aw, Viv, I hardly ever get to see her." Bernard pulled his shirtwaist tails from his trousers while his watery gaze rippled over her form.

Wild-eyed, Vivian pushed her small hand against Bernard's barrel chest and growled at Caitlin. "Get out! I don't want to see you here again! You've done enough!"

Caitlin glared at both of them. Her stepfather, drunk and slovenly, a disgrace to his badge and a desecration to Da's memory. Her mother, birdlike, and crazy-eyed in her insistence that Caitlin leave.

"Fine."

Fuming, Caitlin slammed the door behind her and stood in the hall outside as she coiled her braid up on top of her head.

"Why did you send her away?" Bernard's snarl snaked under the door, and Caitlin stayed to listen.

"You've got no business with her. I'll do my duty to you, but you leave her out of it."

A low murmur, followed by a slap. "Get!"

Caitlin's heart beat in step with the brisk marching outside. All the bruises on her mother's body swam into focus. It had been Bernard, all along. Hadn't she prayed for God to bless her family, help her keep it together? Yet He had done nothing to stop this.

Neither did I.

Her Irish blood surged then, and she burst back into the apartment with no other thought but to end her mother's nightmare. Little did she know it would be the beginning of her own.

Caitlin's stomach groaned, scattering the vivid memories from her mind. But it would take more than cornbread and peanuts to fill the emptiness that cried out from within her.

Missionary Ridge, Tennessee
Tuesday, November 24, 1863

"Withdraw."

Noah Becker could still smell Colonel Nesbitt's bacon and captured coffee as the murmured order clapped his ears like wooden blocks.

"But why?" Ross dared address his officer, perhaps emboldened by the shade of night. "We ain't through with those Yanks yet!"

Though he would not question orders like his backwoods friend, Noah wondered the same thing. Surely the lack of food and sleep was muddling his mind. Yesterday the Union army had emerged out of the fog like an endless blue python wrapping around Lookout Mountain, squeezing the Confederate army out of its impregnable position. The booming of cannons reverberated between the two mountains—Lookout and

Missionary Ridge—until at midnight, after the fusillade had finally ceased, the Sixty-Sixth had pulled away, crossed the valley, and pushed their twelve-pounder Napoleon guns straight up Missionary Ridge. A line of battle rose with the sun today, but from their position over a railroad tunnel, Yankee charges on the Sixty-Sixth's section of the line had been repulsed. Yet the clamor of heavier fighting from the center left the outcome of the contest open to interpretation.

"You idiot." The officer snarled, the glow of a fitful fire yellowing his complexion. "Bragg's headquarters has been captured and the enemy is on the ridge at this very moment. A very thin line holds them back. Colonel Nesbitt says we are to withdraw at once. You'll draw rations at Chickamauga Station."

"Yes, sir." Noah spoke before Ross had a chance, and the officer left, twigs snapping beneath his heavy footsteps.

"How the deuce did them Yanks get up here with all of us across the ridge, anyway?" Ross muttered. "If we go, who's keeping 'em outta Georgia? That's what I want to know."

Noah shook his head, and let the questions fall like pine needles scattering to the wind. Some answers were too painful to voice.

"Ross." A second lieutenant approached them, his pine-torch casting light and shadow on his face. "You're on the picket line tonight. Spread out, keep up a brisk firing until four a.m. to cover our withdrawal, then fall back quietly. Meet us at the station. Do *not* leave your post until four o'clock, understood, private?"

Ross grumbled in the affirmative.

"Becker, you'll come this way. The horses are tired. We've got six cannons to get off this godforsaken ridge, and there's no way the beasts will do it for us. The roads are far too steep. The horses are barely able to stand."

Noah did not point out that he felt barely able to stand himself. The Sixty-Sixth had not slept in almost forty-eight hours, and empty stomachs only added to their fatigue. They hadn't eaten all day. What they'd been eating before that were half-rations only half-worth eating by the time the food reached them after a sixty-mile journey over hard terrain.

"Each company takes a gun. You'll lock the wheels and let the carriages and cannon down gently, all the way to the bottom."

"Yes, sir."

Hunger carved through his middle and the world swayed, yet Noah put one foot in front of the other until he had joined his company. Were they not all exhausted past the point of ordinary limits? Were they not all just as cold as he in the shivering November wind?

At the top of a little old wood road, Noah and his grim-faced comrades clenched stiff fingers around a rope and leaned back to compensate for the leaden burden on the other end. The sky spit sleet into their faces as they began their tedious descent. Noah's palms grew slick against the coarse hemp he clutched, and the earth slid beneath his heels and into the open seams around his toes. Sweat mixed with the cold rivulets tracing down his face as he strained against weight that now seemed to come alive, taunting him silently as it dragged the men down the east side of the ridge.

The rope slid in Noah's hands, stripping his skin with it. *Steady.* Rain and blood mixed to loosen his grip, though he tried desperately to harness the dregs of his strength.

Unbidden, the screams he had heard earlier today and the sharp rattle of muskets coming from the center of the line echoed between his ears, followed by the rushing sound of men running for their lives. According to his officers, Union soldiers had pushed their own cannons up the ridge and fired after the retreating Confederates. How many more cannons had the Rebels added to their number by abandoning them during their retreat? Noah's legs shook, and his hands burned, and the sleet had now soaked into his very bones, it seemed. He knew the same was true for every one of his aching comrades. Steam rose from their bodies, and groans from their lips, but they would preserve their cannon. Too many had been abandoned on the ridge for the Yankees' use already.

A few inches at a time, Noah's company eased the gun and carriage down the five-hundred-foot-high ridge—and right into the frigid, muddy waters of Chattanooga Creek. Shock sliced through Noah as the freezing water swallowed his body. Torchlight wrinkled on water seething and sloshing with men and horses and cannon. With herculean effort, they pushed their guns across the creek and up the bank. Soon the carriage wheels were unlocked and the horses took over the burden once more.

Quaking with cold and gulping the wintry air, Noah forced his chilled, water-logged feet to follow though his sodden body begged to collapse. Another private handed him a torch, and he followed the retreat, the hope of a campfire pulling him forward.

Chills shuddered through him as he waded heavily through the darkness. Seven miles stretched between him and the station where they could finally rest and be fed. As much as Noah tried to hitch his thoughts to that goal, they wandered rebelliously where he did not want to go.

He had retreated before. At the beginning of the German revolution against the oppressive Prussian government, Noah was to march to Siegburg along with one hundred twenty others and seize the armory. About half an hour into their night march, however, one of their horsemen galloped in with the news that dragoons were at their heels and ready to attack the revolutionaries. Some fled to the cornfields, while Noah and others stood silently near the road. But the Prussian dragoons who had scattered them numbered only thirty strong.

Profound shame shrouded Noah. Their mission had come to a disgraceful and ridiculous end, after they had pledged themselves to the cause of German liberty and unity with soul-stirring speeches. Their patriotism flared brightly, but the cold reality was that all insurrectionary attempts in Prussia had failed. Noah could not return to his parents until he had somehow atoned for the inexcusable blunder.

And I believed that so great, so just, so sacred a cause as that of German unity and free government could not possibly fail, and that undoubtedly I would still have a chance to contribute to its victory.

He had been wrong. Noah Becker became a fugitive from the law at that point. Though hope flickered during the course of the next year, it was ultimately extinguished, and he became a political refugee. The revolutionaries failed, and Noah never saw his parents again. His brother Wilhelm's death had been in vain.

The rustle of marching columns mingled with the low snorting of horses and the rattle of sabers and scabbards in the darkness, and Noah reined his thoughts back to the present.

"We did it," a voice breathed.

He turned and spoke toward it. "Do you mean to say we have succeeded? In what?" He did not care that his tone dripped with sarcasm.

"The withdrawal, of course."

"Withdrawal is retreat. Retreat means defeat. We have failed our country and our families. The Union army has Georgia by the throat."

"Our cause is righteous. Ultimately, we cannot possibly fail."

The words fell through him and onto the road, where they were trampled by soldiers retreating to Chickamauga, where only weeks before, they had supposed their Rebel victory had settled the question of Georgian invasion once and for all.

Chapter Twelve

New York City
Thursday, November 26, 1863

℮XTRA EXTRA! GLORIOUS VICTORY IN CHAT-
TANOOGA! Get your *New York Times*, read all about it!"

Ruby's forkful of turkey hovered over her plate as she turned toward the newsboy's cry, muffled by the walls of the house.

"Praise be to God," breathed Vivian as Edward pushed back from
the table and out the door. President Lincoln had declared today one of
national Thanksgiving, and now, it appeared, there was even more to be
grateful for.

Edward returned moments later, his gaze skittering over the headlines.

"Good news for once?" George loaded his fork with boiled ham,
mashed potatoes, and cranberry sauce.

"Very good for the Union. Especially after the decimation at
Chickamauga."

"Please." Vivian's silverware lay idle on a plate still half-full of chicken pie, roasted broccoli, and mixed pickles. "Tell us, dear. Jack was there."

"Was he?" Ruby fed a bite of potatoes to Aiden. She had been careful not to inquire much after Vivian's children, since the topic seemed to pain Vivian.

"After Gettysburg, he reenlisted with the 123rd and now fights under Hooker. Edward?"

He cleared his throat. "Glorious Victory! Grant's Great Success. Bragg Routed and Driven from Every Point. Successful Battle on Tuesday. Gen. Hooker Assaults Lookout Mountain and Takes 2,000 Prisoners. General Sherman Finally Carries Missionary Ridge. Gen. Thomas Pierces the Enemy's Centre. Forty Pieces of Artillery Taken. Five to Ten Thousand Prisoners Captured. Flight of the Rebels in Disorder and Confusion."

"Are there—casualty lists?"

"Not yet. But it says our loss is but little."

Vivian nodded.

"It must be so difficult for you, not knowing exactly where Jack is and how he's doing," Ruby murmured. If she didn't know where Aiden was, but thought he might be in harm's way, she might go mad, no matter how old he was. "How do you manage?"

"I trust that God is able to sustain him, and his sister. Wherever they may be."

"Still no word from Caitlin, then?" Ruby wished there was a more delicate way to ask.

Vivian's head twitched. She resumed her meal. Silence magnified around the scrape of her spoon across her plate, pooling gravy and peas together.

Regret swirled in Ruby's belly then, for the mystery that had caused Caitlin to run away, and for bringing it up to the girl's tormented mother. This was supposed to be a meal of thanksgiving.

Edward folded the newspaper and dropped it on the sideboard

behind him. "Ruby, what do you hear from Mrs. Waverly?"

"She keeps well, and is enjoying her time at Fishkill. Alice is very grateful to have her. She is fatigued." *And so sick the doctors have confined her to her bed until the end of the pregnancy.* But that was not polite dinner conversation in mixed company.

"Does she mention how long she'll be staying?"

Ruby eyed him as he cracked open a steaming roll. Did he wonder how long he'd have to tolerate her and Aiden under their roof? "No. If Alice does not recover earlier, I imagine she may be there some months yet."

"That's fine, dear, absolutely fine," Vivian said. "You're welcome to stay here as long as you need to."

"Of course you are. I didn't mean—" Edward stammered. "You are welcome here."

Aiden clamored for attention, and Edward rose from his seat to clean the boy's face and hands before hoisting him out of his high chair. Ruby smiled as Aiden toddled around the room, happy to be free once again. Silently, she prayed he would not touch anything he shouldn't.

"More turkey, Ruby?" Vivian asked.

"I'm full to the brim, thank you though!" She turned to George. "Mr. Goodrich, thank you so much for allowing us to join your celebration."

"It's nothing," Vivian cut in.

"But it isn't. I'm a maid, and I've not forgotten it. To be invited to dine here—" Her gaze skimmed the bounty of gleaming white porcelain, polished silver, and the steaming food heaped high. "'Tis a gift, and I know it. I won't be putting on any airs after this either. I know my place. 'Tisn't here."

The words were a reminder to herself as much as an assurance to her host, who clearly recognized the yawning abyss between their classes. She was a lowly Irish immigrant with a past so rotten she feared the stench still trailed her. She had no business sleeping in a wealthy business tycoon's four-poster feather bed, with her very own private water closet. For years she had felt dirt between her bare toes in the morning, not the fine wool of an ornate Persian rug, or the smooth surface of waxed hardwood. She didn't belong here. It wasn't who she was. Ruby would do well to remember it. She tucked her hands under the snowy napkin mounded in her lap then.

"At least the girl has sense," George said, huffing.

Ruby should not have chafed. "I'll see to the baby, then, and let the rest of you enjoy your apple pie and coffee in peace."

She scooped Aiden up and retreated to the second floor, where his babbling would not disturb anyone.

Edward's coffee soured in his mouth as he watched her go. "Heavens, what a gracious way you have with our dinner guests."

George's mustache drooped. "All I did was agree with her."

"Some things are better left unsaid."

"The girl knows her place, and rightly so." He cracked his knuckles with a satisfied nod.

Vivian rattled her cup back onto its saucer. "She is a grown woman, a widow, and a mother. I do wish you'd stop calling her 'the girl.' Ruby O'Flannery is sweet as sugar and stronger than steel."

"She's also as Irish as the Blarney Stone."

George's remark scraped Edward's nerves to no end. Condemnation for his father's arrogance boiled in his gut, until bitter judgment formed on the tip of his tongue.

Vivian caught Edward's gaze then, her eyebrow cocked. It stopped him.

Quietly, he excused himself and headed toward the stairs to apologize for his father. With every step, however, his earlier conversation with Vivian came back to him.

We have very different backgrounds, for one thing— he had said.

You mean she is Irish. I see. You are more like your father than I realized.

Edward closed his eyes for a moment, leaning on the banister. Had she been right? Did he harbor, or even lean toward George's prejudice as well? *May it never be.*

Drawing a fortifying breath, he climbed the rest of the flight, and then the next, until he retrieved his surprise from his chamber. He had been saving it for Christmas, but perhaps—yes, this was better. This way she would not feel embarrassed for not having a Christmas gift for him as well.

Back on the second floor, he waited in the sitting room until Ruby had finished putting Aiden down for the night. He could hear her singing to him through the wall. It was not the concert soprano Jenny Lind was famous for—it was far more beautiful for its faltering pitch, for he could guess that it was a mother's love for her son that caused the tears in her voice.

Ten minutes later, Ruby entered the sitting room, and started when she found Edward already there.

He stood. "I do apologize. I didn't mean to alarm you. Please, come in."

She swiped a finger beneath her dewy eye and sat on the sofa.

"My father—he upset you. I'm very sorry."

She waved away his apology. "I've upset myself. I'm not sure staying here is the best thing for us. For you and your family. The lines are blurring. It's confusing."

"Please don't speak like that. I want you to stay. The arrangement has worked well so far, has it not? Besides, where else would you go?"

Her lips quirked up. "Where would I go? It seems to be the recurring theme of my life. You're right, of course. I must stay where I am permitted."

"Please understand, you and Aiden are no burden to us."

"You and Vivian are very generous. Good neighbors." She smiled warmly, without a hint of guile, but he hated the unstated meaning. *Moral obligation.* "Your father has the right of it. No need to apologize, 'tis the way things are. I don't mind being a maid forever, you know. But I did so want more for Aiden." Tears suspended her words for a moment. "I gave up all the money I'd saved for his education. Did I tell you that already?"

"You did what you had to do."

"Aye. But it will take so long to recover those funds. He's not napping nearly so long anymore. Thank goodness Vivian has been watching him for me so much lately."

"I wish there was something I could do to make things easier." Edward clasped his hands behind his back to keep from touching her arm.

"If you're thinking of replacing the money, I'll not hear of it. No more charity from you."

"Oh no, I wouldn't dream of such a thing. I do wonder if you could grant me a small favor, though."

She looked up. "Oh? What's that?"

"Something followed me home from work yesterday and I was so hoping you could take it off my hands. Turn around."

He couldn't see her face, but her hands flew to her cheeks. "A sewing machine!"

"Do you suppose you could work a little faster with the help of Isaac Singer?"

"Aye, that I could." Ruby laughed as her hand glided along the smooth black arm and wheel of the machine before she bent to inspect the foot treadle. She straightened. "I should tell you I can't accept such a gift, shouldn't I?"

"Nonsense. It's not a personal gift. It's a machine that will beg you to work. Many other women would be insulted by it."

She beamed, her eyes flashing in the light of the gasolier. "This gift sings to me. You outdo yourself, truly. You're putting the Good Samaritan to shame."

Edward's countenance fell. Was that how she saw it? "I wish you wouldn't say that." Yet, in truth, he had said the same thing to himself mere weeks ago. *It was not romance he had in mind with Ruby, but ministry.*

"What is it then?" she asked, eyes wide. "Are you being kind to spite your father?"

"No, I—that's not the right reason to—I wouldn't—no." Heat bloomed beneath his collar.

"I see. Then, it must be—aye. You're showing Aiden what it means to be a man. The proper way to treat a lady."

Words refused to come. He nodded, but surely that was not the sum of it. *Then why did I do it?*

"I thank you." Ruby smiled, and Edward's breath hitched. *That's why.*

Ruby was right. The lines were blurring. Or moving.

Maybe one day no line would separate them at all.

———

Atlanta, Georgia
Friday, November 27, 1863

Ouch! Caitlin sucked a pinprick of blood from her fingertip and looked out the workroom window. Her needle and thimble fell idle as she watched a cardinal alight upon a swaying branch outside. Wind switched against the window, but sweet potato putty filled in the chinks around the panes, keeping it out. Fireballs made from coal, sawdust, sand, clay, and water kept up the heat in the fireplace. Still, Caitlin shuddered.

Yesterday's news of the Confederate defeat around Chattanooga had been tempered by the *Intelligencer* editor assuring its readers the defeat was only partial, Bragg could have done no better, and all will yet be well. But Noah had been in the fight, and all was not well until they knew how he had fared.

Worrying does no good, she told herself, and picked up her needle again. *Somehow, we will get by.*

It was a common refrain. Everywhere she looked, callouses formed on hands and hearts of Southern women who were constantly asked to give more of themselves for the cause. With their protectors and providers away in the war, they fed their households with meager resources, and still answered the call to bring milk and food to the hospitals.

And yet it was not enough. Every week, it seemed, there was a new request in the newspaper. The quartermaster general appealed for socks—at least sixty thousand—to carry the Georgia soldiers through the winter. General Beauregard called for church bells to be made into cannons. The Nitre Bureau wanted household potash to manufacture gunpowder. Doctors begged women to cultivate and harvest poppy flowers for their opium, and the country dared to demand patriotism, as if the women were not proving themselves daily.

Caitlin refused to donate potash to be made into Rebel ammunition. But the most recent call from Quartermaster Jones was so pitiful she could not ignore it.

Thousands of our soldiers are without tents, and worse than that, without blankets . . . Ought not the churches, the parlors and the bed rooms to be stript of every carpet, if necessary, and hurried to the army? I think so, and think, besides, that any true-hearted Southern woman will be ashamed to let such articles remain about her premises when she is aware of the necessity to give them up. I believe there are carpets enough in Georgia to supply the Confederate army with blankets. They cannot be procured by purchase. Can I say for you, ladies of Georgia, "They shall be given"?

Caitlin knew what it was to sleep outside, and would not wish the misery of exposure on anyone. As per the article's instructions, she had requested cotton cloth with which to line the carpets, and it had finally arrived.

Her thimble firmly in place, she pushed the needle up through the heavy carpet and pulled the thread through. Until a shadow dropped over Caitlin's hands.

"Do you have any money?" asked Susan, without preamble, a newspaper sagging from her fingers.

Caitlin spared her only a glance before refocusing on her stitches. "Very little. Why?"

Susan sat at the table then and spread the *Intelligencer* in front of her. "A new shipment of goods arrived from Wilmington, North Carolina, fresh off the blockade runners. Just look at everything that's now in stock at P. G. Bessent's on Whitehall Street!" She spun the paper around so Caitlin could read the list advertising flannel, white silk, ladies linen collars, and ladies shoes—Congress Gaiters, English Kid Gaiters, and Morocco boots.

Caitlin shoved the paper back to Susan. "How can you think of a new dress when your army suffers without blankets?"

"The parlor is perfectly desolate without the carpet, you know."

"Better a desolate parlor than desolate men. Besides, I've not taken your bedroom rug."

"Oh no, only every other carpet in the house." She pouted, twirling a lock of her hair around her finger. "Where'd you find the thread for all these so-called blankets, anyway?"

Caitlin pointed under the table to her own skirt, now guiltless of hoops. She'd harvested thread by unraveling her dress from the hem up. Minnie and Naomi had done the same.

Susan gasped. "How could you? Why would you?"

"Without hoops, the skirt need not be nearly as long. I believe the newspaper calls it 'shortening sail in a storm.'" She actually found it quite liberating to be free of the steel contraptions.

"I hate this war," Susan whispered. "I hate moving. I didn't always live in Chattanooga, you know, but during the last seven years, it was home. Until the Yankees decided it was theirs. Nothing is the same since the abolitionists started this unholy mess."

Caitlin cocked an eyebrow but said nothing.

"Men used to line up to court me, and now they are all getting shot up. I just want to feel good again."

"Men made you feel good?" Warning flashed through Caitlin's spirit.

"The attention from them, yes. I was groomed for it. Turning heads was a game I played, and always won."

Caitlin stuck her needle into the carpet and leaned forward on her elbows. "Do not depend on a man for happiness, Susan. Decide to be content in all circumstances even if there's no man in sight."

"I could do that much better in a new dress."

A sigh escaped Caitlin. "You'll have to get one on your own, somehow, then."

"Is that a challenge?"

"Merely a fact. Your vanity is not my concern."

———

Atlanta, Georgia
Tuesday, December 8, 1863

"Too cold." Ana crossed her arms.

"It is *not* too cold, and we could both use the exercise." Caitlin pointed to the azure sky beyond the window. "The mercury shows 54 degrees Fahrenheit!" *Positively balmy compared to New York this time of year!*

Ana put up her hand and shook her head, eyebrows pinched together. "Do you know where Miss Ke—my mama is?"

Caitlin's lips pressed flat. "I believe she's rearranging her hair in her room."

"I'd like to do that, too."

"Ana." Caitlin knelt down to her level. "You don't have to come with me. But if you stay home, I would like you to either do your reading or knit socks for the soldiers."

Ana scowled. "No, thank you. I don't want to read. I'm tired of those stories. And I don't want to knit either—my fingers are too cold!"

A sigh brushed Caitlin's lips as Naomi emerged from the work room and waited in the hall. "I've given you a choice. Read or knit while I'm gone. I'll play Snakes and Ladders with you when I return."

"You're not my mother!" The girl stomped off—toward Susan, Caitlin had no doubt.

"Let her go." Naomi's voice was thick with tenderness. "It is not naughtiness you see, but hunger."

The words cut Caitlin. Exhaustion overwhelmed her—she was tired of calculating and recalculating how far their stores would last, tired of measuring loaves of rice bread and corn bread with a marked string so everyone would get exactly the same allotment. And she was tired of navigating the uncharted terrain of a girl's heart when a long-lost mother replaced a dearly beloved papa.

"I need to get out of here."

"Would you accept some company? I'd love to join you."

Caitlin smiled. "That would be fine. Don't forget your pass." She patted her own pocket, and Naomi nodded.

After telling Minnie and Susan they were going out for a bit, Caitlin and Naomi donned shawls and straw hats and strolled down the lane to the road. A pleasant if strong breeze swirled about them, teasing their hair and twirling the fringe on their shawls. Their plodding footsteps lifted fine red dust from the road.

Silently, she railed against Susan. She refused to make herself useful, disappeared for hours at a time, sometimes came home so late at night that Caitlin had to get out of bed and unlock the door for her. If she had not promised Noah to keep all refugees, and if Susan had not been Ana's mother, Caitlin would have thrown the woman out on her ear weeks ago.

"I don't trust her." Naomi cast a sidelong glance at Caitlin.

"Who?"

"Susan, of course. Don't tell me you weren't thinking about her. Your irritation is written plainly on your face. Right there." She pointed to the wrinkle between her eyebrows. "And there." She tapped her clenched jaw. "I worry about her, you know."

Caitlin snorted. "I worry about the rest of us."

Naomi smiled as they turned right on Fair Street. "It's a different type of worry. That girl is so cunning. I don't know what she's up to, and I bet she doesn't quite know either. I would easily believe that great pain has caused her to go to great lengths to get what she wants. But just what is it she wants?"

"Can it be Ana? She does not seem overly fond of the girl."

"No, she doesn't. I pity her. If she is anything like me, she's headed on a path that will only lead to regret. And she'll have only more pain to show for it, besides."

"Like you?"

"We all have secrets, dear." She eyed the scar on Caitlin's jaw. "Better that they stay that way. Wouldn't you agree?"

Silence her only response, Caitlin looked down at her own shadow, jutting ahead of her. She felt like a shadow herself—two-dimensional, colorless, transient. A mere silhouette of who she really was.

"We're headed to Atlanta Graveyard, by the way. It's the only peaceful place I've found in this crowded, clamoring city. I hope that's all right."

Naomi nodded. "Peaceful is exactly what we need."

They lapsed into comfortable quiet as they continued east. Two blocks north, the Georgia Railroad line ran almost parallel to their path out of the city. The chugging train barely filtered into Caitlin's thoughts. The near-constant noise of the Turntable of the South had simply become part of the atmosphere, along with the dust and soot and flurry of a city running full speed ahead.

Finally, on the outskirts of the city, they reached the Atlanta Graveyard on a ridge overlooking the city. Even in December, the rural cemetery was an oasis after the dusty ascent from town. Inside the post-and-board fence, oak trees clawed the sky with bare branches, while Eastern red cedars perfumed the air with spicy scent. Sparrows and finches rustled in the stiff, brown pasture grasses as they hunted for seeds, while a squirrel scampered across the chert pathway.

A shadow circled the ground, fleeting evidence of a hawk gliding overhead. The fresh air scrubbed Caitlin's lungs as she drank it in. *Funny,* she mused, *that being in a graveyard should breathe life into my spirit.*

"These are the lucky ones, already buried," Naomi said. "If anyone would have told them what has happened to the South, they would've called the prophet a madman."

"Indeed," Caitlin murmured, and they walked further along the path. Until, "Prudy?"

Prudence Periwinkle knelt on the ground before a pair of tombstones, and Caitlin quickly joined her. After briefly introducing Naomi and Prudy, Caitlin turned her attention to the grave. A tangle of spent periwinkle vine wrapped around the headstone in front of her. Caitlin traced the engraving of a lily above the words, the marble cold beneath her fingertip. "Your niece? The one Dr. Periwinkle said I remind him of?"

"The same." She smiled, and wrinkles seamed her face. She had aged so much since taking care of Caitlin eighteen months ago. "Mary Beth was beloved by all, especially her doting father—Lil Bit."

"And today was her birthday."

"And not just that." Naomi knelt and placed her hand on a second tombstone bearing a Periwinkle name.

"Matilda—we called her Tillie—gave her life bringing Mary Beth into this world." Prudy stared at her hands in her lap. "Lil Bit was so broken up about it. I helped him raise Mary Beth and sure as I'm breathing, she was like a daughter to me." Her voice thickened as she spoke. "Lil Bit set such a store by Mary Beth. Never could allow her to be courted by any beaus. I do believe he wanted her to be a spinster, like me, rather than risk her getting in the family way and dying in childbirth like her sweet young mama. But—" Prudence sat back and pressed the heels of her hands to her eyelids. "She did neither."

Caitlin grasped Prudy's blue-veined hand and helped her to her feet as Naomi stood beside them. "What happened? If you don't mind my asking?"

"Smallpox. And her father the doctor couldn't save her. He buried his daughter in this lovely place at the top of the hill soon after this cemetery was established, and he brought Tillie up from the crowded church graveyard to join her. He thought they'd both prefer it up here, together. But has he come back since? No. Too painful, I reckon. And now, her brother will add to their company, if God will only bless my journey."

Caitlin and Naomi exchanged a glance. "Pardon me?" Caitlin probed.

"Her brother, Stuart. Never married, lived with Lil Bit until he signed up for the war. He was killed at Gettysburg."

"But how can you bring his body home? He is buried in foreign soil, is he not?" Naomi's eyes grew large.

"Didn't you hear? Abe Lincoln has consented to an exchange, dead for dead. We are now allowed to retrieve the remains of our loved ones without taking the oath of allegiance to the United States. Lil Bit can't possibly leave the patients here, but I have just secured someone to manage the boardinghouse in my absence. I mean to bring Stuart home, so help me God."

"You're going? To Gettysburg?" Caitlin's words burst out of her, a dangerous reflection of her galloping heart. Her brother's face surged in her mind. If she was going to find him, she could only do it north of the Mason-Dixon line. Quickly, she recovered herself. "It's nearly seven hundred miles!"

"And I am but an old woman, I know."

"Have you traveled much before?"

She shook her head.

"Well then, have you an escort?"

Prudence answered with an amused look. Every able man who was worth his salt was in the army. Every other man was a ruffian, a patient or convalescent, a speculator, or desperately needed on the home front.

The silver-haired woman sought Caitlin's eyes. "You wouldn't— would you have any interest in—escorting me yourself?"

Caitlin's breath seized in her chest while Naomi's hand flew to her heart.

"I know I'm asking much of you," Prudy continued. "But I'd be lying if I said I wasn't afraid to travel north. You—you don't sound like a Southerner, dear. Perhaps you could speak for me, if we are ever in an area that seems hateful against Confederates like myself."

Caitlin's mind reeled. Leave the Confederacy? Could she dare

160

believe this was the escape route from the South, before the House of Dixie collapsed? Ana's face loomed in her mind, pulling her back from the precipice on which she teetered. "I have Analiese to think of."

Naomi found her voice. "Go. I will take charge of the girl myself until your return. You are not abandoning your post; you are doing a service for Prudence. And you can do a service for me, as well." Her eyes shone. "Look for news of my son while you're there. Start at the Lutheran Seminary, ask for Dr. Samuel Schmucker."

"Did he fight there, too?"

"I'm not sure. We lost track of each other." She looked away. "But I'm almost sure he was there, and if he was, he would have gone to Dr. Schmucker, his former professor. I wrote him a letter in care of the reverend right after news of the battle reached me in Tennessee, but since I had to leave my home, he could not have known where to reach me, even if he wanted to."

"Why not come with us?" Caitlin asked.

Naomi shook her head. "Even if Silas was there for the battle, he isn't any longer. Just find Dr. Schmucker. He might know something about him. Even if all he can tell you is that my letter reached the seminary, and Silas was able to read it, I'll be content. I'll stay here and manage your household until you return. Will you do this?"

Two pairs of eyes entreated Caitlin then, eyes that looked haunted and hopeful at the same time. "I'll go," she heard herself say. Butterflies fluttered in her middle.

"Thank you," Prudence whispered, and kissed her on the cheek.

The trio stepped back on the main path, rocks crunching beneath their footsteps. Rather than heading back to the main gate, they walked the length of the cemetery before leaving, from grey, weather-worn tombstones to fresh rectangles of red dirt. Many Johnny Rebs who died in Atlanta's hospitals found their final rest here.

"You know, dear, we may not find Stuart's remains right away when we arrive." Prudy looped her leathery hand through Caitlin's elbow as they exited through the east gate and headed south. "I hear that Confederate graves were not marked well. Some were not marked at all, but were simply buried en masse."

When they neared the southeast corner of the cemetery, Naomi nodded to a long mound of dirt tucked into a wooded area. "Like that?"

It was the grave of the seven Andrews raiders who had been hanged and buried in the shallow trench beside the hastily erected gallows on June 19, 1862, shortly before Caitlin woke up in Atlanta.

"Those were Union spies and deserved no better," Prudence said.

Caitlin shuddered. *How long can I escape a similar fate?*

A whoosh of air turned Caitlin's head in time to see the hawk swoop down to the earth then soar again, this time with a squealing field mouse in its talons.

"WE HAVE HUNG Asafetida-bags around the children's necks as haply it may do some good. My feelings were inexpressibly touched by what our little boy Arthur said to his Mother as she put him to bed tonight: knowing that Johnnie Crankshaw had died and hearing us talk about our children taking it, he asked, 'Mama, are you going to bury us where you did little Alice?' Fat, rosy, full of frolic, he seemed to be taking it for granted that he was soon to die and be buried and it didn't seem to terrify him much. I could not sleep much tonight . . . We see from the Telegraph that James and Mollie have lost their little daughter Mamie that they thot so much of, as she was their only girl."

—SAM RICHARDS, Atlanta bookseller

Act Three

SCOURGE AND SUSPICION

Chapter Thirteen

Atlanta, Georgia
Thursday, December 10, 1863

A train whistled and clattered on the Macon & Western Railroad a few blocks from where Caitlin and Prudence walked, and for the first time, it sounded like hope. Perhaps, if Caitlin dared, freedom. Very soon, she and Prudy would be on a train themselves, hurtling north.

If I can only secure a passport. Worry etched her brow as their heels clicked down Whitehall's sidewalks. Besides the storefronts boasting cigars, glassware, and Negro sales, the street was honeycombed with government offices. The Medical Director of Hospitals, Engineers Department, the Georgia Reserves, the Quartermaster Department, the Transportation Department, and the Commissary Department—including the State Salt Agent—as well as Governor Joseph Brown himself all set up shop above drug stores, hardware stores, grocery stores, and hotels.

When they finally entered the provost marshal's office on Wadley Street, north of the train tracks, Caitlin's nose wrinkled. Tobacco juice stained the wall above the spittoon in the corner, and the distinct odor of corn liquor pervaded the small space. *Ironic,* Caitlin mused, *seeing that the sale of alcohol to soldiers is prohibited.* But she quickly masked her distaste for the man lest her expression jeopardize their errand.

"George," Prudence said without ceremony. "I thought you were transferred to the conscript department."

George Washington Lee coughed into his handkerchief. "True enough."

"Then where is the provost marshal?"

"Mr. Oliver Jones will be back shortly. I was just collecting some paperwork I left behind when I moved offices. Is there something I can help you with?"

"We need two passports." Caitlin let Prudy carry the conversation. "We're going to Gettysburg to fetch Stuart. Haven't got all day for them either, so chop chop, if you please."

He wiped his mouth again before tucking the yellowed square back in his pocket. "What's wrong with Stu?"

"He's dead, that's what." Prudy's eyes hardened. "And I aim to bring his remains home before winter settles in any further. Miss McKae is going to help me."

Lee turned his beady eyes on Caitlin. "Interesting. And why, pray, would you do that, Miss McKae?"

"Miss Periwinkle has shown me great hospitality and I count it an honor to escort her north to recover her nephew's body. She should not have to make the journey herself."

A smile tilted his mustache. "I never tire of hearing you speak. Such a distinctive accent, you know."

Warmth bloomed in Caitlin's chest.

"Really, it's so very kind of you to want to help. Are you sure there is no other reason you might want to cross the lines?"

She schooled her features to reveal nothing.

"Trying to reconnect with family? Friends? Perhaps you'd be content just to get a message to someone up there. Someone who happens to favor the color blue? Hmmm?"

"Oh stop that, George. We've been through all of this nonsense before. Write us the passports before I die of natural causes standing here."

Lee reached into a brown paper pouch and stuffed a wad of tobacco into his cheek before rifling through the newspapers, forms, and envelopes on his desk. Prudence squeezed Caitlin's hand in an apparent attempt at reassurance, but Caitlin's reckless heart would not slow down.

"Date of departure?" Lee asked Prudence.

"Tomorrow."

"Destination?"

"I told you. Gettysburg, Pennsylvania."

While Lee scratched his marks onto the passport, Caitlin's gaze scrambled over his desk.

"Length of stay?"

"Until I find the body and a way to bring it home."

Lee looked up. "A little more specific please."

The door burst open and a cold wind swirled Caitlin's skirt around her legs. All heads turned and found a man dragging a young fellow in by the ear. "Lee. Glad you're still here. This boy has no pass."

Lee stood and circled the desk to face the pitiful creature. "How old are you, boy?"

"N-n-nineteen."

"Old enough to know the law, I reckon. Else, why hide from it if not already convicted by your own guilt? You a ly-out? That why you don't have a pass?"

Lee's back was to Caitlin as he interrogated the alleged deserter. Heart pumping madly, she seized an unused envelope from the desk and scribbled the only address she could think to try—their old apartment in Manhattan. Perhaps it would be forwarded to Jack. Perhaps he was there even now. But what to put inside? No time to write a word! Every thud of her heart seemed to cry out, *No time! No time!*

"Do you know what the penalty is for desertion, boy?"

The questioning sounded far away. With trembling fingers, she tore off as much of the corner of the newspaper as she dared and tucked it into the envelope.

But how to seal it? *No time! No time! No time!*

Hastily, she rolled up the envelope and tucked it inside her left glove just as the boy surrendered to his fate.

"Well well well, this is my lucky day."

Caitlin turned toward the officer and stared into his gleaming eyes. "Pardon me?"

Lee snickered. "Jones, would you believe that Caitlin McKae has requested a passport to travel north?"

Jones laughed. "Just the type of thing I've been waiting for."

"What is the meaning of this?" Prudence's voice trembled just slightly, in spite of her erect posture.

"Take him away, then come on back. This one's for you."

"What?" Fear squeezed the word from Caitlin's throat. "If you are thinking of arresting me, I demand to know the charges!"

"In a word, disloyalty."

"What in God's name have I ever done that ever amounted to disloyalty?" She sagged, and Prudy's arm belted her waist.

"You've kept your head down quite nicely, Miss McKae. A little too far, however. It isn't what you've done so much as it is what you haven't done. Since before he was named provost marshal, Oliver Jones has been following you."

Prudence gasped, while anger fired in Caitlin's veins. "How dare you?"

"You are not a member of the Atlanta Hospital Visiting Committee."

Prudence huffed. "Young, unmarried women do not go to the hospitals; it isn't ladylike!"

"And you are not a member of the Ladies Aid Society."

"I have my own aid society of refugees living under my roof."

"It was reported that on Sunday, September 13, you stormed out of the Central Presbyterian Church right after the pastor prayed for General Bragg."

Caitlin sealed her lips. It wasn't that the pastor had prayed for him, but that he had placed him with the Holy Trinity.

"It was further reported that when said pastor asked his congregation to come to an afternoon prayer service for the Confederacy, you did not attend."

"Did everyone else?"

"No. Neither did Cyrena Stone or Emily Farnsworth, both known Union sympathizers as well."

"A rather flimsy prosecution."

"On October 29, Jefferson Davis came to town. You did not go to see him. The president of our Confederacy visits this city, and you could not trouble yourself to be there for the glorious event? Even if I could overlook your accent and unknown history, the rest of the evidence combines for quite a case against you." Lee scribbled something on Prudy's passport and handed it to her. "I've signed for Jones, he won't mind, especially since I'm delivering Miss McKae into his hands."

Jones appeared in the door again, the sunlight bouncing from his handcuffs into Caitlin's eyes. "I'm escorting you home, where you will stay." He stepped toward her. "I'm taking your pass until further notice. If you're caught walking around Atlanta without a pass, you'll be arrested."

"Wait!" She held up a shaking hand. "Allow me to bid Miss Periwinkle goodbye. In private."

"Out of the question."

Caitlin bristled. She turned to Prudence. "Godspeed. It will be cold in the north this time of year. You must take my gloves." She pulled her gloves off her hands by the fingertips.

"No child, you keep them."

"You heard the man, I won't be going anywhere anyway. I insist." Caitlin pressed them into Prudy's grasp. "I pray you find what you're looking for."

The envelope hiding in the glove whispered under Prudy's thumb, and her eyes grew round. So did her mouth. Caitlin shot her a look of warning.

Prudy frowned as she pulled the gloves onto her hands. "I hope I know what to do when I do."

Caitlin smoothed a smile from her jangling spirit. "Just deliver the package on home. You'll be fine." She hugged Prudence then, whispered "Trust me" in her ear, and felt herself pulled away by large hands.

"Enough. It's time. And I'll not be losing you on your way home, either." Jones yanked Caitlin's wrists behind her and clicked the cold metal into place. To Caitlin, it was the sound of a cage door slamming shut. Memories, long-shackled, broke loose again, battering her heart. Though she prayed her face did not betray her, inside, Caitlin became unhinged.

———

It was the handcuffs, Caitlin decided later, long after the rest of the household had gone to bed. She sat on the bedroom floor in front of the fire, knees pulled up under her chin, rocking back and forth with her hands clasped around her ankles. *The handcuffs.*

It was not merely that her plan to leave had been thwarted and her local pass confiscated, or the humiliation of being escorted home in handcuffs. Jones only used them, she knew, to intimidate her and mark her to onlookers as a suspicious character not to be trusted. But it wasn't his face that loomed before her now. It was her mother's. Yes, this was a guilt she could chew on.

The scar on her jaw tingled, and she buried it into her shoulder, still rocking gently before the popping fire. When she closed her eyes her mind reeled back to April 19, 1861. Memories rained down upon her, slowly at first, then in a downpour.

Get out! I don't want to see you here again! You've done enough!

The slam of the door as Caitlin left, steaming.

Why did you send her away? Bernard's growl.

I had to. You've got no business with her. I'll do my duty to you, but you leave her out of it.

A murmur. A hard slap. *Get!*

Caitlin's blood rushing, her heart pounding right along with the drumbeats rallying the Seventh Regiment to fight. *Women can fight, too.* Cheers reached a fever pitch outside—thousands must have turned out to send the state's first soldiers to the war. The fife and drum, the cheering throng whipped her small swell of courage into a foaming tide. She slammed back through the door, and straight into Bernard's straining uniform, his copper police badge embossing her chest as he caught her to him.

"It's about time," he had whispered, the scent of hard liquor reeking from his rotten mouth.

Caitlin writhed against his hold, lunged backward until his drunken grip on her faltered. Her braid pulled loose from her pins and uncoiled, falling heavily onto her shoulder.

Another step back, and another, until they were out of the apartment and at the top of the stairs in the dimly lit hall. He threw his weight against her, and she smashed into the sconce behind her. When he pressed his face toward hers, she jerked her head away, the jagged glass of the broken hurricane slicing the edge of her jaw.

Lord, help! She prayed, but did not cry out. She would not give her mother another reason to come within arm's reach of this man.

With barely time for a single thought, she broke off the shard of glass that had slit her and brandished it against Bernard.

"Are you assaulting an officer of the law?" A sloppy grin smeared his face as he pulled out his handcuffs. "You will submit to the proper authorities, one way or another. Just like your mother."

Scales peeled from Caitlin's eyes. The marks on her mother's wrists. The handcuffs. They were a match. Visions of her mother suffering untold abuse by this monster ricocheted in her spirit. *What has she suffered while I've been blind to it all?*

Huzzahs and *Hoorays* undulated through the open windows.

172

Strength Caitlin didn't know she possessed flooded her being as she slammed her knee into his groin and shoved him from her.

Bernard stumbled, leaned on the wall for support, then sought her with his bloodshot eyes. Dark, leathery laughter flapped erratically from his throat. "Yeah, your mother used to fight back, too." He shook his head. "Enough. It's time."

Fear seeped from Caitlin's pores, and the glass in her grip grew slick with it.

Dingy light gleamed on the handcuffs as he reached for her again. With the speed of lightning, she slashed his neck with the glass. He cursed, and in the break of his stride, she threw her shoulder against him.

Bernard's hand lashed out, grabbed the end of her braid, but she yanked it from his grip. With her green velvet ribbon clenched in his fist, he staggered backward, until the floor betrayed his step. He crashed down the stairs just as the crowd outside sent up a cheer for the band's performance. Caitlin gaped after him, the throng's *Huzzah!* buzzing in her veins. She only meant to keep him away from her. She had not intended to truly harm him. *Had she?*

At the bottom of the stairs, he lay still, ripping new horror open inside her. *Have I killed him?*

She flew down the steps, her unraveling braid hanging like a rope against her neck. *Or a noose.*

Caitlin knelt by Bernard's body. Booze-flavored breath puffed from his nose. He was still alive, just unconscious. Inebriated. She inspected his neck where she had managed to mark him. It was only a scratch. He may not even need sutures. Relief cooled her flaming pulse, but did not slow its pell-mell rhythm. He would remember this.

Between the jaunty strains of martial music clinging to the April breeze, Caitlin thought she heard muffled voices behind apartment doors. She turned, scanning the hallway for signs of movement. If anyone saw her, a girl with a police officer's blood on her hands, what would they think?

Caitlin fled the building and washed up using a pump a few blocks

173

away before returning an hour later to check on her mother. Her skin tingled with warning as soon as she rounded the corner. A handful of people who had not seen off the Seventh now craned their necks near the front door of the building.

"You can't go in there," one of them said when she tried to pass through. "Coppers are investigating the crime scene."

Caitlin swallowed. "Crime scene?"

The woman nodded. "Someone found a police officer dead on the floor. They're questioning the tenants. Say, don't you live in this building?"

Firecrackers detonated in Caitlin's mind, and she could barely hear herself think. "What? Dead? But he was—" *Alive when I left him.* She bit her tongue. How could he be dead? He was merely sodden with drink, passed out on the floor from a bump to his head! Had there been internal bleeding? Surely it was not the cut on his throat . . .

Heads turned. "What do you know about it? He was what?"

"He was an officer of the law." Caitlin's heartbeat pushed against her corset.

The woman nodded. "That he was. You can bet the police will find the one what did it, though. They look out for their own." She clucked her tongue. "Murdering a copper. Shameful. And stupid."

Caitlin closed her eyes as the world rocked beneath her feet.

"You're bleeding." Caitlin's eyes popped open to see the woman pointing to her jaw.

She pressed a handkerchief to her skin. "Just an accident," Caitlin said, and heard her mother's voice.

"Cut yourself shaving?" The woman laughed, turning back and craning her neck again. "I bet the murderer would just love to disappear right now. If he has any sense at all, he's slipped into that crowd marching the soldiers down to the Jersey City ferry. We'll never see him again, I wager."

Never. Caitlin would follow her mother's advice. She would leave, and never come back, now that she knew Vivian was safe from Bernard. She would depend on no man.

Instead, she would become one. She would enlist, find Jack, and in just a few days she'd be on the ferry crossing the Hudson, and then the train chugging down to Washington. She'd send her pay home to support her mother. It was a desperate escape plan, birthed from a desperate situation.

And now, in Atlanta, she had managed to land herself in another one. Only this time, she could not see how to spring the trap.

Outside Dalton, Georgia
Wednesday, December 15, 1863

"You in or out, Herr Becker?" Ross waved his hand of cards at Noah from his perch on the overturned barrel.

"Out." Noah strolled past the soldiers palming greasy cards, and headed toward the fiddler playing "When Johnny Comes Marching Home" into the crackling campfire. Two letters had arrived by the mail wagon for him today, and waiting until after evening roll call to read them had been torturous.

Settling onto an upside-down crate, Noah opened his hands to the fire for a moment, then fished the letters out of his pocket. When he unfolded the paper, his breath caught in his throat. Ana had improved upon her usual drawing of a little girl and man in front of a house. This time, a woman stood with them. They were holding hands. Caitlin and Analiese got along famously, but he hadn't imagined his daughter would be drawing her into the picture already. He tilted the paper toward the fire to better see the lines Ana had drawn. *Good. Everyone is smiling.* He spread his broad hand over the paper and sent up a silent prayer for Ana before turning it over and reading Caitlin's letter.

Dear Mr. Becker,

We hope you are well and look forward to hearing from you. We are well but surprised that our houseguest Susan Kent tells us she is Ana's mother.

175

No. Noah squinted at the paper, dismay carving his brow. *No. No.* He had cut ties with her cleanly and simply. Right after their civil ceremony, they had moved to Decatur, Georgia, where Noah hoped his immigrant status would not prevent clients from coming to him, as it had in Richmond. Near the end of Susan's pregnancy, he purchased a house in Atlanta for his growing family. A house Susan had visited once, but would never move into. *Until now. But why?* He read on, every line a stake being pounded into his spirit.

Is this true? Her story is convincing but I need to hear the truth from you. Ana tries to please her, but all is in vain. Indeed, it seems none of us can please her. None of us can say what she wants. But to be a mother does not seem to be her heart's desire.

No, it never was. Crumbling logs sprayed sparks into the sky while fire kindled in Noah's belly. Susan never wanted Analiese, even for a moment. She had even left the naming of the baby completely up to Noah, saying she didn't care either way since she would never be part of her life. Noah had had to secure a wet nurse and mammy for her when she was days old, and caring for an infant with a broken collarbone was no small task. As soon as Susan had recovered from the birth, she signed the papers ending their marriage, and fled to Chattanooga to invent a new life for herself. Soon after, Noah and Ana moved to Atlanta.

The campfire flames lapped its logs, and Noah's spirit felt singed. Susan had never loved him. He'd been a fool to be charmed by her. He should have suspected something when her father insisted on such a short courtship and engagement. It had been mere weeks! Before the ink had dried on their wedding certificate, however, she made her revulsion for him crystal clear.

Susan. Her name had curled off his lips like smoke as he reached for her. Elusive. Hypnotic. Toxic.

Stay away from me, you foreigner! She had hissed. He was only window dressing. Susan could not wait to get out of the marriage.

If it was desperation that drove her to me once, she must be desperate to come again. But for what? Perhaps only for a place to stay. If she was still living in Chattanooga up until the battles took place there, she was a refugee, and that was reason enough to look for another roof with which to cover her blonde head. *Why it had to be mine, though, I have no idea.*

At least Caitlin was still there.

He scanned the rest of her letter until he landed on Ana's handwriting.

Dear Papa,

Miss Kent says she is my mama. Why didn't you tell me? I am trying to be very very good so she will love me like you do.

Noah fought the urge to crumble the letter and throw it into the fire. Susan love Ana like Noah did? Impossible. If it weren't for Noah, Ana would have been a ward of the state from day one! But how to explain this to a seven-year-old girl? He seethed.

Do you like my picture? It's you and me and Mama. Some day we will all be together and I will have a real family.

Sorrow ached in his throat. A real family? She was unhappy with just a papa? He shook his head. *Of course a girl wants a mother.* But surely Susan was not fit for the job, her biological contribution notwithstanding. He rolled his neck and stifled a groan as he whipped out the second letter. Any hope he had for better news was soon snuffed out as he skimmed the text.

Dear Mr. Becker,

We thank God we do not see your name in the casualty lists, but look for word from yourself to confirm it.

Prudence Periwinkle is going north to Gettysburg to retrieve the remains of her nephew. She has asked me to accompany her, and I have agreed. You know how much Prudy did for me when I first came to Atlanta. She needs me.

And Ana does not, or so she says. She has Susan. I am "not her mother." I wonder if you could write to your daughter and remind her that I do have some authority in your household while you're gone. Or do you, too, prefer that I defer to your ex-wife in all things? If so, please release me from my obligation. I'd hate to accept pay for unnecessary employment.

Noah could almost see the resentment flickering in Caitlin's brown eyes as he read her words. But as he could imagine the havoc Susan was wreaking on the household, he could not blame her. He only wished he could convince her to stay.

Don't worry about Ana while I'm gone. In addition to Susan, Naomi and Minnie will still be here to manage her.

Ana didn't have time to write you today, but I've enclosed her latest drawing.

Noah's heart plunged when he turned the page over. There was his house. There was Ana. There was Susan. But Noah was nowhere in sight.

———————

New York City
Saturday, December 19, 1863

Edward could taste Christmas in the wind that sighed through the blue spruce, pine, and hemlock trees towering above their sleigh. Freshly fallen snow lay like a blanket of diamonds between the curving pathways of Central Park. With Ruby on the bench beside him, and Biggs up front driving the horses, winter was all beauty and no bite. Sleigh bells tinkled lightly over the snow, while the horses' breath snagged in the air like clouds of glitter.

Ruby arched her neck toward elm and empress branches dripping with icy jewels. "I've never seen anything so beautiful!"

Neither have I. Edward wondered if Ruby had any idea why he'd arranged for their Aiden-free outing. Normally, he welcomed the curly-haired tot. Today, however, he wanted Ruby's full attention. He had been praying about this every day since Thanksgiving, but the idea had planted itself in his heart even before then. He could no longer deny what had been growing within him.

"Have you ever been ice skating before?"

Ruby laughed. "Of course not."

"Well, that's about to change."

Her eyes grew wide. As they rounded another bend, the lake came into view, swirling with color as skaters glided over the ice.

"But I don't have any skates!"

"You do now." Edward pulled out a box and let her open it. She gasped, and satisfaction uncurled inside him. God willing, this was only the start of what he could give Ruby, and the very least of it, at that.

Moments later, Biggs dropped them off and promised to be back in an hour to pick them up. Edward and Ruby exchanged their shoes for skates, and ventured out onto the ice.

Ruby wobbled, and Edward pulled her hand into the crook of his elbow. "Lean on me," he said. She started to pull away, but a small child whisked past her at full speed, providentially sending her back to his arm. "I don't bite." He smiled. "Just walk for now."

Her steps were wooden as she clutched his blue wool greatcoat.

"Why don't you try like this. Step, and slide. Step, slide. Step, slide."

She bent over to watch her feet, but her skirt obscured her vision.

"Don't overthink it, now. Keep your chin up and just walk with me. Look straight ahead, or look at me. I can lead you."

"Like a shepherd leads his sheep, aye?"

"No." Edward's pulse double-timed. "Not like a shepherd. Not anymore."

Ruby met his dark, shining eyes and saw in them something she hadn't seen before. His smile was slow and gentle. When he placed his hand over hers, she did not want to pull away.

"Just walk with me. Let's see where it takes us, shall we?"

Ruby's heart stirred, cautiously wiggling against the walls of its cocoon.

"Look over there." Edward nodded to a boy pushing an earmuffed girl from behind. Her skates didn't steer, but etched their protest into

179

the ice. "I promise not to push you. Now. Do you see that?"

Edward cocked his head another direction. His scarf flying, a young man in a Russian *shapka* and greatcoat skated backwards, grasping the hands of a young lady who awkwardly tried to keep up with him, despite her long skirts and full-length cloak.

"I promise not to pull you. It doesn't work very well and it's selfish. I just want to walk beside you, Ruby. Will you walk with me?"

Ruby hesitated.

"By the way, you're already doing it." He squeezed her hand. "No, don't look down. You're doing fine. Keep looking up."

Her heart fluttered against her corset. "I can't tell if you're talking about ice skating or life itself! I'm a simple girl. Speak plain or I may miss it completely."

"Fair enough. But I believe I'll stand still for this, if you don't mind." His smile wobbled, and he spun around to hold her mittened hands in his. In the edges of her vision, boys and girls, men and women skated in orbit around them. Some had the grace of natural athletes. Some sprawled onto the ice, which was what Ruby felt like doing as her ankles turned to jelly.

"You're right," Edward began. "I'm not just talking about ice skating. I'm talking about us. I—I don't want to just be your Bible study teacher anymore. Or the person whose house you happen live in." A lump bobbed in his throat while Ruby waited, pulse pounding in her ears.

"Who do you want to be?" She could barely breathe.

"I realize you're still in mourning, but I feel it's only fair that I make known my intentions. I promise you, they are honorable."

"What are you saying, exactly?"

"I'm saying—" His sigh froze in the air between them. He looked stripped. "I'm asking if you'll walk with me. I won't push you or pull you. Lean on me. Let's see where God leads us, together. I am hopeful it may one day lead to our union. One day."

Ruby swayed, and Edward circled his arm around her waist from the side. Her knees gave way and she braced herself for the cold, inglorious impact of her rear end to the ice. Instead, Edward caught her beneath her arms from behind and swooped her back up to stand. *Humiliating!*

But Edward beamed. "Does this mean I swept you off your feet?"

She laughed with him and shook her head. Edward Goodrich was like no other man she'd ever met before. So kind, genuine, godly. His sincerity captured her.

But her past crawled up behind her, stabbing her hope. The darkness. The odors of poverty and lust. Rough hands all over her bare skin. Sweaty hulk crushing the life out of her. She was done with all of that. But if she were joined to Edward, would her past somehow poison him, too?

"I'm not good enough for the likes of you." Her eyes and throat burned.

"Don't say that, Ruby, not ever again."

"You deserve a woman who can give you her whole heart. Not just the remnant shreds."

His eyes glazed. "I know you've had a tough life, one that I fail to fathom. But I also know God can heal your hurt and someday, your heart will be whole again."

Ruby searched for condemnation in his face, but did not find it. *If he knew it all, he would condemn me indeed.* "I'm not proud of who I was before I met you. The things I've done—"

"I'm not your confessor. That's between you and God and none of my business, unless you decide to tell me. We are all sinners saved by grace. We are all adopted into the family of God when not one of us deserved it."

She closed her eyes, let the wind caress her face. She had thought she was done with men completely. But perhaps . . .

"We are fellow sojourners through this life. You and me. And Aiden too."

Aiden. The boy could not ask for a better father than Edward Goodrich. How better to mold the lad than for him to have a proper family, with a proper man at the head of it?

"Well?" Edward grew serious again. "What do you say?"

A smile warmed Ruby's face. Perhaps this was the answer to prayers she had not even dared to utter. *'Tis Grace that brought me safe thus far and Grace will lead me home.* Amazing Grace indeed.

She looped her hand through his arm. "Can we take it slow?" *Very slow.*

Edward nodded, eyes shining. "I'm ready when you are."

And Ruby O'Flannery took a step.

Chapter Fourteen

Outside Dalton, Georgia
Wednesday, December 23, 1863

Stomping his tingling feet, Noah turned his gaze south—toward Atlanta—as he sat on a tree stump eating salt pork and beans. The sustenance he craved, however, was word from home.

Winter raked its fingers through camp, stirring the campfires, scraping Noah's face, and cooling the potato coffee swirling in his tin cup. Every fiber of his being yearned to return to Ana. Noah had joined the army to protect her, but the army wasn't protecting anybody. And now Susan was with Ana, probably manipulating her the way she'd manipulated him.

"Acktung, Herr Becker!" Ross jogged up to Noah, a merciful distraction. "Would you biddie be so kind? Never learned my letters, myself, but it looks like the missus found someone to pen a letter to me jes' the same. Biddie."

"Of course." Noah nestled his cup into a bed of pine needles.

"Donkey."

"*Bitte*." Noah chuckled under his breath at the man's crude German pronunciation. He began to read. "Dear husband, Well, me and kids are in a fine kettle of fish. The money you was paid to fight goes only so far now that flour is two hundred dollars a barrel, and a cord of wood is forty dollars. That rich man who hired you to do his fightin' hasn't come by to check on us at all, when he told you he would make sure we was fine. Can't you get off on furlough to come chop wood to see us through the winter? Ain't nobody else going to do it for me, and I know it don't seem right to say it in a letter, but I'm in the family way again and too weak to handle the axe myself."

"Did she just say–"

Noah nodded, smiling. "Congratulations. How many will it make?"

Ross rubbed his hand over his beard. "Kitty and I got five young 'uns already. Jeb's the oldest at fourteen, and the youngest is two. I s'pose it's about time for another, then, isn't it? Go on now, keep reading."

"Jeb says he'll do it but with only one good eye you know he'll cut his own foot off before he'd strike the wood. Write soon, and deliver it yourself for Christmas. As long as you ain't fightin' over winter, you may as well be put to good use at home. Your loving wife, Kitty."

Ross's eyelids hooded whatever he was feeling as he took the letter back from Noah. "You know something? I got a mighty hankering to go to meeting tonight. Care to join me?" Ross nodded to the log chapel the men had constructed. Almost every night a chaplain or pastor from a surrounding town had preached or led prayer services for the soldiers. It had become so crowded that the men eventually took off the side walls of the chapel to accommodate everyone who wanted to attend.

"Hain't you been to one yet?" Ross prodded. "It would do you a heap o' good, Herr Becker, to be in the presence of God."

Noah sighed, the crisp air burning his throat as much as the wood smoke. "To tell you the truth, I'm not sure I'm good enough company for the Almighty right now."

"Well if that ain't just the dumbest thing I ever heard." He laughed. "He's on your side, you know."

Noah eyed him warily. "Do you mean he's on the side of the Confederacy?"

Ross waved the smoke out of his face. "I'm not talking about war—unless you want to talk about the battle for your spirit. What I mean is God is rooting for the sinner to be saved by grace. And He's cheering for the saints to persevere through trials. So if you don't know God, He wants to meet you. If you do know Him, He sure would like to spend time with you. See? Either way, He's on your side, just like I said. Now let's go. We'll bring our families with us in prayer."

Late that night, with Ross snoring on the other side of their crude two-person cabin, Noah could not sleep. His pine needle mattress rustled as he rolled onto his side and stared at the embers glowing in the fireplace.

The preacher had chosen Matthew 11:28–30 as his text for the message. *Come unto me, all ye that labour and are heavy laden, and I will give you rest. Take my yoke upon you, and learn of me . . . For my yoke is easy, and my burden is light.*

Noah Becker was heavy laden, indeed. *What's happening at home? Since we have not been able to keep the Yankees out, even with the help of the mountains, how can we hope to keep them out of the rest of Georgia?* And there wasn't a thing he could do about any of it right now.

Lord, he prayed. *I want that rest You offer. My soul is so weary. Help me find rest in You.* There was much more to pray about, he knew. But for now, he let the words of the hymn they sang tonight wash over him as he drifted off to sleep.

> *Fear not, I am with thee, oh! be not dismayed,*
> *I–I am thy God, and will still give thee aid . . .*

Atlanta, Georgia
Thursday, December 24, 1863

Susan Kent leaned against a lamppost on the corner of Marietta and Peachtree Streets, the cold reaching its fingers through her thin shawl and wrapping deliciously around her spine. It felt so good to feel something—anything—aside from the usual hunger.

The day before Christmas, downtown Atlanta whirled with State and Confederate government officials, soldiers, women, and children running wild. People pointed at storefronts decorated with pine boughs, and pranced out of shops carrying boxes and bags full of untold treasures. Susan didn't need to know what was in them in order to want them for herself. Whatever it was, it was new. *New!* The word itself was a tonic.

Before the war, she never could have strolled about the city unchaperoned. Now, however, the rules of propriety were bending, and she was bending with them. The crowd milling about on the corner quieted as a gentleman drove his horse and carriage down the street. The sunlight gleamed on his spotless white silk suit, blazed from diamonds on his fingers. Susan was nearly blinded by the light, but could not look away. Only vaguely did she hear the jeers being hurled at him, denouncing him as a speculator. So what if he was? It was hypnotizing, this vision of wealth, all the more since it looked entirely out of place.

He stopped his four-thousand-dollar carriage right next to her, and the rest of the crowd fell away from her vision entirely. "How do you do?" He tipped his hat to her. His blond hair was neatly pomaded into place.

"Charmed, I'm sure." She batted her eyes at him, as naturally as drawing breath.

His broad smile flashed in the winter sun. "Are you not ashamed to be seen talking to me? Do you not think it a crime to be rich during a war?"

"A crime to be rich?" She tilted her head. "Why, I see no criminal here. Only a man with ambition, a man who knows what he wants. And how to get it. The rest of us would do well to follow your example." She winked brazenly.

His eyebrows arched, and something uncurled inside her. The game was on. "Zeke Murphy's the name. Can I give you a lift somewhere?" Her eyes brightened as he climbed down to help her up into the carriage and onto the bench beside him. It was scandalous, riding with a strange man like this. But then, she had courted scandal before.

"I'm Susan Kent." She settled herself beside him. "I have some shopping to do at the Richards Brothers' bookstore." She would start small, and see what she could accomplish. She'd been out of practice for some time now.

"That isn't far at all." He smiled down at her, heat radiating from his body into hers. If her stepmother could see her right now she'd either slap her up one side and down the other or lunge for her smelling salts.

But her stepmother was not here. Neither was her father, nor Sophie, the half-sister who had nudged Susan from the center of her father's affections. She was free of them yet. Free of Noah. Free of clinging Ana.

To think, her original plan after being forced out of Chattanooga was to return to Richmond and beg her father's charity. But as they had not parted well, Susan didn't think it likely he would welcome her home. If time had not weakened his resolve against Susan, however, perhaps the sight of a hungry granddaughter would. A granddaughter he didn't even know he had. Perhaps her family would even grow to love Ana, even if Susan hadn't. If they would but take them into their mansion, Susan would never again know hunger or want of any kind.

Neither would she know the arms of another man. Once ensconced again in her parents' home, Susan felt sure no man would come calling, if there were any men left to be had at all. Even if they did, Father would not let them in.

This was the thought that had stalled her. This was what pulled her to Atlanta's bustling downtown for hours at a time. If Susan could just find a suitable beau, she would gladly choose him over the dogmatic rule of her father. And Ana could stay with Noah—assuming he ever came home. The girl simply held no charms for her.

Soon they were outside the Book, Music, and Fancy Store, and Zeke was helping her out of the carriage. When his broad hands lingered on her waist just a touch too long, her imagination took flight.

Inside, the store fairly choked on shoppers intent on finding just the right gift. When they saw Zeke, however, they parted for him. When his hand pressed against the small of Susan's back to guide her to the counter, they stared at her too, scowls slashed on their faces. No matter. She was not invisible anymore.

The store owner, Sam Richards, broke off his conversation with a different patron and hastily approached Zeke and Susan. "Are you two—together?"

"Yes," replied Zeke, and the word rippled through Susan.

"Well then, would the lady be interested in a novel for Christmas? *Les Miserables, Great Expectations, Macaria*? *Macaria* just came out, and it's written by Georgia-native Augusta Jane Evans, a very thrilling and patriotic choice if I may say so!"

"Yes, fine. I'll take that one if you please."

"Excellent. That will be two dollars."

Susan reached inside her shawl, fished dramatically around in her pockets.

"Allow me, Miss Kent."

"Oh, I couldn't!"

"I insist. Do I look like a man who cannot afford a two-dollar book? Especially one backed in—" He turned the volume over in his hand. "Wallpaper?"

The shopkeeper winced. "All the Southern presses are doing it, sir. Saves our precious resources."

"Indeed."

"Will that be all?"

Susan paused. "Mr. Murphy, I can reimburse you just as soon as—"

"Nonsense. What's your pleasure? Anything."

She could not believe her ears. Why, this was far too easy! A price tag attached to a set of twelve bound volumes asked for three hundred dollars.

"That." She pointed to it. "It isn't too much, is it?"

Zeke rolled his eyes. "We'll take it. And now, my dear, I'd like to take you for some real shopping. That is, unless you've got a beau waiting for you somewhere? Dalton, perhaps? Virginia?"

She giggled and shook her head, bouncing the loose curls by her face as she did so.

"Splendid." He paid for the transaction and offered his arm, which she eagerly accepted. "Have you ever had a fairy godmother? Or godfather?" He grinned, and a dimple popped into his left cheek.

Her eyes grew wide.

"Would you like to know what it's like to have one? I'd love to see you out of those rags and into something better suited to you."

A new dress? Such a personal gift coming from a man, let alone a stranger! "Bu-But you don't know me at all!"

"Haven't you noticed? I've got money to burn. I don't care where you came from, who your parents are, whether you can embroider or paint or form flowers out of wax. All I care about is that you're here right now. Let's gather our rosebuds while we may, shall we?"

Now who is playing who? Susan wondered. "No obligations?"

"None." He held his palms open wide. "It's Christmas Eve. Let's make merry."

Exhilaration unfurled within Susan, tingling from her head to her toes, as he whisked her from store to store. On Whitehall Street, he bought yards of Saxony Flannel and black-and-white prints, linen collars, and new kid leather shoes. When she admitted that she had no idea how to sew, he threw back his head and laughed.

"Good girl. Someone else should do that for you, right princess?"

Moments later, a seamstress took her back to get her measurements, and her arms floated, weightless, toward the ceiling. Finally, finally, she felt good again.

The hours passed as mere moments, until the blazing red sun dipped behind downtown Atlanta. By the time Zeke drove Susan back to Noah's house, she was drunk with conquest. A man she had met just today had spent more than two thousand dollars on her.

"Happy Christmas, Miss Kent. May I call on you again? The rest of this town isn't nearly as fun as you are."

Susan's cheeks warmed as she nodded. "I would like nothing better."

He smiled, tapped her on the nose with his finger, then helped her down. He followed, carrying her new books, genuine coffee, and hats. The new shoes were already on her feet, and the new dresses would be ready to pick up by the New Year.

When Caitlin McKae opened the door, the look on her pale and pinched face was worth a small fortune.

"You were wrong, Caitlin." Susan laughed, swaying with giddiness next to Zeke and his tower of packages. "A man—the right man—is the perfect source of happiness." Feeling especially generous, she pulled the box of books and bag of coffee from Zeke's stack and handed the bundles to Caitlin. "Merry Christmas, from Mr. Murphy and me to our humble household. Real coffee and new novels to read!"

"Why, hello there." Zeke bent his head. Susan's heart dropped into her new kid leather shoes when she saw Ana peering out from behind Caitlin's skirt. "And who might you be?"

"She is no one," Susan muttered. "Now I'll take those if you please. You must be on your way."

———

Not even the tantalizing aroma of fresh, real coffee could tempt Caitlin to go downstairs when Ana's shoulders still heaved with sobs in Caitlin's arms. Caitlin cried right along with her. Susan's two little words—"no one"—had ignited a bonfire of fury, burning away the dross of everyday strain and refining Caitlin's love for the little girl more than she thought possible.

"Why–did–she–say–that?" Analiese hiccupped. "When does my

Papa come home? I want my—Papa!"

"I don't know, darlin'. But I know your papa loves you with all his heart and then some. Shall we look at his letter to you again?"

Ana sniffed. "I memorized it."

"You did?"

She nodded, and recited his tender words. "And then he sang me a song. A German Christmas song."

Caitlin's heart caught in her throat as the memory of Noah's baritone reverberated in her spirit. How she wished he was here for his daughter now. "I don't know any German Christmas songs, and here it is, Christmas Eve. Could you teach it to me? I will be your pupil this time, how does that sound?"

Ana nodded. She wiped her face and sat up a little straighter. Her face glowed in the firelight as she sang. "*Stille Nacht, heilige Nacht, Alles schläch; einsam wacht . . .*"

The English translation of "Silent Night" played in Caitlin's mind until Ana's sigh put an end to it, her small body slumping against Caitlin once more. "I like it better when Papa sings it himself, in person. And I don't want to sing about a mother and child anymore. Can you tell me a story?"

"Of course." Caitlin swallowed the lump in her throat and began reciting "'Twas the Night before Christmas." She patted Ana's pillow and tucked her into her covers, silently thanking God she hadn't been allowed to go to Gettysburg. She was right where she was supposed to be. She would never think of leaving Ana again.

Chapter Fifteen

New York City
Sunday, January 3, 1864

We don't belong here. Ruby shifted Aiden to her other hip and followed the tuxedoed waiter to a linen-draped table set with white bone china and crystal. Reverend Herbert and Mrs. Jessamine Lanser had invited Edward to lunch after church today, and insisted that Vivian, Ruby, and Aiden join them.

Tucked between Vivian and Mrs. Lanser, Ruby held Aiden on her lap while waiting for a high chair. Ice clinked in cut glass goblets as Aiden gleefully tugged on the tablecloth. *Lord, if we could get through this meal without making a huge mess, I would be so thankful.* One smile from Edward across the table made the effort seem worthwhile.

The waiter returned with the high chair, and Ruby gratefully set her son securely in place.

"Coffee?" Steam curled from the silver pitcher in the waiter's hands. Ruby nodded, and in a moment, her cup was filled. *Thank heavens.*

Aiden wasn't the only O'Flannery fighting sleep. The bulk of her time was divided between caring for Aiden and sewing for her clients, who never seemed to tire of the latest fashions, even in wartime. Thankfully, between Edward's sewing machine and Emma's surprisingly nimble fingers, Ruby found a way to keep up with the orders, and split her profits with Emma.

When Aiden reached for the pearls swinging from Mrs. Lanser's neck, Ruby quickly tore off a piece of the evergreen centerpiece and tickled his nose to distract him. The spicy scent of the soft needles clearly delighted him as he mashed them in his hand.

"He's adorable." The older woman smiled. "Just look at those curls! Those cherub cheeks! I could just pinch him!"

"Aye—yes. Thank you."

Mrs. Lanser's perfectly shaped brows arched on her porcelain forehead. "Mrs. O'Flannery, is it? And Mrs. McKae? Such fine Irish names. Tell me, how is it you know Mr. Goodrich?"

"I'm his aunt." Vivian spoke over the rumbling voices of Edward and the pastor. "And Ruby here is our very dear friend."

"I see. Have you been in this country long?"

"Fourteen years," Ruby answered.

"How nice. Our family has been here since before the country was founded. Tell me, how are you liking our city?"

As if she had only just arrived in a city that belonged to the old money alone. As if immigrants had no ownership in it, though it was immigrant labor that built the docks, railroads, bridges, and more.

"I like it fine." She forced a smile she did not feel.

"Splendid. Forgive me, I just fail to see how you and Mr. Goodrich became—how did you put it? Very dear friends?"

Carefully, Ruby chose which slice of the truth to serve. "I met him when we both worked in the hospitals in Washington. Now I'm a domestic for Caroline Waverly on Sixteenth Street, not far from the Goodrich house. Edward has been doing Bible studies with me since he came home."

"Ah yes, how lovely. It is unusual, though, for a woman with husband and child to be a domestic. I didn't see him today. Is your husband not a churchgoer?"

Edward's voice broke off midsentence as he turned his attention to the women. "She is a war widow, Mrs. Lanser." His voice was low, respectful.

"Aha! Thank goodness. I was wondering if he'd been involved in that draft riot business last summer, but as you are not in full black, he must have died more than a year ago, at the very least. Oh, listen to me, carrying on when there's a lunch to be decided!"

Ruby's cheeks burned as she hid behind her menu. Aiden played peek-a-boo with the napkin over his head, his small voice blending in with the din of the crowd.

After they placed their order, Reverend Lanser cleared his throat and smoothed his silver whiskers downward. "I know the womenfolk may not like talking business at the table, so you ladies feel free to talk amongst yourselves if this bothers you. But I've got a proposition for our Edward here, and I just can't wait to lay it out for him."

Edward blinked. "Sir?"

Aiden babbled but Ruby tuned her ears to what the pastor had to say.

"You're a godly man, Edward. You've got your seminary degree, you've served as a chaplain down in Washington, Virginia, and now up here in our hospitals. Your reputation is spotless, you relate well to our veterans, and you know how to preach."

"Thank you, sir. But what—"

"The bottom line is this. I'll be retiring from my role as pastor sometime in the next several months, and I'm going to want to know the church is in good hands when I leave. I've had my eye on you for a while, son. The war is bound to end soon, and your work with the wounded soldiers will come to a close. Have you thought about what you'll do when that happens? Have you made any plans for your future?"

Edward found Ruby's eyes and sent her a small smile, the spark in his dark eyes warming her. The future, even if barely believable, had never seemed so inviting. She hadn't imagined being with a man again, but Edward was so different. Surely, if married, she could love and be loved without her past poisoning every touch.

Turning back to the reverend, Edward nodded. "I've always wanted to shepherd my own flock. It's what I trained for. My time with the hospitals has been rewarding, to be sure. I wouldn't trade the experience for the world. But it's just for a season. I'm listening with open ears to where God may call me next."

Reverend Lanser clapped his hand on his shoulder. "I can't tell you how happy I am to hear that. We need not discuss it further right now, but I'd be delighted if you'd consider pastoring my church when I step down. The church would vote on it of course, but with my endorsement, it should be an easy win. I'd be happy to mentor you over the next few months in practical church leadership, if you wish. Pray about it, will you?"

Edward assured him that he would, and Ruby nearly choked on the irony of what was transpiring before her. Would she one day be a pastor's wife? Surely she was disqualified for the title. With nervous fingers, she tore a piece of bread and gave it to Aiden.

"This is marvelous." Vivian beamed. "Edward, did your father ever tell you that it was a Methodist circuit rider that came to our home in Buffalo and led your grandfather to the Lord? Eventually our entire household prayed to receive Christ. George was the hardest to convince, but believe it or not, he did."

Edward's lips quirked, but he said nothing. True enough, George Goodrich's heart seemed to be in a deep freeze. But Ruby had seen evidence of a thaw even in the short time since Thanksgiving. He had started using her name, for instance, rather than calling her "the girl." He had stopped telling Vivian to leave him alone when she hugged him good night. Perhaps most surprising of all, he'd suggested donating funds to Christmas dinners at the hospitals rather than spending money on gifts for one another. It was a lovely idea, and Ruby suspected

Edward was secretly irritated that he hadn't thought of it first, himself.

"Our granddaughter is coming back from holiday soon," Mrs. Lanser was saying. "She had a notion to work with the Sanitary Commission women, but you know how strong-minded that crowd is. Soon they'll be saying women should vote!" She clucked her tongue. "So we've convinced Amy to simply channel her charity into the Women's Central Association for Relief right here in the city, instead. You really should meet her, Edward."

Ruby's glance snapped to the older woman, but she held her tongue. Vivian did not. "Why's that?"

"Hm?" Mrs. Lanser chewed a bite of lamb. "Why what?"

"Why should Edward meet your Amy?"

"Oh! Why, she's beautiful, he'd just love her. Young, sweet, educated, patriotic. She plays the piano, too. A very helpful asset to have around." She dipped her head, her double chin spreading with each nod. "Do you play the piano, Mrs. O'Flannery?"

Ruby swallowed another sip of coffee. "No."

"Amy sings too. She has the voice of an angel, the next Jenny Lind, I tell you! You should hear her sing in the church. The acoustics! Heavenly, I tell you! Do you sing?"

"Only to my son." She smiled.

"Well that's fine, dear. We can't all be songbirds. But between us . . ." She leaned in to Vivian and Ruby. "An upstanding girl who can play and sing would make an excellent candidate for a pastor's wife." She winked and leaned back in her chair. "And a wife is the only thing Edward lacks. A congregation wouldn't trust a bachelor in the pulpit, if you ask me."

"Indeed." Vivian's voice was smooth as silk, but her eyes were sharp. "And is this wife to be of your choosing, or of God's?"

Ruby's face flamed. She was certain Vivian had meant to defend Ruby, but her question snagged Ruby's conscience. Edward was a gift to Ruby. But was Ruby really God's choice for Edward?

After lunch, while Aiden napped and Edward and Ruby shared tea in the sitting room, Vivian found George reading the newspaper in the library, his pipe drooping from beneath his mustache.

"One of these Sundays, I would dearly love to have you in church beside me again, brother." She squeezed his shoulder before sitting in the leather armchair across from him. A vibrant fire danced behind the grate, brightening an otherwise washed-out January day. Wind sighed outside the window, and tree branches tapped their bony fingers against the panes, as if requesting entry into the warm, dark-paneled room.

"Hmph." George snorted, but did not rebuke the idea. "How many saints did the preacher put to sleep today?"

"Now, George." She set her knitting basket on the floor next to her and resumed work on the half-finished sock dangling from her needles.

"Well?"

Vivian bit back a chuckle. "Edward would have done better." She smiled as she settled into the methodical rhythm of her knitting, purling, and slipping. "In fact, there's a possibility that he'll be given the chance—and on a regular basis, too."

"What's that you say?" The sweet scent of pipe tobacco mingled with the aroma of wood smoke.

"Ask him yourself. It's his news to share."

"Ah yes! News!" George's grey eyes popped wide. He slapped the newspaper down on the table beside him, pushed himself up, and walked with his cane to his roll-top desk.

"You need something, George? Let me help."

He waved her away. "Would you have me be sedentary for the rest of my days, until I wither away to nothing? I've got to regain my strength." With one hand cradling his pipe, he rifled through stacks of newspaper and balance sheets until hooking something from beneath his ledger book. "Someone came by for you with this."

"Oh? Who was that?"

"A neighbor from your old building. Said this was mixed in with her mail, thought you might know where to send it." He handed her a letter. "For Jack."

Vivian took the envelope, turned it over to read the address. Dropped her knitting to the floor, felt herself unraveling.

The handwriting snatched the breath from her lungs. "It's Caitlin," she gasped. The envelope trembled in her hands.

"Your missing girl? You're certain?" George, at her side.

"I'd know her penmanship anywhere!" She touched her fingertips to the words.

"Where was it postmarked?" Abandoning his pipe to its walnut tray, he took the envelope. "Gettysburg!"

"Do you think she was there?"

"In December?" He pointed to the date on the envelope. "It's so thin. Can't tell if there's anything in it at all!"

"Open it."

George grabbed a letter opener from his desk and slit the envelope's top. Peered inside. Frowned. The fire hissed in his silence.

"I can't stand it a minute longer!" Vivian's hands twisted in her lap. "What is it? Tell me!"

He fished out a scrap of newsprint, eyebrows plunging. "You're absolutely sure that's her handwriting on the envelope?"

"Yes, yes! What is it? Did she say anything?"

"It's a message all right. But she's not in Gettysburg, Viv."

Alarm jangled in her spirit at the tender use of her old nickname. George handed the torn paper to her.

ATLANTA DAILY INTELLIGENCER   DECEMBER 10, 1863

"She is alive," Vivian whispered, turning the scrap over.

"For now."

Vivian's head snapped up, fear licking through her veins like fire. "How can you say such a thing?"

"She is living in a bull's-eye." George grunted. "Atlanta is the heart of the South, an important railway center. If the Union were to capture it, we would snap the backbone of the rebellion in half."

"What can she be doing there?"

"Hold the envelope and paper in front of the firelight. Do you see anything else?"

Light and shadow tangled behind the paper, but did not reveal further clues. Vivian shook her head.

"No matter," George said gruffly. "It is enough as it is. We know she wanted you—or Jack, rather—to know she was in Atlanta. She could not write anything personal either because it would be incriminating or she had no time, or both. She had to smuggle the letter out of the South in order to reach us."

"But how do you know she did not send it herself from Gettysburg?"

"If she'd been in the North, she'd have been able to write more, or she would have just come home, wouldn't she? Gettysburg is only two hundred miles or so from here. No, she sent it with someone, and there is only one reason a Southerner would go to Gettysburg."

"To bring home the remains of a loved one fallen in last summer's battle."

"Exactly. Which means that whoever sent this is headed back South, with the information that Caitlin has ties to someone in New York." His face clouded.

Vivian locked eyes with her brother. *She will look like a spy.* A log crumbled in the consuming fire, and she twitched. "It's my fault she's in danger now. If I hadn't—" Her shaky fingers pressed her lips to barricade further mutterings.

"What's that you say?"

Vivian's throat tightened. "We did not—part well." It was only a hint at the yawning chasm between them, and yet even now, she felt exposed.

"How did you part?" For the first time in years, George's eyes harbored a spark of the big brother Vivian had adored.

"I can make it right if I can find her." She had driven her daughter away. Somehow, she would find a way to bring her home.

Atlanta, Georgia
Friday, January 22, 1864

No place for a lady, indeed.

Minnie's hollow warning echoed in Susan's mind as she and Zeke Murphy approached the Athenaeum theater on Decatur Street. Yes, its reputation was raucous and rowdy, full of drunken soldiers and the less savory elements of Atlanta society. She didn't care. It was a gay diversion from the humdrum refugee life, and it swarmed with people. It was *exactly* where she wanted to be.

The pungent odor of hay and corn pinched Susan's nose as they entered the brick building. The first floor was used as grain storage and sometime slave auction floor, but it was a small price to pay to be among people who noticed her. Her most charming smile on her face, and her arm looped through Zeke's, she swept up the stairs with the current of the crowd to the second-floor theater already teeming with hundreds of people.

Dazzling with jewels and dressed in luxurious yards of scarlet Saxony Flannel cut in the latest Parisian fashion, Susan turned more heads here than she had in the last three years put together. Her butter-blonde locks were swept into an elaborately braided chignon, with just a few ringlets coiling next to her delicate face. Jeweled hair combs flashed gas light into the beholder's eye.

And all she had had to do to rise up out of impoverishment was give Zeke Murphy a few kisses, and more than a few breathless promises of more to come. She gave him the appearance of class, he had said, and he gave her the appearance of wealth. It was a fair trade for both of them. What did it matter that not all the stares they drew were approving? At least she was someone worth noticing—for whatever reason.

Before taking her seat, Susan's gaze circled the theater. Galleries on three sides squirmed with patrons edging into their seats, or greeting one another across the aisles. They laughed and smiled, as if they were not plunged into winter, or soaked with war. Playbill for the farce

Slasher and Crasher in hand, she eased into her seat and faced the velvet drapes curtaining the stage.

"Say." A thin soldier sat next to Susan and spoke across her to Zeke. "You look to be in fine feather. Why ain't you in uniform?"

Susan kept her gaze straight ahead as Zeke volleyed back, wondering if he would dare admit he'd bribed the conscript officer to keep out of the ranks. "I'm just here to enjoy the play, same as you, soldier. Let's leave the war talk outside, shall we?"

"I don't think so. With the money you spent on those rags you're wearing, you could have purchased supplies for our army in camp or the hospitals here and greatly relieved their suffering."

"Now look here. I don't want any trouble, I'm just here for the show, same as you. Let's leave it at that."

"Your kind is worse than the Yankees, you know that? What do you do? Buy up from the blockade runners and sell the goods at cutthroat prices to your own people, for personal profit?"

His guess was accurate, but incomplete. A large part of Zeke's wealth, he'd confided in Susan, came from buying Yankee greenbacks from Union prisoners with the quickly devaluing Confederate currency. With U.S. dollars, he could afford to purchase scarce items, and then resell them for almost any price he set.

"You selfish son of a—"

"Watch your language, son. There's a lady present here."

"A curse on both of you," he growled, and spit.

It landed on Susan's face.

———

Atlanta, Georgia
Thursday, February 11, 1864

"Hello, Caitlin."

Caitlin's heart wedged itself in her throat. Prudence stood before her in the doorway, her eyes telling more than her words.

Caitlin stood back, motioned her to come inside, and shut the door behind her. She licked her dry lips. "Did you find him?"

"Yes." Prudy followed Caitlin to the parlor and sat at the tea table with her. "I found quite more than I bargained for, in fact."

"Did I hear Prudence?" Naomi hustled into the parlor, eyes wide. "You've made it home! How did it go?"

Prudy clasped Naomi's hands and brushed a kiss on her cheek. "I would never care to repeat the journey. But once in Gettysburg, I found a Southern-born physician named Dr. John O'Neal, who had just finished compiling a list of Confederate dead and their resting places. He led me right to Stuart's burial place on a little farm that was turned into an inn for survivors of the dead. Liberty Inn, it's called. Stuart was there, buried beneath some apple trees."

"And he's home now?"

"Yes. It cost one hundred thirty-three dollars in greenbacks just to get him exhumed, placed in a coffin, and sent to Richmond, and from there it was trains and wagons the rest of the way home." She shuddered. "But, Naomi, Stuart wasn't all I found at Liberty Inn."

Color leeched from Naomi's complexion. "Was Dr. Schmucker there for some reason?"

"Yes—because he escorted me there himself after I inquired about your son Silas. Silas was at Liberty Inn."

Naomi's hands fluttered to her mouth as she dropped onto the sofa. "Beneath the apple trees?"

"No, you goose!" Prudy laughed. "He's alive, and he lives in Gettysburg now! He wrote you this letter." She dipped into her pocket and handed Naomi an envelope.

Caitlin looked on in wonder as Naomi clawed it open and devoured the words with her eyes. As she read, tears traced her cheeks to the corners of her fading smile. At length, she hugged the missive to her chest and bowed her head.

"Well?" Caitlin prodded. "What does it say?"

Naomi wiped her cheeks. "A great many things, things too complicated to make sense to you. But the most important thing is that he is alive, and we are reconciled—or at least as much as we can be from this distance—over what transpired between us years ago. He lost his leg in the battle at Gettysburg last summer, and fell in love with a young woman there named Liberty Holloway. She is—" Naomi swallowed, breathed deeply. "She is the daughter of a mulatto, former slave. I see his tastes follow his father's, God rest his soul."

Caitlin and Prudence exchanged a glance when Naomi buried her face in her hand.

"Forgive me. He's going to marry this Liberty girl, and complete the training he started at the Lutheran Theological Seminary. They mean to live there in Gettysburg. He took the oath to the United States." She cringed as she said it. "And he invites me to come north and live there, too. He says if I can get to Nashville, he will meet me there and bring me 'home,' and take care of me."

Caitlin waited. Then, "Will you?"

Naomi shook her head. "Home, he says. What home? The South is my home. Excuse me, please. Prudence, I'll forever be indebted to you for this." She rose and left the room, still pressing the letter to her heart.

Once alone again, Prudy pierced Caitlin with her gaze. "Home is where the heart is, isn't it Caitlin? And where is your heart? After all this time, was I wrong about you? Is your heart truly in the North after all?"

"I—I—Jack is my—"

Prudence held up her hand. "Stop. The less said the better."

"But did you—"

A nod, and the matter vanished. "My errand here today has another motive."

"Oh?"

She pursed her thin lips. "Lil Bit tells me that smallpox cases are on the rise again. We want you to be safe. I know you'll stay close to home, since your pass has been confiscated, but the members of your household would do well to exercise extreme caution, as well. Some of the soldiers at the hospitals leave before their last scab has fallen off, and they are still contagious. Civilians are catching it, and the medical supplies are all marked for the army. You haven't had it yourself, have you?"

"No." The whisper was dry, brittle.

"Has the child?"

"No, her skin is flawless. But Minnie has had it."

"Then she, at least, will be safe from the scourge. What about Naomi?"

"We can ask her, but I've seen no scars on her."

"And Susan?"

"I doubt it."

"We must know for sure. Where is she?"

"In bed. She's been complaining of a headache and sore throat for the last few days."

Prudy's eyelids flared. "Did she go to the train station last week to meet Captain Morgan?" Thousands had gathered there to see the Confederate hero after his escape from the Ohio penitentiary, and followed him all the way to the Trout House hotel. "I'm sure hundreds of convalescents stole away from the hospitals to see him!"

"No, no, it was too early in the morning. She never leaves the house before noon."

"I must see her." With sudden vigor, the elderly woman swept past Caitlin and started for the stairs. "Stay here."

Caitlin stood alone in the central hall, her gaze following Prudy's rustling skirt. Suspense buzzed in her veins until Prudy returned, eyes dark. "The rash has begun."

Caitlin gasped, fear whisking the breath from her lungs. "You don't mean—"

"Let no one in that room but Minnie. Hang a red flag on your house, allow no one in who has not had the pox or been vaccinated against it."

Terror curled coldly around Caitlin. "But what about you?"

"Vaccinated. I'll be fine. It's you I worry about, and that child in

204

your care. The disease has no mercy, and it is the worst on the young. Lil Bit has nothing to help Susan now. But if I know my own brother, he'll come as soon as her sores are filled with enough pus to be of some good to the rest of you. In the meantime, pray as if your lives depend upon it. They do."

Chapter Sixteen

New York City
Sunday, February 14, 1864

Edward's grip tightened around the bouquet he clutched behind his back for Ruby. Something was wrong.

"I'd rather not dine out tonight, if you don't mind." She cast her gaze downward before peering up at him again, but did not move from the doorway of her room. After spending the week with wounded soldiers still elated about the Yankee prisoners of war who had escaped their Richmond cells five days ago, the contrast of Ruby's sagging countenance alarmed him.

"Are you unwell?"

"I'm tired. Aiden required all my energy today, and now that he's down for the night, I have no desire to go out. I'm sorry, but I'm just not up to pretending to be someone I'm not right now."

Edward blanched. "Is that what you call it?"

"I don't fit into your world, Edward, not like you do. I appreciate your kindness, but really—"

"So help me, if you accuse me of just being a good neighbor to you I'll—I'll—" *Grow a garden of rashes on my neck bright enough to read by.* Awkwardly, he offered his bouquet to her. "These are not the flowers of one friend to another."

A smile flickered on her weary face as she accepted them. "No one's ever given me flowers before," she whispered.

"Not even—" Heaven help him, would he always feel compelled to mention her late husband?

"No one. I thank you."

A stiff smile tipped his lips as he wondered if an Irish immigrant would know the language of the flowers. The red carnations in her hand were for admiration. The pink roses for thankfulness. Red roses, of course, for love. "Happy St. Valentine's Day. Or rather, what would make it happy for you?"

"A cup of tea in front of the fire and the freedom to turn in early. Not very sophisticated, am I?"

Edward drew a deep breath and exhaled slowly. "Actually, that sounds wonderful. Is there room in front of that fire for me?"

She nodded demurely, and his heart relaxed.

By the time Mr. Schaefer came bearing a tray with a vase of water for the flowers, along with tea and biscuits, Ruby was visibly more at ease. Vivian sat in a corner of the room, quietly knitting for the soldiers.

"You've been working so hard lately. How are things with Emma?"

Ruby's eyebrows arched as she sipped her tea. "She is such a big help to me in my sewing business! I don't know what I'd do without her. And now that she's making her money honestly, she has less reason to seek other—means of employment." She hid a blush behind her teacup.

"Emma is so fortunate to have a friend like you."

"But not as fortunate as I wish." Ruby's green eyes shimmered. "She is learning to be industrious, and still her life is not comfortable. Not like this." Her gaze skimmed the wallpapered sitting room. "I fear she is jealous of me, and I can't say that I blame her. Our life stories used to match. And now . . ." Her voice trailed away and she shook her head. Firelight gleamed on her red hair as she sipped her tea.

Confusion rippled his brow. "Are you unhappy here?"

Faint snoring coming from Aunt Vivian's corner punctuated Ruby's hesitation. "Not unhappy. Just wondering when the spell will be broken." A smile tugged at the corner of her mouth. "I tell you, I only fit here as a domestic. You and I were not cut of the same cloth."

Though softly spoken, the words bruised him, a boomerang of his own former argument. *We are very different . . .* "What are you saying?"

Her cup clinked back onto its saucer on the table. She twisted her hands in the folds of her skirt. "Aside from Aiden, you are the single most important person in my life." Her voice trembled, and his heart ached. "A life spent with you would be more than I could hope for, but you would be lowering yourself to take on the likes of me."

Edward balked. "I'm not 'taking on the likes of you.' I want to be with *you*, Ruby. I want you and Aiden to have my last name, to be part of my family. Not as a ministry, but because I—care for you more than you realize." She made him want to be a better man.

"I don't play the piano or sing, and I have no idea how to make small talk with the ladies at church. The last thing I want is to be an albatross around your neck. I'll tell you the truth, I want nothing more in this world than for Aiden to be able to call you his father. But you must know your pursuit of me will surely stir up scandal! Far better for your career if you make a match with Amy Lanser instead." Stunned, Edward raked his hand through his hair and leaned his elbows on his knees. If he'd had any idea that his brief encounters with Miss Lanser—at the church and with the reverend present—would cause such insecurity in Ruby, he never would have mentioned them! Clearly, he had failed to make Ruby understand the depth of his feeling for her. But had she only been interested in him as a father to her son? "Miss Lanser is a fine young woman, but she has absolutely no claim on my heart. Have you no feeling for me, then, as a man?" he dared to ask, silently praying his eyes did not reveal the hurt she had inflicted.

———

Ruby's nose pinched. "My feelings have nothing to do with it."
When it came to men, they never did.

"Yes they do!" Edward jerked his head toward Vivian, but she didn't
stir. "How you feel has everything to do with it. Who taught you otherwise,
Ruby? What happened to you that you should believe this brazen lie?"

His velvety brown eyes were so intent, she almost believed he really
wanted to know. She almost wanted to tell him.

"You matter. Your feelings matter, what you want and who you
want matters." He rubbed a hand over his clean-shaven jaw, and balsam
shaving soap scented the air. "Speak plainly now. If you want me to let
you be, I will, but we cannot go back to the way it once was. Now that
Aunt Vivian is here, and my father has recovered the use of his limbs, I
can request a transfer back down to Washington or Fort Monroe. You
could stay here until Mrs. Waverly comes home, with no fear of my presence. Just say the word and it shall be done."

"Fear of your presence?" she gasped, and the floodgates opened.
She had feared her late husband Matthew at times, and Emma's brother
Sean, and Phineas Hastings, the man who had stripped her to a life of
prostitution the first year of the war. Men took what they wanted from
her whenever it suited them. Not once had anyone cared enough to
leave her alone, until Edward. Would she now turn this man away?

Tears spilled down her cheeks, tasted salty on her lips. "I don't fear
you."

"But do you want me?" he whispered. "Or shall I go?"

Ruby bit her lip. "Don't go."

"Why not? For Aiden's sake?"

Held captive in Edward's eyes, Ruby scrubbed her heart for the
truth. "And mine," she said at length. "Please stay. I suppose it's very selfish of me, Edward, but I do want you in my life."

Edward bowed his head for a moment, his breath released in a sigh.
Then he reached for her hand—and she flinched, erecting a new wall
between them.

"Does my touch repulse you? Is that it?" He edged away from her on the sofa and looked straight ahead into the fire, where flames leapt and danced with reckless abandon.

Heart hammering against its cage, Ruby forced herself to reach out and place her hand upon his shoulder. "No, of course not." His body warmed her clammy hand, and he turned to face her once more. Deliberately, she slid her hand down his arm until she tucked it into his hand. Her spine tingled as he enveloped her hand in his. "The problem I have is not with you."

"Then what is it?" He brought her hand to his lips and pressed a kiss to it, sending shivers through Ruby's body. "Please don't shut me out. No secrets, all right? I've had enough deception from my father." His lips quirked, but he held her hand steady.

Ruby had once believed that truth had set her free. Now, however, she felt trapped by it. Still, she could not lie to Edward. He already knew something was wrong.

Her tongue cleaved to the roof of her mouth, refusing to form any words. Chin trembling, she swallowed the pain growing sharp within her throat.

"Ruby," Edward whispered, moved closer to her until she felt the warmth radiating from his body. Her pulse pounded in her ears. "Darling, it's all I can do to keep myself from kissing you right now."

"Oh no, please don't!" She yanked her hand from his and jumped to her feet.

Edward looked as though he'd been slapped.

"I'm sorry," Ruby gasped, "I'm so sorry. Forgive me, forgive me, I wish I wasn't this way." Fresh tears welled in her eyes.

A lump bobbed in Edward's throat. The stricken look on his face lanced her already blistered heart.

"What happened to you?" he whispered.

Ruby drew a fortifying breath and closed her eyes. "To explain it is to relive it. Please, do not ask this of me. Isn't it clear enough?"

"You were beaten, more than once."

She nodded.

"Physical affection was corrupted into an act of violence against you."

"Many times, and by more than one man." More than two.

Edward's eyes blazed then. "I would never hurt you. Do you believe me? I would never touch you with anything but tenderness. I am not those men."

"I know." But he was still a man. And her body cringed from his touch just the same. "I think I just need time."

Edward clasped his hands behind his back and nodded. "All right. I can be patient. I won't push you, though my arms long to hold you and I dream of kissing your lips one day."

Her eyebrows arched, and a sad smile curved on his face.

"Did you think a chaplain would have no such desire? I assure you, I am made of neither wood nor stone. But I would much rather wait until you are ready than force you to do anything you're not comfortable with. We'll work through this together. All right?"

"Yes." Ruby smiled through her tears.

"Mind if I pray for you?" His voice soothed her spirit as he asked God to heal her heart the way only He could. By the time he said, "Amen," she dared to hope that Edward's prayer would one day be answered.

"And now, I bid you good night. You see? You shall have that early bedtime tonight after all."

He limped to the door, and her heart lurched at the reminder that he had taken a bullet for a friend. What wouldn't he do for his wife? "No more secrets, all right?" he said again, half-turned in the doorway. "We'll weather the storms together."

Ruby smiled but didn't nod. Surely it would be better to leave the worst chapter of her life in the dark. "Good night, Edward." And she took her last secret with her to bed.

New York City
Tuesday, February 16, 1864

It was a bad idea, reading the newspaper right before trying to sleep, but Vivian couldn't help herself. Ever since learning that Caitlin was in Atlanta, she had been scouring all the dailies for any mention of the city. What she'd found last week, official declaration that Atlanta was the target for the Federal spring campaign, had done nothing to assuage her anxiety. But if Caitlin was still there when the Yankees encroached, maybe Jack could find her.

How much better if she were no longer there at all come spring! Sighing, Vivian turned the page of the *New York Daily News*—and almost spewed her milk back into her glass. For there, in the advertising section, among ads for ginger tonic, harnesses, and corsets, ran notices of an entirely different nature all together.

DAVIS C. HUNTLEY, RICHMOND, VA.—FOLKS ALL WELL; NO NEWS FROM KATE; AUNT SARAH DEAD; MONEY IN BANK FOR YOU, HOLMES, EXECUTOR; I AM KEEPING HOTEL AT CATSKILL. HAVE STARTED TWICE TO SEE YOU; COULDN'T GET THERE. HARVEY.

Another ad said:

TO TKJ, NEW YORK. DEAR BROTHER. I AM WELL, BUT HAVE BEEN SEVERELY WOUNDED TWICE. FATHER AND BROTHER WILLIAM DIED DURING THE SIEGE OF VICKSBURG . . . WOULD LIKE TO HEAR FROM YOU.

Vivian pushed herself up in her feather bed, skimming the columns until landing on the small print explaining that the New York paper had reached an agreement with the *Richmond Enquirer*, whereby persons could purchase with two dollars eight lines of space to write to their loved ones across enemy lines. The papers agreed to reprint each other's sections, so an ad taken out in the New York paper could be read in the Richmond paper as well, and vice versa.

"Surely, the newspaper of the Confederate capital would be available in Atlanta, wouldn't it?" Vivian said aloud. She pushed back her covers, swung her legs down, the thick rug cushioning her feet. Hope thrummed through her with every step as she paced the length of her room. *What are the chances Caitlin would see it?*

Still, she had to try.

Vivian slid into her chair at the writing desk, the pencil cool in her warm grip. *C. McKae, Atlanta: Come home. Loving arms await you.* Vivian sat back and stared at her handwriting now swimming on the paper. She crossed out "Atlanta," to help protect her—but would she notice such small print among rows and rows of the same? If she did, would Caitlin finally come home now? Would she be able to if she wanted to? Uncertainty bowed Vivian's shoulders.

We did not part well. Her mild explanation to George echoed between her ears, while the brutal truth stabbed her heart. *I pushed her away. It's my fault she left.* Oh, if that were only the end of it. But God forgive her, it wasn't.

Get out! I don't want to see you here again! You've done enough! Her own words ricocheted in her spirit. Caitlin had obeyed, though fire burned in her eyes. After a preliminary slap from Bernard, Vivian had gone back to the bedroom, then, stripped down to her shift and braced for what was to come. At least Caitlin was gone. *She's safe now,* she had naïvely told herself.

Bernard didn't come right away. Martial music pierced the air above masses of people cheering the Seventh Regiment a few blocks away, making it difficult to hear anything else. Vivian waited, hugging a pillow to her chest, until a sickening thud sounded from the hallway.

"Bernard?" she had called quietly.

She heard nothing beyond the drumbeats of war beating in rhythm with her heart. Vivian sat up, strained her ears. She thought she heard more clamoring—or was that just the music again?

213

Finally, she could stand it no longer. Still using her pillow as a shield in front of her thin shift, she slipped out of the bedroom. "Bernard?"

The front door was ajar. She whipped her gaze around the empty room. Her fists clenched the edges of her pillow as she stepped into the hallway. Peered down the stairs. Saw his hulking form lying at the bottom. And rejoiced.

When Vivian reached him seconds later, she knelt and felt his pulse beneath her fingers. Numbness sank deeper into her being with every beat. *If only the fall had killed him.* Then she saw the blood on his neck, Caitlin's hair ribbon in his hand, and she knew. Bernard had attacked her daughter. Caitlin had fought back, and escaped.

This time.

Vivian tugged Caitlin's ribbon from Bernard's beefy fingers and balled it into her trembling fist. White hot hatred overflowed her heart and spilled from eyes. Rage and fear collided in her spirit, shaking her from the inside out. She could detach herself from her own abuse. But the evidence of Caitlin in danger snapped something inside Vivian.

End it now, a voice whispered to her, *before he steals Caitlin the way he stole you.*

Later, Vivian would often wonder why she did not struggle against this thought. She would beg God for forgiveness for not trusting that He had a plan that did not involve murder. But in that moment, with her pillow over his face, the only thought in her mind was, *It's over.*

"It's over," she said aloud now, and looked up to reassure herself she was not in that dingy apartment anymore, but back in her brother's marble house.

Vivian climbed back beneath the goose down duvet of her canopied bed and wondered. If she were put on trial for her crime, how would she plead? She was guilty. But would she try temporary insanity as her defense, as the famous Union general Daniel Sickles had done when he had murdered his wife's lover on the street just five years ago? A congressman in Washington at the time, Sickles was not insane, his defense claimed, but driven to a momentary lapse in sanity by the heinous sin

214

of adultery. The public had swallowed it for him. Would they accept such a defense for Vivian?

But Vivian knew exactly what she was doing. She had not planned to murder him, but when the moment came, she did it. The police questioned her, but without suspicion. She was so frail, and they were looking for someone with strength enough to overcome Bernard's brawn. They never suspected her.

Bernard was gone, but so was Caitlin. She was in danger again. Vivian could feel it in her bones.

———

Atlanta, Georgia
Friday, February 19, 1864

Caitlin pressed a cool hand to her flushed face as she listened to Analiese recite her lesson in the parlor. Above them, Susan alternated between crying out in pain and ebbing into haunting silence.

"How do you feel?" Caitlin interrupted Ana with the question she now asked a dozen times a day. *Where* was Dr. Periwinkle? "Does your head hurt? Is your throat sore?"

"I'm tired," Ana said, her face pale. Her permanent two front teeth were growing in, but her smile was rarely big enough to show them off. "Can I rest for a while and lie down?"

"*May* I—"

"May I lie down?"

Caitlin nodded and looked out the window once more. Rascal sat on the bare pine floor beside the sofa, and Ana draped her arm around his neck as she stretched out.

Footsteps murmured on the stairs. "How is she?" Caitlin rushed to meet Minnie descending from Susan's room.

"The blisters are ballooning with pus. Some of them are weeping. She is in such pain." Minnie shook her head. "No sign of the doctor?"

"None."

Minnie's eyes glossed as she drew a deep breath. "My dear, you must write to Mr. Becker if you haven't already. Before you fall ill yourself."

"I—I have no paper."

"Have the courage to be honest with him, and with yourself. If any more of you fall ill I will not have time to be writing letters for you. We must pray for the best and prepare for the worst, must we not?"

Dread trickled over Caitlin, but she nodded. After peering out the window one more time, she retrieved a volume of Shakespeare and tore out a page. In the margins, she began her letter. There was little room on the page with which to cushion the news.

"Miss McKae? Judson Periwinkle here, I'm coming in!" Relief streamed down Caitlin's face at the doctor's commanding voice. Quickly she wiped her cheeks and rushed to the door just as he was walking through it.

"My dear girl." His blue eyes brimmed with concern. "I came as soon as I could. You can have no idea how the work has exploded." He shook his head. "Where is the patient? Or is there more than one yet?"

"Just one."

"So far." His countenance hardened.

Minnie hastened to the entrance and greeted the doctor before escorting him to Susan's room. Whether he spent mere moments there or hours, Caitlin could not tell. At some point, Naomi joined her in quiet vigil for the doctor's verdict.

By the time he returned downstairs, Caitlin was nearly breathless with suspense. "Well?"

"The disease must run its course. It will get worse before it can get better—if she is to recover, that is."

"Can nothing be done for her?" Naomi asked.

He sighed, his pipe tobacco scent sweetening the air. "I can spare no opium for the pain. What we have doesn't even cover the wounded soldiers in our official charge. What I do have for you is this." He held a needle and thread into the watery shaft of light.

Caitlin frowned. "I don't understand."

"Inoculation. It's only a matter of time before you catch smallpox living in this house. But if I plant just a bit of the disease in your flesh, your body will better develop the means to fight it off without being overwhelmed. You may expect to suffer some symptoms, but you will likely have a milder case."

Caitlin's mouth went dry. "You're saying I'll have smallpox either way."

"Very likely, you and everyone in this house, save Miss Taylor. The only choice you have is the degree to which you suffer. Decide for yourself, and for the girl."

Her head swam. It was one thing to write to Noah that Susan had taken ill with it and they were steering clear of her. It was another matter altogether to say she had authorized the doctor to plant the disease in their flesh deliberately. Would he understand, or condemn her? What if Ana died as a result of her decision?

"Honey." Minnie laid a hand on Caitlin's arm. "Mr. Becker would want you to do anything at all that might help preserve Ana's life. The greater risk would be not to take the inoculation."

"Fine." Only a whisper.

"Come then, quickly. Men are dying for want of attention."

Three women and Analiese followed the doctor back up the stairs and into the dreaded sickroom. Though a window had been cracked to allow fresh air to circulate, the odor of illness still dominated.

"Mama?" Ana's voice tightened with fright. It was the first time Ana had spoken the name since Christmas Eve. Caitlin tried not to stare at the pustules disfiguring Susan's face and arms. The sores were whitish-grey bubbles ringed with an angry red.

"Who is first?" Dr. Periwinkle said.

Naomi stepped forward. "How will it work?"

The doctor nodded to a chair next to the bed. "I pass the needle and thread through a pustule, then I use a lancet to break the skin on your upper arm, and pass the soiled needle and thread through your flesh. Even if you have already contracted the disease, but have not seen symptoms yet, this should mollify the severity."

Stoically, Naomi nodded and rolled up her sleeve. Ana's chin trembled, and Caitlin hugged her. "Shhhh, it's all right, just think of it as medicine," she said. But everyone in the room knew it was deadly poison, and it was up to each body to fight it off.

Ana chose to go next, sucking in her breath sharply when Dr. Periwinkle slit her skin and threaded her flesh with disease. "I want my Papa."

Bile rose in Caitlin's throat, and she wondered if she would one day look back on this moment with deepest, darkest regret.

Finally, Caitlin's turn. Squinting, Dr. Periwinkle cut into her upper arm, and laced her body with smallpox. She closed her eyes, but still saw the ugly sores pimpling Susan's skin. Then she saw them erupting on her own. *No.* She shook her head. *I can fight this. We all can.* Her eyes popped open and scanned the three red marks on three pale arms, and prayed that the scourge would pass over them, as the Angel of Death had passed over Hebrew homes marked with lamb's blood in the Old Testament.

"Thank you, Dr. Periwinkle," she whispered. "I know it was hard to take time away from the hospitals."

"You're welcome." He gazed at the mark on her arm before placing his rough hand on her cheek. "You know I've never been able to resist a girl with freckles." His voice thick, he tapped her nose. She suspected his smile was meant for Mary Beth.

When Dr. Periwinkle rose, tenderness bowed to urgency once more. "I must be going. There's nothing more I can do. Now we must leave it to your bodies, and to God Himself. May He show you the mercy He withheld from my daughter."

"Indeed." Naomi pressed a scrap of cloth to her arm. "At least we've been inoculated."

"My dear woman," he replied. "So was she."

Chapter Seventeen

Outside Dalton, Georgia
Saturday, February 27, 1864

mack!

A snowball hit Noah Becker square on the jaw, the ice cold crystals burning his skin. Vaguely, he registered teasing voices inviting him to join their wintry skirmish. Wiping the slush from his face, he turned his back to them and squinted at his mail. Caitlin's silent voice pounded between Shakespearean sonnets like some surreal Greek tragedy. *Smallpox* screamed on the edges of love and longing. *If anything happened to Ana, or to Caitlin . . .*

Death and disfigurement were beating on their door, and he was here, marching nowhere in particular and playing at war with handfuls of slush. Heat spiked up his neck and itched across his scalp, until beads of perspiration chilled on his brow. He should be home, to comfort his daughter, to release Caitlin from the nightmare she'd signed on to when she agreed to take the position that tied her to his house.

Setting his jaw, Noah marched to where Colonel Nisbet warmed his hands at a campfire and requested permission to address him.

"Granted."

"I'd like to request a furlough, sir. Just to Atlanta and back."

A grin curled on Nisbet's face. "Ninety miles one way, by foot. Not an easy journey in the best of conditions, let alone winter."

"I am resolved to do it, if you but grant permission. If you'll forgive me for saying so, we march enough miles in camp every day I suspect the distance will not be troublesome." *And we get nowhere, ever.*

"Those who have gone home for furlough do not all make it back safely . . ."

Or at all. Noah finished Nisbet's sentence in his mind. He knew the request for furlough was often denied for fear of desertion. "I would return and fulfill my obligation, sir, if you'll only allow me to take care of a family affair."

Nisbet eyed him warily. "Which is . . .?"

"Smallpox. My daughter—"

"If she has died from it by now, you can be of no use to her. If she is still sick, you cannot improve her condition. You might even bring the pestilence back with you. Two out of every three men who have died while in service to the Army of Tennessee have died slow, agonizing deaths not from bullets, but sickness. No, Private Becker, your request is irrefutably denied. Good day to you."

The words scraped like dry razor blades. Noah lowered his smoldering gaze to the flames tripping in the wind. Though frustration burned in his gut, he saluted and walked away. *And good day to you, sir.*

Noah seethed inside. *I should be home.* Snow crunching beneath his footsteps, he stalked toward his cabin and unfolded Caitlin's letter once again.

This time, however, it was Shakespeare's words that caught his eye.

> *Weary with toil, I haste me to my bed,*
> *The dear repose for limbs with travel tired;*

But then begins a journey in my head,
To work my mind, when body's work's expired:
For then my thoughts, from far where I abide,
Intend a zealous pilgrimage to thee,
And keep my drooping eyelids open wide...

Wind whipping his hair, he stilled his footsteps and lifted his face to the sky, streaked pastel by the fading sunset. *Are Ana and Caitlin looking at the same sky at this moment? Or are one or both of them taken ill to their beds even now?* His chest knotted, and suddenly, he was loath to be alone with his imagination.

From twenty yards away, baritone and tenor voices melded in hymnsong, a prelude for the evening service. *When through fiery trials thy pathway shall lie, My grace all-sufficient shall be thy supply...* Noah followed their harmony until he was sitting on a rough-hewn bench in the log chapel, staring at the cross of pine at the front.

Head in his hands, he prayed for Ana first and longest, and then for the roster of women suffering under his roof. Susan, Naomi, Minnie. When he reached Caitlin's name in his silent prayers, his heart caught in his throat. He should have asked after her family. If she died caring for his child, whom would he notify?

Guilt hovered over Noah throughout the service, clouding his countenance, slumping his shoulders. *How can I think so much of Caitlin when it is Ana, and only Ana, with whom I should be concerned?* His daughter was in danger. The fact that he could think of anything—anyone—else shocked him.

Later that night, he lay sleepless on his mattress. *For then my thoughts, from far where I abide, Intend a zealous pilgrimage to thee, And keep my drooping eyelids open wide . . .* Turning on his side, Noah punched his fist into his pine needle pillow, a scowl on his face. He needed to be home, regardless of what the law said. It was time, he decided, for grace.

Atlanta, Georgia
Monday, February 29, 1864

Wind feathered Caitlin's face, while her raw hands stung from the lye water that sloshed with Susan's soiled sheets in the laundry tub. Fingers clenched on the broom handle, she swirled the linens back and forth under a sky that threatened rain.

The days had inched by since Dr. Periwinkle's visit, each revolution around the sun moving as slowly as a slug through syrup, and now it was Leap Year day, as if this month of scourge refused to turn its page. Susan's descent into the throes of the disease had left her insensible as the smallpox multiplied on her body. Soon not an inch of her face was unmarked by the raised pustules. Her arms and legs were barnacled with sores as well.

For those yet untouched by the disease, one chore bled into another. In the kitchen, Ana ground corn into gruel. Minnie, Naomi, and Caitlin laundered soiled clothes and sheets, or attempted to feed Susan, or pumped water to drip into her mouth. Sleep grew as scant as their strength.

Caitlin threw a glance toward the house before hoisting the sheets into the tub of rinse water. As soon as this chore was done, she could steal a moment to record the day's progress. She kept a running letter to Noah on a page in her Shakespeare volume, while using different pages for her personal use as a journal. She would not burden Noah with the details of caregiving, and her own musings, but neither could she bear to keep her emotions bottled up inside her heart. Thank God that today she could pen good news. *Dear Mr. Becker,* she would write. *Susan is finally recovering, and still we see no sign of disease in anyone else. Our prayers have been answered.*

A moan sounded from inside the house, and Caitlin surmised it was Susan weeping at the face in the looking glass. As her pustules dried, dark red scabs took their place, covering large swaths of her skin with crust. The scabs were beginning to fall off now, but the pitted scars beneath were even deeper than Minnie's. A twinge of pity tweaked Caitlin's heart for the woman who once told her, "You're only as valuable as the man you catch." If Susan did not alter her attitude, her misery would be more contagious than her pox.

A door slammed, and Minnie hurried out to Caitlin. "It's Naomi. It has begun."

Caitlin's heart sank as she plunged her broomstick to the bottom of the tub. Further words unnecessary, she hurried to finish rinsing the sheets as Minnie pumped fresh water to cool Naomi's brow.

Inside the kitchen, a wooden bowl dropped onto the table, and a chair rasped against the floor. Ana staggered outside holding her stomach.

"Ana? What is—"

The girl bent and retched onto the winter-hardened ground. Tears gathered in Caitlin's throat against her will.

"Go to her," Minnie said, peeling the broomstick from Caitlin's stiffened grip and replacing it with the bowl of water.

"I'm scared," whispered Analiese as Caitlin neared. "Can't Papa come home now? I need him more than the army does."

The same question, over and over. "I'm sure he wants to be here, darlin', but I don't think he's allowed to come home. We can write to him, though." The same answer.

Ana groaned. "It's not like having him here."

"No, it isn't." But it's all they had. Caitlin offered Ana a tin cup of the water from the bowl. "But I'm right here, I won't leave you."

With fever-flushed face, Ana blinked up at Caitlin. "I wish you were my mama."

The words expanded in Caitlin's heart until the swelling nearly choked her. "I would be so proud and happy if you were my daughter." She kissed the top of her head.

By the time Caitlin and Ana reached their bedroom, Ana's body radiated heat. Gently, Caitlin helped her out of her clothes and laid her on the bed, wiping the perspiration from her skin with cool rags. "My body hurts!" she whimpered, thrashing about, as if searching for relief.

The doctor had said the joints would hurt and the muscles ache along with the fever. Opium would have calmed her, but of course there was none to be had for civilians, and not much more for the soldiers.

"You are fighting the disease, darlin', and it doesn't feel very good, I know."

"I feel so sorry for my body!" Ana's eyes were closed, and her brow creased even as Caitlin continued gently dabbing her skin.

From across the hall, Naomi moaned in fever's grip. As if on cue, Minnie bustled up the stairs and into Naomi's room with water and rags just as Susan began weeping anew from her room. "Why didn't I die? Why couldn't I have just died?" Her mournful refrain haunted the hall.

Hours passed as Caitlin wiped Ana's fiery skin with rags, held the bedpan for her, and passed Minnie on the stairs several times as they each emptied chamber pots and drew water for their patients. Darkness dropped like a curtain, shrouding the house until dawn lifted the veil, and the boot-black sky faded to Confederate grey.

Caitlin faded, too. Hunger gnawed and her hands shook until she grasped the cold metal of the pump. As fresh water sloshed into her pail, Caitlin pumped a prayer for help from the dormant well of her faith. She believed that God could flood her with new strength. She just did not know if He would.

Atlanta, Georgia
Monday, March 7, 1864

The empty pail in Caitlin's hand might as well have been full of grapeshot, so strong was its pull on her arm. Stiffly, she set it down on the back porch and leaned her throbbing head against the post before fetching more water. Her muscles ached. Her hair needled her scalp, even when she loosened her braid and let her hair fall down her back. *I only need sleep,* she told herself, but just as quickly dismissed the idea, though it was the dead of night. Even Rascal had given up following her and curled into a snoring heap.

Though few pocks had appeared on their bodies, Ana and Naomi were still clutched in the fever's talons, even after eight days. The cool rags Caitlin laid on Ana's steaming body warmed almost as soon as they touched her. Spooning water and tea past the girl's parched lips was painstaking and tedious. No, Caitlin could not sleep yet. Mustering the dregs of her strength, Caitlin plucked up her pail and stepped into the inky night toward the pump.

And froze. Was she hearing things? There it was again. Someone in the kitchen, or in the carriage house right next to it, or in the slave quarters right above it. *Food thief!* Or a vigilante, or a ly-out . . . The empty quarters Bess and Saul vacated were the perfect hiding place for any of them. But what could she do in her weakened state?

The pistol. A thin ribbon of energy trickled back through Caitlin's veins as she set her jaw and spun back toward the house. She nearly lost her balance as she turned, and bit her tongue to keep from growling in frustration.

As though she were walking under water, Caitlin dragged her feet up the stairs, and dug the derringer and its small lacquered box out of Noah's bureau. By the light of the fire, she loaded the pistol with shaking hands before sidling down the steps once more.

Her foggy mind could not keep up with her intentions. Her heart should be racing right now. Instead, it beat only sluggishly, as if there were not an intruder threatening her at this very moment. As if she did not hold in her trembling hand a weapon that she may or may not have loaded correctly.

She stepped out onto the porch, eyelids and pulse fluttering. "Who's there?" Her voice sounded weak and far away. She was an easy target, truly. *Help me.* The only prayer her mind could form.

The derringer grew slick in her palm, and seemed like ten pounds in her outstretched hand. She braced her right hand with her left and scanned the perimeter beyond the pistol's barrel. Though the night air was cool, perspiration sprang from her hairline, beneath her arms, her lower back, until her entire body was filmed with it.

A dark figure emerged from the shadows. She aimed, but her slippery, shaking thumb could not cock the hammer. "Stay back," she gasped. Gulping for air, she was drowning on dry land. Was this the fever that strangled her? Was this how Ana felt, and the rest of them?

The man surged forward, his silhouette rippling before her eyes.

The useless pistol clattering to the porch, Caitlin clawed at the bodice of her dress for breath. "I have the pox!" she forced out. "Stay away or you'll catch it."

Sweat rolled down between her shoulder blades, and slipped into her eyes. Caitlin meant to blink the moisture away, but once closed, her eyelids refused to lift. The floor tilted wildly beneath her feet, as a ship pitching and yawing in the rolling sea.

Caitlin sank down but as through water, her feet swept out from under her. Strong arms cradled her body like a hammock, swaying gently. A trace of alarm swam upstream through her murky consciousness, but the wind blew its lullaby, calming her. *Shhhhhh. Shhhhhhhh.*

Caitlin.

That voice. But it was impossible!

It's me. I'm home. I'll take care of you now.

"But I'm contag—"

Her warning swallowed up in darkness.

Noah's heart buckled as Caitlin surrendered to the fever in his arms. She was as light as cornhusk, and as brittle. Quickly, he carried her into the house and up the stairs to her room, but discovered the room was already occupied. The dying fire cast ghastly shadows upon the gaunt woman's pitted, yellow complexion as she slept. Were it not for the color of her hair, and the letter Caitlin had sent informing him of her illness, he would not have recognized Susan Kent, the woman who had once both captured his heart and shattered it. A bitter cocktail of shock and pity stole a moment at the foot of her bed. His grip on Caitlin tightened.

Then he heard it. A raspy, plaintive plea that sounded more like a kitten than a person. In three long strides, he was in his own room, and there, in his bed, was Ana.

"Papa?"

For a moment, words webbed in his chest. "I'm home, Dear Heart." Carefully, he laid Caitlin down next to Ana on the bed and cupped Ana's face in his hand. "I love you."

"I wanted you," she said. Her eyelids drifted closed, and Noah's love for her cracked open inside him until he could scarcely bear the ache.

Gathering her willow reed body into his arms, Noah pressed his Heart back into his chest, careful not to break her. His tears fell into her hair as he rocked her back and forth on the edge of the bed. Her entire body was soaked with sweat, her muslin chemise stuck to her body. But her skin was not hot. Hope flared, and he dared to believe her fever had broken.

"You're going to be fine now." It had to be true. It must be true.

Caitlin moaned in delirium behind them, and Noah turned in time to see her pulling at her clothes again, strands of hair clinging to her neck and face.

"Oh no." Ana's eyelids fluttered. "She is . . . so hot . . . Papa." The girl slumped against him, asleep once more in his arms. Tenderly, he laid her back down, then circled the bed to reach Caitlin's side. He brought his hand to her brow, and it nearly singed him.

Ignoring the lead suddenly filling his bones, he willed his mind to clear. She needed to be undressed, and quickly. *Minerva Taylor.* Wasn't she here somewhere? Minerva could help. Rubbing the back of his neck, he went in search of her.

He didn't have to go far. In one of the rear bedrooms, another smallpox patient was laid out on the bed. A rag still in her hand, Miss Taylor had collapsed on the floor beside her. Little wonder. From what Caitlin had written to him, the twenty-year-old music teacher had been nursing the sick for weeks now.

"Miss Taylor." Noah gently shook her shoulder, hoping his presence would not startle her out of her wits. His concern was in vain. She could not be roused from her Rip Van Winkle slumber. Giving up his original errand, Noah scooped up the thin woman and brought her to her own bed in the fourth room upstairs. She was doing her patient no good in a heap on the floor.

God, bless the women, Noah prayed, overcome by the hardships they endured. He returned to Caitlin's side and wasted no more time. What would have been criminal before the war now mattered not at all next to life itself. Speaking in low murmurs to her the entire time, Noah stripped Caitlin of her shoes, stockings, apron, skirt, petticoat, and shirtwaist until her limp body steamed beneath only her pantalets and chemise. Her chest heaved and sank with every labored breath, as though the shaft of moonlight that fell across the bed was the Angel of Death, strangling her.

If Noah could have lifted the invisible weight sitting on her chest, he would have. If he could have siphoned her fever into his own body with a kiss, he would have done it. Relief over Ana's broken fever battled with desperation over Caitlin's agony.

How was it possible that he should feel this so deeply? Ana was his Heart, she filled it completely. There was no room for anyone else.

But as he held her head in his lap and tipped water from a nearby tin cup past her lips, Caitlin's likeness, as he remembered her, unfurled in his mind. Sun-kissed and freckled, a rebellious strand of hair sashaying across her face. Eyes sparkling like dark brown sugar. And a scar she never spoke of lining her delicate but determined jaw. He saw her playing chess with Ana, making soap with Bess. He saw her with her nose in a book, or writing—to him.

When the cup was empty, Noah slid Caitlin's head back to the pillow and pumped fresh water outside. Back in his own room, he wiped both Ana's body and Caitlin's to cool and cleanse their skin. The air itself was tainted with the distinct odor of fever-sweat. Noah pushed up the window's sash, and the night breeze tousled his hair before sweeping through the room. The rustle of paper turned Noah's head until he found an open book on his writing table, the wind turning its pages recklessly.

Noah crossed the room, spread his hand on the pages. It was Shakespeare. And it was marked with a ribbon to a letter she had been writing him. With one more glance over his shoulder, he satisfied himself that he was not needed just now, and eased himself into the chair.

Dear Mr. Becker, he read, and dipped the page deeper into the stream of moonlight. It was a running letter, with only a sentence or two written every day for the last week, informing him of Ana's condition. Even though he had just seen Ana take a turn for the better with his own eyes, his heart dropped with every sanitized report.

He turned the page, and continued reading Caitlin's script, winding in and around the text.

Ana is ill, and I fear she is too weak to pull out of this dreadful disease by herself. I don't know what to do. I'm tired but I cannot sleep. I am hollow with hunger but the little nourishment we have must go to the sick. Thank God for Prudy's basket or we would surely starve.

Noah stopped, confusion creasing his brow. It was the first time Caitlin had ever written about herself. Why had she never told him?

I fear Noah misplaced his trust when he put it in me. I have been trying to take care of people since my father died when I was seventeen years old. Inevitably, I fail. God help me, I cannot fail with Ana.

How little Noah knew of this woman! What had she been through before he met her? Why hadn't he asked? *You know why,* the answer came. *You were keeping her at arm's length.* And now, his arms ached to hold her. His gaze lingered on her face for a moment before he turned back to the book.

I had a dream last night from which I was loath to wake. Ana was healthy, smiling, and laughing. Noah was back from the war all hearty and hale, and so was Jack. We were enjoying a picnic in an emerald green meadow under a brilliant, cloudless blue sky. We had chicken and lemonade, cold ham, hard rolls with butter, and even chocolate cake and milk. I was worried Jack and Noah both would hate me, but they embraced me instead, and held my hands, one on either side of me. Their arms were so strong and warm that I cried when I awoke and found myself without either of them . . .

Noah slammed the book closed. She was not writing to him anymore. He had been reading her journal, private words not intended for his eyes to see. *But who is Jack?* Noah scolded himself for even wondering. She had a right to have relationships he was not privy to. She was his daughter's governess. That was all.

Caitlin groaned and writhed under her sheet. Noah knelt by her side, wiping her with a cool rag once more.

"Ana . . . " Her voice was hoarse, her eyes still closed.

"Ana is here, her fever has broken." He circled the rag on her hand, her palm, and in between her fingers.

"Noah? We need you . . ."

His breath hitched at the sound of his Christian name on her parched lips. "I am here, Caitlin. I am here." He swept her hair from her neck, stroked with the cloth from her jaw to her shoulder and downward.

And stopped when his fingertips grazed a bump. Dropping the rag back into its bowl, he looked closer at her upper arm, traced a raised, jagged circle of flesh with the pad of his thumb. As though he'd been stung, he sat back on his heels and stared at the unmistakable evidence. Caitlin had been shot by a .58 caliber bullet, or something very similar. *But why?*

"Jack," she whispered. "I'm sorry . . . I lost you . . . you know . . . always loved you. . . ."

Questions tangled in Noah's weary mind. But none of the answers would matter if Caitlin did not recover. *Please God, bring her back to us. Or to Jack, whoever he is.* Noah had found himself between lovers before. This time, he'd stay out of the way.

Chapter Eighteen

Brooklyn, New York
Wednesday, March 9, 1864

With Aiden tugging on her hand, Ruby stared at Edward, measuring the light in his eyes against the shadows in her soul, and could not guess which way the scales tipped. "Is it very important to you?" she asked, keeping one eye on her restless twenty-one-month-old son.

"I should think you'd enjoy yourself."

"I've never been to a ball before." The mere idea of dancing should not chafe her so, and yet her skin tingled in protest.

"But this isn't just any ball—it's a Calico Ball!" He pointed to the notice in *Drum Beat*, the official newspaper of Brooklyn's Sanitary Commission Fair. "The women are supposed to wear plain calico dresses, you see, rather than silk and satin finery. The idea is that money that could have been spent on gowns and jewels should be donated to—" He underlined the text with his finger. "Ah yes, the families of our soldiers. It is to be the culmination of this grand fair."

He waved his arm, and Ruby followed its arc, craning her neck to appreciate the grand spectacle that surrounded them now. Brooklyn's Academy of Music on Montague Street had been transformed into an eleven-thousand-square-foot emporium sparkling with patriotism. Red, white, and blue sashes draped the soaring ceiling. Gaslights flooded the room with radiance, reflecting on silver and glass until the vast room seemed wainscoted and ceiled with rainbows. All around Ruby, silks and satins shimmered softly. Rare flowers perfumed the air, while piano music tinkled above the tumult.

"What do you think?" Edward prodded, his expression drooping with her hesitation.

"About the ball? It's a lovely idea for a very good cause."

"And will you go with me?" His brown eyes were warm, if wary.

"I'll think about it."

Edward's smile fell flat. "Very well. There is more to see. Shall we?" He scooped Aiden up and held him on his hip as they meandered along.

Crowds buzzed between sales booths of the Great Central Bazaar. Tables fairly sagging with donations were organized into departments: worsted goods; glassware; Parisian fancy goods; baskets; wax flowers; and men's, women's, and children's white goods. A soda fountain had been brought in to quench the fair-goers' thirst, and exhibitions of new homemaking devices attracted women like dust to a sunny parlor. There was enough here to keep Aiden busy looking—and if Ruby wasn't careful, grabbing—for days.

Near the stage wall, a mural of a Sanitary Commission field hospital served as backdrop to a nearby tent displaying the newest war photos and relics, plus wounded soldiers attended by Sanitary Commission workers. Edward caught Ruby's eye, concern etched in his face, as if he knew the scene would whisk her back to the Virginia Peninsula. The place where Matthew had died and Aiden was born. She nodded, and understanding arced between them. Wordlessly, Edward placed a hand on her shoulder. The touch burned through her dress until she could bear it no longer. She shrugged him off, lips twitching into a forced smile, and watched the spark vanish from his eyes.

Silently amid the din, they threaded a path through the crowd, until they neared an optical illusion called "The Skating Pond." Several smartly dressed skaters formed a tableau, mirrors doubling the effect. It was an indoor replica of the very pond at Central Park where Edward had first declared his intentions to Ruby. Her heart ached with the memory as she stood with him now.

Questions swirled in Edward's eyes as he looked at Ruby, and she feared she had no answers for him. Then the sound of his name on another woman's lips snapped his attention away.

"Mr. Goodrich! Oh, Mr. Goodrich!"

Ruby twisted to find the voice's owner.

"Miss Lanser!" Edward said, and Ruby's gut cinched.

Amy edged closer, with roses in her cheeks and fake snow glittering in her raven-black hair. "Mr. Goodrich, it is so good to see you again! My, what a dashing figure you cut in your cloak and top hat!"

"You're looking well yourself." Edward cleared his throat. "Allow me to introduce you to Ruby O'Flannery and her son, Aiden, here."

"Oh! Your immigrant friends, yes, my grandmother told me all about you. Charmed, I'm sure. Grandmother said you're a domestic, correct? Did you see the Hall of Manufacturers? They've got a whole line of sewing machines on display, plus Universal Clothes-Wringers and Hawe's Patent Clothes-Dryer! Wouldn't that make your job so much easier, Ruby?"

She means well. We are immigrants indeed. And I am a domestic. Still, the words were like sandpaper on sunburned skin. "Quite."

"How lovely of you to bring them to the fair, Edw—I mean, Mr. Goodrich. Isn't it marvelous what the ladies of Brooklyn have done? We're sure to beat out the Cincinnati Fair by a heap, and they pulled in $240,000!"

"Let's hope so, yes," Edward sputtered.

"Are you going to the Calico Ball on Friday?" Her sapphire eyes flashed brilliantly. "It's going to be the cherry on top of the whole fair!"

Edward looked at Ruby. "I'm not sure yet."

"Not sure? Whatever could keep you from it? You simply *must* come. But beware! I'll drag you onto the dance floor myself if I have to."

Amy glowed with energy, radiated warmth. She was young, vibrant, beautiful, talented, patriotic, and without blemish—either physical or emotional, Ruby suspected. *So very unlike me.* Perfect for a pastor's wife. And here she was, so ready to take Edward's hand, where Ruby recoiled from his touch. *Let him have her,* a voice whispered. *You could never make him happy.* The words were poison, ready for her to swallow.

Edward turned to Ruby then, the ghost of a smile on his lips, and memories flooded her mind. Edward teaching her the Bible in the garden, digging for worms with Aiden. Standing up to protect her during the draft riots last summer. Bringing her into his home, buying her a sewing machine. Drinking tea rather than dining out. She saw him for what he had been to her, and for what he promised to be.

Tears burned Ruby's eyes, her throat. *There is no fear in love; but perfect love casteth out fear.* Fear told her to give Edward up, but love said he was hers already. It was time to start acting like it.

Above the arch of the stage, in letters formed of tiny gas jets, blazed the inscription, "In Union Is Strength." Did it not apply to Ruby's life as well? In a surge of courage, she grabbed Edward's hand and twined her fingers between his. "We'll be at the ball. Both of us."

Edward clasped her hand, his brown eyes sparkling once again, and Ruby grinned at the pink peeking above his collar. If Amy spoke, Ruby didn't know it. If Aiden reached for her, she didn't notice. All she heard and saw was the man she loved.

New York City
Friday, March 11, 1864

Edward's pulse pounded to the beat of the quadrille music filling Knickerbocker Hall. Still seated at one of the dining tables with Ruby, he sipped his coffee, quail and broccoli cooling on his plate. All he could think about was the ring searing his thigh through his pocket.

"Can you believe what they've done with this place?" Edward asked Ruby lamely. His gaze skimmed the mirror-paneled walls doubling the sets of dancers, the gigantic two-hundred-light chandelier suspended from the ceiling, and the spicy-scented evergreens, woven into stars, twined around columns, and festooned from draperies. Flags, star-spangled bunting, and state coats-of-arms covered the walls and floor, with a handsome portrait of George Washington hung at the southern end of the building. "If you didn't know it, I bet you'd never believe they erected this structure just for the fair."

Stupid. Stupid. Stupid. Edward slumped back into his coffee before glancing apologetically at Ruby. "I rather wish I was debonair in a situation like this." His lips slanted.

Ruby laughed, and he laughed at himself with her. "Debonair? I don't even know what that means, but it sounds out of place for a Calico Ball. This is a charity event, nothing more, remember?"

But it could be. It could be much more, for the two of them. Edward attempted to drown his jangling nerves with more coffee while observing the sets of eight dancers, once more. He knew she wasn't comfortable with group dances, so they sat this one out. But when the song came to a close, he drew a deep breath, searching her face. "Would you . . . care to dance?"

"I would." She smiled bravely, though he knew that dancing would stretch her.

Lord, please give her the strength and courage to do this, he prayed as he led her out onto the floor. *Please don't let any dark memories be associated with my touch. And please—don't let me step on her toes.*

He encircled Ruby's waist with his right arm and held her right hand in his left. "OK?" Edward searched her eyes.

She nodded. Edward exhaled, then completely forgot what to do next. She smiled, waiting for him to lead her, but his feet refused to move. There they stood, in the middle of a room spinning with rustling skirts and flying coattails. But Edward was lost in her dazzling green eyes, the warmth of her body in his hands emptying his mind of all else.

"Forgive me," he stuttered. "I'm not the best partner."

"Yes, you are." A smile curved her lips. "You are the best partner for me. This is just about my speed."

He chuckled. "Quite. But shall we try moving, as well? Just for fun. They seem to like it." Edward nodded at the couples whirling around them, and Ruby laughed.

Finally finding his footing, in the next measure of music, Edward led her into a swirling waltz that even camouflaged his limp, and her red hair shimmered in the light. Ruby was as light on her feet as she was in his hands. He dared to hope that the glimmer in her eyes spelled joy.

This was what he wanted. To hold Ruby without apology, and for her to delight in belonging to him. He reveled in her nearness, and only prayed he could be restrained enough not to draw her closer still. Edward understood her aversion to touch, but in time, surely that would heal. He had faith in her, and in God.

———

By the time the music ended, Ruby's spirit soared. She had done it. By the grace of God, she had waltzed with Edward and not pulled away once. She even enjoyed being whisked around the room. It was methodical, predictable, and temporary. *Nothing to fear. No fear.*

Edward bowed, while Ruby dipped in a low curtsy. "Well done," he whispered to her, his smile as big as his heart. Then a shadow passed over his face. "Walk with me?"

"What's wrong?" But she let him lead her off the floor and out the door until they were on Montague Street, next to the covered bridge connecting Knickerbocker Hall with the Academy of Music. He shrugged out of his jacket and draped it over her shoulders, wrapping her in his scent and warmth. Ruby's heart thudded. "I—I thought you wanted to go to the ball."

"I did. We went. I wanted to be with you."

A carriage trundled over the cobblestones, and Edward waited until it passed. "I *want* to be with you."

"I want to be with you too, Edward."

"Then be my wife."

He pulled a ring from his pocket and slipped it on her trembling finger.

"Are you—are you sure?"

"I wouldn't ask you if I wasn't. Please. I will never lift a finger against you. I won't leave you. You'll never have to worry about money again, or about Aiden's future. I love you, Ruby. And I'll spend the rest of my life showing you how much." A lump shifted in his throat. "Please say yes," he whispered.

Hope went to Ruby's head like champagne. "Aye," she whispered. "Yes, yes."

Edward opened his hands, and she placed hers in them. Slowly, he pulled her closer. "May I?" His voice was husky, and she did not have the strength—or the will—to refuse him. She stepped into his embrace, felt his arms wrap around her, her head tucked under his chin.

"You are safe," he murmured. "You are mine." His heart pounded in her ears, matching her own quickened rhythm.

'Tis Edward, she reminded herself when her blood rushed in her ears. *I'm not trapped, I am loved. It is affection, not violence.* He pressed a kiss to her hair—and stopped. "Thank you," he said, and released her.

Ruby's heart squeezed in her chest. He loved her, yet did not take from her what she was not yet ready to give. Someday, Ruby would be able to love him with all she had. She was sure of it.

Someday.

Atlanta, Georgia
Saturday, March 12, 1864

Susan watched from the doorway as Noah bent his ear to Caitlin's chest, listening for her heartbeat, no doubt. It had been five days since he had swooped back into town like some old-fashioned fairy-tale hero, and exactly thirty-nine days since Susan had seen Zeke Murphy. Truly, she should stop counting. She'd never see him again. If, by some chance she would have that opportunity, she would spit in his face the way that diseased soldier at the Athenaeum had spit on her. If it wasn't for Zeke, none of this would have happened. *Too bad I can't spit on Zeke myself.*

Susan brought her hand to her cheek, each pit in her complexion a fingertip-sized crater. It would be a miracle indeed to get any man now, even a foreigner with a German accent. *Look at him, hovering over that girl like she's Varina Davis herself.* The lines etched into his face, the tenderness in his strong touch—it scorched Susan's eyes. What had Caitlin McKae ever done to lasso the man that way? He could fall ill, himself, could even die from nursing Caitlin!

Even more troubling—why had no man ever shown that kind of concern for Susan? Watching him day after day carved out a piece of her soul, or perhaps just reminded her of what was already missing. She had known lust. She had known pleasure. Certainly, she had known power. But in Noah's quiet, selfless vigilance, he showed Susan—flaunted the fact, really—that she had not known love. Even after Noah had offered it to her so many years ago.

Until now, she'd almost always gotten what she wanted. Now, Noah Becker made Susan wonder if what she craved, and received, had been shoddy—a worthless imitation that falls apart at the slightest strain. She hated him for that.

Rascal kept vigil alongside Noah for the woman who had replaced Susan in the dog's affections. She had never liked that dog, and both the canine and his owner knew it. Against Susan's wishes, Noah had accepted him from a cash-poor yeoman farmer as payment for legal services. The dog had pursued Susan's attentions so much, and she called him a rascal so often, that soon he believed it was his name and answered to it. Rascal represented the first time Noah had not bowed to her wishes. The dog's presence grated her pride now as much as it had then.

Susan's chest constricted, squeezing her heart into an unnatural shape like the corset compressing her middle. "Good to see you, too," she finally said to Noah's back, the lie slippery on her tongue. It wasn't good at all unless she could maneuver him the way she once had.

He turned, his tobacco-brown hair disheveled from his lonely vigil, and years peeled away between them. Noah had wanted her once, and she'd teased him mercilessly. Today, it was pity, not longing, that flickered in his steel-blue eyes. It infuriated her.

Noah approached her then, and she recoiled, though it was he who ought to cringe from her. "It's good to see you up."

"Honestly, Noah, one would think you were in love with her, the way you're acting."

A sad smile curved his lips, and comprehension glimmered in Susan's muddied mind. By mere accident, she had spoken the truth.

"It isn't decent! She's the governess, and she talks like a Northerner!"

"Country of origin has never held the same import for me as it has for you, Miss Kent."

"Do you love her?" She was aghast.

"Not that it's any of your business. It doesn't matter, anyway."

"It matters to me."

He frowned, crossed his arms. "I cannot think why. It certainly didn't matter to you when I loved you."

Susan paused, disarmed for a moment, before taking up a different tack. "You never touched me with such care."

"You never let me. But I *treated* you exactly the way you wanted to be treated. I left you alone. Hid your shame behind my name. Raised your daughter. In fact, my care has never ceased. Now, speaking of Ana, I'd like to go find her if you don't mind."

"Minnie is reading to her downstairs. Naomi is there, too." Both Naomi and Ana were recovering now, with only a few marks on their faces to show for their ordeal. Not like Susan, whose entire face had been almost one solid crust of scabs. The itch alone had nearly driven Susan mad. "Ana's fine. But I'm not."

Noah's eyes glinted as he rubbed a hand over his sandpaper jaw. "I can see that."

Susan clenched her teeth, shored up her courage for her next performance. "Noah, please. I didn't mean to argue. Why do you think I came here to your house in the first place, if not to find you? I missed you, Noah. I—" She cast her lashes down out of habit before peering up at him again. "I need you."

Rascal sauntered between them and leaned into Noah's leg, groaning absurdly when Noah scratched behind his ear. "You do not need me."

"Yes, I do!" Susan ratcheted her voice above the ridiculous canine ruining the mood. "And Ana needs a mother. Have a care, Noah."

"Please. Such familiarity is no longer appropriate. If you must address me, you will call me 'Mr. Becker.'"

"Oh come now, there's no need to be so cross." Susan's heart galloped after him. He was slipping through her fingers like melted beeswax, when he had been so moldable in her hands when she met him. Her father had played him like a pawn, and forced her to marry and move away with him to Georgia, a banishment for her wayward behavior and tendency toward scandal. *I'll not stand by and watch you drag our family name through the mud,* he'd told her. But nothing could induce her to love Noah Becker when her heart already belonged to another. It was hardly Susan's fault that her lover was already married.

Looking at Noah, now, though, his face settled into tense lines, Susan could barely detect the young man she once had eating out of her hand.

"It is enough that I allow you into my home until you can find more appropriate housing elsewhere."

Susan blinked. "And leave Ana? How could I?"

Noah stepped closer, towered over her. "It is my understanding, Miss Kent, that Analiese means very little to you at all." His voice was as dark as the shadows beneath his eyes. "So then, how is it that you are here at all? What is it, exactly, you hope to gain from us?"

240

"You took me in before, I assumed you'd take me in again." She held her breath, her ideas of using Ana as a bargaining chip with her father locked safely within her mind.

"I beg you, do not trample upon my hospitality further. I would hate to cast out a convalescent refugee."

Susan gasped. "Is that what you think of me?"

"That is what you are. I mean no disrespect, but you cannot think to conjure up any warm feelings whatsoever by bringing up our abbreviated history. Now, I believe we are quite finished."

"You would not separate me from my own daughter!"

"You separated yourself from Ana the very *day* you were strong enough to walk away." Thunder rolled in Noah's voice, lightning flashed in his eyes. "She is more my daughter than she is yours."

"How dare you!" Susan cried. "She is nothing to you."

"She is my very heart. You granted me legal custody of her when she didn't even know night from day. This conversation is pointless." He began to descend the stairs, knuckles white on the railing, then turned back to her. "I'll not evict you while you are still recovering. But please, make a good faith effort to find other arrangements for yourself."

"Where, *Mr.* Becker? Hotels are charging forty dollars *per night*. On eleven dollars a month, even you could not afford it, and I have no income at all. If you throw me out, I will be destitute. And as my pockmarks will attract no suitors, if there are any out of the army anyway, I shall be forced into an occupation in which one's face can remain in the dark."

Noah dipped his head.

"Are you bowing to me now?"

"I am praying, Miss Kent, that I will learn to love grace more than I love the law."

"Capital idea, since you broke the law to be here." If he truly had furlough, Colonel Lee would not have come pounding on the front door looking for him the other day with a telegram from Dalton in his hand. And Minnie would not have shouted through the door that to search the house would mean certain contagion for the intruder.

"You may stay. For now." Somehow, he did not look beaten.

And yet, she had won. "I knew you wouldn't turn your back on me."

But he walked down the stairs and did not look back. Susan was alone with her scars in his wake.

———

Atlanta, Georgia
Thursday, March 17, 1864

Jack smiled at her, then, but shook his head. *What have you done?* He flipped the ends of her freshly cropped hair, then turned her face with his thumb to her chin. The smile vanished when he saw the ragged cut on her jaw. *Caitlin, what have you done?*

Shhhhh! She cut her voice low. *My name is Davis Walker now, and I've just enlisted, same as you. Mother will be glad for the income.*

What do you mean you've enlisted?

Caitlin shrugged. *You should know. The medical examination consisted of a few questions and a listen to my heartbeat. I'm strong and healthy, and Lincoln has asked for 75,000 volunteers.*

Men. Jack shot back. *He asked for 75,000 men. This is not a game of dress-up, you know.*

But she did not back down. *I am not the first woman to serve and I certainly won't be the last. Deborah Sampson, Revolutionary War. Lucy Brewer, War of 1812. Eliza Allen, Mexican War.*

Jack rolled his eyes. *Save your history lesson for your students.*

But Caitlin had no students. She only had regret for opportunity lost, and guilt for a murder she did not intend to commit. She also had Jack. She would not fail him the way she had failed her mother. *I am my brother's keeper.*

I am a man.

You are seventeen.

I don't need a keeper.

Then accept me as your friend.

They shook hands then, but an earthquake split the ground between them. Caitlin tightened her clutch on Jack's hand, but it was slipping. The earth plunged beneath him, even as it surged up like a cliff under Caitlin.

Release me! Jack yelled, wiggling free of her grasp. *I can take care of myself!*

The world groaned apart, an abyss dividing them in mere seconds.

Jack! She splayed herself on the ground, reaching down into the void but could not see him. *Where are you? Are you hurt?*

Get back from the edge!

But she could not see him. *I won't leave you!*

The decision is not yours to make! We are already parted. Have faith! God will not waste this great divide.

The cliff began to crumble beneath her, and she scrambled backwards to keep from falling in. She should never have let him go. *Jack!* She cried again, tears glazing her cheeks.

Caitlin. The name rumbled on someone else's lips, calling her back from the brink. Where was the voice coming from? Wrapped in darkness and pressure, she was suddenly standing on the ocean floor, yet somehow able to breathe. All was madness.

Caitlin, it's all right. Come back to me. Please. Please don't go. Noah was with her. Why could she not see him? His hand was on her brow. Her cheek. Brushing her hair from her face. Gently pressing her hand.

She caught it, squeezed it, would not let go. It was an anchor, pulling her up through leagues of muddied coherence.

I'm here now. And I'll help you find Jack.

With a gasp, Caitlin broke through the surface and splashed back into wakefulness. Shock jolted her weary heart. For there was Noah Becker, kneeling beside the bed, his bowed head atop her hand.

Please, Noah prayed, *bring her back.* Flames licked in the fireplace, but did little to thaw his weary body. Stubborn winter had poured half an inch of ice on Atlanta yesterday, and the chill probed every corner of the house. Would spring never come? Would Caitlin never awake?

Noah kissed the top of her hand, then held it against his cheek. When her slender fingers twitched, he looked up. Her face blurred in his vision before he could blink the moisture away.

"Caitlin," he whispered. "Thank God."

She reached out and patted the empty bed beside her. "Ana . . ."

"She's fine." He still did not release her hand. "You did well caring for her. I thank you."

"Naomi? Susan?"

"All recovering. It is you we are most concerned with now."

She pushed herself up to sit and lifted trembling fingers to her face.

"Just a few tiny bumps is all. You are just as beautiful as you ever were." The words slipped out before he could catch them. His face burned. It was Jack she wanted. Not him.

Caitlin licked her lips, and he handed her a cup of water, then sat on the chair near the bed. After taking a drink, she cradled the cup in her hand. "I—I'm sorry I tried to shoot you." She cleared her throat. "That was you, wasn't it?"

Laughter rumbled in his throat. "I was not in much danger, despite your best efforts."

"But you are now—aren't you? Have you had this disease before?"

Noah shook his head.

Panic flared in her eyes. "Then why on earth are you here?"

"My daughter was in trouble. Did you think I would not move heaven and earth to come to her side?"

"Of course. I know why you would come for Ana. But why are you *here* in this room with me? Has Minnie collapsed?"

A smile tugged at his lips. "Miss Taylor is fine, although exhausted from her monthlong vigil. I insisted on caring for you myself, with minimal help from her."

Logs snapped in the quiet between them. Until, "How long?"

"You've been out ten days. I was so afraid you were slipping from me. From us." He looked away, lest she see in his eyes the longing that seared his heart. "This is my fault," he said at length. "I release you from your contract as Ana's governess. Miss Taylor says she will assume the role if you choose to leave."

"You want me to leave?"

Of course not. "I want you to be safe, and happy. Surely you have— family—or a loved one to whom you can go?" *Someone named Jack?* "Some place other than Atlanta. The city is the known target of the Federals' spring campaign."

She blinked. "I don't want to leave you. Or Ana. I told her I'd be with her, and I intend to keep my promise."

"Your sense of duty does you credit," said the soldier who was absent without leave.

"Not just duty. Love." She locked eyes with him for a moment. "For Analiese. I love her, truly. I want to stay. But—"

———

She should ask about Susan. But the last thing she wanted was to bring another woman—even her name—into the room with them. Through the open window, bitter wind sliced through the room, awakening her senses. Noah knelt beside her, his blue eyes glittering, with a smile on his face she wished was for her alone. Did he feel something toward her, or had it all been a mirage? Her name on his lips, his lips on her hand, his hand on her face . . . Even if those things were inconsequential to him, he risked his very life by being with her. Surely that meant something. *Doesn't it?*

"You asked for Jack."

Oh. Her eyelids dropped as quickly as her stomach.

"Would you like to tell me who he is?" Noah's voice was kind, but insistent.

Caitlin's mouth felt as though it was filled with cotton. "You're sure I said 'Jack'?"

"Yes."

"When?"

"More than once. Including just now, before you woke up. If you love him, I will do what I can to help you find him."

Love him? Of course she loved Jack, but it was not what she felt for Noah. Her fingers flew to her unraveling hair and began braiding the plaits once more. "I was delirious, you can't trust what I said."

"But I trust what you say to me now." He returned to the chair next to her bed and leaned forward, elbows on his knees, hands clasped together. "Jack is important to you, isn't he? You must want to be with him."

Tears bit her eyes. *You are important to me. I want to be with you, and Ana.* But her tongue refused to say it.

Noah raked his hand through his hair and sighed. "I must know your answer before I go."

Caitlin's fingers stilled. "Go?"

"And soon. I must return to my regiment, now that you and Ana are no longer in danger. I took an oath. For better or worse, my word is binding."

"So is mine," Caitlin managed to say. "I'm staying here with Analiese until you return."

"I know Ana will be thrilled to hear that, Miss McKae."

Formality snapped back into place, an invisible shield between them. *Fine.* She had no place to go, anyway.

But you would not leave now even if you could, her heart whispered. *You would stay in enemy territory, where food and medicine are scarce but suspicion and crime are rampant, in a city sure to meet with destruction. And for what?*

Maybe Mother was right. Love would be her undoing.

Atlanta, Georgia
Tuesday, March 22, 1864

And then he was gone. Though Noah had been home for two weeks, it felt like only the beat of a heart. The groans tearing from Ana's throat bent the girl in half. Caitlin's heart felt as though it was being ripped from her chest. Ignoring the calendar, snow fell as he stole away, and did not stop until the ground was covered with a blanket four inches deep, suffocating the fruit just beginning to grow. Moonlight doubled itself on the thick layer of white, illuminating Atlanta's night sky with the fairy glow of a million sweet gum globes. Caitlin could not help but think that when Noah left, spring vanished with him, and that this winter would never end.

———

Outside Dalton, Georgia
Saturday, March 26, 1864

Shirtless, Noah collapsed to his hands and knees on the frosty ground as soon as the officer cut the rope from the tree trunk. The metallic taste of blood filled his mouth, streaming, it seemed, from both inside and out. His nose was broken, and his eyes so blackened one had swollen shut completely, the other a mere slit. But it was his back that screamed in agony. Every lash of the leather whip filleted his flesh into a map of crimson gullies and streams. His body shuddered with cold and pain.

An officer squatted beside him, leaning in until Noah could smell the tobacco on his breath. "This is how we treat runaways when we're playing *nice*. Next time, you'll be facing a firing squad." He stood, slammed his boot into Noah's ribs before leaving, spiking darts of pain through his core.

Gradually, the ring of muddy shoes surrounding Noah dispersed, save one pair. Ross, his old friend, came near and bent down. "Are you all right, Herr Becker?"

"Ach." Noah winced as he drew a breath, and spat a mouthful of blood on the ground. In truth, just drawing air was excruciating. "Paper cuts and bruises. I've hurt myself worse learning to ride a horse."

"Would you do it again?"

He grinned, though every inch of his face protested the slight movement. "Without question, Ross. Without question."

"TIME AFTER TIME had we been told of the severity of General Sherman until we came to dread his approach as we would that of a mighty hurricane which sweeps all before it, caring naught for justice or humanity. Our fear of his coming, however, did not prevent it."

—MARY RAWSON, 16-year-old resident of Atlanta

"WE CAN HEAR THE CANONS and muskets very plane, but the shells we dread. One has busted under the dining room which frightened us very much. One passed through the smokehouse and a piece hit the top of the house and fell through but we were at Auntie Markham's so none of us were hurt."

—CARRIE BERRY, 10-year-old resident of Atlanta

Act Four

ENEMY AT THE GATE

Chapter Nineteen

Outside Dalton, Georgia
Wednesday, May 4, 1864

*P*ine-scented wind swirled Noah's hair as he watched fifteen barefoot soldiers being tied to the stake. Fifteen coffins lay before them. The blood-red ground yawned expectantly, waiting to swallow their bodies whole.

Impotent anger flashed through him. *They are not the enemy.* But they had broken the law, as Noah had. Their crime: attempting to reach families who depended on them for life itself. Their mistake was getting caught before they could return—if they ever planned to. Their sentence: death.

Now Ross stood along with fourteen others, all uneducated and poor, each of them no doubt thinking of the mouths at home he would never help feed again.

Fifteen rifles cracked the air, and fifteen bodies jerked and slumped against their stakes. With no loved ones surrounding them, with no tombstones to mark their graves, with absolutely no glory enshrouding them, the earth received their flesh.

With the taste of saltpeter stinging his throat, Noah stepped forward to help shovel dirt atop Ross's coffin. Each spadeful of soil he dropped in the grave thudded in his own heart, as if he were burying his former self along with Ross.

———

New York City
Monday, May 16, 1864

"Such a bonnie bride you'll be!" Emma gushed as she sewed buttons onto a gown for Ruby's trousseau.

"Well, the dress will be beautiful, at least." Ruby glanced at the wedding gown now draped over the ironing board, waiting to be pressed. Since she could not wear white for a second wedding, she had chosen a light violet shade of serviceable linen, not silk, in keeping with the spirit of the times.

"Aye, but the lass inside the gown is what your Edward will have his eye on, he will!"

"Emma." Ruby let the wristband of Edward's shirt fall into her lap. "I'm terrified."

All jauntiness vanished from Emma's face, then. "You don't mean he's hurt you—"

"No, no, nothing like that. It's just that—I don't desire marital intimacy. At all. I have no appetite for it. All those memories come flooding back and I—it just makes me feel sick. I don't know how I'll ever be a good wife if I don't get over this, but I don't see how I can."

Emma nodded. "Aye, I do understand. But surely he does, too. Doesn't he know why?"

Ruby slanted her a gaze before picking up the wristband again. "He knows half." She plunged a needle through the buttonhole. "The half before Matthew went to war."

253

Emma's eyes widened. She whistled, low. "Bedad, Ruby! I thought you said Edward was a good man, with no reason to fear a life with him!"

"True enough."

"Then why do you fear telling him your whole truth?"

Ruby pulled the thread through another hole and pulled it taut. "I *hate* my whole truth. Right now he believes I was wronged, and that's the end of it. He has no idea how I put food in my belly those awful months after Matthew left. I don't want him to know. I don't want to remember it myself, let alone talk about." Tears burned her eyes. "I don't want to see the look on his face. I don't want to lose him, Emma."

Emma shook her head. "I'm a wee bit shocked at you. Or maybe I just didn't hear you right all these months we've been sewing together. This thing called grace. You say it's changed your life, changed who you are."

"It has!"

"Then why be afraid to tell him something that has already been—what's the word you like to use? Redeemed. Aye, that's it. Aren't you redeemed?"

Ruby's pulse quickened. "Yes. I'm redeemed. But to name my past is to relive it! I only want to move on and never look back."

"You're lookin' back now, Ruby Shannon. And on your wedding night, it's going to come back to you clear enough. Don't you think that if Edward understands grace, he will give some to you, when you tell him the truth? He adores you, you know."

Warmth spread in her cheeks. "It will hurt him, immeasurably."

"Better coming from you than from someone else."

Ruby locked eyes with Emma. "What does that mean? Are you going to take it upon yourself, like Sean did?"

"No, darlin'. It's not my place. It's yours."

Ruby sighed. "What he doesn't learn won't hurt him."

"If you don't mind my sayin' so, it already has. You can't think he enjoys that cold shoulder you're so fond of turning, can you?"

"He is very patient."

"He won't be forever."

Further argument refused to form on Ruby's tongue. Emma was right. But, "I can get past this."

Emma cocked an eyebrow. "Your wedding is not three weeks away."

Ruby swallowed the anxiety growing sharp against her throat. "I'll be all right and there will be nothing to explain. He never has to know."

———

New York City
Saturday, June 4, 1864

"I now pronounce you man and wife. You may kiss the bride."

Edward's heart tripped over itself as his lips met Ruby's. The touch of her sweet lips sent desire charging through his veins, and for the first time since he'd started courting her, he was not afraid of it, or ashamed. She was his wife now. Soon they would be bonded in God's eyes, too.

Just a little while longer, he told himself as they stood apart from each other and faced the people who had gathered for the wedding. As the reverend introduced "Rev. and Mrs. Edward Goodrich," every smile he saw tugged on him. For there, in the garden of the Waverly brownstone, were the people he and Ruby held most dear.

Dappled with sunlight, Caroline Waverly and her daughter Charlotte beamed, two-year-old Aiden waddling back and forth between them, bunches of grass in his fists. Alice and Jacob Carlisle took turns cuddling their cooing three-month-old baby girl, Josephine. Nose red, Aunt Vivian dabbed her eyes with a handkerchief, and Edward thought he even saw George smile. Rounding out the group was brave Emma Connors, Ruby's oldest friend.

The rest of the celebration was a blur to Edward. The summer evening whirred with cicadas and laughter, and glowed with sunset and congratulations. During the feast, Jacob had said something about the campaign for Atlanta being critical to Lincoln's reelection, and Aunt

Vivian had whitened. Though Charlotte must have longed for Caleb Lansing, her fiancé in the Army of the Potomac, she had flashed Edward a brilliant smile and warmly squeezed his hand. Thank God she did not affect him the way she once had. Edward only had eyes for Ruby.

My wife. He rolled the words over in his mind as he watched her with Aiden and the rest of their guests. He could scarcely believe she was the same woman she was when he met her two years ago. And he could hardly believe she was his. Truly, the Lord had blessed him with a woman who was both upstanding and beautiful. The violet gown she had made for herself skimmed her curves perfectly before the skirt draped becomingly over their hoops. His hands burned to draw her close. But if he had waited this long, he could wait a few hours longer.

"Did you get lost in there, darling?" Edward's voice prodded gently from the other side of the water closet door.

Ruby stared at her reflection in the mirror. "I'll be right out." *Lord, help me.* Her hair fell in a curtain to her waist, draping the ivory satin nightgown Caroline had given her for her wedding night. *I love him,* she reminded herself. *I love him. I can do this.* Though they had agreed not to spend money on a true honeymoon, he had surprised her with this night at the St. Nicholas hotel, and had arranged for Aiden's care during their absence.

When she emerged, Edward rose from his perch on the edge of the bed, his merlot-colored robe falling open slightly to reveal his bare chest. Her breath hitched and she fought the urge to look away.

"You look—you are—so beautiful." His deep brown eyes captured hers. He cupped her face in his hand and bent his head to hers. Heart pounding, she told herself to return his kiss, and her lips obeyed. His hand slid to the back of her head, his fingers plunging deep in her hair while his other arm circled her waist and pressed her gently to him. His tenderness was unparalleled by any man she'd ever been with, and Ruby's spirit soared with hope. Of course she could respond to Edward.

"I love you," he whispered before kissing her ear, her neck, her shoulder. Her knees weakened, and he guided her to the bed and turned the gas lamp down low. "I'm not going to hurt you. We won't do anything you don't want to do."

Ruby nodded, though tears threatened. She took a deep breath and let her head rest on his outstretched arm upon the pillow. "Just give me a minute."

He did. And then, to her utter shock, he prayed. "Lord, You know what Ruby's been through. You know how deeply she has been hurt. Please bind up her wounds, and cast the past behind her as far as the east is from the west. Help us, Lord, to enjoy the gift of intimacy as You designed it to be enjoyed between a loving husband and wife. Amen."

The tears broke free, then, and slid down Ruby's cheeks as she silently thanked God for Edward's care.

"Is it too much?" he asked, and she answered him with a kiss. This time, she did not have to tell her body what to do. Her hand cradled the back of his neck before sliding down to his shoulder, inside his robe. A faint moan sounded from his throat as he covered her hand atop his thudding heart. He deepened the kiss, and she breathed him in—until the smell of his hair pomade pried her back like a crowbar.

Suddenly, it was no longer Edward who held her in the shadows of a rented room, but another. The memory, now triggered, was so strong it stole her breath. Her skin crawled as if his mustache tickled her body once again. She felt exposed. Endangered. Vulgarities hissed so loudly in her ears she could barely hear Edward ask what was wrong.

"Stop, stop!" she cried to both memory and Edward. Only her husband obeyed. "I can't, not yet," she whispered. "I'm sorry."

"Don't be," he said, but his stricken face betrayed him.

Hot tears coursed down her cheeks and into her ears as she stared at the ceiling, covers pulled up tight beneath her chin. Edward had not hurt her. But her past was enough to hurt them both.

Kennesaw Mountain, Georgia
Saturday, June 25, 1864

After seventeen days of hard rain earlier this month, Noah was grateful for today's sunshine—even though now his clothes were plastered to his body with sweat instead. While other soldiers felled trees with which to construct defensive works, Noah's muscles strained against their seams as he heaved his weight into a cannon and shoved it up the rocky slope. The skeletal Rebel mules could not handle the eight-hundred-foot-high camel hump called Kennesaw Mountain. The Yanks would not take it either, some said.

Of course, that's what they had said about Lookout Mountain and Missionary Ridge, and here he was, shouldering another cannon up another hill, but much farther south and closer to home. Kennesaw was only twenty-two miles from Atlanta.

"Steady, Becker." An officer muttered next to Noah as he mopped his brow, but Noah did not need the reminder. Sherman had 254 pieces of artillery, Colonel Nisbet had said, while General Johnston, who had replaced Bragg after the failures at Chattanooga, had 154. "That hunk of iron might save your life."

And it might not, Noah mused. The Rebel ammunition was just as inferior in quality as it was in quantity. The range on some of these guns was morbidly laughable. Many shells refused to explode at all even if they did reach their targets. Johnston had done as well as a general could be expected to do in his position. The army loved him. *But are popularity and valiant efforts enough?*

For more than three weeks, the Confederate army had bloodied the pursuing Yanks, felling thousands of their men before falling back themselves. At Dalton. Resaca. Cassville. Allatoona. New Hope Church—now known by those who fought there as Hell's Hole—Pickett's Mill, Dallas. The Rebels were outnumbered, 70,000 Confederates to the 90,000 Federals whose pursuit would not relent. Though more Yankees than Rebels had been slain, the Union army seemed to regenerate itself like a giant blue lizard, snaking south over everything in its path. Seventy-five miles of "terrain that could not be crossed" had, indeed, been lost to the Northern army. Sherman would stop at nothing.

The Confederacy, however, stops at one meal a day. Noah's stomach growled audibly as he shoved the cannon into place at the top of the hill. While the Yankee supply line delivered ample food to them, even in enemy territory, Confederate Congress had passed a bill this spring slashing their already meager provisions. One ration a day for every soldier. No matter how many miles marched, or gallons perspired, or rounds fired. One meal was all. One and a quarter pounds of meal, a quarter-pound of hominy, and one-third pound of bacon. *Union blockades, loss of farmland, and restrictions on transportation mandates the reduction,* Congress said.

Noah's frustrated sigh sounded more like a growl. Weren't the odds against them high enough? The next time battle broke, would the hungry men fight harder for their homes, or faint in the Georgia sun?

Atlanta, Georgia
Monday, June 27, 1864

"When will we stop retreating?" "Where will we go if they come to Atlanta?" "Is my Papa coming home?"

Questions flapped madly in the Becker household while black-bordered death notices spread like sores in the newspapers. Fear played upon nerves like a bow screeching across violin strings until Caitlin's head ached with the clamor.

The world was shifting beneath their feet. Thousands of slaves, impressed from owners all over the county, had trudged by with picks and shovels on their shoulders, and sweat on their brows. Among them, with more swelling in his arthritic knuckles and more salt in his pepper-black hair than Caitlin remembered, was Saul. They were digging more ditches encircling the city, though miles of breastworks already ringed it, farther out. *Merely a precaution,* the newspapers said. *I can hold Atlanta forever,* Johnston said, as refugees poured in from upper Georgia, and the backwash of battle's carnage flowed into Atlanta on railroad tracks that never cooled. Naomi and Minnie nursed in the hospitals, while Caitlin and Ana made biscuits by the wheelbarrowful to send with them, and to the slaves digging ditches, who received no rations at all. Susan did nothing to help.

And then, one grey morning, they heard it.

"Is it thunder?" Ana's face was white.

Caitlin shook her head, flashes from Bull Run, Williamsburg, and Fair Oaks washing over her, as she whisked batter for corn pone. It was cannon. It was Noah. *Was it also Jack?*

Later, the din of a crowd drowned the roll of artillery, drawing Caitlin and Ana out from their home. They followed the noise to the City Hall Square and across the railroad tracks, stopping on Peachtree Street just south of its intersection with Marietta. Rain fell in silver gossamer threads, and it seemed that the whole town had packed itself beneath the wooden awnings of the stores.

Some of them tried to cheer for the motley parade blurring in Caitlin's vision. A lump wedged itself in her throat at the sight of the state militia and the Home Guard bobbing down Peachtree and out of Atlanta via Marietta. They were smooth-cheeked boys and grey-bearded men with faces seamed with age. Some of the men were shielded from the rain by umbrella-wielding slaves, marching along beside them. Scattered between were precious few young men wearing the cadet grey uniform of military academies. The fortunate ones carried old flintlocks. Others had shovels and hoes. Many carried bowie knives in their boots and Joe Brown's Pikes in their hands, as if long sticks with iron-pointed tips could be a match for shot and shell. Many had no weapons at all, but would have to arm themselves from killed and captured Yankees. Johnston had called for men to replace the thousands he'd lost in retreat. And these were the troops he was getting.

Caitlin shuddered, vivid images splashing against mind. Her own crisp blue regiment marching beneath its emerald-green flag on the Virginia Peninsula. Yellow-faced soldiers tortured by fever and dysentery, mosquitoes, and black flies. The battles that followed anyway, leaving human wreckage in garish shades of red and black. Her hands felt leaden with the memory of the broken bodies she had helped carry off the field as their blood trailed recklessly behind them. *You'll be all right,* she had told them then, and was surprised to taste the lie on her lips even now, as she watched the Southern soldiers pass.

Ankle deep in the red mud road, their stamping feet seemed to stomp upon Caitlin's chest. The hidden piece of her heart now throbbed with hope for Union victory. But the other half bled for the coming slaughter of boys too young and men too old to play at war, and for their families whose brave smiles crumbled as soon as the columns passed them by. Longing for Jack battled yearning for Noah until she feared her aching heart would surely be rent in two.

With Ana's hand in hers, and tears and rain mingling on her face, Caitlin sent up a desperate prayer, not for victory or defeat, but for the end, and that God would be her anchor in this storm.

———

Kennesaw Mountain
Monday, June 27, 1864

Cautiously, Noah raised his head over the ditch, feeling for all the world like a sleep-deprived gopher just waiting to be stomped on by a blue-clad giant. His nerves pulled tight as he scanned the horizon beneath the glaring sun. The earth looked as if it were made of iron, the sky as though made of brass. Sweat rolled down Noah's face and spilled between his shoulder blades. The mercury was 110 degrees in the shade. Not a sound could be heard, save a peckerwood tapping an old trunk for his breakfast.

Then hell broke loose in Georgia.

The high-pitched yipping of the Rebel Yell rent the air as, up the hill, the Yankees came. Closer and closer, on and on, massed in columns forty men deep, until it seemed the entire Union army was hurling itself head-on up the hill. *Foolhardy!* Noah's revolver spent of its bullets, he grabbed a musket from a dying comrade nearby, ripping the cartridge box off his belt as well. Rebel fire lashed out from the ditches, cutting the enemy down like wheat before the scythe. Before Noah's eyes, hearty Yanks with repeating rifles were mown down by gaunt Rebs with revolvers and muskets that took at least twenty seconds to load for each shot. The ditches filled up with Yankee prisoners, but still they came marching on, and still they dropped, bleeding, to the ground.

It was slaughter.

Sweat stung Noah's eyes and sulfur filled his mouth and nostrils. A haze of gunpowder hovered above the entrenchments, amplifying the stupefying heat even further, until he could not see the muzzles spewing their fire.

Minié balls whizzed and zinged over his head, while artillery continued to tear the sky above. Pain slashed Noah's neck as he loaded the rifle, and blood splattered his face. *I am a dead man.* But when he brought his hand to the burn, it came away dry. He had only been singed by a passing bullet. The bullet had killed the man next to him, spilling the dead man's life in a scarlet arc from his neck.

Noah slammed his ramrod down the barrel, then yanked it back out. Before he could pull a cartridge from the box, the earth exploded next to him, ripping his weapon from his sweaty grip, and hurtling him, as though weightless, through the spray of dirt and shrapnel. Noise dimmed as though the battle suddenly raged underwater, and he alone floated above it, between waves of lead and the unblinking eye of the sun.

He landed, pain shuddering through his body. The sharp taste of metal. His face and neck slick with bubbling blood. This time it was his own.

Chapter Twenty

Atlanta, Georgia
Tuesday, July 5, 1864

The panic that had pulsed just below the surface of Atlanta now erupted in reckless gaiety. Johnston had defeated Sherman at Kennesaw Mountain! Atlanta was saved after all! Yet for the first time in years, Susan Kent did not join the merrymaking.

The newspapers jumped from discussing General Johnston's "retrograde movements" to praising the godlike qualities of the Southern army. "There is an invincible host still between Atlanta and our ruthless foe, which, like a wall of fire, will resist his advance into it," the *Intelligencer* stated, expressing "the utmost confidence that if battle is made before the city, we will scatter the enemy like leaves before an autumnal frost." And the people were converted.

The city grew drunk on relief and hope. Rashes of parties broke out quicker than smallpox while Susan sulked with her scars in her ex-husband's house. When any soldiers were in town from the fighting, dinners were given in their honor, followed by dances where the ladies outnumbered the men ten to one, everyone said, and fought for their attention. Revelry rattled the windows, taunting Susan. She could not decide which was worse: the day last month when the deceased Bishop General Polk had lain in state and Atlanta choked on dour mourners, or this raucous pursuit of pleasure, whose wild crush she did not enter.

If Atlanta was full before, it was absolutely glutted now. In addition to government officials, refugees, and wounded, families of the men entrenched at the mountain came to be nearby in case their soldiers were injured. Hordes of girls came in from the country—where all the men between sixteen and sixty years old were gone—to bat their eyes in thrice-turned frocks.

If it weren't for her pocked skin, Susan would be out there, too, flirting with the men alongside seventeen-year-old belles ten years her junior. She would have been shameless. And she would have won.

A cold, wet nose suddenly tickled Susan's fingers, and she jerked back. "Oh, you rascal!" But he stood there still, seeking her companionship. *He is the only one who wants me.* Hesitantly, she laid her hand on his back, his spine bony under her palm. His eyes rolled back and he groaned happily, tugging a rare smile from Susan's lips.

Then Caitlin entered the parlor and Rascal trotted away to her. Tears burned down Susan's textured cheeks.

Caitlin's eyes grew round. "Are you unwell?" A shrieking rage would have concerned her less.

Susan's blue eyes bore into hers. "I am alone. And I always will be. Even the dog will not stay by me."

Rain pattered outside, dimpling the puddles forming in the dirt road. "I'm here, so are Naomi and Ana. And let us not forget you have Minnie to thank for your life. She faithfully nursed you back to health."

"Then I have her to blame for not letting me die."

"You are not the only one who has been marked, you know."

Susan's laugh was shrill against the thunder's roll. "Oh, so true, so true. Naomi, you, and Ana do appear to have been bitten by about three mosquitoes each. Even Minnie's pocks are nothing compared to mine!"

Caitlin dropped her gaze. "You could melt beeswax and fill the divots if it bothers you that much."

"Beeswax! We don't even have enough for candles. And if we did, it would melt off my face as soon as I spackled it on. Any more bright ideas, you goose?"

Caitlin's cheeks warmed, but it was more likely from the simmering July heat than Susan's barb. Ana now slept on the drugget beneath the dining room table, so sweltering was the second floor.

"Yes. Try thinking about something other than yourself for a change. I'll read to you from *Macaria*. We're almost finished."

Caitlin turned to page 412 in the novel, her eyebrows raising in amusement at the dialogue unfolding on the page. "Irene is speaking here." She began reading the text.

Electra, it is very true that single women have trials for which a thoughtless, happy world has little sympathy. But lonely lives are not necessarily joyless; they should be, of all others, most useful. The head of a household, a wife and mother, is occupied with family cares and affections—can find little time for considering the comfort, or contributing to the enjoyment of any beyond the home circle. Doubtless she is happier, far happier, than the unmarried woman; but to the last belongs the privilege of carrying light and blessings to many firesides— of being the friend and helper of hundreds; and because she belongs exclusively to no one, her heart expands to all her suffering fellow creatures.

Susan groaned on the sofa, but Caitlin silently reread the passage. Her mother would have liked it, even if this fictional heroine—and the author—was a staunch Confederate woman. The argument fell right in line with single blessedness, which Caitlin had been so intent on pursuing. At least, she had been before Noah had carved a place for himself

265

in her heart. His face surged in her mind, his voice whispered in her spirit, yet he still called her Miss McKae in his letters and signed off only as Mr. Becker. Truly, she should not allow him so much space in her mind.

Just then, Minnie burst in through the front door and entered the parlor, face glowing with more than just summer's heat.

"What is it?" Caitlin asked.

"I'm married!"

"What?" Susan cried, jumping to her feet.

"It's true! I'm Mrs. William Iverson now, and I couldn't be happier!"

Susan fled down the hall and slammed the back door behind her, leaving only Caitlin to gape at Minnie's announcement.

"I am astonished! Whatever do you think you're doing?"

Minnie crossed the room and grasped Caitlin's hands in hers. "Listen, honey, I'm not Irene what's-her-name from *Macaria*. And I'm not Caitlin McKae."

"What's that supposed to mean?" Caitlin gasped.

"You're so strong and confident on your own, you act like you could be unmarried forever. But all I ever wanted was to be a good, true Southern woman and wife. My hands have grown rough and calloused, but William doesn't care. He says my refinement is in my heart, not the texture of my skin, nor in the clothes I wear. My husband loves me, scars and all. Do you see?"

Caitlin nodded, wiping the tears from her cheeks. "You're leaving—now?"

"Aw, be happy for me, honey. You know I couldn't live here as a refugee forever. Now I have a husband. I'm one of the lucky few. We are a generation of women whose men are being eaten up by this horrid war."

"Is he not a soldier himself then?"

Minnie smiled. "Wounded veteran. Nursed him back to life myself during the last few weeks at the hospital. He's got one eye now, which is good enough for living but not good enough for fighting. Oh, I'm sorry to surprise you like this but it's all happened so suddenly! I felt a

266

connection with him right away but wanted to make sure it was real before mentioning anything about it to you—you know how hospital romances come and go so fast. But this one's genuine, we're married, and we're going to the Car Shed now to catch the next train out of here. And don't call me rash, there must have been a dozen other couples getting married at City Hall today!"

"Oh!" Caitlin cried, the suddenness almost too much for her to bear. Aside from Prudence, Minnie was her first and best friend in Atlanta. "I'll miss you so much!" She threw her arms around Minnie's neck.

"I love you, honey, and I'll miss you too. But singleness is not so blessed. You should think on it yourself."

Caitlin pulled back and searched her friend's sparkling grey eyes. "Why bother?"

"I've never seen a man so pulled apart by worry as Noah Becker was when you were sick. Do yourself a favor. When the war is over, you marry that man."

"Minnie! You act as though the entire matter were up to me."

"It's more up to you than you realize." She winked, and then went upstairs to gather her meager belongings, singing "When This Cruel War Is Over" as she went. When she departed Noah's house, her echoing voice was all she left behind.

Smyrna, Georgia
Wednesday, July 6, 1864

Bloodred mud squished up between the branches Noah had laid on the floor of his ditch. Logs raised a few inches above the lip of the trench had protected their heads as they fired rifles through the gap. Bush arbors offered patchy shade from the merciless sun. But nothing had been able to shield them from the rain.

Every day since Johnston had withdrawn his army to Smyrna, rain had fallen on the entrenched troops, as if nature itself would scrub the residue of war from their bodies. The dirt, blood, sweat, and soot that had rinsed away contaminated the puddles filling the four-foot-deep-by-four-foot-wide trenches the men now occupied. Noah—and the rest of them—were wading in battle's dishwater.

The blow that had sent blood gushing from Noah's nose and ears did not seem to exact damage beyond ringing ears and headaches. Miraculously, his only visible souvenir from the mighty contest was his bruised and bloodshot arm from wrist to shoulder due to firing the musket more than 120 times.

Noah slicked his hair back from his forehead and glanced up at the pewter-grey sky. The rain had stopped.

"Oh, Johnny!" cried a Yank. The enemy line was so near that between firing upon each other, they volleyed conversation back and forth instead. Normally, they taunted each other to show themselves and have a real fight outside these oversized prairie-dog holes. But tonight, "We want to hear that cornet player!"

"He would play," yelled back a Georgian soldier, "but he's afraid you'd spoil his horn!"

"We'll stop shooting."

"All right, Yanks."

And so the cornet player from Savannah mounted the works not far from Noah's ditch to play familiar airs from operas, and sing in his trained tenor voice, "Gone Where My Love Lies Dreaming" and "I Dreamt That I Dwelt in Marble Halls." On both sides, weary, sodden troops nesting below ground were carried away from their stinking ditches on the wings of the heavenly music soaring above it.

"Becker. You read?" A bearded private nudged Noah in the ribs.

Noah replied that he did.

"The Ladies Relief Society sent a bundle. *Les Miserables, Macaria,* and a bunch of newspapers from Richmond and Atlanta. Want any?"

Noah accepted a stack of weeks-old newspapers. In an April issue of Atlanta's *Intelligencer*, Noah scanned a speech given by Vice President Stephens at the Georgia state capitol, a list of blockade goods for sale, and descriptions of runaway slaves. A May issue of *Southern Confederacy* warned that the wheat harvest must not be lost just because all the men who would reap their own grain were gone in the service. The Atlanta Sabre Factory, being all out of charcoal anyway, offered twenty hands to help with the harvest and challenged other government workers to do the same.

The *Richmond Enquirer* contained predictable stories—until Noah turned to a four-page section of cryptic messages from family members to other subscribers. *When did they start doing this?* Noah wondered as he perused column after column of the notices. The fine print explained the agreement the newspaper had with the New York paper, in which they reprinted each other's ads to aid loved ones communicating across the Mason-Dixon line.

And then he saw it, reprinted from the *New York Daily News*.

To C. McKae: Come home. Loving arms await you.

Noah frowned. *C. McKae? Certainly there are dozens of C. McKaes in the Confederacy. Still . . .* He looked at the date on the paper. February 25, 1864.

The next paper was an edition from March 5. He turned to the family notices section and found the exact same ad. The same wording was reprinted yet again in the March 25 paper. *Whoever C. McKae is, he or she is not responding.*

Noah turned to the same section in the next three editions of the *Richmond Examiner*. He felt the color drain from his face with each successive notice.

To Caitlin M: Come home. Loving arms await you.

C. M., Atlanta: Must talk in person. Get out before it's too late!

To C. McKae: Stay well. Watch for Jack. Be ready.

Noah finished reading just as the opera singer's last tremulous note faded. Though thunderous applause from the Yankees spilled into the trench around him, it was nothing compared to the newsprint words now echoing in his mind. *Jack.* The man Caitlin loved was from the North, and he was coming to Atlanta. Leaning his head back against the ditch wall, Noah saw all over again the waves of bluecoats coming up the hill at Kennesaw. A sickening feeling washed over him then, both at the thought of Caitlin in another man's arms, and the possibility that Noah had shot him.

———

New York City
Wednesday, July 20, 1864

Cook faster, cook faster! Edward was due home any minute and dinner was nowhere near ready. Aiden had skipped his afternoon nap today and left a path of destruction wherever he went, leaving Ruby worn out and behind on her dinner preparations. *The house is a shambles.*

Mrs. Waverly's house, she corrected herself. Ruby stirred the potatoes as they fried in the skillet. When Caroline heard they were trying to save money for a house, she offered them the use of her brownstone. She was too in love with her granddaughter to leave Fishkill, she had said, and would stay there indefinitely. So now, in the very house where she had once been the domestic, Ruby was its temporary mistress. She felt like an imposter. Though she appreciated the cost savings, she longed for the day when she and Edward and Aiden could start afresh in their own home.

The door unlatched, and weary footsteps came toward her.

"Welcome home, dear," she said.

"Mmmm." He kissed her cheek, then stood back and crossed his arms. "Potatoes again, darling?"

Her face burned. "And a roast in the oven. Only . . ." she cringed. "It won't be ready for another hour. I'm so sorry I didn't get it in to start earlier."

Edward's shoulders slumped and he rubbed a hand over his face. "Busy day, was it?"

She offered a lopsided smile. "Aye. Aiden has worn my patience to a thread. He wouldn't sleep, so I had no break, and had to pick up after him all day!"

"Really?" He looked at the toys scattered on the floor. "I never would have guessed."

Ruby set her jaw. He didn't understand. He wasn't even trying to.

"Where is he now?" Edward's hair fell onto his forehead. Thank heavens he only wore that pomade for their wedding.

"He finally fell asleep a little bit ago on the floor."

"So what does that mean? When he wakes he'll be up until we all go to bed at ten o'clock? You know I look forward to having some time with my wife before I sleep."

"Well, I'm sorry, Edward, he was exhausted, and I could not have made dinner if I didn't let him just rest for a wee spell."

"But dinner isn't ready anyway. And I have to leave again for prayer meeting in thirty minutes. It's Wednesday. I have this meeting every Wednesday. Did you forget?"

Ruby winced. "Aye. I'm sorry." *I'm sorry. I'm sorry.* All she had done since Edward came home was apologize! Was everything really all her fault?

Edward sighed, and placed his hand on her shoulder, even though he knew she didn't like that. "I had hoped you could come with me."

She stared at him. "Go with you? Aiden cannot attend prayer meeting. He'd scream and fuss the entire time."

"Then ask Aunt Viv to watch him."

Ruby shook her head. "I use her too much as it is, and frankly, I'm not up to going, myself. I'm exhausted." Not to mention she never felt welcome there.

"You're tired? Me, too, honey. And oh, by the way, my day was rotten, thank you for asking."

"Was it? Why?"

"If you wanted to know, you would have asked me yourself."

Chills rippled over Ruby as she took in his rumpled shirt and haggard expression. *What is it?* Edward had never spoken to her this way before.

"I'm sorry," she whispered, again. "I do care. I want to hear all about it as soon as you get home from prayer. I'll keep the roast warm for you."

"It'll be completely dried out."

Her brow creased with frustration. "Have some potatoes, at least, before you go."

Edward tossed a glance into the skillet. "No thank you. I guess I'll just take care of myself." He trudged to the doorway, then turned. "You and Aiden have a good night. Don't wait up. I wouldn't want you to be tired."

"Stop." Ruby dropped her spatula and stepped toward her husband. "You can't leave like this."

He cocked an eyebrow at her while smoothing his caramel-colored hair back into place. "I'm going to prayer meeting, not a brothel, you know."

Heat singed her cheeks. Tears gathered in her eyes as guilt crashed down on her afresh.

Edward's eyes softened. "Look. We'll sort it out. Later. I promise. I love you."

The staccato words matched the staccato beating of her heart. *I can't lose him. I can't.* "I love you, too."

Lips quirking in an unconvinced smile, he released a breath she hadn't realized he'd been holding. He clasped his hands behind her waist. "Then why won't you let me into your heart?"

Edward's eyes misted, and Ruby hated herself for being the cause.

"You must believe, I love you!" Her voice tightened in desperation. "Would you believe me if I was a better cook? Or mother?"

"The food is not the problem, and I don't need you to be my mother." His voice was husky.

Ruby knew what he needed, and begged God to help her give that to him. "I—I—"

He silenced her with a kiss as tender and gentle as the Edward she had known for the last two years. His hands pressed her close and she melted into the warmth of his body. Though her arms felt leaden, she forced them to wrap around his waist. *Why is the one thing that is so hard for me to do the one thing he wants most?*

"Ruby," he whispered. "Don't you know you're the only one for me?" He kissed the top of her head, her cheek, the tip of her nose. Then his lips took hers with an urgency that startled her. His hands roamed the hourglass curve of her corset until they rested on her hips.

"Potatoes are burning." Ruby pulled back from his kiss, but his hands did not let her go.

"Let 'em burn." He kissed her from ear to shoulder, sending shivers down her spine.

"Aiden will wake any minute!"

Edward groaned as he plunged his fingers in her hair. "It's good for him to see a man love his wife. We're only kissing, dear. What we're doing isn't wrong. It's very, *very* right."

She giggled, and his eyes sparkled endearingly. "So does this sort of . . . business . . . agree with you now?"

"So far, aye." *Please God, give me desire for my husband!*

Edward couldn't believe it. Was Ruby really warming to him? He kissed her once more to find out. *That would be a yes.*

"Don't you need to go to your prayer meeting?"

He smiled into her gemstone eyes. "Meeting? What meeting?"

She coughed on the smoke now clouding the air, and he crossed the kitchen to turn off the fire beneath the burner and move the skillet from the heat. Edward never did care for potatoes anyway, though he'd never tell her that. *At least, not now.*

"Suddenly, I don't have much of an appetite." *For food.* Edward grasped her hand and pulled her out of the kitchen and into the rear parlor. He didn't bother turning any lights on.

"You're going to be late!"

"They can start without me." He sat on the sofa and pulled her onto his lap. "I'm not the pope."

"Obviously." She covered a laugh with her hand, and he laughed with her.

"I miss you, Ruby." He grew serious. "It seems like the last few weeks, our married life has just been—"

"Not what you expected," she finished for him.

He shrugged.

"*I* am not what you expected."

Warning flared in her eyes as she wiggled off his lap and sat beside him. *Please don't shut me out already. Not now.* "I didn't say that." *And if you would stop putting words in my mouth this would be so much easier.* "I had hoped . . ."

"For more."

He clamped his mouth shut, irritation twitching behind his eyes. But she was right. He had hoped for more love, more passion, more closeness. More of his wife. Could he even call her that if they had not yet consummated their vows?

"All right." Ruby pressed her lips together. "Then tell me. What is it you had hoped for?"

She scooted from him, but he caught her hand in his. "This." He pressed a kiss to her hand. "You."

Her nose pinked, and her chin quivered. "I know," she whispered. "But I can't."

"There is no fear in love. No fear, darling. No fear."

Tears spilled down her cheeks, and Edward swiped them away with his thumbs. His heart squeezed as her forehead knotted, and leapt when she threw her arms around his neck and cried on his shoulder.

"Shhhh, it's all right," he murmured to her as he wrapped his arms around her waist. He could be her rock. But the fire inside him burned for more. Her green poplin gown was smooth beneath his hands as he slowly skimmed up her sides from her waist—and grazed the swell of her breasts with the heels of his palms.

Eyes suddenly wild, Ruby reared back like a skittish horse and slapped him clean across his face. "I told you I can't!"

Edward was off the sofa in a flash, his hand covering his stinging cheek. "That was an accident, *dear*, and by the way, a man should not have to apologize for coming into contact with his wife's body, fully clothed or otherwise!"

His blood boiled. He had done nothing wrong—if anything she should apologize for her unreasonable restrictions—and yet she would make him feel like a lecher if she could! She was his *wife*, hang it all!

"I can do nothing right by you, I see that now. Why don't you do us both a favor and hang a sign when you're open for business, all right?"

She gasped. "You said you wouldn't hurt me."

"You said you'd be my wife." *So we're both liars.*

Tripping over Aiden's blocks, Edward stumbled out of the room, grabbed his hat and Bible from the hall rack and escaped into the evening air, slamming the door closed behind him. The humidity was a relief compared to the oppressive atmosphere in his own—borrowed—house.

Absently, Edward fiddled with the bookmark dangling from somewhere in Proverbs. It was a braid of Ruby's hair, tied at both ends with satin ribbon, given to him during their engagement.

Lord, was I wrong to believe this marriage could work?

Chapter Twenty-One

Atlanta, Georgia
Thursday, July 21, 1864

July dragged by on blistered feet while Rebels ran roughshod over it. The sky to the north had burned red on July 9 when Johnston fired the Chattahoochee bridge behind him, but the Yankees crossed the murky river anyway. Three days ago, President Davis replaced Johnston with John Bell Hood. A general who would yield no more ground, or die standing.

"Atlanta will not, and cannot be abandoned," touted the *Southern Confederacy* as Rebel soldiers filled fortifications ringing the city, and hundreds of deserters and stragglers slinked south through the streets. Many of Atlanta's refugees and residents vied for space on trains already clogged with the wounded being evacuated to points farther south. Markets crowded with housekeepers, but soaring prices turned many away. A barrel of flour: $300! A pound of sugar: $15! Locally grown sweet potatoes at $16 a bushel, and no other vegetables or chicken to be had in the city at all. In a restaurant, a plate of ham and eggs with a cup of coffee went for $25—more than two months' pay! The uproar of a city turning inside out provided easy cover for robbers who smashed open and looted houses, depots, and stores in the darkness. Starving stragglers and hungry residents broke into any place that promised food. The arsenal, commissaries, and factories had moved to Macon, and the railroads ceased to run for anyone outside the military. The swollen war-time population of 22,000 was now reduced to 4,000 stalwart citizens. Houses were deserted, their gardens blighting in the sun. The newspapers evacuated, leaving Atlanta riddled with rumor and speculation. Even Col. George W. Lee had left.

The air pulsed with the sound of cannon that could only be a few miles away. Still, Caitlin McKae would not leave. This was Ana's home and Noah's, and she would not abandon them even if she could.

Susan, however, I could do without. But she'd never say it aloud. Susan was obviously unhappy. The best remedy Caitlin could suggest—helping someone else in need—had been stubbornly refused every time. Naomi seemed to make up for her lack by doing the work of two. In fact—

"Susan." Caitlin knocked on her bedroom door, nudging it open with her knuckles. "Have you seen Naomi today?"

"No." She rolled over in her bed, unhelpful as usual.

Caitlin's mouth screwed to one side as she looked out the window into the inky darkness. Had Naomi really not been home since yesterday morning? "I'm going to go look for her. She never came home to sleep and pick up the baskets of biscuits for the patients. I'll take them with me. If Ana wakes, please go to her." The poor girl had been having nightmares of Noah dying in battle ever since they had been able to hear the cannons.

She did not relish moving around the city at night, but it was the only time guards did not stop citizens for their passes—sometimes every two blocks. *Fine idea,* she thought sarcastically, *to remove the guards in time for the rowdies to have full run of the streets.* Hidden in her apron pocket, her loaded derringer flopped against her leg with every step. She prayed she would not have to use it on the battlefield.

The city had long since run out of gas for the street lights, so Caitlin made her way across the railroad tracks by the light of the moon. The bright sound of breaking glass jerked her head to the right, where a Confederate cavalry team raided stores and impressed everything they took a fancy to, scattering clothing, stationery, and pipes on the street to be trampled by their own horses. Quietly, she turned left, ducking into the shadows until she arrived at the railroad depot known as the Car Shed.

Lanterns flickered beneath its vaulted ceiling like fireflies as dark-skinned women tended a floor paved with moaning, bearded patients. The hospital staff was so limited, Naomi had told her, that eight out of ten volunteers were impressed slaves. Mutely, Caitlin wondered how they felt aiding men who had fought for the right to keep them enslaved.

Nose pinching with the smell of human waste and blood, Caitlin waded into the churning sea of men, thankful that after her service on the battlefield, nothing would shock her. Flies swarmed and mosquitoes dipped in and out of wounds, most of which were in the head and arms, since the armies had been fighting in trenches. Many men had lost at least one eye. A man screamed several yards from Caitlin, and she jumped, nearly tripping over a coffin at her feet.

"Gangrene," she heard someone say. "The only thing for it is to pour nitric acid right on it. Fries the skin to a crisp."

Tears bit Caitlin's eyes even as she muscled through her gag reflex. She realized then, that even worse than the fresh wounds she had seen in every variety, were old ones.

"Caitlin!"

She turned toward the voice, but did not dare move, waiting instead for Naomi to come to her.

"What are you doing here?" Naomi asked. She looked yellow in the lantern-light, framed by wisps of untidy hair.

"You didn't come home. I was worried." She handed the baskets of bread to Naomi.

"Thank you. Yesterday's battle at Peachtree Creek—there are eight hundred here just on this floor, and I have no idea how many elsewhere. It seems as though we just finish evacuating patients when more come in. All that can be moved, must be moved. Atlanta will not be held."

Spewing wood cinders, a train of boxcars ground and wheezed its way into the station, and Caitlin waited until her voice would be heard. Divided loyalties tugged on her heart as she processed the news. "Will you go with them? With your patients?"

"I've run twice already, and I'm tired of it. I've got no place to go and I'll not be a permanent 'runagee.'" She leaned in. "Besides, if my son took the oath to be a Yankee up at Gettysburg, surely there must be some gentlemen in the lot of them."

The train cars clattered open. "Naomi, do you need help? Loading the men in the cars? I daresay I have more strength than you, seeing as you haven't slept in almost two days."

"If you like, I'll not stop you."

"Let me take your place. Please. You'll be no good to anyone when you faint."

After a moment's hesitation, Naomi nodded. "I just might deliver your biscuits and collapse somewhere. That's Dr. Welford over there. Take orders from him, and tell him I sent you."

Caitlin did.

Urgency surged in her veins now just as it had when she had evacuated Union wounded from the fields of battle. They were men, and men in mortal danger still, which was far more important than the fact that they were Southern. How many Southern women had her regiment alone rushed into widowhood?

"Do you mind if I help?" Caitlin approached a Negro woman crouching beside a patient. When she lifted her kerchief-covered head, a white smile flashed on her face.

"Don't mind if you do."

"Why, Bess! How can you be doing this?"

Bess stood and pressed her hands to the small of her back as she

279

stretched. "Easy answer is that I've been made to. But the truth is, helping those who can't help themselves is the right thing to do. Haven't you ever heard of the Good Samaritan?"

"But you're—you're—" *A slave*, she wanted to blurt out. *And the Confederacy means to keep you that way*!

"I know who I am, Miss Caitlin. Can you say the same?"

No answer formed save the erratic beating of her disoriented heart.

"Mm-hmmmm." Bess shook her head. "Well, the Lord knows who you are, even if you don't, and He loves you. He loves me as much whether I'm slave or free, and yes, He loves these pitiful creatures at our feet. 'There is a balm in Gilead, to make the wounded whole.'" Bess's rich alto voice rose in song as she motioned for Caitlin to help her lift the broken man at their feet. "'There is a balm in Gilead to heal the sin-sick soul.'"

Until her limbs burned and her back ached, Caitlin helped Bess heave groaning men into rickety boxcars, packing them like sardines on scant straw. The odors from their bodies magnified in the hot, confined space, until it coated her mouth and nostrils. As they worked, dozens of other slaves joined their voices to Bess in soothing harmony.

Sometimes I feel discouraged,
And think my work's in vain,
But then the Holy Spirit
Revives my soul again.

With her throat too tight to speak, Caitlin dared to pray that the God who could revive the discouraged slave would revive her heart as well.

Caitlin arched her back before bending one more time to lift yet another patient beneath his knees, his bare feet pitiably cut up and blistered. Bess helped Caitlin swing their patient up onto the car floor, then Caitlin climbed up after him to help move him to the back.

"Halt! Caitlin McKae, you devil Yankee spy, halt in the name of the law!"

Chills swept her sweat-filmed skin as she rounded on the car's gaping doorway. In an instant, Oliver Jones leapt into the car after her.

"Just where do you think you're going?" the provost marshal snarled.

Caitlin drew a foul-tasting breath. "I am simply helping the wounded onto the car, as this woman can tell you." She nodded at Bess.

"Their testimony don't stand in court. You ought to know that by now. You are hereby under arrest."

"On what grounds?"

He yanked her arms behind her waist, twisting unnecessarily, and latched the handcuffs into place. "On the grounds of the Confederacy."

"What is the charge?" she tried again, willing her voice to remain low, controlled, though the weight of the metal on her wrists made her want to fight. He hopped off the train first, and she followed.

"You got no pass. I took it away myself. You're not carrying a forged pass, now, are you?"

She grit her teeth as his hands skimmed her body, falling still on the pistol in her pocket. "Looky looky, what do we have here?" He retrieved the gun and aimed it at her. Cocked it. "It ain't already loaded, is it?"

Caitlin's breath came faster now, pushing against her stays. "Is it a crime for a woman to defend herself?"

Jones laughed. "You've saved me the trouble of using my own bullets. How thrifty." He poked the barrel into her spine. "You're coming with me."

Inside the Atlanta Hotel, several pinched-looking ladies sat with their hands folded tightly in their laps, including known Unionists whose husbands had already fled town. Caitlin felt their eyes on her as Jones yanked her up the stairs and into a room.

Jones leaned against the bedpost, while a youth with scant hair covering his upper lip slouched against the wall between two chairs and a washstand. It was such a strange place for a military tribunal hearing that Caitlin hardly knew whether to take it seriously.

"Do you promise to tell the truth?"

"I promise not to lie. But I also invoke the Fifth Amendment."

After a string of choice words, Jones shoved a newspaper under Caitlin's nose. *Richmond Enquirer.*

"Is this supposed to mean something to me?"

"I would say so." Jones spoke around a cigar drooping from his mouth. "Leastwise, it has your name on it."

"Pardon me?"

He jabbed a finger on the print. *To C. McKae: Stay well. Watch for Jack. Be ready.*

The words crashed in Caitlin's mind. Quickly, she scanned the text surrounding the message and surmised these were messages from Northerners to Southern loved ones. "This is a Richmond paper," she said. "C could stand for Charles, or Carl, or Cathleen, or any number of other names."

"But it doesn't." Jones stepped forward with two more papers, folded into squares, and marked with indigo circles. "These are from two other papers, published in March."

To Caitlin M: Come home. Loving arms await you.

C. M., Atlanta: Must talk in person. Get out before it's too late!

"Someone sure is trying hard to reach you, Miss McKae. What I want to know is, who? Why? Who is Jack?" Jones blew cigar smoke in her face.

Visions of her mother and brother swam before her. But she would not give them up for anything. Just as Union spies were known to be in Atlanta, Confederate spies were very likely planted in New York City, too. Wouldn't they come after Vivian if given a reason?

"I asked you a question, 'C. M., Atlanta.'"

She answered with stony silence.

"It's a code," Jones said, and Caitlin almost laughed. "C. McKae . . . Caitlin M . . . C. M., Atlanta . . . What does it mean?"

Caitlin watched with some fascination as the paranoid Jones explored aloud all sorts of possible meanings for the simple message. *It means my mother, finally, wants me back.* A lump formed in her throat. Still, she said nothing.

Blue smoke puffed from his cigar as he crossed his arms. "You ought to think mighty hard about your situation, little miss. You were caught walking without a pass. Concealing a weapon on your person. Boarding a train to escape the city. You are named three times in this here paper by an agent in the North. And an anonymous tip told us you sent a code north to a Jack McKae. Taken together, we have no choice but to conclude otherwise but that you are an agent of espionage."

And just how did you come by that tip? Caitlin's scalp tingled at the idea that perhaps Jones had threatened Prudy somehow in order to get that information. Or worse still, that she willingly volunteered it. Still, "I vow, I am not a spy."

Jones clucked his tongue. "And you said you wouldn't lie to us."

"I am not lying. I'm not a spy. I am a governess for Noah Becker, a soldier in the Army of Tennessee. Tonight I delivered food to the soldiers at the Car Shed and stayed to help load them into the train for their evacuation. That's all."

"Mm-hmmm. And the newspaper ads. Explain those to us, if you will."

"This is the first time I have seen those papers. I'm as surprised as you are."

"But what do they mean?" Jones' smoldering eyes bore into hers, and she held his gaze.

"Are we quite finished then?" she asked at length, her voice calm. "I've told you what you need to know. I am not a spy. Now you will please release me."

"I don't believe I will."

"Search my house if you like. I'll escort you myself."

"I think not."

"Please. There is a little girl in my charge I cannot be away from for long, and the hour is late."

But Jones was already pulling Caitlin to her feet, out the door and into another room. After removing the handcuffs, he shoved her forward with the barrel of her own pistol. The door closed and locked from the other side.

Atlanta, Georgia
Friday, July 22, 1864

Susan covered her ears to mute Rascal's nervous whine as much as to muzzle the fear ongoing inside her head. "Hush!" A swat against the dog's protruding ribs sent him scurrying, tail between his legs.

The Yankees had come. The cannons sounded as if they were on Whitehall Street this very day, and Susan was sure she could hear the scream of men being shot to pieces. A shell burst inside the city this afternoon. No one was safe! And Caitlin McKae had vanished, leaving Susan alone with a child she had never wanted to begin with. She especially did not want her now! What she wanted was to get out of here, like all the other sensible citizens and storeowners who had gathered up what they could and hightailed it to the train station.

"Where is Miss McKae? Why isn't she home yet?" The girl's face pinched as she asked the same questions she'd been asking since she woke up this morning.

"She left us!" Susan burst out, not caring one whit how it must have sounded to the child, not even bothering to measure her reaction. It was the truth. Caitlin had left, selfishly, irresponsibly, and without warning. She said she'd come back, and she didn't. *Liar.*

Was this to be Susan's lot in life, to be left alone when she needed help the most? Truly, she should be used to it by now. This time, it was her turn to leave.

"Annie, I'm stepping out," she called out. "Naomi will be home soon." *Probably.*

She let the door slam behind her without looking back.

———

Susan's breath shortened as she drew near to her escape, so terrified was she of her lifeline being yanked from her grasp. Life and death mingled hideously together in the Car Shed. Convalescent soldiers buzzed between moaning patients awaiting treatment, evacuation, or merciful sleep from which they would never wake. Haggard white women crooned to their children, and rich women were followed by their entourages of colored folks shouldering whatever their white folks asked them to: a huge parlor mirror bound in gold, pots, kettles, baskets, bags, barrels, kegs, bacon, and bedsteads. A pet goat bleated on the end of its rope, and birds in their cages added their shrill songs to the cacophony. The smells were as layered as the sounds.

Just outside the depot, wounded Union prisoners were laid on the unshaded grounds of the City Park between corpses already straining their buttons. Some were missing legs, some their arms. The stench of gangrene was their only covering beneath the blistering sun. Only a couple of Negro men worked frantically among them washing and dressing their wounds while heavily armed Confederate cavalry galloped by.

"I'll pay you! In greenbacks!" One of the Negro men looked up from a maggoty stump and called out to other dark-skinned folks looking on. "Buy some food, bring water, tell the slaves at the Ponder estate to come help!"

Susan turned from the ghastly scene. She had her own problems to worry about.

Between the train whistles, frantic voices caught in Susan's ears until she had no choice but to interrupt them. "What are you talking about?"

"That explosion today."

"Yes I heard it. What of it?"

"Why, Sherman's begun shelling the city, that's what!"

"It was not an accident?"

"No. It's Sherman, and I vouch he'll do it again. Killed a little girl out walking with her parents today. War on the doorstep is one thing, but bringing it inside our city—uh-uh. Atlanta is too hot for me—but there's no place in hell too hot for Sherman!"

A tide of terror bore down upon Susan. She was perfectly right in fleeing, she could not stay, not now that she was in danger! She would beg her father's forgiveness if she could just get out of this fiery path of war and stop running! Though she once thought she needed Ana for her family to take her in, now, surely, her smallpox scars would be enough for them to take pity on her. Traveling light suited her. A child would only slow her down. Her lips set firmly, she elbowed her way to a railroad official.

"Please, sir." Susan grabbed his arm, schooling her features to manipulate. "I need to get on that train." It did not matter where it was headed, as long as it was away from here. She could worry about connections to other cities later.

"Sorry, lady. This here car is carrying the wounded away. There's just no more room."

Susan glanced past him. This was a coach car, with actual seats. How badly could the men be wounded if they could sit like proper passengers? "I have a passport! And I have barely any luggage at all!"

He brushed past her to help a different woman and her two children climb aboard. *What?* Susan seethed. Hadn't he just told her there was no more room? Sullenly, she crossed her arms and glared at the homely woman bouncing a toddler on her hip while the other child hid behind her apron. They would steam away soon, and Susan would still be stuck in this quagmire of refugees and stick-thin wounded men, where the air was a liquid stench and the sky was on fire around them.

Then hope sparked in her chest. If it was children that now trumped charm, Susan Kent was still in the game. Hoisting her skirt above her ankles, she jockeyed her way out of the depot.

"Annie, put your shoes on," Susan called out as soon as she entered the house. "Annie! We are going. Make haste."

Rubbing her eyes, Ana appeared from the doorway of the dining room where she'd been sleeping on the floor. "Going where?"

"Away from here. The Yankees are coming."

"But where is Miss McKae?" Her eyes were hooded, Susan suspected, with distrust. She had no time for arguing.

"I have no idea where she is, so you might as well forget about her. We're getting out of here tonight; I can't stand this place a moment longer!"

"No thank you."

Susan glared down at the child. "What did you say?"

"I want to stay and wait for Miss McKae. And Papa. He said he would come back. I have to be here when he comes."

Susan gripped Ana's shoulders and shook her. "Do you know what happened today? A little girl was killed by a shell here in Atlanta. The Yankees are bombarding the city. Who do you think will keep you safe? Not your Papa. He left you, like he left me. Caitlin left for God knows where, Minnie is gone with her new one-eyed husband, and if Naomi went on the train evacuating patients to Macon, she'd be a fool to come back to Atlanta now. You and I are the only ones left."

Ana frowned. "My Papa is coming back. I want my Papa. I want to stay here."

Anger boiled in Susan's breast. She could be bested by smallpox, by an invading army, by a lover who broke his promise to her. She would not be bested by an eight-year-old child. *My child.*

Susan bent, her face just inches from Ana's. "You listen to me, you little brat. I am *your mother* whether you like it or not, and you will come with me even if I have to drag you kicking and screaming."

"I am not a brat! Why do you say such mean things to me? I don't believe you're my mother at all! Mothers love their children! You're nothing like Papa!" Her bright blue eyes glittered with tears, her face knotted in defiance.

Susan balled her hands into trembling fists. "I'm the only person you've got in this world, and we're leaving this horrid place right now. If you don't put your shoes on this instant, I'll take you barefoot."

Ana's lips screwed to the side, but she stomped up the stairs, presumably to obey. But when she didn't return soon enough, Susan marched right up and retrieved the girl—with shoes and scowl both firmly in place—and dragged her out the door.

Chapter Twenty-Two

Atlanta, Georgia
Saturday, July 23, 1864

*T*he hotel windows rattled with the crescendo of activity outside as more and more people fled town. Caitlin had spent two nights here, waiting for Jones to release her, but Jones had never returned. Now that the city was under fire, he may have evacuated Atlanta and left her here for all she knew.

Convinced she was no longer a primary concern, she picked up the washstand and battered it, legs first, against the locked window until it broke. The sound of slivering glass fit right in with Atlanta's ambient noise. Fearless for her own safety, she climbed out and jumped to the dirt below without incident.

Hunger nibbling at her strength, thoughts of Ana pulled her down Decatur Street. *What must they think has become of me?*

The rumble of black-covered ambulances turned her head. Blood trickled from the backs of the wagons, turning the mud road a crimson hue. Grown men and one boy clung to the sides, fanning slit-paper fly brushes at the open windows, trying to keep away the terrible swarms that hovered over wounded men.

Mere blocks from home, City Hall Square had been transformed into an open-air, mass operating room. Stretcher bearers unloaded their moaning, shrieking cargo from ambulance wagons and laid them on long wooden tables. The green grass beneath grew red as the surgeons hastened in their work, for surely more were coming. A gravedigger paced by the open windows of City Hall, now a hospital, calling out: "Bring out your dead! Any dead in there?"

"Please, not Noah. Not Jack." Her whisper cracked on the thick stench of bodies being cut open.

A low-pitched "oooooooooo" sailed overhead and crashed into the road not ten yards from her, spraying dirt and shrapnel in concentric circles. The gaping hole that was left beneath the sulfurous plume was large enough to swallow an army wagon and its mules. Anger licked through Caitlin then, and propelled her home double-time.

She found it empty, except for Rascal, whose clicking claws on the hardwood floor only magnified the silence in the house.

"Lord!" Caitlin cried out as she fell to her knees. "I can't do this alone! Any strength and courage I've ever had is from You. I need You now, Lord. I can't lose Ana. Keep her safe, wherever she is. Hold her hand. Wrap her with Your love. And please show me where to look!"

———

Susan was beyond exhausted. They had not been permitted room on any train all night, and had spent it sitting up inside the Car Shed and being stepped upon. "Hush up." Susan whipped her words at Ana for the hundredth time since leaving Noah's house last night, but the girl would not stop crying. Her nose ran, her eyes watered, her entire face was one soggy mess. "Wipe that snot off your face. Use your sleeve if you have to." But she only cried harder.

A railroad official cast a pitying glance at Ana, and Susan leapt to lasso that sympathy and steer it to her advantage.

"All of this is just too much for the girl." Susan swept her arm in a wide arc over the depot. "Can't we board soon?"

He cocked his head, and she seized once more upon his hesitation. "Her father is fighting in the army, but if he can't protect us from Sherman, he would want us to be safe." Susan pinched Ana, hard, and the girl wailed right on cue. "That little girl who was killed by a shell on Wednesday—that was her best friend." Plausible, though untrue. "We really must scuttle away from here."

The gullible man was putty in her hands, she could see that in the twitch of mustache. "All right. But this is a hospital car. Squeeze on if you can, but it's not the travel you're used to, I assure you."

"Fine. Thank you."

The man swung Ana up into the boxcar, and then helped Susan in after her. Confusion rippled her brow as her eyes adjusted to the darkness. There was nowhere to sit in this car. Ana pulled at her skirt, and she swatted her away like the droning flies. *Oh no.* The drone was coming from the floor. A layer of broken, bleeding men covered it. The ones who hadn't passed out moaned faintly inside their blood-stiffened bandages.

Before she had time to second-guess her mode of transportation, the door rattled shut, enclosing her in this tomb of the living dead.

"Air," one of them rasped. "Air! Just a little!"

Susan couldn't agree more. With trembling hands, she grasped the door's metal frame and pushed until it screeched open about a foot. The air that stirred was hot, but at least the fetid car was no longer as breathless as Susan.

Finally, the train lurched and squealed into motion.

"I don't want to go!" Ana wailed as she stumbled to keep her balance in the swaying car. "I want my Papa!"

"Susan! Ana!" Caitlin's voice rose above the grinding wheels of a train chugging to life. "Analiese Becker! Don't go!"

Astonished, Susan peered through the opening in time to see Caitlin jostling through the crowd to be closer to the train. In her wake, a slave lost his grip on a ten-foot-tall parlor mirror and it struck the floor, shards of glass splintering from the frame. A woman, who Susan guessed was the mirror's owner, shrieked in dismay.

"Ana! Stay with me!" Caitlin's voice faded into the tumult as the woman grabbed her by the wrist and spoke in shrill tones, pointing to the shattered mirror. Caitlin tried, but in vain, to lunge free. "Ana!" But the train was leaving the station, as indifferent to Caitlin's plea as Susan was.

Ana pushed herself next to Susan, both of them rocking with the car's motion. "Miss McKae? She's here?"

Susan chafed at the hope in Ana's voice. "She left you, remember."

"She got my note!"

"Your what?"

"Upstairs, before I put my shoes on, I wrote her and Papa a note that you were taking me from Atlanta and she came back! She's here! She wants me!"

"Well, thank God someone does." But no one wanted Susan. How had life come to this, that Noah should have the undying love of a child not his own, and a woman who stayed in harm's way for him? Susan Kent had no one. How was it that she was the only one who knew this pain? It wasn't right. Noah should hurt the way Susan had been hurt. It was only fair. A smile curled on Susan's scarred face. She would break his heart, indeed. Ana looked up at her. "But you begged me to come with you."

"As my ticket aboard this train. Feel free to leave any time."

"I don't think I can jump!"

Susan glanced through the one-foot-wide opening once more. Amid the commotion all about them, a knot of women looked up at the sound of Ana's fragile cry, scanned the train briefly, then turned back to their own babies crying in their arms and to their toddlers tugging their skirts.

And Susan turned back to Ana. "Let me help you. Remember this as you go. Your mother never wanted you, and neither did your father."

"Papa loves me!"

"Noah Becker isn't your father. He's just a man who took pity on you! *Your* father is married to another woman and has his own children with her. Your *real* father never cared to even meet you once! That's who *your* father is!" Susan raked her gaze over the soldiers lying at her feet. Clearly they were too sick to take an interest in the drama unfolding above them. Or at least, too sick to comment.

Tears streamed down Ana's face. But, "You're lying. My Papa is my Papa, and he loves me."

"He isn't." Noah's love for Ana was irrelevant and irritating. "I am your mother, and even I don't want you." As they neared the end of the platform, Susan budged the rickety boxcar door open a little further.

A shove and the sniveling girl was gone. Screams pierced the air as Susan leaned back against the inside of the boxcar. A thud. The sound of running feet faded as the train juddered away. Maybe now they would know her pain.

Fort Lafayette Prison, New York Harbor
Tuesday, July 26, 1864

The gentle dip and ripple of Edward's oars through the New York Harbor soothed his spirit with every stroke. Seagulls stood sentinel on the pier behind him, but their squawk, like his worries, faded as he crossed the two hundred yards from the Brooklyn coast to the fort-turned-prison. After being at the hospitals all day, even the brackish water smelled sweet.

Inside Room No. 3, however, the air soured with the odor of poorly cooked rations and seven men who had no real reason to clean up. *Make that six dirty men.* One man in this breathless casemate had made a point to groom himself, a fact which Edward fully appreciated now as he sat across the table from him.

"Edward Goodrich." Edward shook the prisoner's hand. "I'm a

chaplain, and I've come to see if there is anything I can do for you. Something I can pray about with you, or for you, perhaps." He laid his small Bible on the rough wooden table and waited.

"I don't suppose you could get me out of here." A dull gleam glimmered behind his brown eyes. "Not that I have anything to return to."

Edward smiled. "I can give you something better. Freedom from spiritual bondage."

The prisoner's lips curled. "Hmmmm. I must confess I'm much more interested in freedom from physical bondage. You know, the literal variety. An escape plan."

"God has an escape plan for you. For all of us."

"From Lafayette Prison? Well done!"

"From death itself." Edward opened his Bible to where Ruby's braid marked the book of Romans at chapter 6. "For the wages of sin is death but—"

"Oh yes, yes, the gift of God is eternal life through Jesus Christ our Lord. I know all about it." His gaze flicked to Ruby's hair. "Say, that's quite a striking shade of red hair you've got in your Bible there. It's the color of rubies, isn't it?"

Edward grazed the braid with his thumb and smiled. "Quite. She was named for her hair, in fact."

"Ruby? Her name is Ruby?" He leaned forward, elbows on the table. "I once knew a seamstress named Ruby."

Edward blinked, wondering at the sudden interest. "Why, yes. Her name is Ruby and she was a seamstress, too. Still is, in fact."

"Well chaplain, I had no idea you had it in you!" He slapped his hand on the table and laughed. "And how does the good Lord view a man of the cloth sticking his finger in that pie, however tasty it may be?"

"I beg your pardon, sir! Just what are you insinuating?"

"Gracious, have I assumed too much? I'm thinking of an Irish immigrant woman who also tried her hand at domestic service. Ruby O'Flannery is her name. She has a bastard son who should be—let me think now—just over two years old now."

"He is no bastard. His father died in the war and I am adopting him as my son. Ruby is my wife." Edward's response went against his strict policy of not discussing his personal life while on duty. But how could he let such a statement slide?

The man's jaw dropped for a moment. "So you really believe what the Bible says about forgiveness of sin, redemption, and all that? You really believe that God can snatch people from their downward spirals and set them on a course of righteousness?"

"Of course I do." Edward's forehead furrowed. Obviously, this man with blazing eyes knew something about his wife's burdened past. "Although I fail to see how Ruby's past abuse constitutes sin on her part."

"Abuse? I'm referring to her voluntary prostitution . . . Isn't that somewhat—frowned upon—in your circles?"

Edward's mouth went dry. "You are mistaken."

He shook his head, eyes wide. "I don't believe it. You didn't know? Oh!" He slapped the table again and hooted with apparent glee. "The chaplain married a prostitute and didn't even know it!" All heads in the casemate turned to stare.

Heat crept up Edward's neck. Poor Ruby! First Sean accused her of this very thing, and now this perfect stranger! "She is and was no such thing, sir. I would beg you to keep a civil tongue in your head!"

"Oh no, you are the one who is mistaken, you pitiable fool. She has played you like a harp, I see, to improve her social standing."

"I don't believe you. You know nothing about her."

"There is a birthmark in the shape of a butterfly on her left breast. Now. How would I know that unless I had seen it myself?"

Edward stood, knocking over his chair as he did so, visceral rage eating through his veins like acid. "*What* birthmark—" he blurted out, barely able to see straight, let alone think.

"Oh no, this is just too much. Don't tell me you haven't seen it yourself! Oh how rich! She sold herself to countless men and now won't let her own husband have a go? Oh!"

Edward's fist flew into the man's jaw to silence the maniacal laughter.

Six bearded men now dropped their cards and newspapers and formed a circle around the two, obviously hoping for a fight.

Breaking through them, Edward stormed out of the casemate.

"Goodbye, Mr. Goodrich! Tell the little missus Phineas Hastings says hello!"

It isn't true. It can't be true. He was lying.

By the time Edward let himself into the brownstone on Sixteenth Street, at least he could breathe again. But Mr. Hastings' voice was entrenched in his mind, his words a perfect abatis puncturing his soul. *Why let a prisoner's barbs bother you so much?*

Because Hastings had no reason to lie. Ruby, however, did.

Cicadas and crickets droning in his ears, Edward hung his hat on the hall rack and tugged his jacket off. The red crosses on his collar mocked him as they slid past his bruised knuckles. What sort of chaplain resorted to violence?

What sort of chaplain marries a prostitute—and doesn't even know it?

Teeth clenched, Edward grasped the banister and pulled himself up the stairs toward the bedroom. It was unfair to take a prisoner's word over his wife's. Hastings was wrong about Ruby. He had to be wrong.

Steadying his breath, he entered his bedroom—and found Ruby undressing for bed.

"Oh!" She jumped. "You startled me." Ruby's hunched her back as she hastily slipped on her nightgown. "Hard day?" Her eyes searched his as she faced him again.

Edward rubbed his hand over his face. "Does it show?" He forced a smile.

She squinted at him. "What happened to your hand?"

He shrugged. "Nothing." He removed his shoes, then unclasped his belt and stepped out of his trousers. Ruby averted her gaze. "Come now, darling, surely this is nothing you haven't seen before."

296

She jerked her head around. "And just what is that supposed to mean?"

"We've been married almost eight weeks."

Her brow wrinkled. "And?"

"And you've seen me in my drawers before."

Ruby's shoulders relaxed. "Aye. True enough."

"And I've been waiting long enough." Hadn't he? Even without the treasure hunt for a birthmark, a man had a right to his own wife.

She climbed under the covers, said nothing. Until, "I'm very tired."

"So am I." He was tired of being patient, of putting her needs on a pedestal and denying that he had any of his own. Tired of treading lightly in his own marriage. Tired of wondering exactly what happened to Ruby before he met her. Without ceremony, Edward threw his clothes in a pile on the floor and joined Ruby in the bed. "It's time." How utterly unromantic. *Romance never worked anyway.*

Ruby closed her eyes. "Wait."

"For what?"

"Brush your teeth?"

Grumbling, Edward rolled out of bed and padded, barefoot, to the water closet. There had been a time when he would have done anything to woo his wife. Now he had to be reminded to brush his teeth. He glared at his reflection in the mirror. *Come on. You can do better than this.*

He half expected Ruby to have vanished by the time he returned to the bed, but she was still there. As still as a corpse, but there, nonetheless. Edward dimmed the kerosene lamp, but did not extinguish it.

Ruby slid him a sideways, skittish gaze. "Please," she whispered. "Be gentle." Tears already glazed her eyes.

Edward's heart was as disoriented as a wildly swinging pendulum. It was impossible to know just what he felt, and why. "I never wanted to make you cry. What have I done wrong, Ruby? Tell me. I have no idea how to fix whatever is wrong."

"It's not your fault."

"Then what? What is it?"

Ruby shook her head, eyes closed. "It's not your burden. It's mine." *And I mean to keep it that way.* It was her fault Edward was so desperate right now. He deserved far more than she had given him. If she wasn't going to tell him the root of her problem, she had to get over it and perform the duties of a wife. God knew she had performed before.

She pulled him close, her lips swaying against his, and wrapped her arms around his neck.

He pulled back for a moment. "Who is this in my bed with me?"

"Your wife." *And from now on, I'm going to act like it.*

Edward kissed the smile on her face, and she swirled her fingers through his hair, while his hands swept the satin curves of her figure. She did not push him away this time, though a frightening mixture of pleasure and shame exploded in her spirit. *This is dirty, this is wrong. No it isn't, it's God-ordained in marriage!* Her internal tug-of-war clamored so loudly she almost did not notice when Edward began unbuttoning her nightgown at her throat.

Ruby's breath heaved as she fought off images of every other man who had done this to her. She forced her eyes open to reassure herself this was Edward. This was love. Still, her body shuddered with every button undone, until Ruby felt she was becoming undone herself.

Edward's kisses wandered from her mouth to her ear, then trailed down her throat. Gently, he slid her nightgown over her shoulders and smothered her with tenderness—

Then he stopped. Drew back, eyes were suddenly hard.

Instinctively, she refastened the buttons on her nightgown and pulled the sheet up to her chin. "What?" she whispered.

"Never did tell you where I was today."

She eyed him, dread chilling her.

"Fort Lafayette Prison."

"Oh?" It meant nothing to her.

"Had some interesting conversations with the inmates there. Phineas Hastings sends his regards."

Darkness crowded the corners of her vision until all she saw was Edward's hollow eyes. *He knows.* And then her world went black.

––––

Atlanta, Georgia
Wednesday, July 27, 1864

BOOM!

"Are you sure we're safe here?" With her hand buried in the scruff of Rascal's neck, Ana scanned the ceiling as if expecting a shell to fall through it at any time.

"This is where the doctor says we must stay," Caitlin replied. After Ana broke her legs on the platform last week, Dr. Periwinkle said she was not to be moved once a litter had borne her home. Now Ana's bed was made right next to the parlor's empty fireplace, her legs tied to broken chair legs with strips of the sofa's slipcover. If her bones were jarred out of position before they were fully healed, she could be crippled for life.

But Ana's broken heart concerned Caitlin just as much. Even the exploding shells could not drown out the echo of Susan's vicious farewell Ana had relayed to Caitlin. What would Noah do when he learned his daughter, his Dear Heart, was not his own? Had he suspected Susan's infidelity? Or was Susan lying just from spite? Questions without answers circled and swooped until Caitlin batted them away.

"I'll be right back." Caitlin kissed Ana's forehead, uncertain whether it was physical or emotional pain that wrinkled it.

"Five minutes."

"I know." Timing the intervals between shells had proven a reliable pattern.

Caitlin stepped into the sunshine, the July heat beating down upon her shoulders in shimmering waves while honeysuckle cloyed in the

299

steamy air. *This is my fault,* Caitlin thought as she pumped water into a pitcher. If she had just left the hotel earlier, Ana never would have gone with Susan on that train. She never would have had to jump, or to hear those venomous words. And they could be in a hole in the ground even now. *Grand reward, indeed.* Yet there was no doubt that the safest of Atlanta's citizens were in backyard bombproofs.

One shell blasted through a roof and cut in half a six-year-old girl and her father, killing them in their beds. A refugee woman from Rome, Georgia, was killed while ironing outside. When a neighbor girl died from typhoid she'd contracted at a soldiers' hospital, the family buried her without a coffin in their backyard rather than risk the exposure required by a trip to the cemetery.

Caitlin shook her head as she carried the water back into the house. Atlanta was as helpless against the shells as it was against pestilence. *One might as well try hiding from lightning strikes.* Naomi was a saint for going every day to nurse at the Car Shed, ducking into bombproofs every five minutes along the way. *There are no strangers,* she had said, *when we face a common danger.*

"Thirsty?" Caitlin helped Ana sit and handed her a cup of water. She drank, and soon lay back down. "Read to me?"

Caitlin took a draught of water, too, then opened a Bible to Psalm 91. "He that dwelleth in the secret place of the most High shall abide under the shadow of the Almighty. I will say of the Lord, he is my refuge and my fortress: my God; in him will I trust. Surely he shall deliver thee from the snare of the fowler, and from the noisome pestilence. He shall cover thee with his feathers, and under his wings shalt thou trust: his truth shall be thy shield and buckler. Thou shalt not be afraid for the terror by night; nor for the arrow that flieth by day; nor for the pestilence that walketh in darkness; nor for the destruction that wasteth at noonday—"

BOOM!

Five more minutes.

New York City
Wednesday, July 27, 1864

Ruby wiped her watering eyes and tucked her handkerchief back into her sleeve as she looked out the window for a husband who did not appear, though night had already arrived. When she had woken up this morning before dawn, Edward's side of the bed was unrumpled. He must have slept somewhere else, but where, she had no idea.

She was shattered. A pile of brittle shards of glass. That was all.

If Edward would only come home, she would tell him everything, from the beginning, the only way the story could ever be told. Oh, if only Caroline were here, or Charlotte, or Alice! They had understood when she had told them. *But they were women, not your husband,* a voice reminded her. *And they heard it from you before finding out from anyone else.*

Guilt reduced her to her knees on the parlor rug. Edward did not deserve to learn her darkest secret the way he had.

"But how could I tell him?" she sobbed to the crickets chirping outside the window. "I knew he would react this way, I knew I wasn't good enough for the likes of him!"

You didn't trust Me. It was not an audible voice, but it pierced her, just the same. *Is anything too big for Me to take care of? Do I not have your future in My hand?*

"But Aiden needs a good father . . . "

I know what your son needs. Don't you believe I want the very best for him? I know what you need, too, Beloved, and I know what Edward needs. For are you not both My children?

Fresh tears coursed down Ruby's cheeks. How selfish she had been! What did Edward need? A wife who loves him for who he is, not for what she hoped to gain from him: security without intimacy and respectability without honesty.

Lord, she pleaded. *I've wronged him, and I'm so sorry. Please, help me somehow make this right as soon as he comes home!*

But Edward did not come home.

301

Chapter Twenty-Three

New York City
Sunday, August 7, 1864

$\mathcal{V}$ivian McKae sat mutely in the pew, unable to sing the "Battle Hymn of the Republic" around the lump wedged in her throat. Perhaps she should not have read the newspaper before church this morning. But after six months of scouring them for news and word from Caitlin, it was a habit she could not break, even if she wanted to—and sometimes she did. "A lady on the train was killed by a shell at Atlanta this morning." Vivian had spewed coffee over the words. Could it have been Caitlin, who had finally gotten her messages and decided to escape?

The hymn ended. After the pastor's closing prayer, which seemed more intent on guiding the hand of God to destroy Atlanta than guiding the congregants' hearts to God, the service dismissed. Vivian placed her hand on Edward's knee before he could steal away.

"Where is Ruby today? Not sick again?" She and Aiden had not come last Sunday, either.

Edward's face was drawn. "Not feeling herself these days."

Vivian frowned. Then, "Oh! You don't suppose—" She dropped her voice down to a whisper. "Could she be in the family way? I was terribly sick with—"

"Decidedly not." His sharp tone cut through the low buzz in the sanctuary as he stood. "Absolutely, certainly, the answer is no."

Unless she has yet another secret I'll be learning about later . . . Edward's hurt seemed to swallow his reason almost as completely as it had shattered his pride.

"Goodrich, my boy." Reverend Lanser clapped his hand on Edward's shoulder. "Might I have a moment?"

"With pleasure." Edward followed the man's rotund form out of the sanctuary and down the stairs to his office, grateful to not be faced with any more of Aunt Vivian's questions.

"Sit down."

Edward did so. "Sir?"

Elbows on his desk, Reverend Lanser tented his fingers and sighed. "I've never been one to mince words, so I'll just come out with it. It has come to my attention that Mrs. Goodrich is not what she appeared to be."

Dread shortening his breath, Edward braced himself.

"I have heard reports that she was a working prostitute this side of three years ago. Why, that's almost yesterday!"

"Reports from whom?"

The minister waved his hand as if to swat the question away. "Irrelevant."

"If you please. It is relevant to me."

"If you insist. It seems you made a bit of a scene when you punched a prisoner at Fort Lafayette a couple of weeks ago. Naturally, the guards wanted to know what the man had done to provoke it. He told them.

303

The guards told others, who then told others—you know how this works. Eventually word got back to me. You were surprised by the news, then?"

"As shocked as you are." Edward clenched his jaw.

"Well, it's a hard knock, son. It's no way to start a marriage, that's for sure. Does she exhibit a lingering appetite for the baser pleasures?"

"Not in the least. In fact, it's quite the opposite."

"I see." He nodded. "And when you've talked to her about this, does she demonstrate remorse and redemption?"

Edward shifted awkwardly in his chair. How could he admit he had not had a genuine conversation with his wife since the night she fainted at the mention of Phineas Hastings? That he had deliberately stayed away from dawn until dusk, filling his time with meetings and ministry to avoid her? *Coward.*

"Well?" the pastor prodded. "What does she have to say for herself?"

"It's quite a personal matter, don't you think?" The truth was, Edward had no idea. He'd never given her a chance.

"Ah, my dear young man. When you are in ministry, your personal matters become public matters."

Edward's brow creased. "How public?"

"I have no doubt you and Mrs. Goodrich will work through this. If she has left her life of sin, then we must—you must—forgive her for her dishonesty and restore her to your trust. Your marriage is not doomed. However, I'm withdrawing your name as a candidate for this church's pulpit upon my retirement. It's for your own protection."

Edward's heart sank as his head bowed. "How's that?"

"People in the church will want to know all about both you and your wife before they submit to your leadership. Let us not give them opportunity to further comment on the past. I do not judge a repentant sinner. Nor does God. But, though it pains me to say it, there are some in this church who will, with pleasure. The maelstrom of gossip would be more devastating to you both than you can imagine. Even if ultimately found blameless, you'd never be welcomed in another pulpit in the city."

Nodding, Edward stood, spinning his hat by its brim. "So let me ask you this. If I would not make a good candidate here, where is the church where the past would not be a black mark on my application?"

Reverend Lanser shrugged. "You will find it, Edward. God's plan for your life does not end here."

The pastor was right, of course. But as Edward left the church, his heart was not convinced.

———

Confederate works, north side of Atlanta, Georgia
Tuesday, August 9, 1864

Day dawned beneath a veil of rain, turning the dusty trenches ringing the city into slick, bright red gashes in the earth. Noah Becker heard no cannon. Except for a fireworks display last night, the shelling had lightened up considerably during the last few days. Federal guns had been silent now for several hours. Peering over the top of his lice-infested trench, he dared to hope that water would be the only shower from the sky today.

Maybe Hood was right. No army ever formed could possibly come up against Atlanta's fortifications. All they had to do was snip Sherman's tenuous supply line stretching to Chattanooga. Without food and ammunition, what else could the Yankees do but starve, scatter, or surrender? Both armies had already picked the countryside—and the rural homes—clean of all the food that could be foraged.

The rain stopped around eight o'clock in the morning, and still no sound came from the Union line. *Have we done it? Is it over?* Hope dawned inside him as the clouds parted for the bright red sun in the east. Soon he could hold Ana in his arms again.

And release Caitlin to find her Jack. If, in fact, he was still alive. For Caitlin's sake, Noah prayed he was. For his own sake, he stuffed down the bitter disappointment that when this was all over, he could not invite her to be part of their lives forever. *It would have been so wonderful for Analiese.* He would not admit how wonderful it would have been for him.

A chilling blast from the north shattered Noah's daydreams, as Sherman's guns thundered to life. In seconds the sky writhed with screaming lead and twisting fire, arcing like hell's rainbows over the Confederate trenches and directly into Atlanta. The earth shook and the heavens roared furiously as ten Confederate and eleven Federal batteries squared off along the north and west of the city. Twelve-pound chunks of iron ripped through the air, coming within five feet of Noah's position in the works. All hands not employed at the artillery guns grabbed their weapons. The picket lines popped and rattled with fire as men fought it out beneath the flaming sky.

Before the exhortation arrived from General Hood, every soldier knew what the general did not need to write. They were to hold their positions to the very last. "The destiny of Atlanta hangs upon the issue."

———

Atlanta, Georgia
Tuesday, August 9, 1864

BOOM! B-BOOM BOOM! BOOM!

Stunned, Caitlin locked eyes with Naomi at the table. After a lull in the shelling for a few days, war exploded once more above their heads. Rushing in to Ana in the parlor, they squeezed hands and watched silently through the window while Rascal whimpered and emptied his bladder on the floor.

The inferno of noise swelled at intervals by the roar of a falling building. All the fires of hell and all the thunders of the universe seemed to blaze and roar over the city. Caitlin's well-trained ear heard four-and-a-half-inch guns and twenty-pounder Parrots firing, as quickly as they could be loaded.

Great volumes of sulphurous smoke rolled over Atlanta and trailed down to the ground. Through this stifling haze, the sun glared down as a great red eye peering through a bronze-colored sky.

In a terrible crash, lead and light broke through the ceiling on the other side of the room. Plaster dust danced in the air before coating Caitlin's, Naomi's, and Ana's skin. Yelping, Rascal ran out of the room with his tail tucked between his legs.

White-faced, the women wrapped their arms around Ana in a protective huddle, but did not seek a safer place. *Only the hand of God can shelter us.*

"Be merciful unto me, O God, be merciful unto me," Naomi quoted from the psalms, "for my soul trusteth in thee: yea, in the shadow of thy wings will I make my refuge, until these calamities be overpast."

Only when the shelling ceased did Caitlin realize Rascal was gone from the house completely.

Confederate fortifications, north of Atlanta, Georgia
Saturday, August 27, 1864

Noah Becker felt as though he'd been holding his breath ever since he awoke yesterday morning to the most foreign sound of all: silence. As far as the eye could see to the north and the west, the Union trenches running parallel to the Confederate works were empty. No smoke rose from the bivouacs beyond. There were no flags shuddering in the hot breath of summer. No tents. No glint of sun on steel.

Throughout the day yesterday, the batteries on the defense line sent cannonballs out to feel for the enemy. No Union guns responded. It appeared as though the entire Federal army had emptied overnight. *Was it a trick?*

But today, word came down from General Hood in no uncertain terms: "Sherman has been starved out! We have won!"

Finally, Noah dared to breathe again. It was over. The emaciated Confederate army had held their own against superior numbers, saving

Atlanta after all. The tens of thousands of Rebels who had died had not done so in vain. The moment was bittersweet. Atlanta was safe, and so was slavery, for as long as the Confederacy lived.

The breath Noah drew now as he inspected the abandoned Union trenches was decidedly sour. Black dog flies covered everything—bowls, chairs, ammunition boxes. Discarded clothing, new and old, crawled with lice. Also left behind were small brick furnaces where they must have heated their cannonballs into "hot shot," spreading fire as well as debris upon impact.

Between Yankee and Rebel trenches, scavengers hunting relics joined rats and crows, and the occasional fox scouring the torn-up land.

Farther north, behind the trenches, were crude bunks. Apprehension carved Noah's brow when he came upon crates of abandoned hardtack and desiccated vegetables. *Strange leavings for a starving army.* On a headboard, a note was written with coal in large bold letters. "Goodbye, Johnny. We are going to see you soon, and when we come to Georgia we will remember Kennesaw." It was signed, "YANK."

Instinctively, Noah cocked the revolver in his hand.

"Hold it right there, Johnny Reb. I've got a bead on you so put your hands where I can see them."

A straggler. Armed and aiming right at Noah. Without turning around, Noah said, "It's over. We need not continue this pointless bloodletting."

"I feel the same way, but here you are with a revolver in the enemy camp."

"It's deserted. Except for you. Now why do you suppose that is?" Noah's voice held steady, but sweat slicked his palms. The fight was over. The Rebels had won. Atlanta was saved. He did not escape death thus far just to be killed by some disgruntled Yankee deserter mere miles from his home!

"Never mind that. Just put your weapon down."

"Capital idea. You first."

The Northerner chuckled. "You mean you don't trust me?"

"Not with a threat like this staring me in the face." He nodded to the charcoal message scrawled on the bunk in front of him. "You write that?"

"No. Drop your weapon."

"You going to shoot me in the back?"

"No such thing."

But who could trust a man who spent the last several weeks bombing innocent civilians? Clenching his jaw, Noah whirled around, his barrel pointed at the Yankee sidestepping toward a bunk that stood between them. Noah's revolver remained trained on him. "You shelled my city. I ought to shoot you where you stand for that."

The young man swallowed. "Not all of us wanted to do that, you know. Sherman's orders."

"You must have dropped four thousand shells in the city on August 9 alone."

"Five thousand."

Noah stepped closer. "God knows how many women and children you killed."

"I swear I didn't want to do it."

"So you knew there were noncombatants in the city?"

The Yankee shrugged. "Sherman said they'd been ordered out, that as a military post, they had no business being in there anyway."

"Have you any idea what it's like to have the ones you love in harm's way?"

"Yes." The Yankee swallowed. "I even know what it's like to be the cause. Now tell me. Is there anything worse than that?" Slowly, he lowered his weapon, and Noah did the same.

They stood there for a moment, the Billy Yank and the Johnny Reb, the hunger and weariness of one reflected in the other.

"Care to tell me your story?" Noah asked.

"I don't know where to start."

"Well, how is it that you are here, when the rest of the bluecoats have vanished?"

The young man sighed. "I hid when they left during the night. I've got business to attend to in the city."

Noah raised his eyebrows.

"Yesterday, though, I didn't dare go anywhere for fear of those wretched shells and cannonballs you all were tossing over here throughout the day." He half-turned and nodded at a large black orb on the ground. "That one over there scared me half to death when it rolled on through. Thank God it was a dud. Not unlike so many of your others, I must say." He brought his canteen to his lips, but finding it empty, tossed it aside.

The explosion that followed lifted Noah off his feet on a wave of pressure before sending him to the ground in a shower of red dirt and gravel. His vision spun like a reckless carousel for several moments as he lay still. Hands covering his ears, he waited, wincing, for the ringing to recede.

When his stomach settled back into place, Noah slowly pushed himself up, shaking his fingers through his hair. "Funny thing about those duds, eh, Billy? Never can tell when you might tap one back to life." His voice sounded faraway, muted by the clanging between his ears.

Pressing his hand against the pain expanding in his head, Noah cautiously walked between the splintered remains of two bunks. "Hello, Yank?"

Hang it all. Noah found him, alive, but injured. Below his knee, blood turned his Union blue trousers dark purple. Shrapnel had peppered his chest and blasted through his thigh, taking a chunk of flesh and muscle with it.

Oh no. Noah sank to his knees beside him. "It's not bad. Hang on." The man needed medical care, and he would not get it way out here. He would have to be treated in Atlanta. But he'd not get in wearing blue.

Noah peeled the man's Union jacket from his body and began rolling it into a tourniquet for his leg.

The Yankee whispered, and Noah asked him to speak louder.

"Atlanta," he tried again. "Your city?"

"Yes, that's right." Noah leaned in to read his lips.

"Then you can help. There is a letter in my pocket . . ." He winced. "Can you see . . . that it's delivered? Afraid I don't . . . have address."

"A letter?" Noah hoped he wasn't shouting.

The young man nodded.

Noah fished out an envelope and turned it over.

Caitlin McKae, Atlanta.

Atlanta, Georgia
Saturday, August 27, 1864

Caitlin hardly knew how to feel as martial music blared on the streets and neighbors emerged from perforated houses and steamy gopher holes with tremulous smiles. Most everyone was smiling. Atlanta had survived without surrendering like Vicksburg had.

Caitlin's heart had been so battered during the siege she could barely trust its conflicting beats. She was livid the Union army had targeted a civilian population, grateful the shells had stopped, and suspicious of Sherman's so-called defeat. Vivian had told her to watch for Jack, but her brother had never come. And what of Noah? Was he safe? Would he come home soon?

Idle thoughts, useless questions. Caitlin and Naomi tidied Noah's house the best they could, sweeping plaster, wood splinters, and brick rubble out the door. The kitchen and carriage house had been demolished by a shell, and the garden seemed torn up beyond repair. Nothing could be done about the hole in the roof and the second floor. Ana mourned Rascal's departure as yet the loss of another friend from her crumbling world. *But*, Caitlin told her own stinging heart, *at least we survived.*

Twenty-two others had not. Some said at least 107 residents of Atlanta had suffered through amputations without anesthesia, same as the soldiers. Dogs and cats had disappeared, and Caitlin wondered if they had found food, or become it, during the five-week siege. Thoughts of Rascal were swept away as quickly as they alighted.

"I bet you wish you'd gotten on that train to Macon, Naomi." Caitlin leaned on her broomstick as she stood on the back porch.

"And leave you and Ana? After all you've done for me? Not a chance."

Caitlin looked past the woman, focusing instead on two raggedy male figures coming through the splintered trees at the back of the lot.

Naomi followed her gaze. "Ah. More bummers. Do you want me to tell them we've got no more food to eat than they? If it weren't for General Hood sparing some rations for those of us families who stayed, I don't know what would have become of us. Wait a minute—one of them's hurt."

"How is it they came all the way down to the southern part of the city?" Caitlin shielded her eyes from the sun.

Naomi shrugged. "Maybe the northern section's all filled up. Every house on Peachtree took in patients and convalescents, it seems."

Nodding, Caitlin stepped off the porch, tossing her fraying braid over her shoulder. The man supporting the injured one halted when he saw her stride forward. Then the wounded soldier collapsed, and the other hoisted his limp body over his shoulder like a sack of grain.

"Naomi, some water." But the faithful nurse was already at the pump.

Caitlin quickened her pace, lifting her skirt above the late August jungle of thistles underfoot. And then she stopped. "Noah?" she gasped, then jogged toward him. "Is it really you?" His body was sinewy beneath his rags, his eyes piercing, electrifying blue.

"And Jack."

Her heart nearly stopped. "What?"

"He was looking for you," he panted. "I told you I'd help you find Jack. Is Ana—"

"She's fine, thank God. But is Jack—is he—"

Noah closed his eyes for a moment, the lines of his face visibly relaxing. "Injured. Passed out." He pushed past her. "He will live."

Long-bottled tears overflowed in sweet release as she trailed them into his house. *Thank You, God, thank You, thank You.* She wiped her face with her apron and hoped she had not made the mess worse. To have Noah and Jack both, it was a dream. *Her* dream come true.

————

To be so near Caitlin after wondering if he'd ever see her again, to watch her shed tears of joy for another man, was almost more than Noah could bear. *She was never mine to lose.* Noah laid Jack on the dining room table and backed away, allowing Caitlin and Naomi to tend his wounds.

"What happened?" Naomi asked while Caitlin bent over him like a willow to the river, whispering in his ear.

Noah looked away as he answered. Perhaps he should not be here for their reunion. "A shell exploded. Shrapnel struck his leg."

"Raked his chest, too, I see. His leg bandage is already sodden . . ." she murmured.

"Papa?" He heard Ana call. "Papa?" But why didn't she come running?

Heart thundering, he strode across the hall toward her voice. His knees nearly betrayed him when he found her in the parlor, both legs tied to broken pieces of furniture. In a fraction of a second, he was at her side, barely registering that a shell had plowed through the room. "Ana, what has happened? Are you in pain?" He crouched on the floor beside her, wrapped his arms around her thin body. Her sobs shuddered against his chest.

"Susan said you're not my Papa!"

Anger licked through Noah's veins. "You are the daughter of my heart. I chose to be your Papa, and I will be your Papa for the rest of your life." He kissed the top of her head and prayed she would believe him.

"She tried to take me away even though I said I didn't want to go! I said I would wait here for you but she didn't listen! Miss McKae found me at the Car Shed and—and—I jumped off the train but my legs broke when I fell!"

It was too horrifying to be true. "You jumped from a train? It wasn't moving was it?"

She nodded, and visions of her on the tracks, mutilated by the iron horse surged in his mind. Thank God it was only two broken legs!

Caitlin appeared in the doorway. "I am so sorry. I tried to catch her—the doctor said her little legs were just too weak for the angle at which she landed."

Too weak. Because of smallpox, likely, but also because there had not been enough food for a growing girl. "I made the wrong decision," he said into his daughter's hair. "I should have been here the whole time. None of this would have happened if I'd been here." His head ached with growing pressure.

"But, Noah." Caitlin knelt beside him. Did she realize she was using his Christian name again? "They would not have allowed you to stay home. And you did it. You stopped Sherman's army at the gate." Tears filled her sparkling brown eyes again. "If it weren't for you, I never would have found Jack. I don't know how you did it, but I am forever in your debt. I thought I'd never see my brother again."

Noah's eyebrows plunged. "You have a brother?"

Her eyes widened. "Yes! Jack! I thought surely he told you."

"Jack. Jack is your brother?"

"Yes! Who did you think he was when I first mentioned—oh." Her cheeks bloomed pink. "Of course not. I mean, of course, Jack is only my little brother. There is no other man—except—oh dear. You've only just come home. Spend some time with Ana, she has missed you so." She pushed herself up to leave, but Noah caught her hand.

"But you did not?"

A lump bobbed in her throat. "I missed you." Her voice was but a whisper.

"Caitlin, I—" Words failed him, utterly and completely.

She smiled. "We have time. You're home now. We are all together

314

at last, the way it should be. There is time, and I will answer all your questions." She gave his hand a light squeeze and returned to the dining room to see Jack. Her brother. Noah remembered then, what joy felt like.

"I—I suppose Ana told you. What Susan said on the train?"

Noah unlatched his gaze from the rubble that had once been his kitchen and turned to Caitlin. "Yes, she told me."

She blinked, looked down at her fingers pleating and unpleating her apron. "So . . . how are you?"

He concentrated on her lips to filter her words through the relentless ringing in his ears. "Susan was completely out of line." He sighed and leaned against the porch column, the sharp edges of its peeling paint prickling through his shirt. "Nothing will change my love for my daughter, and thank God, Ana seems convinced of it now."

"That's wonderful. But it isn't what I asked." A strand of hair blew across her freckled face before she hooked it behind her ear. Her eyes held his steady. "It must be so difficult for you, having doubt cast upon your relationship to Ana."

He smiled. "There was never any doubt."

"But—"

"I owe you an explanation." His vision beginning to spin again, Noah sat on the porch steps and patted the rough boards next to him.

"It's such a personal matter, please, if you'd rather not . . ." But she stepped closer, and he took her hand as she sat beside him.

"I want you to know. " He pressed a kiss to the back of her hand, then released it. "Once upon a time, I was twenty-four years old, had been in America for four years, and all I did was work and study. I had no time to learn the rules of courtship in the South, let alone actually try my hand at it. I was as naïve as they come. But having left my entire family in Germany, I longed to one day have my own. I was so lonely. I longed for intimacy—not just the physical aspect, understand—but to know another person on the deepest level, and to be known, truly known, in return. I craved companionship and love." Indeed, he was starved for it.

"Go on."

Noah picked up a broken branch of boxwood and absently plucked the glossy leaves from it, one by one. "Susan's father was a city council member who I had often seen and spoken with in city hall, where I worked as a legal clerk. One day, after I mentioned I'd be leaving soon to practice law in Georgia, he told me I was to court his daughter. That she was too shy to tell me herself, but she had fallen in love with me, and he was giving his permission and blessing to marry her. She was young and beautiful. Scores of men flocked to her all the time. I could hardly believe my good fortune, that of all those men, she wanted me. I'd assumed her to be a girl of froth rather than of substance, but if she saw something in me when so many shunned me for being an immigrant, perhaps I had misjudged her. Turns out, I hadn't."

Caitlin nodded, and Noah felt like the fool all over again. Shame wormed through his middle even now.

"We had a whirlwind courtship, her father pressing for a wedding right away. I was so blinded by her charm that I did not stop to ask why. And in that short amount of time, she had made me believe she loved me, though not nearly as much as I thought I loved her."

"Thought?"

"It was the haze of infatuation. True love needs time to cultivate and grow, to be tested and refined, to mature." He dropped her gaze like a hot coal, tossed his stripped branch to the ground.

Crossing his arms, he focused on a knot in the pine floorboard. "Well. It was not happily ever after for us. On our wedding night, she turned her back, both figuratively and literally. Other than a few chaste kisses before the wedding, I never touched her. She pushed me away completely, said I disgusted her."

"But why?" Caitlin's eyes were wide.

"Isn't it obvious?"

"No, it is not!"

Noah stifled a chuckle when Caitlin's cheeks flamed red. "I was not the man of her dreams. I was a nobody, from a foreign land, with no real money or family name to speak of. And she was in love with someone else."

"Truly?"

"Truly."

"But she must have had a change of heart about you."

Noah shook his head. "She never did."

She frowned. "Not one time?"

"No." His eyes bore into hers, willing her to understand what he was loath to say. "The marriage was never consummated."

Her hand covered her mouth. "But—but—"

"At nineteen years old, Susan was in the family way, courtesy of another woman's husband. It wasn't until we had moved to Decatur that I learned of her delicate condition, a secret she said even her father didn't know."

"Then why did he rush the marriage?"

"It would seem he had read the writing on the wall, so to speak. He decided to get her safely married off—and quickly—rather than risk the scandal she seemed so bent on creating. I was a convenient groom for the purpose, with my relocation already planned." A grim smile bent his lips.

Caitlin whispered something he couldn't hear, then nodded for him to continue.

"I told her I'd remain her husband, for what was a girl in her condition to do?" He shook his head. "She chose independence over motherhood. Susan was not ready to be—how did she put it? 'Locked away in domestic isolation.' So, no sooner was Ana's name written in the family Bible than did we have our marriage annulled. We had a lawyer draw up paperwork renouncing any legal claim Susan had on Ana. She signed it without a backwards glance, went north to Chattanooga, and I brought Ana with me here, to this very house, along with a mammy to

317

be her wet nurse. That was supposed to be the end of it."

Noah risked a glance at Caitlin.

She shook her head, pressed her fingertips to her eyelids before speaking. "You could have given up the baby to an orphanage," she said. "She is not your blood."

He smiled. "No. But she is my Heart. After Susan, she was all I needed." Noah's heart was in his throat as his broad hand swallowed Caitlin's. "Until now."

Chapter Twenty-Four

Atlanta, Georgia
Thursday, September 1, 1864

*H*ow is he?" Noah laid a hand on Caitlin's shoulder, and she covered it with her own.

"I fear he is worse." The cuts in Jack's chest had been superficial, but the ragged wound in his leg gaped, the edges bruised. Fever sweat soaked Jack's saddle-brown hair, and delirium wagged his head. "Should we fetch a doctor?"

"No doctor would come, my dear." Naomi soaked another strip of a parlor slipcover in fresh water and mopped the beads from his face. "Those that are left are stretched beyond their limits with cases far more severe than this. Let me tend him for a while. Ana will read and keep us company, won't you, dear?"

Propped up in the corner, Ana held up *Robinson Crusoe* and grinned.

"I'd offer to take you for a walk to get some fresh air, but there is nothing fresh about Atlanta." Noah's lake-blue eyes soothed Caitlin's raw nerves.

"I'd have to decline anyway. You aren't exactly presentable." She smiled and cocked an eyebrow at the hair overlapping his ears.

"Aha!" Naomi fished in her apron pocket. "There's the scissors, dear."

Warmth spread across her face.

"You were saying?" Noah winked.

"Yes, please, cut Papa's hair, Miss McKae, he looks like a coondog!"

The reminder of Rascal's absence darted through Caitlin and everyone else in the room, though no one spoke of it. Recovering, her lips tipped in a smile as she accepted the scissors and led the way to the back porch, ignoring the tripping of her heart.

"I'm not going to find any lice in here, now am I?" Caitlin teased as she pulled a comb through Noah's hair, sending shivers down his spine.

"Oh no, they all evacuated along with the Yankees. Ana even confirmed it yesterday."

"Did she now?" Caitlin's laughter tickled his ears. "I can just imagine her inspecting you as if you were both chimpanzees."

"That's about the way it went, too." He closed his eyes as the comb and Caitlin's fingernails raked through his hair down to his neck. The ringing in his ears had receded, but his head still ached—less so, however, under Caitlin's touch.

"The change in her spirit is remarkable since you've been home," she murmured. "Her little heart was wasting away for missing you, I think."

Noah started to nod, but she placed her palm against his brow. "Don't move. I'm cutting now."

"Not too short."

"Don't you trust me?"

If he could only see her face. "Trust is a fragile thing."

"Look down please." She tipped his head until his chin dipped almost to his chest. The cool blade of the scissors ran across the nape of his neck as she snipped. "It is indeed." Her breath feathered his skin.

"I've had a hard time trusting ever since Susan."

"For good reason." She combed and tugged his hair, snipping here and there.

"I had a hard time trusting you. You had secrets."

"But is it any wonder I kept them?"

"No." Caitlin had explained them to him shortly after he'd shared about his artificial marriage. The scar on her jaw. The scar on her arm. Her reckless enlistment. The Rebel's New Testament found in her hand after the Battle of Fair Oaks, which had caused the misidentification that sent her to Atlanta. He had suspected she was from the North, but her soldiering had come as a shock. It also meant she could understand him, and what war did to a man's soul, without him needing to explain himself.

"And are you quite disappointed I'm a—" She bent to his ear. "Yankee?"

There was nothing about her that disappointed him in the least. "Remember I told you I enlisted to defend my homeland. And the men I fought beside were some of the bravest I have ever known. But if I lived in the North, I would have fought with as much vigor to defend the Northern ideals of freedom and a united nation. That's why I fought in Germany, with *my* brother, you know. For democracy and equal rights for all citizens."

" 'There is an unseen battlefield, In every human breast, Where two opposing forces meet, And where they seldom rest.' Sound familiar?"

"Yes!"

"It was printed on a page you tore from *Balm for the Weary and The Wounded*, on which you wrote one of your letters to me. I've always thought the lines were beautiful."

"Now a Yankee is quoting from a Confederate devotional book.

Maybe there is hope for this country yet." He chuckled.

Caitlin circled to his front and cocked her head as she measured the length of his hair on both sides. "To tell you the truth, I wouldn't care if I never heard about North, South, Union, Confederate, Rebel, or Yankee again. I'm more than ready for this war to be over." Her tone carried the conviction that only a veteran could feel. He understood her. Finished trimming, she stood back. "The question is, are you?"

She handed him a looking glass and he inspected his reflection. What he saw—other than a man with a tidy haircut—was a soul conflicted. An unseen battlefield, indeed. He set the mirror down.

"I just—I just need to know if I should be bracing myself for you to go away again." Caitlin dropped her scissors in her pocket and folded her hands in front of her apron. "If we should be preparing Ana for another departure." Her gaze skipped his eyes and darted between his ears, instead, apparently still judging her handiwork. When she reached out to measure the lengths one more time, he caught her wrists, and stood.

Finally, her eyes met his. Her fingers twined in his hair. "I just don't want the lengths to be uneven," she whispered.

Noah felt somewhat uneven himself.

"Are you leaving again?" She repeated the question.

"I don't want to."

"But does that mean—"

Noah bent his head, kissed the freckles on her nose. His lips brushed hers as she turned her face to the side. Her hands slid down his arms, fingers digging into his biceps.

"Noah Becker, if you kiss me right now my heart will be yours forever whether you live through another battle or not. So please, have mercy. Don't take my love until you know you can keep it safe." Her pulse beat visibly in her neck. "I want this moment as much as you do," she whispered. "But I don't want to be made useless pining away for you if this is all I'll ever have. A kiss would ruin me with longing for you." She turned to face him once more. "Don't you know I ache for you enough already?"

Noah's heart seized as tears glossed Caitlin's eyes. At length, he released her, though his arms felt hollow without her.

She nodded, lifting her chin in that determined way of hers. But her trembling lips said nothing.

"Caitlin! Mr. Becker!" Naomi burst onto the back porch. "The government warehouses have been thrown open to the city! We are free to carry away as many sacks of grain as we can!"

Noah frowned. "They are giving the food away?"

"Come see!"

Noah and Caitlin looked at each other, then hustled through the central hall and out the front door of the house. Sure enough, a handful of residents were carrying grain home, either on their shoulders or with wheelbarrows.

Naomi volunteered to go, and Noah pulled Caitlin back in the house. "They are evacuating the city."

"Who is?"

"The government! The soldiers! They are giving Atlanta up! There is no other reason to abandon such a precious commodity. If I'm right, the army will march south out of the city yet this day."

Noah was right. In fact, they marched out of town on McDonough Street, just beyond his front door. Battle raged afresh inside Noah. He wanted to stay home. But were his wants relevant? Didn't every soldier now tramping south with bare feet and broken spirit long for their own family and hearth? What gave Noah the right to enjoy the comforts of home—even a torn-up home—when thousands of other men still marched though the fight had gone out of them completely?

The Confederacy was a lost cause now, anyone could see it. But Noah had committed to it.

I've also run from it. Twice. Visions of the fifteen deserters being executed scrolled across his mind. *They will shoot me on sight if they recognize my face.*

A dull headache pounded at his temples as he glanced at Jack's young face. What was he, all of twenty years old? Noah had risked his life to bring Caitlin's brother here, and he was hanging on to life by a thread. When Wilhelm had died, the grief had all but crushed Noah. How could he leave Caitlin to suffer this loss alone?

Noah's gaze moved to Ana, his little girl with broken legs. How would the Yankees treat the people of Atlanta when they arrived? For certainly, they were on their way. Noah set his lips in a firm line. He could not stay, nor could he leave. Not yet.

The weary, mournful cadence of Noah's comrades carried on the sticky breeze as they trudged past his house and out of Atlanta.

> *A hundred months have passed, Lorena,*
> *Since last I held that hand in mine;*
> *And felt the pulse beat fast, Lorena,*
> *Tho' mine beat faster far than thine . . .*

———

Night was a void of both sight and sound. Not even crickets chirped. Everything in Atlanta was death-still.

Especially Jack.

By the light of the moon, Caitlin unwound the bandage from his leg, the odor becoming sharper with each layer removed. By the time the cloth was fully off, she could not help but cover her nose. Her stomach twisted as she bent closer. The bleeding seemed to have stopped, but—what color was the skin? *Oh, for a decent light!*

"Still up, I see." Naomi's soft voice drifted from the doorway. "And how is your patient?"

"Come look at this, if you can, please. I can't make it out, but—"

Naomi's stride hitched several feet from the table. "Oh no. That smell."

Caitlin backed away, eyes wide, as Naomi swept closer to the table. "What do you need? More water?"

Shaking her head, Naomi released a weary sigh. "Water will not help him, now. It's gangrene."

Dread corkscrewed through Caitlin. "What do we do?"

"Nothing. You must brace yourself, dear. It will play out cruelly."

"Surely you don't mean—isn't there anything that can be done?"

"Nitric acid might kill the infection before it eats away his leg. I heard the doctor say that iodine worked well, but we never had any of that at the Car Shed. An amputation would remove the infection before it could take his life."

Caitlin's pulse rocketed.

"Prepare yourself." Naomi laid a hand on her shoulder. "I fear this is one battle he will not be able to win."

Shock rippled over Caitlin's skin, raising goose bumps on her arms. "No. This does not end here, not like this. I'm going for a doctor. Dr. Periwinkle will come, I know he will. Stay with him?" She did not wait for Naomi's response before running out the door. Her little brother had come for her. She would not fail him now.

The Car Shed. Whatever patients were still left in town would be gathered there for evacuation, Caitlin guessed. And where patients were, there was bound to be a doctor. She would start there, at the depot.

With her skirt in her fist, and her heart in her throat, her feet carried her north, around holes blasted in the streets during the siege, and over ruts carved by army wagons giving up on Atlanta. Gravel entered her shoes at the seams and ground her feet as she ran, but she did not stop. Her stays cut into her ribs as her lungs sought breath. Jack could not die. Dr. Periwinkle would help. He had to.

But before she even reached Hunter Street, a quarter mile south of the train tracks, an explosion ripped through the night with the force of a runaway locomotive, jolting the earth beneath her feet. Tongues of flame erupted skyward. Caitlin covered her ears against the tremendous noise and watched in awe as buildings rocked like cradles, the glass in every window shattering. Chinks of light appeared through brick and wood as shrapnel pierced the walls.

Suddenly rooted in the dirt road, Caitlin clapped her hands over her ears, waiting for it to end. The ghoulish red sky pulsed with flame and arcing rockets. Crash followed desperate crash while sparks filled the air with countless spangles. Time disappeared.

Strong arms circled Caitlin's waist, pulling her back, away from the trembling buildings, breaking the spell that had bound her. It was Noah, she knew without looking. She would find no doctor tonight.

The explosions lasted for hours, the astounding booms punctuated by the rapid-fire rattle of musketry. The Rebel army was destroying its own munitions that had been loaded into the remaining trains.

To Caitlin, every hour lost was an hour closer to Jack's death.

————

Atlanta, Georgia
Friday, September 2, 1864

Morning dawned in a haze of smoke over a city panting between two flags. Abandoned by the Confederacy, not yet taken by the Union, Atlanta was without police protection, a municipal government, and practically without any law, for how long no one knew. As Noah Becker stepped outside in search of a doctor for Jack, he carried his revolver with him.

This is my fault. If Noah hadn't stopped Jack and talked to him, he wouldn't have tossed his canteen onto the waiting shell. How cruel and pointless, that a man could survive three years of battles and be brought to death's door by a wayward canteen. Noah pinched the bridge of his nose, the bump from its break pushing against his thumb. He would find a doctor before Caitlin awoke.

Striding up to Dr. Calhoun's residence, Noah knocked on the door and waited. A Negro man cracked it open a few inches, scanning Noah up and down. "Any Yankees out there?"

"Not that I can see. Is the doctor in?"

"Yessir, but he sick in bed. Tumor on one side of his face. You sick too? You sho nuff don't look it."

"No. I have a friend, though, who needs a doctor's care. Is there any other doctor in town?"

The Negro shook his head of tightly coiled grey hair. "No how. Our doctor is the only one left, and that only because he can't get up."

Noah tipped his hat. "Thank you kindly."

The door clicked shut.

Moments later, tramping feet could be heard before their owners could be seen. From the porch of the doctor's residence, Noah watched dusty blue columns march into town until the order to halt and rest scattered them like ants from an anthill just destroyed.

There were surgeons among them.

Noah was their enemy. *But Jack is one of them.* So was Caitlin.

Slipping away between the houses and bombproofs, Noah quickly arrived back home.

"Caitlin." He shook her awake by her shoulder.

She startled beneath his hand, then right away, checked for Jack's pulse. The air in the room was fetid. Gangrene had a voracious appetite.

"The Yankees are here." He kept his voice low. "They have surgeons, medicine, everything Jack needs, and they are only blocks away. In fact, they will be coming through here any moment. All you need do is step outside and hail a congenial-looking fellow. Your accent will protect you as soon as you speak, I wager." *And who wouldn't want to help a beauty like you?*

"They are here?" Her hand fluttered to her heart. "You'll be their prisoner, you must go!"

"Tell Ana I love her—"

"Papa? You're leaving again? But I need you here!"

Noah's heart buckled at the tremor in Ana's voice. He flew to her side and wrapped her in his arms for but a moment. "The war cannot last much longer, now." He kissed the top of her head.

"Go!" Tears swam in Caitlin's eyes.

"I'll come back." Noah stood, though Ana's wail nearly broke him in half. "Stay safe. We'll be together again."

327

A hard knock sounded on the front door.

"It's for you," he whispered to Caitlin, and stole out the back door before his lips could steal her kiss.

Caitlin's voice floated down the hall as Noah left, her Irish lilt thickening as she spoke. She was keeping the Yankees busy for a moment, giving him time to sneak away. It was time to rejoin Hood's army, though wrenching himself from Caitlin and Ana took all the strength he had. *Lord, bless them and keep them. Make Your face shine upon them and give them peace. Give us all peace, in Jesus' name.*

"Halt!" The cocking of a hammer behind Noah stopped him cold. "Put your weapon down, slowly, and turn around."

"OH WHAT A NIGHT we had. They came burning the store house and about night it looked like the whole town was on fire. We all set up all night. If we had not set up our house would have ben burnt up for the fire was very near and the soldiers were going around setting houses on fire where they were not watched. They behaved very badly."

—CARRIE BERRY, 10-year-old resident of Atlanta

Act Five

REFINED BY FIRE

Chapter Twenty-Five

New York City
Saturday, September 3, 1864

*F*rom inside the brownstone on Sixteenth Street, Edward and Ruby Goodrich could hear the guns saluting Sherman's victory and the bands striking up "Hail, Columbia" in Union Square, where George and Vivian were sure to be. They could hear the crowds cheering as much for Lincoln as for Sherman, since Atlanta's fall was a thunderbolt to any peace negotiations. "Let the war go on!" they could hear the people shout.

"I imagine Reverend Lanser will be utterly rejoicing over this in church tomorrow," Edward muttered over his newspaper.

"And why not? Isn't it a great victory for the Union?" Ruby sat on the floor, rolling a ball back and forth to Aiden.

"Yes, of course. For the Union. But for humanity, I'd consider it a failure. Are you forgetting my cousin Caitlin was living in Atlanta? We still don't know if she survived that senseless shelling. Aunt Viv is absolutely beside herself until she hears from her, or from Jack."

And that is the most you've said to me in a week, thought Ruby. After Edward had been withdrawn as a candidate for the pastorate, tension dripped between them. Hot words and cold silences pushed them to separate bedrooms. Refusing to hear her story, Edward drowned himself in his work and Ruby gave all her attention to Aiden. It was easy to do, especially since several of her sewing clients had withdrawn their business from her.

"Aye, I remember Caitlin. I used to watch her and Jack when they were children in Seneca Village. I do pray they are both safe."

Edward grunted. "How holy of you."

Ruby whipped her head up, skin tingling. "You know darlin', it was not so very long ago that you were nurturing my faith instead of mocking it."

"Ball! Ball!" Aiden protested her brief pause in the game. She rolled it back to him.

"Ah yes," Edward said behind his paper. "I'm the one who's changed, then, am I?"

"Aye." She swallowed. "Yes. You have, and not for the better."

"Funny. In my estimation, it's my circumstances that have changed, not me. You may say *you* are not different, but the information I have certainly is. Wouldn't you agree?"

"You don't have the whole story, Edward. I want to tell you, if you'll promise not to interrupt, and not to hide behind that newspaper." *Even though you once told me you were not my confessor. That we were all sinners saved by grace.*

"Mama! Ball! Roll ball!"

Edward folded his paper and dropped it to the floor. Quickly, Ruby rolled the ball back to Aiden.

"I'll start with the war. Matthew left, and I was on my own to make ends meet. His pay was delayed by months." Aiden rolled the ball back, and she returned it to the boy. "I took in as much sewing as I could, but it wasn't enough. I was evicted from my apartment and looked in Five

Points for lodging. But I couldn't bring myself to stay in the only flophouse I could afford."

She hazarded a glance to Edward and saw that his eyes had lost their hard edge. He appeared to be listening. Ruby caught the ball and rolled it back once more. "I tried applying to the Five Points House of Industry, but was denied for lack of references. Then I begged some Moral Reform Association ladies to give me a chance and place me as a domestic somewhere." She rolled the ball to Aiden.

"It was while I was there, that Phineas Hastings—"

Crack! A wail erupted from Aiden, who held his head with both chubby hands. He had stumbled into the corner of a table while chasing the ball.

"Oh, did you hurt your head? Let me see." Ruby scooped him up and tried to console him, but the boy would have none of it. She bounced him on her hip and paced the parlor, murmuring in his ear.

Edward just sat there, watching. "Story time is over, I see." He stood.

Ruby frowned over Aiden's head at him. *Unfair.* "I can't very well finish it while he's upset now, can I?"

"Course not. Just drop everything and take care of his needs. Seems to be your specialty."

Tears bit Ruby's eyes. The man was impossible.

Atlanta, Georgia
Monday, September 12, 1864

"Caitlin." Jack's voice was edged with impatience. "It is the best way. It is the only way."

"I'm not leaving," she said again. The Union doctor had successfully treated Jack's leg with nitric acid before the gangrene had spread too far. His recovery, though incomplete as of yet, was enough for Caitlin to have no qualms about arguing with him now.

"Then you are at odds with Uncle Billy, and I sincerely doubt you'll win."

Uncle Billy. Such a congenial-sounding label for such a battle-hardened general. William Tecumseh Sherman may be a military genius, but his recent order for a forced evacuation of every civilian still in Atlanta marked the first of its kind since the forced removal of the Cherokees from Georgia. Certainly it was the first time such an order was imposed on white people, to Caitlin's knowledge.

"It's for your own good. Don't you see? Atlanta is a worn-out, used-up town. There's not enough food to feed you, and the Union army can't be handing out rations to all four thousand of you every day." He flipped a piece of hardtack in the air and let it clatter on the table. "And think of the wood! Winter is coming, and where is the wood with which to keep you warm? Every stick of it is in the miles of abatis and fortifications left behind by your city's fair defenders."

Caitlin struggled to maintain an even tone. "The city's defenders bore their breasts to shot and shell for six grueling weeks of siege. Their courage outlasted their odds. And you forget, this city is not 'mine' by choice."

"Yes, it is. You are making the choice right now."

"It's not that simple. I have a responsibility to Ana. And to Noah. He said he'd come back, and he deserves to find his daughter when he does."

"Noah, is it?" Jack raised an eyebrow.

"Yes. The man who brought you to me. Remember him?"

"I remember I told our mother I'd see you to safety. Her heart bleeds for you every day you're gone. And now Sherman is offering free transportation to Nashville, and you thumb your nose at it, as though it were nothing. I won't be here forever to watch out for you."

Did he not realize how much she had endured without him thus far? "What about Ana?"

"Bring her with you. Mother would love her to pieces, you know she would."

"Jack." She pinned him with her gaze. "I'm not leaving."

"Not for me? Not for Mother?"

Caitlin pressed her lips resolutely.

Sparks burned in Jack's eyes. "Did you ever stop to consider how terribly selfish you are being? There are people who love you. And they aren't here, they are home. That's New York, in case you've forgotten. You have family, Caitlin. Me, Mother, Uncle George, and our cousin Edward. Go home."

"I'm glad Mother has been reunited with her long-lost brother and nephew, I truly am. If she's well taken care of with her family, then she doesn't need me, too." Caitlin drew a breath. "This is my home now," she whispered.

Jack's nostrils flared as he looked out the window. Brassy strains of "Yankee Doodle" floated on the breeze from the band playing at City Hall. He turned back, eyes flashing. "And what will happen to you after we leave Atlanta, and its former citizens return? How do you think they'll treat you when they come back and see you're a Unionist after all?"

Caitlin swallowed. Licked her lips. "You may be right. But Noah—"

"'But Noah.' Always Noah. He is a Rebel soldier, sister. Or did this somehow escape your notice? He is the enemy!"

"He is not!" She dropped her eyelids. *He is . . . a phantom. A hope. A dream.* "He is not the enemy."

Caitlin met Jack's gaze once more. He did not need to speak for her to read his thoughts.

Traitor.

———

During the next ten days, thirty-five hundred people departed Atlanta. Families with relatives in the Rebel army or farther South, were taken to Rough and Ready. Those with family in the North, or strong Union sentiments, were taken north. Naomi Ford was among them, on her way to her son in Gettysburg, and yet another hole was carved from

Caitlin's life, until her heart felt as riddled as Noah's shell-blasted, wind-swept house.

Still, she stayed. By virtue of Caitlin's relation to Jack and Ana's broken legs, they were among the fifty families allowed to remain, on one condition. They would not be a burden to the Union army.

But the Union army was a burden to its host. Tens of thousands of Union troops built camp homes for themselves by pulling planks of wood off houses and harvesting bricks for their own stout chimneys. Pulled up fences provided wood for their floors. Villages of these little cabins now crowded together in front of City Hall and spread across open fields.

Every other day, the army sent foraging wagons to scour the deserted countryside. The train always returned after three or four days replete with corn, sweet potatoes, flour, chicken, hogs, cows, and whatever else the quartermasters could find to confiscate.

Caitlin asked for nothing—except for the soldiers to stop pulling Noah's house apart for their cabins. While bands played and generals smoked cigars from the grand porches of her neighbors, Caitlin picked corn from ruts in the road like a dog lapping at crumbs from the table.

Noah would come back. They would be there for his return.

———

Rock Island Prison Camp, Illinois
Thursday, October 13, 1864

The rags draping Noah's gaunt frame shivered against his skin while trees dripped with curls of sunshine and fire. Below autumn's majestic canopy, he sat in the dirt, his back against the wooden planks of his barracks. In one hand, he held his day's ration: a two-inch square of pungent salt pork and a one-third pound loaf of stone-hard bread. *Man does not live on bread alone . . .* But without enough bread, men died.

Noah tossed the sick-smelling pork aside and slammed his loaf against the wall to break it into more manageable pieces. A gunshot cracked the air, spraying dirt all over Noah when the bullet hit the earth beside him.

Noah dropped his bread and spread his hands to show the guards he was no threat. He should have remembered loud noises were grounds for being shot. In fact, since he had arrived at the camp, Noah had counted six prisoners who had been shot inside the fence, not trying to escape. At least one of them had been shot while he was inside his own barracks.

Between six and eight thousand Southerners were imprisoned on this three-mile-long, half-mile-wide island in the Mississippi River between Rock Island, Illinois, and Davenport, Iowa. Surrounded by a twelve-foot-high fence and guarded by the 108th U.S. Colored Troops, Noah had never felt so far from home.

What's left of it. Was his house even still standing? Were Caitlin and Ana scratching out their survival from Atlanta's ruins? When would a letter be able to get through the lines to them?

Noah had nothing but the threads on his back. Everything he'd worked for since coming to America was gone. The Confederate currency and bonds were worthless now. How could he hope to provide for his family even after the war was over?

Forgive me, he prayed silently. *I am grateful for life itself.* He would get home to Caitlin and Ana somehow. Someday.

"Becker."

Noah squinted into the sun to find Col. Andrew J. Johnson, commanding officer of the prison camp, and quickly scrambled to his feet. "Sir?"

"Hungry?"

Noah returned his gaze, but said nothing. Of course he was hungry. He was wasting away.

"You're foreign-born, isn't that right?"

"Germany." Would his immigrant status never fade?

The colonel cocked an eyebrow. "Did you happen to have any connection to the 1848 revolution over there?"

Wilhelm's face surged in Noah's mind. Yes he and his brother had fought for the unification of Germany, and a democratic government and for the equal rights of all people. "Yes," he conceded, cringing inwardly. The irony that he was now a prisoner for siding with secession and slavery was not lost on him.

"Did you know Davenport is full of your old comrades?"

Noah frowned. "Pardon me?"

"The Forty-eighters. German revolutionaries, intellectual and political refugees. They came to America via New Orleans, then sailed up the Mississippi until landing in Davenport, just across the river from us now. One-third of the city is German, they still speak the language. You'd fit right in."

I doubt it. While a twinge of nostalgia washed over him, Noah had not come to the United States to be part of a German enclave. He had come to be an American. And now, neither North nor South would claim him. "Will that be all?"

"No. It's just the beginning. I suspect you fought to protect your state against invading troops more than for the principles of the Confederacy."

Noah waited.

"How would you like full rations and a new set of clothes to keep you warm this winter? How would you like to get out of here, away from this constant armed surveillance? How would you like one hundred dollars bounty and a regular paycheck—in greenbacks?"

"I don't understand."

Johnson cut his voice low. "I'm recruiting you into the Union army."

"To fight against the South?" Noah could never make war against his former comrades.

"Never. You have my word."

Noah's brow furrowed. "Then what?"

"Our military presence in the West needs reinforcements. You'd have to swear allegiance to the United States of America, but then you'd trade your rags for a soldier's uniform. In blue. We'd feed you well."

Noah pinched the bridge of his nose, the bump beneath his thumb a reminder of his previous transgressions. Temporary desertion was one matter, but literally turning coats another. No matter what he chose, he'd be hated by one government, and disposable to the other.

Johnson left, and Noah scuffed a slow circuit around the barracks. Rounding building number sixteen, a lively conversation between two imprisoned Southern officers met his ears.

"The justification of slavery in the South is the inferiority of the Negro. If we make him a soldier, we concede the whole question. And if slavery is to be abolished then I take no more interest in our fight."

"But Washington used Negroes as enlisted soldiers in the Revolutionary War, and they have advanced in intelligence very much since that time."

"I say again, if the Negro is fit to be a soldier, he is not fit to be a slave."

"There is no doubt that the proposition cuts under the traditions and theories of the South. But I am for it. Set free all who will enlist, and let us prosecute this war on something like an equal basis."

Noah nodded to them in greeting as he passed, though it was not their faces he saw. Instead, Saul, Bess, and a host of dark-skinned souls loomed before him. His stride quickened along with his resolve. Noah had defended his Southern homeland. Now it was time to side with freedom once again.

Chapter Twenty-Six

Atlanta, Georgia
Tuesday, November 8, 1864

*Y*ou still haven't heard from him?"

Not trusting her voice, Caitlin simply shook her head. Dreaming of Noah did not count.

Jack sighed. "I need to go, too. Just finished voting for Lincoln's re-election, and now I am to join General Thomas's army up in Nashville. Sherman's getting ready to move out for his winter campaign, too." His crisp blue uniform reminded Caitlin that he was a man, and not still the fourteen-year-old boy who looked to her for mothering when Vivian's grief stole her from the task. "Don't you think you should go back to New York now?"

"You know I can't." Even if she wanted to leave, the union provost marshal's offer for transit north had expired.

"Poor Mother. She wanted both of us home, and instead she gets neither."

Caitlin's nose pinched as she grasped his hands and looked up into his shining hazel eyes. "I'm sorry I left you." Her words barely fit around the sorrow clogging her throat.

"When you were wounded in Virginia? And they mistook you for a Confederate soldier?" A smile curled on his lips as he shook his head. "That wasn't your fault. And you forget, I never asked for your company." He winked, softening the sting of his words. "You are not your brother's keeper."

"Because I failed."

"No, sister. Maybe God had something else in mind for you. And He is more than able to be my protector without any help from you."

Caitlin cocked her head. "This doesn't sound like the Jack I remember."

"Like I said. God is able. Maybe you're the one who could use a lesson in trust now." A roguish grin on his face, he handed her his copy of the *Union Soldier's Prayer Book*, along with a stack of greenbacks. "Back pay. I won't be needing it. Go home when you're ready. You and Ana both."

————

Atlanta, Georgia
Saturday, November 12, 1864

Something's burning.

Caitlin wrenched awake and leapt out of bed. The cold wood floor slapped the soles of her feet as she ran to the window, and gasped. Though dawn was hours away, the sky glowed orange behind red tongues of flame and boiling, billowing smoke.

Heart racing, she grabbed her cloak and shoes and dashed out of the house and through the streets until she reached the encampment at City Hall Square, mere blocks away.

"What are you doing?" Pointing to the sky, she shouted at the soldier standing guard in front of City Hall.

"It's unauthorized, ma'am."

"What is?"

"The fires breaking out among the private residences. Demolition is only scheduled for structures of military use. Depots, machine shops, warehouses, that sort of thing. We've been ordered not to touch dwelling houses, but some of the fires will spread by accident."

"And by arson." Caitlin's voice quavered with anger. "Is it not enough that you shelled the city for thirty-seven days already? Will you now burn the homes left standing?"

The soldier cleared his throat. "Some soldiers will be undisciplined. General Slocum is offering a five hundred–dollar reward for catching arsonists. We'll make sure it doesn't happen here. We've got sentries posted."

"Not at my house, you haven't." She gave him her address.

"We'll send one right over. And if any incendiaries come through this way, we'll stop them. Go on home and get some sleep, now."

But Caitlin did worry, and she didn't sleep, though an armed guard in Union blue now patrolled Noah's property. Rattled by the smoke and roar of fire, she traded slumber for vigilance while the horizon crackled and flashed.

For three more days, Sherman's engineers destroyed whatever could be used for war, and by night, wayward soldiers torched or ransacked private homes. With Ana huddled next to her on the bare parlor floor, Caitlin kept her shoes on and her senses on high alert.

Atlanta, Georgia
Tuesday, November 15, 1864

Finally, inexplicably, there is wood for the fireplace. Warmth spread throughout Caitlin's body, relaxing muscles kinked from weeks of shuddering in the drafty house. She stepped closer to the fire, smiling as the heat caressed her face. *Finally, the chill is gone.*

"Wake up! Wake up!"

Caitlin jerked awake to find Ana yanking on her arm. Wraiths of smoke crawled across the ceiling. The fire was not in the parlor hearth, but on the floor, spreading in a crackling pool from a blackened pine torch. The clock's chimes jarred Caitlin's nerves once, twice, three times, as flames flashed on its face.

Scrambling to her feet, Caitlin grabbed Ana and stepped backwards, away from the searing heat. "Out!" She scooped up the girl, worried that a trip could break her brittle legs, and rushed her across the street to safety. No Union guards were in sight. "Stay here."

"What will you do?" Ana's voice trembled as they faced their burning house.

"I don't know." *But I must do something.*

Dashing back to Noah's backyard, Caitlin pumped water into a bucket, soaked her apron and tied it around her nose and mouth. Bursting back inside the house, she doused the floor. But by then, the flames had spread.

November wind rushed through the holes in the roof and walls, whipping every spark into a blaze. Velvet curtains were fiery rags dripping from the rods. The oil painting melted and bubbled on its canvas, releasing noxious fumes as it burned. Flame sizzled across the picture molding until Caitlin was surrounded by a ring of fire.

Shimmering waves of heat crowded her. Acrid smoke stung her eyes and clogged her throat through the fibers of her apron, which had already cooked dry as though she stood baking in an oven. Pulse loud in her ears, horror rooted her to the planks now hot beneath her feet as though hypnotized by the destruction.

Only when the windows began exploding, and the second floor creaked and splintered above her head, did she turn her back on the rising inferno.

Escaping into the night air, she crossed the street and captured Ana to her.

"You shouldn't have gone back!" Ana sobbed. "What would I have done without you?"

Burying her face in Ana's smoke-scented hair, Caitlin's shoulders shook with grief for everything that had been taken from her, and from all the children of war. Wordlessly, she grasped Ana's hand and hurried up McDonough Street.

Dense, black columns of smoke were pillars on the horizon, and waves of fire rolled up into the sky, growling, blazing, furious. They receded, like an ocean tide, but still hung suspended over the city. Explosions and shattering glass punctuated the low roar of fire. As they turned left on Hunter and passed City Hall, rousing strains of "John Brown's body goes marching on" met Caitlin's ears. By the light of a flaming sky, a regimental band was serenading Sherman outside the house he had made his headquarters.

Was this the army she had fought with? Did they still sing of the righteousness of their cause, even as they ruined the homes of civilians? Right and wrong tangled in Caitlin's mind until nothing seemed right at all. Everything was wrong. Her father's death; her mother's abuse; this wicked war that separated parents and children, siblings and sweethearts; made widows of young women, and turned innocent people homeless by the thousands. Caitlin had seen death and disfigurement on the battlefield, and those images were burned forever into her mind. But nothing had prepared her for this willful burning of a ruined city.

"God!" she cried out, though her body could spare no tears. "Will this war never end?" The music of the *Miserere*, now played by the regimental band, was the haunting reply. The Italian opera song gave melody to Psalm 51:

Have mercy upon me, O God, according to thy lovingkindness: according unto the multitude of thy tender mercies blot out my transgressions.

Wash me thoroughly from mine iniquity, and cleanse me from my sin.

For I acknowledge my transgressions: and my sin is ever before me.

"Ma'am?" A soldier touched Caitlin's elbow, and she turned her glassy stare upon him.

"Our guard is gone, and our house is on fire." She pointed to the fire now leaping into the sky from Noah's roof.

Within moments, a hastily assembled crew of Union soldiers rushed to contain the blaze.

When morning came, Caitlin squinted with burning eyes through air that was peppered with ash. Noah's house was half-skeleton, stained with soot, and sagging. As the last of Sherman's troops marched out of the smoldering ruins singing, "Glory, glory hallelujah," Caitlin and Ana scrubbed smoke from a shell they still called home.

New York City
Friday, November 25, 1864

"And don't come back until you've talked it out!" Aunt Vivian practically pushed Edward and Ruby out the door, insisting on watching Aiden for the evening. Since she had received letters from both Jack and Caitlin, assuring her of their well-being, she had much more energy to nose into her nephew's marriage.

"Did you tell her?" Edward asked Ruby as he helped her into the carriage.

"I didn't have to. I think yesterday's Thanksgiving dinner was even more uncomfortable than last year's, when your father insisted on calling me 'the girl'!"

A rare smile cracked Edward's stony face.

"Of course, that was also the day you gave me the sewing machine. The perfect gift. Thank you."

Her lips tipped up, and Edward nodded as he hitched the carriage up to the horse. "I was happy to give it to you." He would have done anything for her then. *And now?* Things were different. Edward climbed up next to Ruby, reins in hand, and clucked his tongue to the horse.

"I—I miss you." Ruby's voice was soft, but weighted.

"I miss you, too," he admitted.

"You can forgive your father for keeping your aunt a secret. Can't you forgive me for keeping mine? I'm sorry, Edward, you can have no idea how sorry I am. Please. Don't let this ruin us."

He steered toward Broadway and let her words settle on him like snow. "I don't suppose I ever gave you a chance to explain yourself." The carriage wheels jolted over the cobbles. "Well, I'm listening."

"Thank you," Ruby whispered, and Edward could not tell if she were speaking to him or to God. But when she draped her hand on his knee, he knew she was trying. He smiled to encourage her, and her eyebrows arched.

"Let's see," she began. "I was hungry. Starving. And then I met Phineas . . ." In bits and pieces, her story came out, revealing the whole truth about the role Phineas Hastings had played. Posing as a respectable fellow, he had once courted Charlotte Waverly, who later befriended Ruby in Washington. But before that, his mother had employed Ruby as a domestic here in New York. When Phineas suspected Ruby had learned of his illegal profiteering in shoddy uniforms, Phineas had raped her, and ruined her character for any sort of decent work. She had turned to prostitution thinking she'd already been soiled, and at least one act would buy her a few weeks in which to figure out a new way to survive. Only, without Matthew's financial support, and without a job as a domestic, there was no other way to eat.

"Then Aiden was conceived."

So Phineas had been right. Aiden wasn't Matthew's son.

"And I wanted to die. I wanted him to die inside me."

If Edward had read this awful tale, shock and judgment may have prevailed. But the way Ruby told it, with such brokenness, it broke his own condemnation apart. As her story unfolded in tearful tones and halting rhythm, he finally heard it for what it was. This was a story of a woman redeemed. Ruby, like the woman in John 8, had chosen to go and sin no more. She had grasped onto grace and allowed God to transform her.

Phineas Hastings' words rushed back at Edward now. *So you really*

believe what the Bible says about forgiveness of sin, redemption, and all
that? You really believe that God can snatch people from their downward
spirals and set them on a course of righteousness?

"I believe. Ruby, I need to ask your forgiveness. I've been mean and spiteful lately, only confirming that you had a good reason to keep this from me. I'm sorry you were so fearful of my reaction that you carried this burden alone." He shook his head, conviction snatching his words for a moment as he realized how closely he'd resembled a Pharisee. "I was full of Bible knowledge, yet quicker to judge than to love. I am deeply, deeply sorry."

Ruby wiped the tears from her eyes. "I'm sorry I deceived you! It was selfish of me, and—"

A scream split the air, then another, then more, until the night was shredded with them. Shrieking women streamed out of one Broadway hotel after another, including the Astor House, the Metropolitan, and the St. Nicholas, snapping Ruby's and Edward's attention toward the billowing plumes of smoke coming from the windows. Throngs packed the street to see the commotion, until the clanging bells of horse-drawn fire engines split them apart. Wooden houses were evacuated, and the crowd whipped into a frenzy.

"It's a Confederate plot!" someone shouted. "Find the Rebels!"

"Hang them from a lamppost!"

"Burn them at the stake!"

Edward watched the color drain from Ruby's face. *The Washington Infirmary. She almost burned down with it in November 1861.* Was she reliving that horror right now? "That's enough. We're going home."

———

Atlanta, Georgia
Wednesday, November 30, 1864

Hunger clawed Caitlin as she marched with a case knife in her apron pocket, and two baskets in her hands. Lone chimneys from burned-down houses—Sherman's sentinels—marked her path as she trudged toward the barren Atlanta battlefield. Forests that once obscured the view to Stone Mountain had been cut down by the armies' fierce fight, and the bitter wind swept through the land, uninhibited. Caitlin's skirts beat around her legs, and her hair whipped into her eyes. When she came to a marshy spot, she knelt and carved into the ice-encrusted earth, until minié balls were freed. *This is bread for Ana,* she told herself as she dropped the lead into the basket.

A commissary relief store had been set up in a tent back in town, announcing it would trade food for lead. *Never mind that the lead will be formed into more Confederate weapons.* In the face of starvation, patriotism mattered little. This lead that had been forged to kill would now sustain their lives. This is what mattered. That they would live.

Another woman and her slave were on hands and knees digging for lead as well, crying audibly as they did so. The white woman choked back a sob and said, "Lord of mercy, if this be Thy holy will, give me fortitude to bear it uncomplainingly..."

Caitlin's throat tightened. But she must hurry. Ana, on crutches provided by the Union doctor, and unable to stand the hike, was waiting in a half-burned home where no fire was lit to keep her warm. Cold needled Caitlin's feet, and her dry hands cracked and bled as she scraped at the frozen earth.

But when she brought the baskets to the commissary ten hours later, the kindly gentleman in faded grey emptied them of lead and returned them full of coffee, sugar, meal, and meat. They would live another week.

New York City
Saturday, December 10, 1864

Six inches of snow turned New York City into a scene from Currier & Ives. Vivian McKae delighted in the refreshingly clean mantle, though she knew beneath it, the metropolis was as dirty as it ever had been.

Her smile faltered. Could the same be said of her? On the outside, everything sparkled. Her brother had been restored to her, she was welcome to live in his fine home, and she had been assured that both Jack and Caitlin were well.

Yet a single, unconfessed sin sullied her spirit. *Bernard.* She had killed him, and she had meant to. She was a murderer. Yes, she had brought this to God and believed He forgave her, but keeping the truth from the civil authorities was a sin she could live with no longer. Neither Jack nor Caitlin depended on her anymore. In fact, no one needed her at all. Her imprisonment would hurt no one but herself.

Quietly, Vivian donned her cloak and crunched the snow beneath her feet as she stole away to the precinct. A brief prayer, combined with the crisp air scraping her skin, invigorated her for the task ahead.

Once inside the warm building, memories surged around her. This was where Bernard had worked. This cigar-tobacco scent hanging in the air—that was his scent, when it wasn't masked by whiskey. She shuddered even now. The man had been a monster.

"Can I help you?" A young man scratched his jaw.

Vivian stepped forward. "I need to speak with a detective, please."

"Regarding?"

"A murder."

His eyebrows shot up. "A moment, please."

He disappeared around a corner, then returned with an older man with a grey mustache, tugging at his collar as he walked. "This way, please."

Vivian followed him until he plopped down at his desk and motioned for her to be seated opposite. "Now. What's this all about?"

"The untimely death of Officer Bernard Wilkens. April 19, 1861."

"I remember Bernie. You have some information on his passing?"

She swallowed, gripped her hands together. "His murder. Yes, I have information on his murder. I did it," she added in a whisper.

The officer stared at her, face a complete blank, until it creased into smiles. "Go on. How could a little wisp like you best a burly man like Bernie?"

"I was his wife."

"Well, my condolences. God rest his soul. He was a hard drinker. Wicked temper, too."

"So you see. I had motive."

He squinted at her. "He beat you, lady? I always suspected he was the type."

"He did." She held her chin higher.

"I see. And you wanted him out of the picture."

"He went after my daughter."

Grunting, the officer excused himself for a few minutes before coming back with a file. He jabbed some text with a stubby finger. "Says here he died of liver poisoning."

"Who did?" Vivian's brow puckered.

"Your late husband. Bernard Wilkens. Not surprising with the drinking he did. Someone was supposed to notify you of these findings immediately." He flipped through another page. "Oh. This case was closed by a bloke who enlisted right afterward. Scrambling to be one of Lincoln's seventy-five thousand before the war's end stole his chance to fire at some Rebels. Remember those days?" He shook his head. "Well, I see he neglected to have you informed, and for that I do apologize."

His words swam in Vivian's foggy mind. "I don't understand. He was alive when I found him at the bottom of the stairs. He had a pulse, but he was unconscious, I assume from his fall. I—I held a pillow over his face."

"Did he try to fight you off?"

"No, I told you he was passed out."

"Hm. Well, this here coroner's report says plain as day he died of poisoning of the liver. That's liver poisoning. Too much drinking. Do you recall, was he intoxicated that night?"

"Of course he was. He was drunk every time he set foot in our apartment."

"Well, there you go. The straw that broke the camel's back. It caught up with him." He tucked his papers back in the file. "You're free to go, in case you didn't catch that."

"You're certain?" Hope fluttered in her chest.

"Yes. Now don't go making more work for me by trumping up a fake murder when there's none to be reported. Good day to you."

Atlanta, Georgia
Saturday, December 10, 1864

From somewhere outside, howling sliced through the winter night. Dogs abandoned by their Atlanta owners during the siege or occupation now roamed the country in packs. The baying of the now-feral animals scraped Caitlin's nerves. Was Rascal among them?

"Papa isn't coming." Ana's hollow eyes looked haunted by her admission, and hunted by despair. "I am tired and I'm cold. No one likes us here. My tummy hurts."

Caitlin bowed her head to hide her tears. Because of her, they were pariahs, more than she ever had been before the siege. Her decision to stay during the Federal occupation had been interpreted by those who were just now returning to town as a cardinal sin against the Confederacy. She was spit upon in the streets. The newspaper called her out by name, along with several others who stayed, whether they still remained in Atlanta or had refugeed North. The words "traitor" and "Yankee spy" had been written in coal on the white boards of Noah's house.

"I don't want to be here anymore," Ana whispered.

Caitlin held her hand, kissed her forehead. "Where do you want to be?"

"Away from the fighting, and from hospitals. And away from fire. I want to be where I can be warm again, and eat cake. And I would love to have a new dress and something to wear on my feet. Do you suppose there is such a place in the world anymore?"

Not in your world, darlin.' Caitlin sighed. These were outrageous requests only in the South. "There is a place we could go, but it is North. New York."

Ana frowned. "Yankee land?"

"It is far, far from the battles. You could meet my family."

"You have a family? I thought we were your family."

The innocent question squeezed Caitlin's heart. "You are."

"Then can I please call you Mama?"

Caitlin's eyes popped open, and her nose pricked. The letter Noah left for her the last time he left echoed in her mind. *I want you to be Ana's mother. If I don't come home, please take her in. I have updated the enclosed will accordingly.* Was Ana's request a foreshadowing? Or just a simple grasping for connection?

"You may call me whatever you like, love."

Ana wrapped her arms around Caitlin. "Then take me away from here, Mama. I will go wherever you go."

Atlanta had long since fallen. It was time to climb out of the rubble.

Chapter Twenty-Seven

New York City
Thursday, December 29, 1864

Vivian's teacup and saucer clattered to the floor, spilling steaming Earl Grey down the front of her tartan plaid skirt. In the periphery of her vision, Mr. Schaefer scooped up the china and bowed out of the front foyer. But her gaze remained fixed on the bone-thin woman and little girl before her.

"Mama."

A cry burst from Vivian's heart as she captured Caitlin into a fierce embrace. "You're home, at last! Oh thank God, you found your way home!" She pulled back to look at her.

"Jack gave me the address . . ." Her chin quivered. She looked absolutely exhausted. "Mama, I'd like you to meet Analiese Becker. Ana, this is Mrs. McKae, my mother."

"Pleased to meet you, ma'am." The girl's forget-me-not blue eyes were enchanting, even if they looked too big for her face.

Vivian bent down to her level. "It's my pleasure. How would you like to have some bread with marmalade and a little milk while we draw a nice warm bath for you?"

Her eyes grew even wider. "You have bread and milk here?" Wonder laced her voice.

Vivian's throat constricted as she nodded. Were bread and milk really such delicacies? "Yes. Come, you must be hungry from your journey. I'll have Mr. Schaefer bring in your things."

Caitlin shook her head and raised a single satchel. "I have a few books. That is all."

Vivian clamped down on her surprise. "No matter. We'll take care of everything you need. Well, your Uncle George will, anyway." She smiled, though she felt like weeping for the poverty that stood before her with large eyes and empty hands. "Come, come. You're home now. Everything is going to be fine."

"When I said 'go away,' I didn't mean forever."

Caitlin closed her eyes and let her mother brush through her hair while Analiese was in the bathtub down the hall.

"I was trying to protect you from Bernard."

Tears gathered in Caitlin's throat as she remembered the birdlike woman her mother had been beneath his domineering hand.

"Why, *why* did you disappear?"

Caitlin glanced into the mirror. The hurt reflected in Vivian's eyes sliced to her heart. Now Caitlin understood just what it was like to be left behind, to never know whether the one you love is dead or alive, or whether he thinks of you at all. But, "You told me to make my own way, didn't you? Without depending on a man?"

"I didn't intend for you to become one in order to do it."

Caitlin looked down at her hands, still cracked and rough from harvesting minié balls. "There is a bigger reason. I—I tried to protect you from Bernard too, Mama."

Vivian's brush stilled on Caitlin's hair. "What did you do?" she whispered.

"I wanted to get him away from you."

"He was three times your size, child, what were you thinking you'd do? Oh such Irish impulsiveness!"

"I know." She shook her head. "But it worked. I lured him away from you, but he attacked me and I—I fought back."

"Good girl." Vivian's voice was steel.

With halting voice, Caitlin choked out the rest of the story. She had committed murder. "Are they still looking for me?" she whispered. "It was an accident. Do you think they'll believe me?"

Vivian knelt in front of her now, grasped her hands. "You did not kill him."

"But he was dead! I'm the one who pushed him down the stairs, and I cut his throat with a piece of glass!"

"It's not what killed him," she said again.

"How do you know?"

Vivian drew a breath, released it slowly. "I went to the precinct a few weeks ago, and they told me the cause of death was liver poisoning. He drank himself into his own grave."

Caitlin blinked. "Are you sure?"

"That's what I asked them. I couldn't believe it myself."

Caitlin drew back, withdrawing her hands from Vivian's hold. "You suspected I murdered him, and you went to the police to tell them, now?" Her heart skipped a beat.

"No, darlin'. I suspected *I* murdered him, and I couldn't live with that guilt any longer. That's why I went—to confess."

"But how—"

"I found Bernard at the bottom of the stairs where you left him. I could see you two had been struggling, and I—" Her face knotted. She swallowed, smoothed away the wrinkles in her brow. "I couldn't stand the thought of him doing to you what he'd done to me. I wanted him dead." She locked eyes with Caitlin. "I suffocated him with my pillow. Or at least, I thought I did."

Shock shuddered through Caitlin. "You tried to kill him? With a pillow?"

A nod.

"But he killed himself with drinking?"

Another nod.

A brittle laugh slipped from Caitlin's lips. She covered her mouth with her hand. "All this time, I stayed away—"

"Would you have come home if you knew?"

The last three and a half years scrolled through Caitlin's mind. Her army days, the tedium in camp and terror in battle. Her two and a half years in Atlanta, teaching at the Institute, then her spartan life in Noah's home with Ana, Naomi, Minnie, and Susan. "Home from battle, yes. Home from Atlanta—not until now."

Vivian's eyes sparked. "You love him, then. Ana's father. Though he fights against your brother? Your country? Freedom itself?"

"Don't." Caitlin's skin crawled at the speed at which Vivian judged Noah. "It's complicated. He is an immigrant, like Da, but from Germany. A lawyer and languages instructor before he enlisted, which he did only to defend his home. In fact, he came to America for asylum after he fought to unify Germany—and failed."

"And he loves his daughter," Vivian prompted.

"As much as Da loved me." Tears glazed Caitlin's eyes.

For the first time since his death, Vivian did not swat away the reference to her late husband. Instead, she only nodded, a fragile smile on her face. "Does your Noah love you, too?"

"I thought he did." Her heart flipped. "But I don't know where he is, or when—or how—I'll see him again."

"You will find each other. His daughter calls you Mama. You will find your way home again."

Caitlin shook her head, fatigue suddenly weighting her body. "We have no homes."

Chocolate eyes twinkling, Vivian cupped her chin in her hand. "I know you, daughter. You will make a new one."

New York City
Sunday, January 1, 1865

"More cake, dear?" Vivian served up another slice and passed it to Analiese, her heart swelling at the grin on the child's face. She turned to Caitlin. "How about you, birthday girl? We're making up for four years of missed celebrations here, so don't be shy." Vivian could hardly believe her daughter with the freckled nose was twenty-five years old already. And yet the depth in her eyes, the faint lines on her brow showed she had aged far more than that.

"No more cake, thank you, but I'd love some more coffee, if you don't mind." Caitlin held out her cup, and Ruby poured, the servants being dismissed early for New Year's Day. "You've no idea how I've missed it."

Sunshine poured in between velvet curtains and bounced off the silver service. Yesterday's fierce snowstorm had draped a plush white rug over the city, but today dawned clear, a fresh, bright beginning for a new year. Vivian had never been so glad to turn the calendar.

"How about some more potatoes? Or brisket? Let's put some meat on those bones!" George teased the niece he'd only just met, clearly smitten with both her and her tiny Southern shadow. *You had two broken legs!* he'd said to Ana earlier. *Why that's just like me, but my arms were broken too! But look at me now. Fit as a fiddle!* George insisted they take the master suite that Ruby and Aiden vacated, denying he was strong enough to reclaim his old room just yet.

"So, Caitlin." Edward rested his fork on his plate with a clink. "Do you plan to register on the list of Southern refugees?" He winked, but Caitlin did not return the smile. Vivian shifted in her chair, irked her nephew had brought up the distasteful topic.

"What's that?"

"I'm only teasing. I wouldn't expect you to, really."

Caitlin shook her head as she looked around the table. "I don't understand."

Edward kissed Aiden's cheek as Ruby guided him down from the table. "Sorry. A band of Confederates plotted to burn down New York by starting fires in a dozen or so hotels last November. Some said it was in retaliation for Lincoln winning the national election—even though he lost to McClellan by a landslide here in the city. If McClellan had won nationally, there may have been peace negotiations that would have recognized the Confederacy as its own nation. Obviously, Lincoln's re-election means the war goes on. Others say the hotel fires were in retaliation for the burning of Atlanta."

"Could be both reasons," George added. "If Atlanta had not fallen when it did, Lincoln very likely would have been defeated. He needed that victory to defeat the 'four years of failure' plank of the Democratic platform."

"Quite." Edward stirred cream into his coffee. "Thankfully, the plot to burn down New York City fizzled out with no lives lost and only four hundred thousand dollars' worth of damage. Anyway, ever since the fires, especially, New York has been nervous about Southerners coming into the city. They want a list of names so they can feel better about the copperhead population."

George snorted. "Feel better! Ha! They'll feel better all right, once they come after those Southern gents and use them to fill up the Union quotas!"

Caitlin's eyes grew round. "Would they?"

"It has already been tried elsewhere in the Union." Edward sipped his coffee. "Civilian men of a certain age are eligible for the draft throughout the Union, but they harvested new soldiers from prison camps, as well. From what I've heard from the officers at the hospital, however, the strategy was not successful."

"They forced Confederate prisoners to turn and fight against their own people?"

"Recruited, not forced. But yes, and therein was the problem. Once in the Southern states, they very often deserted, presumably to get back to their own homes. Those who met with the misfortune of capture by the Confederate army were treated worse than regular Yankee prisoners."

Vivian glanced at Ana, but the girl did not seem troubled by the fates of her fellow Southerners. Perhaps she was too busy licking the icing on her cake to notice.

"They've locked up some Southern civilians at Fort Lafayette, too," Edward continued.

Caitlin wrapped her fingers around her coffee cup. "On what charge?"

"No charge, the writ of habeas corpus being suspended. A fellow named Amherst Stone has been stowed away for more than a year now."

"Amherst Stone! Why, I knew his wife Cyrena in Atlanta! They are both loyal Unionists who lived in Vermont before moving to the South!"

"Well, he came north with a half-baked blockade-running scheme that just seemed suspicious."

Caitlin's eyes glowed in her gaunt face. Vivian worried about her health. "And what else can a Southern refugee expect from New York?"

"Cake!" Vivian jumped in. "Lots and lots of cake. And unlimited supply of coffee." Caitlin's lips bent in a weary smile, but Vivian knew it would take more than food to make her daughter—the Union veteran from the South—feel welcome in a city that fed on war.

Rock Island, Illinois
Friday, January 27, 1865

Cold burned Noah's bare feet and bit his nose as he waited, shivering, for a turn in front of the barracks stove. Wind burst through the door, scraping his face and piercing his rags like a bayonet, and he wondered if this frozen purgatory was punishment for his answer to Colonel Johnson's proposal that he enlist with the Union army. No longer prisoners but not yet soldiers, he had been here, crammed into a forced huddle with hundreds of other men, for nearly four bitter months, with no new clothing issued to them. A thousand pinpricks needled his skin every moment he was not before the stove, unless numbness brought sweet relief.

Longing for Caitlin and Ana swirled like snow. Noah's memories were growing brittle. He'd held Caitlin in his arms, hadn't he? *Why didn't I kiss her?* Had Caitlin said she loved him? Did she even say she would wait? It would not have been fair to ask her to.

The bleak winter days dragged their frostbitten feet and still Noah Becker went nowhere.

———

New York City
Monday, March 6, 1865

"Please don't drop him."

Edward tightened his grip on Aiden's legs and slanted an amused gaze at Ruby's pinched face. "I won't drop him." Besides, the crowd was so tightly packed around them, even if he lost his grip, Aiden would never hit the ground.

All necks were craned toward the seven-mile-long procession now snaking its way through lower Manhattan. It was a National Jubilee in honor of Lincoln's second inaugural and the recent Union victories, and in anticipation of impending Confederate defeats.

"It's a shame Ana isn't here, she would have enjoyed this too," Ruby said.

"Unless, of course, she learned we're celebrating the demise of her homeland. Look! Here come some elephants—and what are those animals with the big humps on their backs?"

"Camels!" cried Aiden, and Edward patted his leg.

"Good boy."

Besides the exotic animals, soldiers, volunteer firemen, and ethnic community organizations joined businesses and banks in marching. McAuliffe's Irish whiskey held a sign that said, DON'T AVOID THE DRAUGHT. Sailors carried ship models, including one of the ironclad *Monitor*. One placard boldly proclaimed: OIL IS KING NOW, NOT COTTON.

"I suppose it doesn't exactly put out the welcome mat for the Southern families in our midst, eh?"

At least Edward could talk to Ruby again. Their relationship had healed tremendously since their carriage-ride conversation the night of the hotel fires. Still, they felt more like amiable housemates than husband and wife.

Edward caught Ruby watching him, and matched her smile with his own. They were the smiles of friends. Not lovers.

"Ruby?"

Emma Connors emerged from the crowd and Edward stifled a groan. He had never been quite sure how to conduct himself around her.

"Why, Emma!" Ruby looped her arm through her friend's elbow. "So good to see you here!"

Emma kissed her cheek, then shielded her eyes as she squinted up at Aiden. "Oh my, no. This canna be the bonnie wee laddie named Aiden, can it?"

Ruby beamed with pride over her growing son. She tapped Edward's arm, then reached up to take Aiden down. "Aye, this is him!"

"Oh look at you now!" Emma ruffled his curly locks with her hand, and for the first time, Ruby wondered if she pined for a family of her own.

"Would you like to hold him? He's heavy. Aiden, would you let Emma hold you, darlin'?"

Emma hoisted him onto her hip, and he draped a chubby arm

around her neck. Ruby could almost see her friend melting. "You're not too heavy for me!" She bounced him just a bit. "You are just exactly the way you should be. Perfect."

Ruby laughed. "Not always." She sought Edward's eye, but he was staring straight ahead at the parade.

Emma noticed. "Why don't I walk around with him for a wee bit? Give you and Edward a little time to yourselves."

Ruby laughed. "To ourselves? How many thousands of people do you suppose there are here?" But she knew what Emma meant. It might be nice to interact without frequent interruptions from Aiden. "All right, you win. Don't feel like you have to stay away long, though. Ten minutes? Right back here on this corner?"

"Aye, see you then!"

Ruby smiled as she watched them sway through the crowd and out of sight.

"Don't look now, but someone just walked off with your son," Edward teased.

Ruby slipped her hand into his and squeezed. "Nothing gets past you, does it?"

Ten minutes flew by.

And then five more. Then ten. By the time thirty minutes had passed, Edward looked as anxious as Ruby.

Then, "Ruby!"

"Oh thank God, Emma, you scared me! Twenty minutes late, did you get lost? Where's—Where's Aiden?"

Emma's eyes hardened. "He's safe. With Sean."

A ridge popped between Edward's eyebrows as Ruby grasped for his arm. "Excuse me?"

"Just while you and I take care of a little business is all. But not here. Much too noisy. Shall we go back to your place?"

Edward leaned in. "Whatever game you're playing, you can stop right now. Where's the boy?"

"I told you. You'll not get him until you all take care of something for me." She cocked her head in that self-assured way Ruby had never learned to master. "Let's go."

Ruby looked up at Edward, shook her head. She was just as confused as he was, and likely ten times as alarmed.

Back in the Sixteenth Street brownstone, Emma walked to the front parlor and sat.

"What do you want?" Edward growled.

"Only what's rightfully mine. I've been sewing with you more than a year now, Ruby Shannon, and I don't believe I've collected a fair share."

Ruby spread her hands. "Well then, what's fair?"

"I'll tell you what isn't fair. 'Tis a crying shame you got a husband, a son, a house, and a business, and all I got is a brother who can't pull himself out of the bottle and a disease I'll never be cured of. And are we so very different, you and me, after all? How is it you got all the blessings, and I got only curses?"

Ruby gasped. "Are you ill? I didn't know!"

Emma rolled her eyes. "Think on it, Rubes. A girl in my line of work? Bound to happen sooner or later."

"But I thought you—"

"Gave it up? Not soon enough. And since our sewing business dried up I had to go right back to it."

Ruby's stomach turned, and she feared it would reject its contents. Emma had reverted to prostitution.

"Now. As I said, I want what's mine, I do. But don't worry. This won't hurt a bit." She pointed to an expensive painting in a gilt-edged frame. "She'll never miss it."

"I can't give you that, it doesn't belong to me." Her voice shook with both conviction and fear.

"Jewels, then. What did the old missus leave behind?"

Edward put out his hand. "We're not giving you Mrs. Waverly's things."

"Then cash will do nicely. Five thousand dollars, if you please."

Ruby blinked. "Are you in earnest?"

"No cash, no boy."

"This is ridiculous." Edward hooked Emma's arm. "We're going for a walk."

"Where?"

"The police station, where I'm reporting you and your brother for extortion and kidnapping. I'm sure they'd be very interested in hearing about your disease while we're at it too, and just exactly how you contracted it. Let's go."

"Oh, all right, all right!" Emma fought against Edward's grasp. "We were just shaking the tree to see if anything would fall out. I'll take you to Sean, no need to get the police involved. Bedad!"

"Where is he?" Ruby asked, nerves jangling.

"Back at Five Points."

Ruby's spirit groaned in protest. Every fear she had harbored for Aiden had its root in that nest of crime and sin. The worst thing that could happen was that he would develop a fascination, and then an appetite for that kind of life. And that was where Sean had him. He could be giving him nips from his flask right now!

With his face as much like a thundercloud as Ruby had ever seen, Edward hitched the carriage to the horse.

"How *could* you, Emma?" Ruby whispered as they climbed up into the Concord.

"Sean. He says he needs the money, although I don't know where he puts it. Gambles it all away. I'm likely as mad at him as you are."

Not likely. "It was a vicious trick. If any harm should come to his body or spirit—" She would not know how to fix it. There was little else to say as they rode south on side streets parallel to the procession route. It was two and a half miles away, but it felt like the entire length of Manhattan.

Emma directed Edward to the intersection for which Five Points was named. Ruby craned her neck, heartbeat thrumming above children hawking apples, and unshaven men joking coarsely with bright-cheeked women. "Where is he?"

"I—I don't know, he said he'd be right here at this corner!"

"If this is another trick, Miss Connors—" Edward growled at Emma, but Ruby could read in her wild, darting eyes that it wasn't.

Dread spiraled through Ruby as Edward steered the carriage through decaying vegetable matter, apple cores, horse manure, and pig droppings. Splattered with filth up to his fetlocks, Justus zigzagged the Concord up Baxter Street, across Park Street, through Mulberry and Mott. They checked every street corner in the Fourth and Sixth Wards, calling out Sean's name into the erratic dissonance of Five Points. Pressing her handkerchief to her nose, Ruby fought to keep from gagging on the odor of the open sinks behind the tenements. Weathered wooden flophouses, gropshops, and brothels leaned drunkenly into each other. Yawning doorways seemed to mock Ruby, who had been loath to live here herself, and was now searching this den of vice for her son.

"He might have gone back to our rooms," Emma offered.

But he hadn't. They found Emma and Sean's apartment as hollow as Ruby's hope. Her knees weakened with growing despair, and Edward caught her waist to his side.

"We're going home." His voice was gruff. "They might be waiting for us there." But his eyes were dark with doubt.

When they found the Waverly brownstone and gardens just as empty, fear wrapped coldly around Ruby. "They might still come . . ." she rasped.

"I'm going to the police." Edward's breath came shorter. "Miss Connors—"

"Please don't take her." Ruby grabbed Emma's arm. "I don't want to be alone with Sean if he comes while you're gone!"

Face ashen, Edward raked his hand through his hair. Tension puckered his brow. "You'll forgive me for not quite trusting you, Miss Connors."

"I'm sorry, Mr. Goodrich, I don't know what's gotten into Sean! But you'll not be leaving Ruby alone like this, and someone needs to be here in case the boys do come this way."

He flicked his gaze heavenward before meeting Ruby's gaze with troubled eyes. "I'll stop at Father's on my way to the station. He and Aunt Vivian will come back to sit with you. After the station I just might search Central Park. Will you be all right with Aunt Viv and Father?"

Ruby nodded, but did not feel his lips brush on her cheek. She was numb, and she could not stop shaking.

The door latched behind Edward and Ruby stood there, staring at its walnut panels and seeing nothing. *Aiden is gone.*

"'Twas never supposed to go this far, darlin'." Emma gently guided her to the sofa in the parlor. "You have to believe me. Sean'll come blowing in any minute, he will, and your bonnie wee laddie with him."

He is gone. My son is gone.

"I'll—I'll put on some tea."

Ruby blinked, and suddenly a hot cup was in her trembling hands, steam breathing into her face. "Emma." Her voice was flat. "I've never mothered a child past the age of three." Meghan had died an infant. Consumption took Fiona when she was only months older than Aiden.

"Bedad, Ruby Shannon! Aiden's not dead, you goose!" Her laugh was shrill. "We just don't know where he is!"

"Then find him!" Ruby jerked, and her tea sloshed out of its cup. The burn was nothing against the desperation now boiling beneath her skin. "I can't stay here when my son is out there somewhere. You know your brother better than anyone else. Where is he? Where is my son?"

Emma's eyes grew wide. Her lips were a thin red line. "If he's not home, and he's not here, there's only one place he would be."

"You're sure?"

"If he isn't, there'll be someone there who's seen him."

Ruby clunked her cup onto the table and stood with shaky legs. "I'm coming with you."

Emma plucked her shawl from the hall rack. "Will you not stay and wait for Edward's father and aunt?"

"I can't stay here," Ruby said again, tears coursing down her cheeks.

"I'll go mad." She followed Emma out the door to chase a gossamer thread of hope.

———

"Sean! Bedad! What in the name of St. Patrick can you be doing?"

Ruby's limbs turned to stone as Emma flailed against her brother. He had staggered out of Fatty Walsh's saloon. Alone.

"Where's the boy?" Emma shrieked.

"Where's the money?" His speech slurred around his swollen tongue.

"They haven't got it, you dolt! Give Aiden back to his mother now, it was a stupid plan!"

"Maybe." Puffy eyes drooped with drink. "But looky here." He withdrew a wad of cash from his trouser pocket and thumbed through it with grimy fingers. "Sort of worked out, see? And this isn't even the whole of it. Figured it wouldn't hurt to celebrate with some refreshments right away."

"Who'd you steal that from?" Emma asked.

"Nobody. It's a bonus. Yeah, that's what he called it, a bonus."

"But *where* is my *son*?" The pressure of the unknown ballooned inside her until her head felt like it would burst.

Sean shrugged, smelled his money. "Ask him who paid me for him."

"What?" Horror strangled Ruby's voice.

"Aw, don't worry. 'Twas not a thug who bought him. 'Twas Pease. Lewis Pease."

"Of the Five Points Mission? The House of Industry?" Slowly, the cogs of Ruby's mind turned. She had met him once. Charlotte Waverly had worked with him in the House of Industry before the war started.

"The same. Said I wasn't fit to care for the lad, he did. He asked me to hand him over. I said no, that the lad was going to make me some money. He offered to pay me this bonus so he could take care of the lad at the Mission. So you see, lassies? Everyone is happy." He tipped a bottle to his mouth again, then swiped the back of his hand over his face. "Aiden is safe, and I still got paid."

Ruby gasped with relief so intense it nearly swept her off her feet. With new energy trickling through her whiplashed spirit, she wordlessly headed for the Mission. Aiden was safe, and mere blocks away.

Bursting through the doors of the Five Points Mission, Ruby scanned the Spartan foyer with eyes ravenous for sight of her son.

"Can I help—ah. So you've come. Hello again, Ruby." Mr. Lewis Pease loomed before her, as did their conversation from three years ago. Obviously, he had not forgotten it, either.

Desperate for income, Ruby had applied to be a sewing instructor at the House of Industry. The only name she'd been able to supply as a character reference was Emma Connors. When Mr. Pease learned that Ruby had withheld the fact that Emma was a working prostitute, he had labeled her a liar and turned her out. He rubbed his jaw as he assessed her now. "Is this about the boy I found with Sean Connors?"

"That boy is my son. I thank you for keeping him this afternoon, but I'll take him now. Please." *He must be terrified after this ordeal.* "He's my son."

But Mr. Pease made no move. "Do you know how I found him? Drinking whiskey from Sean Connors' flask. Making mud pies from animal droppings."

Revulsion wrenched Ruby's gut. "I thank you for removing him from such a depraved influence, truly. I'll take him back, now."

"Where's the laddie, Mr. Pease?" Emma piped up beside Ruby. "Didn't you hear her? That's her son you've got."

"I heard her." He leveled his gaze at Emma. "I already learned from Mr. Connors that Aiden is Ruby's son. And I already know Ruby's a prostitute, another reason I removed the boy."

Fire blazed in Ruby's cheeks. "I'm not a prostitute," she gasped. "Not anymore."

"I've heard that before. I didn't believe you three years ago, and I don't believe you now."

"I've changed!"

"Yet here you are, in the company of Emma Connors, another who famously plies the same seedy trade. And your son was left in the company of a drunk. What kind of mother would do such a thing?"

Aiden was kidnapped. It wasn't my fault. But the words cleaved to her tongue.

"Ruby's no prostitute, Mr. Pease, I'll tell you that. She's married to a chaplain, she is!"

Mr. Pease narrowed his gaze. "Edward Goodrich, yes, I know. Just lost a chance at the pastorate of my mother's church because of his wife's—that would be you—prostitution. Am I right? So you see, I still have trouble trusting you."

His words whipped the breath from Ruby's chest. Mute with shock, she slumped against Emma for support.

"I don't believe Aiden is in a suitable home. I believe he would do better raised by another family, somewhere far from the city."

"The Goodriches live in the finest home I've ever been inside," chimed Emma. "The Waverly brownstone, 16th Street!"

"Waverly?" Mr. Pease frowned. "As in, Charlotte Waverly?"

Ruby nodded.

"Charlotte used to work in the House of Industry with us before the war started. Why are you now living in her home?"

"I—I was a domestic there for her mother, Caroline. We live there still."

His eyebrows arched. "You don't say. Then you won't mind if I speak to Mrs. Caroline Waverly to confirm this."

"You can't." Emma's voice grew shriller with every word. "You'll just have to trust us, you will! Mrs. Waverly doesn't live there right now, neither does Charlotte. It's just Ruby, Edward, and Aiden."

"Squatting on the property, are you?" Mr. Pease shook his head, muttered something Ruby could not hear over the rushing of her blood in her ears.

"No, no, you don't understand!" Ruby cried. "It was Mrs. Waverly's idea in the first place!"

Mr. Pease barked a laugh from his throat. "Caroline Waverly? Oh no. Absolutely unbelievable. Charlotte's mother forbade Charlotte to continue working with us here in Five Points. If she couldn't abide her daughter serving in the House of Industry once a week, she most certainly would not leave her home in the hands of a prostitute."

Ruby flailed in the tide of distrust. Swirling half-truths crashed and roared in her ears. *Enough of this!* Desperation curled her fingers as she latched onto Mr. Pease's arm. "Where is my son? Give me my son!" Her tone was as raw as her heart.

"He's gone."

Air crushed from her lungs, Ruby's cry died in her throat.

"I put him on a train this afternoon along with a dozen other orphans and half-orphans. He's headed to Iowa as we speak, where a nice farming family will adopt him and give him the wholesome upbringing you never could, away from the city's filthy influence. He will forget you, and grow into a decent man."

The room spun, grew dark, and disappeared.

Aiden! I'm here! Ruby dropped to her knees and spread her arms to her son. His eyes were bright, his cheeks ruddy, and he smelled of hay and clover.

Mama?

Yes! I've come back for you at last!

Mama? He said again, louder this time. But why was he looking over his shoulder? Why—why was he walking away? *Mama! Mama! I'm right here!*

But he shook his head furiously, chubby legs pumping to carry him away from her, until he reached a sun-browned woman milking a cow.

Mama! he said again, and she caught him to her bosom, laughing.

371

There you are, my sweet! Did you find a fox in the henhouse? Or are you just happy to see your mother?

"Aiden!" Panting and damp with sweat, Ruby heaved out of her dream.

Edward jerked in the armchair next to her bed. Though the room was layered in shadows, she could see his rumpled clothes and haggard expression. She had awoken from only one nightmare.

"It will be all right," he told her, but she wailed into her pillow.

"Aiden is out there somewhere, wondering why I don't come to him, and I have no idea how to get him back!"

"Ruby, darling, listen to me, please." He turned up the lamp, chasing the darkness to the corners of the room. "Emma told me everything. We'll sort it out. As soon as day breaks, Father and I will go have a talk with Mr. Pease while Aunt Viv stays with you. She's in Charlotte's old room even now. We'll have Mr. Pease telegram Caroline himself—Charlotte, too, if he likes—and when they clear your name, he'll have no choice but to get Aiden back for us."

"Wh—what if he won't?" she sobbed.

"He will. Of course he will, once he knows the truth. The Five Points Mission partners with the Children's Aid Society to send orphans west, and I went to the same seminary as the Society's founder, Charles Loring Brace. I'll talk to him. Brace's best friend is Frederick Law Olmsted, and you know Mr. Olmsted would vouch for you, too, if need be."

Hope glimmered. Ruby sat up, pushed a strand of hair from her forehead. *Yes, Mr. Olmsted.* The executive secretary of the Sanitary Commission, and the landscape architect of Central Park. He'd taken a special interest in her when they'd worked together for the soldiers in Washington and on the Virginia Peninsula. *Probably because he felt guilty I'd been evicted from Seneca Village to make way for the park.* Surely their mutual friendship with Charlotte helped, too. "You'll talk to Brace? And Pease?"

"As soon as the hour is decent. Mr. Pease means well, and I don't doubt that most of the children on that orphan train will, indeed, be better off in the country. But Aiden belongs with us. Those half-truths were quite condemning. But the truth—the whole truth—will set us free."

New York City
Wednesday, March 8, 1865

Spice-scented steam curled and divided above the teacup in Vivian's hands, as Caitlin's murmuring to Ana floated through the wall to the sitting room. Vivian's heart squeezed. Caitlin sounded like a mother, indeed. She sounded like Ruby when she had put Aiden to bed so many nights in that very room. And now Aiden was gone. *But surely, he's coming back.* Mr. Pease had telegrammed Caroline Waverly, and if she hadn't already responded, certainly she would soon, and then Aiden would come home. Ruby's agonizing ordeal dwarfed Vivian's own dilemma.

The letter lay heavily on Vivian's lap. Placing her teacup back on its saucer, she fingered the edges, and the grey scrawl blurred on the paper. *No more secrets,* she told herself, and prayed for strength to do the right thing by her daughter. Clinging to her, even after such an excruciating separation, would be utterly selfish.

The door latched in the hall, and Caitlin entered the sitting room, unpinning her braid from its coil on her head as she did so.

"Tea?" Vivian nodded to the silver tray on the table.

"Yes, thank you!" Caitlin helped herself and settled into the sofa with a sigh. "And shall I find some Shakespeare to read aloud, as well?"

Vivian smiled at the reference to their long-ago tradition. "Actually, I've brought different reading material tonight."

"Oh?" Caitlin popped a piece of shortbread in her mouth and leaned her head back on the sofa, eyes closed. She seemed so tired lately.

Vivian worried it was more an exhaustion of spirit than body.

"I took the liberty of writing to your former instructor at the Hartford Female Seminary. I thought she'd like to know you put your training to good use teaching down South for a time."

Caitlin's eyebrow spiked. "And?" She ducked back into her tea.

"And she wrote back. With an idea." She tapped the letter in her lap. "The National Popular Education Board—you remember, the board that partnered with your alma mater, the Hartford Female Institute—well, the board sent a teacher out to Astoria, Oregon, some years ago, and she has decided to come back east. She was too lonely for her family. They need a replacement."

Caitlin swallowed, and lines grooved her brow. "Why tease me so? You know the board no longer finances transportation to the sites."

"True. But your uncle would." The spark of hope in Caitlin's eyes drew a smile to Vivian's lips.

"What are you saying?"

"You've always wanted to teach out West, and I've always been sorry that opportunity was lost—but now we have another one. There is still a surplus of teachers in New York, but the need in the West only grows greater, though the teacher placement program is defunct. Since the Homestead Act went into effect two years ago, settlers have been flocking west to claim their free land. Their children need teachers. Miss Dunn is ready to appoint you the post, especially now that you have professional experience on your resume."

"But—Astoria! It's on the other side of the country completely!"

Vivian knew. Nestled on the Pacific coast, it was three thousand miles from New York, more than three times the distance to Atlanta. And yet, "You were gone three and a half years without a word. I suspect homesickness will not impede your success." Vivian hoped her smile looked sincere, not sarcastic.

Caitlin dropped her lashes to her cheeks. "I did miss you, Mama. Remember, you were the one who told me to leave. I would have stayed and taken care of you, you know." She looked up with hooded eyes.

"And now you're telling me to leave again."

"No, child. This is not a forced evacuation. It is an invitation to follow your own dreams. I'll miss my girl, to be sure. But who am I to keep you here if God is calling you somewhere else?"

"Would you really be all right if I left again?"

"I won't be alone. I think George needs me, though the old grouch would never say so. And you have Ana to think of. She isn't happy in New York, is she?"

Caitlin shook her head and sipped her tea. "I wonder if she will be happy again until she sees her papa." Her shoulders drooped.

"She is happier with you than she would be with anyone else. But what about you? Are you still waiting for word from Mr. Becker? Have you hung your happiness on this man?" Vivian could tell her questions trod upon her daughter's brittle heart. She hoped it would hold firm.

"I'm trying—" Caitlin's voice caught. "I'm trying to hope."

"My darlin' girl." Vivian placed her hand on her daughter's knee. "I understand. But don't let that hope hold you captive. Move forward with your life."

"But if I don't have hope—" Her composure cracked, and she held open empty hands, palms up.

"Hope! Always hope, but in God alone. Wait, yes, but on the Lord. Expect Him to do great things, and trust His timing rather than demanding that He follow yours. He will renew your strength. You will rise again. You will run, and not be weary, walk, and not faint. If Mr. Becker is meant to find you, he will find you." Vivian wrapped her arm around Caitlin's shoulders. "Now. What will you do in the meantime?"

The mantel clock ticked inside Caitlin's pause, and Vivian held her breath. Then, "Ana can come with me?"

"Indeed. And you'd not be without an escort. Miss Dunn writes of a Union veteran from her church—Alan Wilcox—arranging to join his brother on his homestead in Oregon. She vouches for his character. But I do believe—he fought in the Atlanta campaign."

A wry smile tipped Caitlin's lips. "We'd have plenty to talk about."

Vivian chuckled. "I have no doubt of it. The road would not be easy. But as I'm sure you already know, sometimes the most challenging journeys are the most rewarding in the end. Now. Mr. Wilcox leaves in three weeks, so you have some time to decide."

Closing her eyes, Caitlin leaned her head on Vivian's shoulder, and Vivian stroked her hair as she had done countless times before. She spoke the words of the prophet Isaiah, as much for her own ears as for Caitlin's. "Remember ye not the former things, neither consider the things of old. Behold, I will do a new thing; now it shall spring forth; shall ye not know it? I will even make a way in the wilderness, and rivers in the desert."

In the quiet that followed, she wondered if Caitlin had fallen asleep. Until, "I'll miss you, Mama."

Tears gathered thickly in Vivian's throat. "I'll miss you, too. But you'd miss so much more if you stayed." She pressed a kiss to her daughter's temple and wondered how she would bear the ache of this new thing springing forth.

New York City
Thursday, March 9, 1865

"Don't be nervous," Ruby said, though her own hands still trembled with suspense. Caroline and Charlotte Waverly had both telegrammed Mr. Pease yesterday, and Mr. Pease had sent word to the agent on the train to turn around and fetch Aiden back to New York. All Ruby and Edward could do now, was wait.

In the meantime, Ruby took a cue from Vivian, who still cared for the people within her reach even when her own daughter had been missing. "Dr. Blackwell is an excellent doctor." Ruby spoke to Emma in low tones in the waiting room of the New York Infirmary for Women and Children. Edward, who had insisted on taking them in the carriage, sat across from Ruby with his newspaper.

Emma's forehead knotted as she twisted her hands in the pleats of her green merino wool dress. It was the first she had sewn for herself, with Ruby's help, back when Ruby had thought sewing would save her life. She'd been wrong.

"You're making me crazy, you are." Emma sniffed, eyebrows darting toward her trembling mouth.

Ruby flinched. "Why?

Her chin trembled. "'Tisn't right, lass. What I did was awful. I don't deserve your concern. I don't deserve anything good at all."

"Nonsense." Ruby handed her a handkerchief even as she battled her own tears. "You didn't know how things would turn out. Sean—"

"Sean didn't need to put pressure on me so much as you might think. I wanted you to steal for me and spread the wealth around. I meant to do you wrong, even after all you've done for me. And now your son is gone." She covered her face with her hands.

"He's coming back," she whispered, an echo of the constant mantra in her mind. But her hands would not stop shaking until they held her son.

"I can't understand why you don't hate me. I hate myself, and I could not be sorrier for the pain I caused."

Ruby squeezed her hand. "I forgive you."

Ridges seamed Emma's brow. Her eyes narrowed into glittering slits. "Why? How?"

"Ah, Emma. None of us is without guilt. You know my wrongs— you even tried to talk me out of deceiving Edward! I didn't listen to you, and I broke my husband's heart. But he forgave me, too."

Emma's gaze flitted to Edward, who kept his nose buried in his paper, though Ruby suspected he heard every word they spoke.

Ruby smiled at the obvious confusion swirling in Emma's eyes. "And do you want to know why and how Edward could forgive the likes of me? It's because Jesus forgave him, too. Yes, even chaplains do wrong. Jesus forgives all of us if we but ask Him to. Then, not only does He withhold the punishment we deserve, but He invites us to be His children. He can heal your deepest hurts and replace them with peace and joy. That, dear Emma, is grace." She held Emma's red-rimmed stare.

"Can He heal this diseased body of mine?"

"If He chooses." Ruby nodded. "But even better, He can heal and restore your soul."

At length, Emma thinned her lips and nodded. "All right, lass. Tell me again how this grace can be mine. This time, I'm listening."

Chapter Twenty-Eight

New York City
Monday, March 13, 1865

*R*uby could not get out of bed. Not since Mr. Pease had crushed her with his pronouncement that Aiden could not be found. A farmer took Aiden from the train station in Cedar Falls, Iowa, but no one knew how to reach him now. "Farmers travel up to twenty-five miles to choose children, you understand," Mr. Pease had said. "But we'll find him. It will just take time."

The voices in Ruby's head were deafening. *There is a reason they have not been able to find Aiden again. You almost killed him before he was born, you do not deserve this child. You do not deserve any happiness at all.*

Moaning, Ruby writhed in condemnation's clutch. *I can never be free of my past. I may be forgiven, but there are consequences for what I've done. If I hadn't kept company with Emma and Sean, none of this would have happened. My sins have ruined Edward's reputation and taken Aiden away from me.*

Faded images of Aiden on a farm bloomed in her mind. He was safe, and happy. Without her.

"Ruby?" Edward appeared in the doorway with a tray of tea, toast, and applesauce. "Will you eat?"

Oh. Did people eat so often? She could not imagine why. Her appetite had vanished and she hadn't even noticed. "Aren't you going to the hospitals today? Or the prison?" She licked her dry lips, and he passed her the cup of tea.

"Not today. I'm needed here." A ridge between his eyebrows, he sat in the chair beside the bed. He leaned forward, elbows on his knees, his caramel hair tousled the way it always was after he'd been deep in thought. "Aunt Viv is here, too, if you'd rather talk to her. Caitlin will be coming soon to sit with you, as well. Did you sleep last night?"

She blinked, her eyelids weighted with exhaustion. "Of course not." Fatigue cloaked her but could not blot out the one idea that had been crowding her consciousness for days. "Edward," she whispered, eyes burning. "What if this—Aiden growing up in the country—is really meant to be?"

"It isn't." He frowned, the very likeness of his father.

"My worst fear is that Aiden would lose his way and love the world. But a life in the country, away from the city's temptations and rough edges—what if that's the answer?" Her voice trailed to a croak.

"A life without us? His parents? Surely that is *not* the answer."

Tears slid down her cheeks and beneath her chin. She was so tired. Tired of waiting, tired of trying to be a good wife and mother and failing at both. She was exhausted from being a constant disappointment to Edward. This marriage wasn't what a marriage should be. But Caitlin's story about Noah Becker annulling unconsummated vows had inspired her. All that had stopped her from suggesting it was Aiden. *How selfish I've been.*

But now . . . The lump in her throat grated as she swallowed it. "You entered this marriage not knowing what it would be. I have not been a true wife to you. I release you from this arrangement, if that is what you want. Annul the marriage. Do not feel obligation to me, or to Aiden."

Edward shook his head, began to speak, but Ruby plunged ahead like a river towards the falls. "He will grow up where the air is fresh and the work honest. I can go back to Mrs. Waverly if she'll have me. We have burdened you enough." Her breath shortened with every sentence that spilled from her.

"Is that what you think? You've been a burden?" Edward's voice wavered as he stood and paced the room.

"Aye, I know it and so do you. I was so afraid of being hurt, I didn't realize—I never wanted to cause you such pain. I've been the black sheep in your fold." Her words rushed and tumbled over themselves, careening toward her own martyrdom. It was only what she deserved.

"No, my dear." He clasped her hand in both of his, looked deep into her eyes. "You've been the one sheep for which I would leave the other ninety-nine."

"You'd do better with another." A fresh wave of grief swallowed her, and she turned from his stunned expression.

He dropped her hands. "What—what are you saying? You want to dissolve the marriage?"

She sluiced the tears from her cheeks with trembling hands. "Consider it. For your own good."

Edward dropped into the chair once more. "What about Aiden? You would just pretend you don't have a son anymore?"

She fought to keep from covering her ears. This conversation was strangling her soul. "He is not quite three," she gasped. "He will forget me."

"Like I forgot my mother." His eyes were rimmed with red. A sigh broke from his lips. "I miss her, Ruby."

"What?"

"I don't remember her and yet I still *miss* my mother. I don't have memories of her singing to me, or wiping the dirt off my knees or kissing away my tears. I am told that she loved me, but I never felt it—at least not that I recall. I don't know if she held me close even when I wasn't crying, just because she loved me. I don't know if she scratched my back to help me fall asleep, or if she tickled my belly to make me laugh." He swallowed, dipped his head for a moment before straightening again. "I turned out fine, I suppose. But I did not know my mother's love, and that will always be a gaping hole in my heart."

Even in the midst of her aching for Aiden, Edward's words peeled the scales from her eyes. *I am told that she loved me, but I never felt it.* It was his mother's touch that he missed. The physical contact was a conduit of love. It was the very thing Ruby had withheld from him, too, and not just in the bedroom. She had told him she loved him, but he never felt it. She closed her eyes as the realization pierced her weary mind.

Still, "Your mother didn't have a choice."

"I know that. But you do."

The words sliced through Ruby's spirit.

"Aiden might be in a good home where his needs are met by good people who will teach him well. They might even pinch his cheeks and kiss the curls on his head. But *you* are the only mother he has. Will he grow to manhood wondering why his mama gave him up?"

A sob caught in her throat as she buried her face in her hands.

"I know you want to do right by him. But trust that God can help you raise Aiden wherever you live. Some trials are blessings in disguise, and God uses them for our good. But sometimes, people just make mistakes—like putting Aiden on that train. We'll get him back. We just need to keep looking. I'll go to Iowa myself if I have to."

Silence wrapped them as Edward's words dangled in Ruby's mind.

Until a rap on the door ushered Vivian, wide-eyed, into the chamber. "That was Mr. Pease at the door," she gasped, breathless. "They found Aiden!"

———

382

Cedar Falls, Iowa
Friday, March 17, 1865

"Breathe, Ruby." Edward's warm brown eyes crinkled as he removed his hat and dropped it on the bureau. "Holding your breath won't make the sun rise any faster."

Nervous laughter tripped from her lips as she removed the pins from her derby-style hat. They had just arrived at the Carter House Hotel after days of train travel, but though the hour was late, she had no plans to sleep a wink. Aiden would be brought in from his farm in the morning. Crossing to the window of their second-story room, she looked out over the lamp-lined Main Street toward the river mere blocks away, and wondered where Aiden was sleeping tonight.

Edward hung his jacket in the armoire before joining her at the window. Moonlight gleamed on storefront awnings, and gaslights glowed like fireflies, spreading pools of light on a quiet street still patched with snow.

"Does he know I'm coming for him, do you think?" Itching to hold Aiden, Ruby touched her fingertips to the cool glass pane, instead.

"I would think they would have told him. I'm sure he's just as eager for morning as we are. As you are."

Ruby caught Edward's gaze in their reflection in the window, and noticed the distance he'd placed between them. Now that she understood that touch was how he had been trying to show his love, she felt keenly that he no longer touched her shoulder, or her waist. He did not even reach for her hand. Perhaps he had decided to dissolve the marriage after all. She certainly wouldn't blame him. But oh, how she would miss him. "I have to know," she blurted out.

He looked down at her. "Know what?"

"When this is over, and Aiden is safely with me again. Will you take your leave of us?"

All the color drained from Edward's face. He rubbed his hand over his jaw and eased himself into the armchair with a ragged sigh. No

383

matter. Sharing a room for the first time in months, they'd have to sort this out tonight.

"Is that your desire?" he asked at length.

Ruby rolled her lips between her teeth before replying. "I desire whatever is best for you. And as I've said before, I fear that Aiden and I have not made you happy."

"Happy? Did you think marriage was only about happiness?" He raked his hand through his hair before leaning forward. "God has used you to show me my own sin, to chip away at the barnacles that have grown, unnoticed, on my heart. Though the process has been painful, I am a better—and far more humble—man now than I was before we wed."

"But, Edward." Tears bit Ruby's eyes. "You know we are not truly married." And the blame was hers alone.

A sad smile bent his lips. "But I believe there is love between us yet, for all our trials and misunderstandings. Look here." He opened his Bible, and her heart flipped at the sight of her braid she'd given him as a bookmark. "I read from 1 Corinthians 13. 'Charity suffereth long, and is kind; charity envieth not; charity vaunteth not itself, is not puffed up, doth not behave itself unseemly, seeketh not her own, is not easily provoked, thinketh no evil; rejoiceth not in iniquity, but rejoiceth in the truth; beareth all things, believeth all things, hopeth all things, endureth all things.'" He looked up, his coffee eyes slick. "'Charity never faileth.'"

Ruby's breath caught when his gaze caressed her face, but her feet remained rooted to the floor.

"I love you, Ruby. God knows it would be easier if I didn't, but I do. I rejoice in the truth. I believe, I hope, I endure."

And heaven knows you suffereth long.

"I want our marriage to succeed. But you are still at arm's length, beyond my reach." He stood and held out his hand to her. "If we dissolve our vows, it won't be because I want to."

"You still want me?" Hope pounded against her corset.

"More than I did a year ago today."

Ruby covered her lips with trembling hand. *How could I have forgotten?* One year ago this very night they had danced together at the Calico Ball. He had asked her to marry him. *And I told him yes.*

"You are my wife." His voice was husky. "I want . . . my wife."

Courage swelled within her, and she bridged the chasm that had divided them all these months. She placed her hand in his, and his fingers wrapped around it. "I take thee, Edward, to be my wedded husband." She grasped his other hand, as well. "To have and to hold—" She squeezed his hands, utterly convicted of what she'd withheld from him, and he pulled her into a tender embrace. Her tears soaked his shoulder, but she was not finished yet. "From this day forward, for better for worse, for richer for poorer, in sickness and in health, to love, cherish, and to obey, till death us do part, according to God's holy ordinance."

She pulled back and searched Edward's face. *Does he know that I mean it this time, truly?*

His eyes swam in tears of his own. "I take thee, Ruby, to be my wedded wife—"

Raising herself on her toes, she covered his lips with a kiss that could leave no doubt. With one hand, she unpinned her hair, then whispered in Edward's ear. *I'm ready.*

By the time the Illinois Central chugged back east across the Mississippi River, Aiden had fallen asleep on his mother's lap, his fingers clutching hers. Arm draped over her son, Ruby's silky head rested on Edward's shoulder while wooded hills rolled by outside the window. The journey they had taken together was far more arduous than this peaceful ride through the Midwest, and in truth, he did not know where it would take them from here. But while Edward wasn't certain what their future would be, he knew Ruby would be by his side. She was his wife, indeed.

Leavenworth, Kansas
Saturday, April 1, 1865

Now that the train travel portion of their journey was complete, and the frontier stretched before her, bottled excitement now surged in Caitlin's chest. Hitched to three matched pairs of gorgeous horses, the bright red Concord Stage Coach stood before her, trimmed in yellow and ornamented by an exquisite landscape painting on the door. Finally, she was on the threshold of her new life in the West.

"You'll want to secure a seat, Miss McKae. You'll be most comfortable at the front." Ever attentive, Mr. Wilcox loaded their meager luggage into the top rail while Caitlin and Ana climbed inside.

Leather curtains were rolled up and tied at the top of each window, allowing sunlight, dust, and wind through the damask cloth-upholstered interior. As soon as Caitlin and Ana seated themselves on leather-covered pads just as hard as the wood beneath them, six more passengers swarmed in around them, the unluckiest settling on the middle bench, that had no back save a leather strap that could be hooked from one side of the coach to the other.

"What do you think? Are you ready for this?" Mr. Wilcox flashed a smile at Ana as he eased himself down on the middle bench across from Caitlin, his knees nearly touching hers. The slightest groan escaped him as he rubbed his thigh above its connection to an artificial leg.

"Does it trouble you?" Caitlin asked.

He shook his head, the hair beneath his hat the color of wheat before the harvest. "Think nothing of it. I barely do myself." An easy grin pushed laugh lines into his tanned cheeks and a sparkle into his eyes. "Cozy, isn't it?"

Nine people in a box that was four feet wide and four and a half feet tall? Caitlin chuckled. "Quite."

"OK folks, listen up, because I'm only going to say this once." The stagecoach driver hollered at the passengers as he climbed up to his box, the shotgun who would keep an eye out for bandits following behind

386

him. "Number one! When I ask you to get off and walk, which I most certainly will do, do it without grumbling. I will not request it unless absolutely necessary. Number two! If our team runs away, sit still and take your chances; if you jump, nine times out of ten you will be hurt. Three! Don't growl at food stations. They give you the best they got, and if that ain't good enough for you, you might as well head back east."

The coach lurched on the rutted road, rocking like a cradle on its leather thorough braces. Facing the rear, the sudden motion pitched Caitlin forward, right into Mr. Wilcox's arms.

"Pardon me," she gasped, righting herself and straightening her hat on her hair.

"Quite all right." His eyes told her he meant it. The way the passengers were packed in, mere inches separated them as it was.

"All right, folks, I'm getting wore out so I'm going to make the rest of this quick." Caitlin hitched her attention to the driver's speech. "Don't keep the stage waiting. Spit on the leeward side of the coach. If you have anything to take in a bottle, pass it around or be hated by all. Don't swear, nor lop over on your neighbor when sleeping. Don't ask how far it is to the next station until you get there. Never attempt to fire a gun while on the road, it may frighten the team, which will frighten you, I guarantee. Don't linger too long at the pewter wash basin at the station. Don't grease your hair before starting or dust will stick there in sufficient quantities to make a respectable 'tater' patch. Most of all, don't imagine for a moment you are going on a picnic; expect annoyance, discomfort, and some hardships. If you are disappointed by the mild nature of your trip, thank the Maker. Got it? Let's ride."

Not the least bit intimidated, Caitlin leaned down to Ana. "Are you ready for our adventure?" Traveling at five miles an hour, it would likely be more than a month before they reached Astoria, but the prospect still tingled Caitlin's spine.

Ana's braids bounced on her shoulders as she nodded. "I only wish Papa were here. He'd like this too."

Caitlin pressed a smile from the ache in her heart. "You'll have so much to tell him. Do you have your journal?"

Another nod.

"Good. Chronicle everything. This is a once-in-a-lifetime experience!"

Adjusting now to the coach's sway, Caitlin looked past Mr. Wilcox to watch the dust slowly obscure Leavenworth from view. Only when she realized her escort was watching her did her smile falter.

"You're uncomfortable," she said. Surely it was more difficult to maintain balance with a prosthetic leg. "Trade places with me."

"Now what kind of gentleman would I be if I let you have the worst seat in the coach?" He clucked his tongue. "Besides, I rather prefer the view I have." His lips tipped in a playful smile, and she prayed the wind would cool her burning face.

———

Fort Kearney, Nebraska
Monday, April 10, 1865

Wind rushed across the plains, whipping the breath of a prairie spring about Noah Becker's face, and the U.S. flag flourished against an endless blue sky. With buckskin-gloved hands, he tugged his kepi into place and mounted his horse. His gaze settled on the horizon now billowing with dust as he waited for the coming wagon train. And smiled.

It had taken four grueling, shivering months in Rock Island's "calf pen" before the Union army organized last winter. Finally, in late February, Noah and more than seventeen hundred other Confederate prisoners at Rock Island took the oath to the United States of America, and were put into service on the frontier. The "Galvanized Yankees" worked alongside seasoned Union regiments from Nebraska and Iowa to provide escort service to stagecoaches and wagon trains on the Overland Trail, protecting them from both bandits and Indians.

As recently discharged veterans passed by on their pursuit of homestead sites, words from the Old Testament scrolled through Noah's mind: *The people which were left of the sword found grace in the wilderness . . . and they shall beat their swords into plowshares, and their spears into pruning hooks: nation shall not lift up sword against nation, neither shall they learn war any more.*

In addition to the veterans and other settlers, politicians, land speculators, parties of Mormons, theatrical companies, railroad surveyors, and government contractors comprised a steady stream of humanity trickling from East to West. Canvas-covered Prairie Schooners, Conestogas, and freight wagons labored under loads of corn, hardware, groceries, whiskey, clothing, kerosene, and machinery. Some days, the trains stretched as far as the eye could see. Fort Kearney was a weathered outpost dotted with broken-backed sod buildings squatting in a sea of rippling grass. But the trail the soldiers protected was the highway to tomorrow.

The work suited Noah, and when his enlistment was up, he'd have some money with which to begin a new life. He could only pray that Ana and Caitlin would be in it.

Drumming hoofbeats yanked Noah's gaze as a soldier from the east galloped pell-mell toward the fort, shouting like a madman. Confusion rippling Noah's brow, he pressed his heels into his mount and trotted toward him until the words on the wind untangled.

"Lee's surrendered!"

Noah nearly dropped his reins. Were his ears playing tricks on him?

"Lee's surrendered! Lee surrendered! The North has won! The war is over! The Union forever!" The soldier burst past him and thundered to the fort. Shouts multiplied as men emerged from the barracks, the officer's quarters, the hospital, and the sutler's store.

It's over. Stunned, comprehension drizzled over Noah until his chin dropped to his chest in wordless prayer. Finally, finally, the bloodletting would stop. His throat tightened as he grieved for lives and homes destroyed. How long would it take for man and country to heal?

A tumult erupted and Noah wheeled toward the noise. Celebrating soldiers ran to fill the sixteen blockhouse guns, two field guns, and two mountain howitzers with a good charge of powder before cramming them to their muzzles with wet gunny sacks.

"That's our wagon train coming with our supplies!" One of them pointed to the wagons drawing closer. "We'll tell them the news with a bang!"

Noah rounded back toward the train, scanning the line of wagons. Army mules should not be bothered by the impending noise—but that bright red coach traveling with them was surely civilian, driven by horses that would surely startle. With spurs to his horse, Noah galloped toward it to warn them.

Dozens of supply wagons flew past his vision as he leaned forward on his mount. But before he could reach the end of them, the gunners fired their cannon. Noah glanced over his shoulder in time to see the gunny sacks hurtle into the air, catch on the wind and open up before floating off.

The strange apparition in the sky triggered the animals—even the mules—into chaos. The lead wagon team broke formation and stampeded, panicked, across the prairie, followed by others, the drivers either thrown to the ground or leaping off their mounts to save themselves. The ground shook with the force of a buffalo herd as more than eighty wagons and hundreds of stock pounded the prairie. Unmanned runaway wagons of supplies bolted from the line. *Inconvenient, but not life threatening.* Noah ignored them. But when a driver jumped from the Concord stagecoach careening past Noah, he slammed his heels into his mount and thundered after them. The painted door burst open, swinging wildly on its hinges.

"Stay in the coach!" Noah shouted, his voice muffled by the crescendo of the runaway train. "Hang on!"

A cry pierced through the roar of the stampede. A child's cry. Noah clenched his jaw and squinted through the swirling dust as he rode after them, his kepi surrendering to the wind. A braid the color of pecans flapped out an open window, and Noah's heart lurched. *It couldn't be.*

Caitlin's heart hammered against its cage as she gripped Ana's and Mr. Wilcox's hands. The jangle of the horses' harnesses and bridles rattled her core. What had she been thinking to bring a nine-year-old child on this journey? The coach rocked wildly, throwing passengers against each other as if it were a ship tossed by the sea. *Lord, protect us!*

Outside the window, dust rose in a choking cloud that invaded the coach. Through the swirling grit, Caitlin watched, breathless, as a lone Union soldier spurred his horse past the coach.

"Easy, easy," she thought she heard him say as he approached the panic-stricken team. With knuckles whitening on the edge of her bench, she prayed their rescuer would succeed.

"Whoa . . ." his voice rumbled among the hoofbeats. "Whoa," he said again, and Caitlin's heart turned violently in her chest. She looked at Ana, whose eyes were wide, her face white.

"Papa . . ." Ana's mouth formed the word, but no sound came out. When she turned to the window, Mr. Wilcox caught her wrist.

"Don't lean out," he instructed. "Stay in, or you'll topple head over heels. Just wait."

Wait. Caitlin squeezed her eyes shut, and swallowed the scratching dust. *They that wait upon the Lord shall renew their strength; they shall mount up with wings as eagles; they shall run, and not be weary; and they shall walk, and not faint.*

"What's happening?" Ana asked.

Mr. Wilcox squinted past Caitlin, through the window between the coach and the empty driver's box. "Looks like he's taken the lead. He's got himself in front of the lead pair of horses so the middle post between them is bumping up against the rump of his own horse. He's trying to slow them down."

"Whoa . . ." That baritone voice, again, bellowing above the frantic hoof beats. By degrees, the horses eased their pace. "Whoa. *Gut.*"

Caitlin's mind whirred as as she stared at her knees, unseeing. In that one word, Noah came rushing back to her. In his carriage after Gettysburg.

You need a place to live. I just so happen to have a house. Leaving for the war. *I'm giving you my Heart, you know.* Kneeling by her sickbed. *Come back to me. Please. I'm here now. And I'll help you find Jack.* After the dreadful siege. *Ana was all I needed. Until now.* And the last time she saw him. *We'll be together again.*

"Don't be frightened, Miss McKae." Mr. Wilcox offered his hand-kerchief, and only then did she realize she was crying. "The Lord has placed us in good hands."

At last, the stagecoach ground to a halt. Dazed, the passengers stumbled out until only Caitlin and Ana were left.

Caitlin swallowed the ragged heartbeat pulsing in her throat. "It might not—be him, you know." *For in thee, O Lord, do I hope.*

"It's him!" Ana cried, pushing past her and leaping out the door. "Papa! Papa! It's Ana!"

Hornets swarming through her middle, Caitlin pressed her hand to her chest and prayed her knees would hold her up. *They shall walk and not faint. Walk and not faint.* Then Ana's weeping lanced Caitlin's heart. So they'd been mistaken, after all.

Biting her lips to keep from crying, she wiped the dust from her face and neck with her handkerchief. When she leaned forward on the bench and peered outside, an electric shock coursed through her. For there was Ana, sobbing in the arms of the Union soldier. He was on his knees in the dirt, his uniform straining against his biceps as he gently swayed with the little girl. "Papa," she hiccupped, and a hoarse voice replied, "My Heart."

Impossible! Caitlin braced herself in the coach's doorway, frozen in its frame. Then he looked up, lassoing her heart with his steel-blue eyes.

"Caitlin."

The breath whisked from her chest.

He stood, and Ana stepped away from between them. Dropping his gloves to the ground, Noah stepped up to the coach, eyes bright and cheeks ruddy from his ride. "My love," he whispered, and reached for her. With trembling hands, Caitlin held his shoulders as he lifted her down by her waist. When her feet touched the ground, he did not let her go, and she did not pull away.

"It's you." She laid her hand on his faintly bristled jaw, then lightly grazed the bump on his nose with her finger. Fleetingly, she rued her disheveled state, but the look in Noah's eyes told her it didn't matter. New life swept through her as fiercely as the prairie wind whipping her skirts around them both.

With his thumb under her chin, Noah gently tipped her face to his. Last time they were together, she had begged him not to kiss her. Now, she slipped her arms around his neck, and he circled her waist. The earth fell away from beneath her feet, and Noah took her lips in the kiss she'd been dreaming of for months. He was worth the wait.

"Heavens. If I had known that was to be the reward I would have stopped the coach myself."

Caitlin giggled under Noah's soft lips, and he gently put her down.

"This is Alan Wilcox, our escort on the trail to Astoria," she said, turning toward the veteran. "For a teaching job."

Noah's eyebrows arched as he extended his hand to Mr. Wilcox, who shook it amiably. "Much obliged. I'm Noah Becker. I see you've met my daughter Ana—" He cupped her shoulder in his hand. "And this woman here is going to be my wife, if I can persuade her."

Caitlin's knees weakened again, and Noah pressed her to his side. The warmth radiating from his touch burned her cheeks. Ana squealed, and Mr. Wilcox pumped his hand once more before he tipped his hat and left them alone.

"Got rid of the competition, anyway." Noah grinned.

Caitlin shook her head. *There is no competition.*

Eyes growing serious, Noah grasped both her hands. "I am yours, Caitlin McKae, if you can accept a man as complicated and flawed as me."

Her heart grew wings. "And can you find a way to love a Yankee who fits neither North or South?"

"I have loved you since I first left you. But war will not separate us again." Noah penetrated her with his gaze, now suddenly bright. "Caitlin," he whispered. "It's over."

She gasped. "Are you sure?"

"News galloped into the fort just before you arrived. That's why they fired the cannons that caused the stampede! There is no more Union versus Confederacy. There is only the United States of America."

Tears burned Caitlin's eyes as she searched Noah's face. She had expected news of victory to resound like a gong, detonating a riot of joy within her. But that was before she'd made the South her home, before Rebels had names and faces. *Prudence and Judson Periwinkle. Naomi Ford. Minnie Taylor. Noah.*

"Everything you fought for . . ." Her voice trailed off.

"I fought for my home. I fought for us, and you are both safe, despite my failure. If the Confederacy had won, Bess and Saul and all the rest would still be slaves. Now they are 'forever free,' as Lincoln says, though their struggles are far from over. The South must reinvent itself."

Caitlin nodded. "Are you all right?"

A sad smile played on his lips. "I'm ready to move on."

"Will you go back? To Atlanta?"

"After wearing a Union uniform?" He shook his head. "No. I will make a new life. I have done it before. Surely I can do it again. Will you start over with me—with us—in the West?"

"Please, Mama?" Ana tugged on her hand, and Caitlin bent to pull her into an embrace.

Sunshine edged Noah and Ana in gold and Caitlin saw them for the treasures they were. Hope unfurled within her, as boundless as the prairie sky. "Of course I will." She kissed Ana's cheek, then stood and pressed another to Noah's willing lips. The end of the war was not the end at all. "This is only the beginning."

Epilogue

Cedar Falls, Iowa
Thursday, January 17, 1867

*H*er breath a glittering cloud before her, Ruby Goodrich stamped her feet on the train platform to keep warm. They'd been standing in the cold for an hour, but she'd been anticipating this moment much longer than that.

Four-year-old Aiden jumped up and down beside her. "When's it coming?" he asked again, though only a minute had passed since his last query.

Edward laughed. "We're just as excited as you are, son, but have patience. Good things come to those who wait. Isn't that right, Grace?" Mischief sparkled in his eyes as he bounced their daughter on his hip. Just over one year old, the cherub-faced toddler with her daddy's chocolaty brown eyes and caramel-colored hair was adorable proof indeed.

"Look, Gracie!" Aiden grabbed his little sister's shoe and pointed at the locomotive chugging into the station.

Mr. Stone, one of Edward's congregants, turned and smiled. "Evening, Reverend, Mrs. Goodrich. Ready to add to your family?"

"Absolutely," Edward replied, but Ruby's attention was fixed firmly on the train. As it screeched to a halt, she reached for Edward's hand and squeezed.

Moments later, an agent of the New York Children's Aid Society paraded five boys and one small girl across the platform.

"That one," Ruby whispered, her eyes locked with the girl's. Black hair, freckles, and eyes too old for her face, she looked to be only a few months older than Grace. There was something special about her.

"What can you tell us about the girl?" Edward asked the agent, who flipped through a stack of cards. "Mother died of venereal disease. Father unknown."

"Is the girl healthy?" Edward prodded, and Ruby heard the agent say she was.

Then her eyes grew round. "Do you know the mother's name?"

The agent looked again at her card. "Emma Connors."

Ruby's breath skidded.

"Ah yes," the agent continued. "I remember her. She'd had an abortion or two before Shannon was born. It's really a miracle she was able to give birth. Clearly something in her life changed from the time Miss Connors conceived and the time Shannon was born. She was full of faith when she died. Are you quite well? You look—"

But Ruby had walked away and was kneeling in front of Shannon. "Hello darlin'. Did you know Shannon is my name too? My middle name."

"This girl was named for you." Edward, behind her. "Surely it's no coincidence."

Tears bit Ruby's eyes. "I bet you miss your mama very much."

Shannon's grey eyes were luminous in the gaslight.

"She loved you, and I love you. We'd love to take care of you from now on. Would you like to be part of our family?"

Shannon blinked, then turned her gaze on Edward, Grace, and a very bouncy Aiden.

"I could be your big brother!" Aiden piped. "I'm very good at it. And Gracie can be your sister. We have a nice house with a big yard to play in. Mama has lots and lots of flowers and when we visit Uncle Jack on his farm, he lets us ride a pony and milk cows. There are always kittens around. Do you like kittens?"

"And you'll have cousins!" Ruby added. "They are practically our neighbors."

Edward lit up. "Cousins! I almost forgot. Don't be cross with me, dear, but Ana came bursting into the church office right before I left today. She said you and the kids weren't at home. Seemed rather agitated about something—only I can't seem to recall what the fuss was all about."

Ruby gasped. "Edward Goodrich, if you don't tell me right this instant, I'll—I'll—"

Eyes twinkling, he knelt in front of Shannon, Grace sitting on his knee. "Have you ever seen a brand-new baby?"

———

Propped up with pillows on her canopy bed, Caitlin Becker ached with love as she gazed at her newborn son. Ever vigilant of her comfort, Noah fed a log to the fire, and shadow and light waltzed together on the wall. Analiese placed a cup of tea carefully on the nightstand.

Returning to Caitlin's side, Noah planted a kiss on her forehead before turning his adoring gaze on his son. "Well, my love, have you decided on a name? I don't suppose he'll be very pleased with us if we call him Peanut forever."

"Wilhelm James." For Noah's brother, and Caitlin's father.

Soft lines framed Noah's eyes as he nodded. "William James Becker," he said, choosing the English variation. "It suits him." He wrapped his arm around her shoulders, his fingers brushing the scar they had both grown to love, for the bullet that created it had sent Caitlin to Atlanta—to Noah and Ana—years ago.

"Will." Ana's tone was firm. "After all, he is just a tiny boy."

"Fair enough." Noah laughed, and then a knock at the door drew him away.

When he returned, pride shone on his face as he led the Goodrich family—plus one more little girl—into the room.

"Say hello to Will!" Ana beamed at her red-nosed cousins.

Caitlin's eyes went wide. "I completely forgot! Tonight you met the train, didn't you? You must be frozen."

"I'll make some hot chocolate!" Ana bounded out of the room, clearly satisfied with her position as the eldest cousin.

"Oh, he's so perfect! Just look at that little mouth!" Ruby rubbed her hands together to warm them. "May I?" She gently lifted the baby from Caitlin's arms.

"And who is this?" Caitlin smiled at her cousin Edward, who looked so at home with a child in his arms.

"This is Shannon." He beamed.

"You're home at last." Caitlin's voice was gentle. She knew what it was like to be suddenly transplanted. "I hope you like it here as much as we do. You can call me Aunt Caitlin, and this is Uncle Noah."

"And who am I, chopped liver?" Jack blustered through the doorway, Ana riding his back. "Well, sister, you've lost weight since I saw you last." He bent to kiss her cheek and Ana slid to the floor. "Special diet? Do tell me where you put the pounds."

"She gave them to me, you rascal!" Ruby laughed, her gaze still pinned to William's face.

Jack wiggled his finger into the baby's tiny fist. "Look how strong he is! Watch out, Noah, he might not be satisfied to work in a courtroom like you. He might want to plow a field like his Uncle Jack!"

"But look at those wise eyes," Edward teased. "He might want to be a preacher."

"His fingers are so long!" Ruby said. "He'd make an excellent tailor."

"Or a teacher!" Caitlin smiled, thinking of her own students who had knit so many blankets for the baby he'd surely stay warm for years.

Noah laughed. "William will be anything he wants to be. This is America."

Caitlin reached out, and beckoned Shannon to her side. Holding the girl's hand, she whispered, "Do you know the best thing about living here? Family." Overwhelmed with gratitude, Caitlin's eyes welled with tears as she gazed upon the faces of all those she held dear. Noah, Ana, Jack, Edward, Ruby, Aiden, Grace—and now Will and Shannon too! Yes, she could have been teaching in Oregon right now. But when she and Ana had found Noah at Fort Kearny, Caitlin let the wagon train go on without them. Ruby and Edward had settled down in Cedar Falls by the time Noah was discharged from the army, and choosing to join them was the easiest decision Caitlin and Noah had ever made. Living in a town with railroads meant Vivian and George could reach them in days, not weeks. Cedar Falls needed teachers and lawyers, too. And Caitlin needed family.

"God setteth the solitary in families," Edward quoted from Psalm 68:6. War divided them no longer. The pieces of Caitlin's heart had come together at last.

The History behind the Story

Though *Yankee in Atlanta*'s main characters of Caitlin McKae and Noah Becker are fictional, their struggles represent those experienced by real people living in Atlanta during the Civil War. Caitlin's character was inspired by the hundreds of women who disguised themselves as men and enlisted in the army on both sides. Caitlin also represents the Northern natives and Union loyalists who lived in Atlanta during the war. Thomas Dyer's book *Secret Yankees* sheds light on the small band of Unionists living in Confederate Atlanta. Cyrena Stone's journal, quoted in Dyer's book, lends valuable insights. The *Yankee in Atlanta* scene in which Caitlin is arrested and questioned in a hotel room was inspired by Cyrena's account of the same surreal experience as it happened to her. While the secret Yankees in Atlanta are long forgotten, several place-names of the modern city are named for them: Markham, Dunning, Hayden, and Webster Streets; Angier Avenue and Lynches Alley; and the suburban towns of Austell and Norcross.

Noah Becker represents another minority—the German immigrant living in the Confederacy. A wave of German immigrants did come to

America after the Revolution of 1848, but most settled in the North, including Union general Carl Schurz, whose early years in the Rhineland inspired Noah's specific backstory. Between 176,817 and 216,000 German immigrants fought for the North. In the South, only between 3,500 and 7,000 Germans fought for the Confederacy, but of that number, many were conscripted, and a large number deserted.

The "Galvanized Yankees," officially known as United States Volunteers, were made up of six regiments of Confederate prisoners recruited from Point Lookout, Rock Island, Alton, and Camps Douglas, Chase, and Morton. Many were immigrants, Irish and German predominating. During the spring and summer of 1865, they restored mail service between the Missouri River and California, continually fighting off raiding Indians. They escorted supply trains on the Oregon and Santa Fe trails, and rebuilt hundreds of miles of telegraph line destroyed by Indians between Fort Kearney and Salt Lake City. The U.S. Volunteers guarded surveying parties for the Union Pacific Railroad, helped protect Minnesota settlements, and searched for white women captured by hostile Native Americans. Though little remembered, their service was vital to the homesteaders settling the frontier.

The major events in this novel, both in Atlanta and New York City, were depicted as historically as possible, including the National Board of Popular Education's efforts to send female teachers to frontier towns, the Panic of 1857 and subsequent mass prayer meetings, the razing of Seneca Village to make way for Central Park, the hanging of the Andrews Raiders in Atlanta, the draft riots in New York City, the Southern army revival during the winter of 1863–1864, the refugees flooding Atlanta, the battles of the Atlanta campaign, and the Confederate plot to burn New York City after Lincoln's re-election. Due to the high population of sick soldiers in its hospitals, Atlanta civilians were also victims of epidemics such as smallpox and scarlet fever. The concert above the trenches in Smyra, Georgia, and the prairie stampede triggered by exploding gunny sacks celebrating the war's end also reflect real events.

The Children's Aid Society in New York City operated orphan

trains for decades. Partnering with the Five Points Mission, nearly one thousand children per year were sent west just from 1865–1874. We know of thirteen of these orphans adopted in Cedar Falls, Iowa, which was the western terminus of the Illinois Central Railroad during the war. Nearly 60 percent of the children put up for adoption by Five Points Mission had at least one living parent. Lewis Pease did, in fact, pay cash to destitute parents for giving up their children on at least a few occasions. He was also taken to court by parents who wanted their children back—but he usually won.

The text from Southern textbooks and newspapers are direct quotes. The arrangement between the New York and Richmond newspapers to print "family ads" lasted only about a year. By the end of 1864, and after two thousand family ads had been printed, war officials North and South put a stop to it, suspecting the ads contained coded messages of espionage.

Several historical figures also appear in these pages, including Col. George Washington Lee, Oliver Jones, Col. James Nesbit of the 66th Georgia regiment, Col. Andrew J. Johnson, Sam Richards, Cyrena and Amherst Stone, and Lewis Pease. Other historical figures referenced were Dr. Elizabeth Blackwell, Frederick Law Olmsted, and Charles Loring Brace. Brace and Olmsted are said to have been best friends. The man tending the Union wounded outside the Car Shed on July 22 was an enterprising slave named Robert Webster, who organized a team of former slaves to get the neglected Yankees to a hospital. The woman Caitlin saw digging lead from the battlefield with her slave was Decatur resident Mary Ann Harris Gay, who recorded her experiences in *Life in Dixie during the War*.

The blood spilled for Atlanta was staggering on both sides. Union forces suffered 31,687 men killed, wounded, or missing during the campaign, and the Confederates 30,976. More than two-thirds of the Rebel losses came after Hood took command from Johnston. The surrender of Atlanta bolstered Lincoln's public approval in the North, which clinched his reelection. The 1864 election was the first time soldiers were allowed to vote from the field. Any hope of peace negotiations evaporated along with any doubt that the war would be fought to its conclusion.

Primary source material, photos, and other resources may be found at www.heroinesbehindthelines.com.

Selected Bibliography

Anbinder, Tyler. *Five Points: The 19th Century New York City Neighborhood that Invented Tap Dance, Stole Elections, and Became the World's Most Notorious Slum.* New York, New York: Penguin Group, 2002.

Bennett, William W. *The Great Revival Which Prevailed in the Southern Armies during the Late Civil War between the States of the Federal Union.* Philadelphia, Pennsylvania: Claxton, Remsen, & Haffelfinger, 1877.

Blanton, Deanne and Lauren M. Cook. *They Fought Like Demons: Women Soldiers in the Civil War.* New York: Vintage Books, 2003.

Bonds, Russell S. *War Like the Thunderbolt: The Battle and Burning of Atlanta.* Yardley, Pennsylvania: Westholme Publishing, 2009.

Brown, Dee. *The Galvanized Yankees.* Lincoln, Nebraska: University of Nebraska Press, 1986.

Burrows, Edwin G. and Mike Wallace. *Gotham: A History of New York City to 1898.* Oxford: Oxford University Press, 1999.

Carrie Berry papers, MSS 29F, Kenan Research Center, Atlanta History Center.

Current, Richard Nelson. *Lincoln's Loyalists: Union Soldiers from the Confederacy*. New York, New York: Oxford University Press, 1992.

Davis, Robert S., ed. *Requiem for a Lost City: Sallie Clayton's Memoirs of Civil War Atlanta*. Macon, Georgia: Mercer University Press, 1999.

Davis, Robert S. and Douglas W. Bostick. *Civil War Atlanta*. Charleston, South Carolina: The History Press, 2011.

Davis, Stephen. *What the Yankees Did to Us: Sherman's Bombardment and Wrecking of Atlanta*. Macon, Georgia: Mercer University Press, 2012.

Dyer, Thomas G. *Secret Yankees: The Union Circle in Confederate Atlanta*. Baltimore: The Johns Hopkins University Press, 1999.

Edwards, Laura F. *Scarlett Doesn't Live Here Anymore: Southern Women in the Civil War Era*. Chicago, Illinois: University of Illinois Press, 2004.

Farnham, Christie Anne. *The Education of the Southern Belle: Higher Education and Student Socialization in the Antebellum South*. New York, New York: New York University Press, 1994.

Fraser, Walter J., Jr., R. Frank Saunders Jr., and Jon L. Wakelyn, editors. *The Web of Southern Social Relations: Women, Family, & Education*. Athens, Georgia: The University of Georgia Press, 1985.

History of the Brooklyn and Long Island Fair, prepared by the Executive Committee. Brooklyn: "The Union," Steam Presses, 1864.

Hoehling, A. A. *Last Train from Atlanta*. New York City: Thomas Yoseloff, 1958.

Holt, Marilyn Irvin. *The Orphan Trains: Placing Out in America*. Lincoln, Nebraska: University of Nebraska Press, 1994.

Jabour, Anya. *Scarlett's Sisters: Young Women in the Old South*. Chapel Hill, North Carolina: University of North Carolina Press, 2007.

Levine, Bruce. *The Fall of the House of Dixie: The Civil War and the Social Revolution that Transformed the South*. New York, New York: Random House, 2003.

Marten, James. *The Children's War*. Chapel Hill, North Carolina: University of North Carolina Press, 1998.

Massey, Mary Elizabeth. *Ersatz in the Confederacy: Shortages and Substitutions on the Southern Homefront.* Columbia, South Carolina: University of South Carolina Press, 1952.

Massey, Mary Elizabeth. *Refugee Life in the Confederacy.* Baton Rouge, Louisiana: Louisiana State University Press, 1964.

Mobley, Joe A. *Weary of War: Life on the Confederate Home Front.* Westport, Connecticut: Praeger Publishers, 2008.

Nisbet, Col. James Cooper. *Four Years on the Firing Line.* Chattanooga, Tennessee: The Imperial Press, digital edition 2012.

Noe, Kenneth W. *Reluctant Rebels: The Confederates Who Joined the Army after 1861.* Chapel Hill, North Carolina: The University of North Carolina Press, 2010.

Ott, Victoria E. *Confederate Daughters: Coming of Age during the Civil War.* Carbondale, Illinois: Southern Illinois University Press, 2008.

Rable, George C. *Civil Wars: Women and the Crisis of Southern Nationalism.* Chicago: University of Illinois Press, 1989.

Rose, Michael. *Atlanta: A Portrait of the Civil War.* Charleston: Arcadia Publishing, 1999.

Schurz, Carl. *The Reminiscences of Carl Schurz.* New York, New York: McClure Company, 1907.

Taylor, Amy Murrell. *The Divided Family in Civil War America.* Chapel Hill, North Carolina: The University of North Carolina Press, 2009.

Time-Life Books. *Atlanta (Voices of the Civil War).* Alexandria, Virginia: Time-Life Books, 1996.

Venet, Wendy Hamand, ed. *Sam Richards's Civil War Diary: A Chronicle of the Atlanta Home Front.* Athens, Georgia: The University of Georgia Press, 2009.

Weitz, Mark A. *A Higher Duty: Desertion Among Georgia Troops during the Civil War.* Lincoln, Nebraska: University of Nebraska Press, 2000.

Wortman, Marc. *The Bonfire: The Siege and Burning of Atlanta.* New York, New York: PublicAffairs, 2010.

Discussion Guide

1. When we first meet Caitlin, she believes she is better off handling her own problems, rather than depending on anyone else. How do you balance personal responsibility with leaning on others for support and wisdom?

2. Caitlin changed her appearance and behavior more than once in order to survive. When have you had to reinvent yourself to adjust to a new situation or environment?

3. Atlanta Mayor James Calhoun voted against secession, but when war broke out, his own son enlisted, and he did everything he could to support the Confederacy. Have you ever had to support a decision with which you didn't initially agree? What happened?

4. There had been a time when Edward Goodrich would have done anything to woo his wife. Later, he had to be reminded to brush his teeth. Why do you think we sometimes stop trying to impress those who matter most to us?

5. Ruby didn't tell Edward the truth about her past until someone else exposed her. Would you ever keep a secret from your loved one? Why or why not?

6. First John 4:18 says, "Perfect love casts out fear." What does this verse mean to you?

7. After his wedding, Edward discovered it was easier to minister outside his home than it was to tend his broken relationship with Ruby. Why do you think this was true?

8. Desperate for her mother's love, Ana grasped after Susan's affection, though Susan did not reciprocate. How important is parental approval to you?

9. The characters in this book felt loved through different expressions. Edward felt loved by physical touch. Ana craved time. What makes you feel most loved?

10. Noah felt torn between antislavery principles and an obligation to defend his homeland. When have you felt conflicted about something you did? How did you handle it?

11. If you were displaced from your home like the Southern refugees, and could only fill two suitcases from your home, what would you pack?

12. Noah juggled his duty to country with his duty to Ana, which included going AWOL. When have you had to reevaluate your priorities with work and family and make changes?

13. In what circumstances would it be more honorable to break the rules than to follow them?

14. Caitlin's loyalties and perspectives shifted during the story. What was the most surprising change of heart you've ever had?

15. The ideal woman in the antebellum South possessed qualities of amiability, piety, a desire to please others, cleanliness, neatness,

patience, industry, kindness, modesty, politeness, respect for elders, and obedience. How does this differ from today's standard of the ideal woman?

16. The Southern home front learned to live with far less than they had been accustomed to. What have you learned to live without? How did that affect you?

17. Vivian tells Caitlin, "Don't let that hope hold you captive. Move forward with your life." Have you ever been held captive by hope?

18. Caitlin struggled to wait on the Lord instead of just waiting for Noah. When have you had to wait on the Lord?

19. Ruby and Noah experienced prejudice because they were immigrants. How have you seen immigrants treated in your own community?

20. At both the start and the close of the book, Caitlin says, "This is not the end. It is only the beginning." When has one painful end in your life led to a new chapter?

Acknowledgments

I could never bring *Yankee in Atlanta* to life without the help of many others. My gratitude and appreciation go to:

Moody Publishers/River North Fiction, for their dedication to bring the Heroines Behind the Lines series to life.

My agent, Tim Beals of Credo Communications, for his steadfast support.

Rachel Hauck, author and consultant with My Book Therapy, for helping me brainstorm the plot.

My husband, Rob, and children, Elsa and Ethan, for sharing me with a rigorous writing schedule, and for coming along to historic sites across the country while on vacation: the Chickamauga & Chattanooga National Military Park (Tennessee), the Rock Island Arsenal Museum (Illinois), The Museum of the Confederacy and The Siege Museum (Virginia), The National Homestead Monument (Nebraska), Western Historic Trails Center and Cedar Falls Historical Society (Iowa). For the record, I did visit Atlanta for research too, I just didn't have my family with me. Special thanks to Elsa, whose speech and mannerisms inspired the character of Analiese.

My parents, Peter and Pixie Falck, for watching my kids and bringing several meals over so I could write with minimal interruptions. Food preparation is the bane of my existence while on deadline.

A host of friends and experts whose research across the country I could not do without: Trevor Beemon of the Atlanta History Center and Amy Reed of the Marietta Museum of History for information about Civil War Atlanta architecture and upper middle class lifestyle; Bettina Dowell for scouring the Library of Congress for Atlanta newspapers; Laura Frantz for help understanding the course of smallpox; Chief Wesley Harris for being my Civil War firearms expert; Peter Leavell for acting as both research assistant and critique partner; Sheila Usher Mounce for her lessons in horse behavior; Jordyn Redwood for answering my medical questions; Nora St. Laurent, Lyn Vivenzio, and Gail Mundy for help with Atlanta's vegetation; Larry Upthegrove and Sara Henderson from Atlanta's Oakland Cemetery for offering details about what the graveyard looked like in December 1863; and Mindelynn Young for researching prairie history in Independence, Missouri. Thanks also to the Civil War History and Nineteenth Century writers groups for their reliable guidance.

My prayer team, for holding me up during the writing and editing process.

L. L. Bean for making the best writing pants ever.

Above all, I thank Jesus for the gift of words, for the power of story, and for being the Author of life itself.

About the Author

Jocelyn Green is an award-winning author of multiple fiction and nonfiction works, including *Faith Deployed: Daily Encouragement for Military Wives*, and *The 5 Love Languages Military Edition*, which she cowrote with Dr. Gary Chapman. Her first novel in the Heroines Behind the Lines series, *Wedded to War*, was a Christy Award finalist, and the gold medal winner in historical fiction from the Military Writers Society of America. A native Northerner, she and her Southern-born-and-bred husband live in Cedar Falls, Iowa, with their two children. Her goal with every book is to inspire faith and courage in her readers. Visit her at www.jocelyngreen.com.

MORE FROM
THE HEROINES BEHIND
THE LINES SERIES

978-0-8024-0576-0

978-0-8024-0577-7

978-0-8024-0578-4

COMING SOON

Spy of Richmond

FEBRUARY 2015

Also available as ebooks

IMPACTING LIVES THROUGH THE POWER OF STORY

www.RiverNorthFiction.com | www.MoodyPublishers.com

midday connection

Discover a safe place to authentically process life's journey on **Midday Connection**, hosted by Anita Lustrea and Melinda Schmidt. This live radio program is designed to encourage women with a focus on growing the whole person: body, mind, and soul. You'll grow toward spiritual freedom and personal transformation as you learn who God is and who He created us to be.

www.middayconnection.org

MOODYRADIO

Where you turn. For life.

IMPACTING LIVES THROUGH THE POWER OF STORY

Thank you! We are honored that you took the time out of your busy schedule to read this book. If you enjoyed what you read, would you consider sharing the message with others?

- Write a review online at amazon.com, bn.com, goodreads.com, cbd.com.

- Recommend this book to friends in your book club, workplace, church, school, classes, or small group.

- Go to facebook.com/RiverNorthFiction, "like" the page and post a comment as to what you enjoyed the most.

- Mention this book in a Facebook post, Twitter update, Pinterest pin, or a blog post.

- Pick up a copy for someone you know who would be encouraged by this message.

- Subscribe to our newsletter for information on upcoming titles, inside information on discounts and promotions, and learn more about your favorite authors at RiverNorthFiction.com.